GHOST WRITER
IN THE SKY

GHOST WRITER
IN THE SKY

A XANTH NOVEL

PIERS ANTHONY

OPEN ROAD
INTEGRATED MEDIA
NEW YORK

Cover design by Amanda Shaffer

978-1-5040-3877-5

Published in 2017 by Open Road Integrated Media, Inc.
180 Maiden Lane
New York, NY 10038
www.openroadmedia.com

GHOST WRITER
IN THE SKY

Chapter 1

NIGHT COLT

Goar was in a foul mood. He hated his job as Night Watchman and Cleanup Man at the local Fracking Complaints Office, partly because teens liked to throw anonymous stink bombs, but mostly because it was a urine-poor chore in itself. When a bomb got through, not only did Goar have to clean it up, using caustic floor wash that burned his eyes, he got the blame for the remaining smell that could not be completely extinguished. But what could he do? It was the only night job available in town, and he was a dedicated night owl. It gave him time to be by himself and dream his dream of becoming a famous writer. If only he had time for that.

He had tried small pieces and submitted them to publishers. He had real hopes for "The Head," about a headache as a life form that kept seeking new heads to honor for a while, but whose aspirations were in the lavatory. Pretty much like his literary career, actually. Then there was "Camelflage," wherein a camel was really good at hiding, confounding its mean master. What genius ideas! But the rejections arrived almost before the pieces went out. So he tried posting some free on story comment sites, to garner reader comments. One was "Demon Sun," phrased as an adventure of solar exploration, whose protagonist kept finding himself mysteriously changing sizes. The key was in the pun: Demon Sun = Dimension. What a phenomenal surprise ending! Yet online reviews had suggested that he should try tasks more appropriate to his intellectual capacity, like ditch digging or castrating chickens. So that was no good; story sites were evidently ruled by jealous idiots. What he needed was to get into a novel, where his full range of talent could be exploited. But that would require more focus than he could muster at the moment.

This night there had been two stink bombs and a firecracker that landed in his pail and blasted soapy water all over his legs. What a mess! And of course he hadn't caught the guilty teens, who zoomed by in silent cars, tossing their missiles out the windows as they sped by. Sure there was a curfew, but they ignored it with impunity. The police had better things to do than chase after boys who would be boys.

Goar's name meant "fighter," but the only fighting he did was in his imagination. One day he would write the Great American Fantasy Novel with plenty of magic combat, adventure galore, and breathtakingly lovely damsels. If he ever got time to write. As it was he worked by night and slept by day, with the interstice time spent on the dull details of mundane existence. It felt like a treadmill going nowhere.

His romantic life was no better. His last attempted date had quoted from a popular song: "Catch yourself a trolly car that goes into the sea." He wasn't sure what she meant by that, but it sounded negative.

There was a letter in his box with a lawyerly return address. Was somebody suing him? That might at least make life more interesting. Goar opened and heated a can of mushroom soup for breakfast, not bothering with a bowl or spoon—why generate more dishes to wash, when he lacked a woman to wash them?—and settled down to read the letter as he sipped.

Then his jaw dropped almost into his soup. It was a notice relating to the estate of Great Uncle Hoarfrost, who it seemed had recently died. Goar had known him only vaguely, and the crusty old man had never liked him. But it seemed Hoarfrost had mentioned Goar in his will, with this terse message: "Now you will suffer as you deserve, you poor excuse for a cow-flop. Make the most of it." Par for that course. So had the ornery character willed him a white elephant?

Then it described the inheritance: a generous amount in the form of interest from untouchable principal that would pay Goar enough each month to live on, indefinitely. As long as he focused on writing, producing at least a token amount each month, which he would have to send in to a listed Cloud office. When he missed a month, the allowance would be cut off for that month, and if he stopped entirely the account would be terminated. That was what was astounding. Uncle Hoarfrost was in effect paying him to be a writer.

The old man thought that was punishment? "Please don't throw me in that briar patch, Unc!" Goar murmured, smiling.

He called the lawyer's office, just to be sure this wasn't a practical joke. He didn't get the lawyer, of course, but the secretary had anticipated him. "Your uncle says in a codicil, no, it's not a joke. I quote: 'Look at page two, dumbbell.'"

Goar flipped the page. There was a check for the first month. It looked authentic. The behest was real.

Well, now. He would certainly take advantage of this amazing opportunity to become a successful and maybe famous writer. But first things first. He typed an email to his employer: "Take this job, liquify it, and shove it up your leaky tubes. Find someone else to mop up your fecal matter. In sum, frack it! I quit."

Then he turned in for the day. Better to sleep on it before he tackled the writing itself. Just in case this was actually a glorious dream.

He slept well, waking in the afternoon for a lunch of canned spaghetti with chocolate crackers. They were running low; he would have to get out and shop for more. The message and check remained. The deal was real.

Instead of heading off to work, he sat at his computer, ready to start typing his masterpiece. And discovered that his mind was blank. It was as if a stink bomb had scored on his imagination, making it reek. He had no idea of a title, let alone a story line. It seemed he had dreamed of having written a wonderful novel without actually working out its details. Such as a plot. Such as characters. Such as a unifying theme.

Oh, well. He tried. *The Great American Fantasy Novel*, he typed neatly in italics. *Once upon a time there was a poor excuse for a cowflop—oops, writer—whose fabled ability as a storyteller was all in his weak imagination.*

He didn't even need to reread that before deleting it. For one thing, the main text shouldn't be in italics. He tried again.

*Once upon a time there was a handsome prince who—*Who did what? Well, maybe it would work better with a pretty girl.

*Once upon a time there was a lovely princess who—*what, lay down in her own loveliness? And why was he still in italics?

A wee small voice in the murky back of his mind tried to hint that maybe uncle Hoarfrost had known what he was doing. Forcing Goar to put up or shut up, and so far he was shutting up. He was indeed starting to suffer.

Maybe princes or princesses weren't sufficiently magical. Try something that was all magic, like a genie. *Once upon a time there was a family of seven genies. G Ermaine was the Genie of Relevance. G Olf was the patron of little white balls. G Nius was the most intelligent. G Ode did his magic with crystals. G Mini was a small pair of twins.*

Oh, wait—that would add a genie, making the total eight. All right, so make it eight genies. Or was the plural still genie? He would look it up in due course.

G Em Stone was rare and precious, but her brother G Eneric was rather common. So one fine day the seven or eight genie(s) went out to have a great adventure.

The text stalled. What adventure? He was back to square one. Just when he was going so well. Sigh. Delete.

Well, maybe a different protagonist. *Once upon a time there was a walking skeleton with fat bones. Worse, he suffered from osteoporosis. All of the other skeletons used to laugh and call him names. They never let poor—*

Delete.

Maybe something less ambitious, to start?

Once there was some pocket change that was constantly changing pockets. All it wanted was to rest in the same pocket for a while. But then it wouldn't be change.

Delete.

He struggled all night, determined not to give up, but just got more frustrated. He generated unprinted reams of deleted efforts that hardly deserved the name of prose. He seemed to have a huge mental block that prevented him from writing. In fact, it was Writer's Block. He had thought that was humor, but it was turning out to be deadly serious.

As dawn approached, he fell into a daze, as this was normally the time he came home and got ready for sleep. Then something weird occurred.

There was the sound of horse's hooves echoing on his roof, which was odd because he lived in a basement apartment; the roof was ten floors up. Then a black horse came through the wall as if it were made of smoke. The horse halted right in front of Goar as he sat facing the computer, but now the computer wasn't there, just the horse.

"We must talk," the horse said.

Goar focused on what he could manage at the moment. "Your lips didn't move. How can you talk?" Let alone the fact that few if any horses talked at all; if you asked them to they said "Neigh!"

"Telepathy," the horse said. "My projected thoughts are entering your mind, and your mind is translating them to your familiar words. Similarly, your thoughts are reaching me, your words being superficial."

Oh. Nice to have an explanation. He was obviously imagining this. Give his imagination some credit for making a modicum of sense. "Um, I never heard of a talking horse, outside of old TV humor programs, and anyway, you don't look like Mister Ed. So what's happening here?"

"I am the Night Colt. I have a deal to propose that may significantly benefit us both, if you are interested."

Goar had been schooled never to look a gift horse in the mouth, but he had never been much for schooling. "Why should I make any deal with an imaginary horse? It will dissipate the moment I wake up. I may be a fool, but there are limits."

"I see you desire more background, but I don't want to bore you."

Was that a warning? "Bore me," Goar said.

"I come from the fabled Land of Xanth. Are you familiar with it?"

"Zanth? No."

"It's a magic realm resembling the state of Florida with added dragons, tangle trees, nickelpedes—"

"Whoa, there, horsie! I know what dragons are, but then you veered to left field. Can you flash me pictures, maybe?"

"Yes." The Colt flashed him pictures of carnivorous trees with green tentacles instead of leaves that grabbed unwary passers-by and hauled them in for meals. Also of bugs like giant centipedes with pincers that gouged out nickel-sized chunks of flesh. "Many Mundanes are eager to visit Xanth."

Goar was taken aback. "Why should anyone ever want to go there?"

The Colt flashed another picture, this time of attractive nude nymphs running around, screaming cutely, kicking their lovely legs high, and swinging their long hair around fetchingly. "They love to celebrate with men in the natural way."

Goar licked his lips. It had been some time since he had had a girl-friend, even one wanting to put him on a trolley to the sea, and she hadn't looked remotely like that. Nor had she been eager to "celebrate." In fact it was just after he had made his interest known that she made her remark. Possibly that was not coincidence. "Point made. Go on."

"Xanth is a kingdom where every citizen has a magic talent, ranging from the simple ability to make a spot on a wall, up to making motions slow or even freeze, or even Magician caliber transforming to other shapes. It is also largely made of puns."

"Oh, crap. Right when it was getting interesting." He had just spent the night trying to wrestle puns into a writable story, and was sick of them.

"You might like some of the puns. Shoes grow on shoe trees. Panties grow in pantrees. Zombies live in Zombie Houses. Step on an Infant Tile and turn into an infant. Shin digs."

"What digs?"

"Music that lures you in, only to feel a kick in the shin. A little like Boot Rear."

"Root Beer?"

"It's a pun. You get a kick out of it."

"I see. Continue."

"Then there's the husky tail that lends people different talents, the Tail Lent. Lots of people would like to grow one of those. And some folk dwell in cheese cottages."

Goar grimaced. "Cottage cheese?" But he was becoming intrigued. Maybe this land would be worth visiting, if only for its weirdness. "How could I get there for a look-see?"

"You can't. Not physically. Only in your imagination."

"Double crap!" Goar swore. "If I had imagination, I'd be writing my novel."

"Yes, I sensed your frustration. That's what summoned me."

"Okay, you call yourself the Night Colt. Exactly what does that mean?"

"As I said, I don't want to—"

"Bore me," Goar commanded.

"In Mundania, which is the dreary realm you occupy, folk mostly gen-erate their own bad dreams. But in Xanth these dreams are crafted under the direction of the Night Stallion, and delivered to worthy dreamers by the Night Mares. It's quite an industry, as they devise the screenplays and get them acted out by licensed actors, then deliver them to each sleeper. Similarly the Day Mares deliver daydreams to waking clients. Those are generally pleasant, such as finding patches of jelly bean plants, each bean a different flavor, like grape, strawberry, cherry, or other jelly, and completely non-fattening. The Night Stallion has a comprehensive catalog of sleepers who deserve punishment, so as to know exactly when and to whom to make every delivery. Timing is vital. It's an essential job." The Colt paused. "One I would very much like to assume, one day."

"Oho! You crave advancement."

"Exactly. I'd love to rule the herd, and have access to all those mares, apart from the importance of the position. But the Night Stallion is jealous of any possible competition, and ruthlessly eliminates any males that make the scene. I dare not go abroad by night lest he catch me and destroy me. But neither can I go abroad openly by day, where the day horses are; I'm a night horse. I have to remain completely silent and invisible, on pain of extinction."

"So you're up the creek without much of a paddle, let alone canoe."

"Exactly," the Colt agreed again. "I need to survive until my time comes, but I am severely constrained. I can risk it only between shifts, when neither the days nor the nights are out. That's half an hour before dawn and half an hour after sunset."

"What do you do in those limited times?"

"So far, nothing. But I could deliver bad dreams, if I had them. I can't craft them, because I'm a deliverer, not a creator. I need a private source."

"I think I'm beginning to get a glimmer. You want me to craft you some dreams to carry, so you can torment sleepers."

"Almost," the Colt agreed. "I can't deliver bad dreams, because that's the province of the mares. Also, if I go abroad before dawn, many of my subjects would wake before the dreams really take hold, wasting my effort."

"So you're screwed," Goar said.

"Gelded," the Colt agreed. "But there may be a loophole. Suppose I deliver a dream of any type just before the client wakes—to take effect in the waking state? Not a daydream, but a happening? It would give me valuable practice without technically violating either the night or day realms."

"Maybe so," Goar agreed thoughtfully. "But tell me this: why should I bust my behind crafting dreams for you to take the credit for? What's in it for me?"

The Colt hesitated. "May I speak candidly?"

"Speak," Goar said. "I really want to know."

"You are a failed writer. You have never written anything worthwhile, and now have walked smack into a Block so you can't write even bad stories."

That was more candor than Goar had sought, but he had to concede its accuracy. "So I'm a dismal flop as a writer, just as my scheming uncle said. How can I prove him wrong?"

"By doing what you *can* do, which is devising apt titles and opening situations, then letting them play out with real people in Xanth. Let them work out the continuations for you, because they will have no choice. You can put them into situations that they must find their ways clear of."

Goar considered. "It might be like seeing my stories made into movies, and I could watch what happens and make notes."

"Exactly," the Colt said once more. "Then you could write the full stories, having seen their continuations, and be on your way to success and fame."

"If I can't go to Xanth myself, how will I know what happens there?"

"You can't go there, but I can. I can't show myself by day, as I explained, but I can be there, and watch what happens, then tell you in the dusk session."

The notion had its appeal. "But suppose—"

"Oops, my time is up," the Colt said. "I shall return at dusk." He faded out.

And Goar woke up. Had it all been a dream? More correctly, had it been real? The Night Colt visiting him in the dream state, but with a real deal? This seemed likely, because otherwise it evinced more imagination than Goar had managed all night, literally.

Well, he had about twelve hours to prepare for the next stage, assuming it was real. He needed to devise some story titles and settings for the Colt to deliver.

What titles? What stories? His Block remained in force.

Maybe he could get an idea by checking some real stories. He checked his bookshelf and picked up the first book he saw. *Relentless Fairy Tales.*

Well, maybe it would do. He started reading—and promptly fell asleep. Because daylight was his normal sleeping time.

He woke in the afternoon, hungry and with a pressing bladder. And with his mind full of punnish takes on the fairly tales. Such as "The Princess and the Pee." Well, why not? It wasn't as if he would have to work out the main story himself.

At dusk he fell into another daze, and the Colt did come. "Bad news," the horse said. "I remembered a crucial limitation: only the mares can actually carry the dreams. I don't qualify."

Ouch! But Goar, in his sudden desperation, actually came up with an imaginative answer. "But surely I can carry them, since I'm inventing them. So I can ride you, in my dreams, and you can take me to Xanth and to the places we need to be, where I can sow my stories. You will still be instrumental in delivering them."

The Colt considered. "There was a time when a girl managed to ride a night mare. I suppose a man could ride a night colt. But only in your dreams; I have no physical substance here in Mundania, and not much in Xanth."

"Then let's do it," Goar said. "I'm asleep now. Let's do a test ride."

"Do you know how to ride a horse?"

"No. I suppose I can hang on to the saddle horn."

"I don't wear a saddle."

"I have to ride you bareback? That's beyond credence."

"That complicates it," the Colt agreed. "I will be leaping into the sky. What happens if you fall off?"

"I guess I'd wake from the dream as I hit the floor. But since this *is* a dream, let's amend it: I will imagine that my legs stick firmly to your hide, so I can't fall."

"At least, not without pulling my hide off. Why not simply imagine you're an expert rider?"

Goar's jaw dropped. "Why not, indeed! Okay, I'll be a fine experienced rider." He promptly jumped onto the Colt's back.

The Colt leaped up through the ceiling. They passed through all ten floors and out the roof, leaving some folk staring. This was a realistic dream!

Then they entered the Fantasy Land of Xanth and galloped through the sunset. The sky was turning red. The Colt jumped from cloud to cloud, gaining elevation.

"Yahooo!" Goar cried, waving his imaginary cowboy hat as they soared. "Yippee ti-yi, or whatever."

"Let's get down to business," the Colt said a bit sourly. "Spread some dreams."

"Okay. How about 'Goldilocks and the Three Beers?'"

"How does that go?"

"Goldilocks is a little girl. She wanders into this bears' house while they are out taking a walk. She finds three beers on the table, and sips from each. One is super spicy so she can't drink it. The next is so bland she spits out the sip. The third is just right, so she drinks it down and gets instantly drunk. That makes her sleepy, so she tries the three beds. The first is hard like a board. The second is so soft she's afraid she'll sink to the bottom of the earth. The third is just right, so she lies down and falls asleep. She's still there when the three bears return. 'Someone sipped my beer!' the papa bear exclaims. 'Someone sipped mine too, and spat it out,' says momma bear. 'Someone sipped my beer, and gulped it all down,' says Baby bear. Then—"

"We have a problem," Colt said. "We don't have any bear family like that in Xanth, and bears here don't drink beer."

"Well, find any three bears, and we'll make them fit the story."

The Colt swooped down low over the green jungle, and soon did find three bears who were snoozing near a honey pot. "The story of Goldilocks and the Three Beers!" Goar called. The words drifted down and sank into the bears.

Nothing happened. Was something wrong?

"Maybe the timing is incorrect," the Colt said. "This is the evening, when they're sleeping. We need to catch them just before they wake. Because this isn't a real dream, for them; it's supposed to be a story for them to act out awake."

"We'll try it again in the morning," Goar agreed, nevertheless disappointed.

They returned to Goar's apartment in Mundania. At least they had had a trial run, proving their ability to fly through the sky of Xanth. Great things might be in the offing.

"I will return in the morning," the Colt said. "Maybe you should have a different story ready."

"I will," Goar promised as the Colt leaped back through the ceiling and disappeared.

He spent the night, his normal waking time, refurbishing the stories suggested by the fairy tales. He decided to try 'The Three Little Prigs' next.

In the morning Goar was ready. "I have a different story," he said as he mounted the Colt. "It's about three little prigs. Three teenage girls, each of which is fussier about minor deals than the others. Then comes the Wolf, who wants them for a nefarious purpose. But he's big and messy and has carrion breath, so they're not interested. When he comes after the first girl, she slams the door of her straw house in his face. But he huffs and he puffs and he blows her house down and catches her. Then he goes after the second prig, and she hides herself in her wood house, but he huffs and puffs and blows it down too, and gets her also. Then he goes after the third prig, but she barricades herself in her brick house, and he can't get her. So she lives and dies an old maid."

"That's not much of a story," the Colt said as they flew across the landscape of Xanth.

"Well, it's what I got." Goar didn't want to admit that it was rather freely adapted from a fairy tale, his own imagination having failed him. "Find me three prigs near a wolf."

The Colt swooped down over a village. They could see into the houses as if they were roofless. Some villagers were out and about, but though they glanced at the sky, they obviously didn't see anything unusual. Goar and the Colt were invisible. Which was fine. It allowed them to do their business without fear of interference.

And lo, there were three houses near the edge where teen girls slept. "The Tale of the Three Little Prigs!" Goar hollered as they passed over the houses. He saw the girls stir as they received the dreams.

They flew back to his apartment. "I will watch and report what happened, tonight," the Colt promised.

Goar waited impatiently for the night report, meanwhile adapting more fairy tales to his purpose. But when the Colt came, he was disappointed. "They woke up and shook off the dreams," the Colt reported. "Nothing interesting happened."

"What are we missing?" Goar asked.

"I think your stories lack sufficient definition. You need to nail them so they can't be dismissed. Maybe if you wrote the title where folk could see it, so they know it's a story setting."

"And maybe I can name the girls, for this purpose," Goar said. "So they're tagged, as it were, and can't move on until they have fulfilled their roles."

"We'll try again tomorrow," the Colt said.

Before dawn, they flew to the village again. This time Goar made a smoking torch—in his dream he could conjure things as needed—and held it aloft as the Colt made letter patterns in the sky right above the three houses.

THE THREE LITTLE PRIGS

"Who are named Eenie, Meanie, and Minnie," Goar pronounced. "Who are about to encounter the Big Bad Wolf."

Then they hurried back to Mundania, because making the aerobic title had taken time and they had to be gone before dawn.

The Colt appeared that evening. "I have good news and bad news," he said. "The story worked. But it didn't play out exactly as you had plotted it."

"I will endure," Goar said, secretly relieved, because what he really needed was not a timid adaptation but an original story.

It turned out to be some story. It seemed that the first Prig, the one named Eenie, woke first, got up, opened her door, and was confronted by the Wolf, exactly as specified. The Wolf was dressed like a big lunk of a neighbor boy. "Well, little girl," Wolf said with a lupine smile that showed too many teeth. "You and I are about to have a fine time. Let me into your house and we'll indulge on your bed." He eyed her contours, which actually were good ones.

Eenie considered that for all of a microsecond. But Wolf was shaggy, and his teeth weren't clean, and his breath smelled of carrion. That turned her off. She was very fussy about such details. "Not by the hair of your chinny chin chin," she replied, and slammed the door in his face.

That annoyed Wolf, for some reason. "Well, I'll huff and I'll puff and I'll blo-o-ow your house down," he growled.

"Get lost, fur-face," Eenie called from inside.

So Wolf huffed, and he puffed, and he blew out a blast that compared pretty well to a hurricane. It blew the house apart, exposing Eeenie. "Well now," Wolf said, licking his chops. "Shall we get to it, you delectable morsel?"

But Eenie's talent was the Flee Market. The one magic thing she could do was flee fleetly to that market. So she fled to it, with the Wolf in slavering pursuit. Unfortunately he mistook it for the Flea Market, where fleas went to pick up their dogs, and the fleas mistook him for a dog and leaped on. It took him an hour with noxious chemicals to get free of fleas.

But the Wolf had by no means given up the chase. The first little prig was gone, but there was another next door. She lived in a wood house, which she was now busily cleaning, being persnickety about such details. Wolf pounded on her door. "Open up," he cried. "I have urgent business with you, you tasty little twerp."

Meanie had a certain streak, and she didn't much like being termed a twerp. "Forget it, hair for brains," she called without opening the door.

So Wolf huffed and puffed and it was like a tornado blasting the house to smithereens. Meanie was exposed in more than one sense; the wind had also blown away her clothes. That annoyed her.

So when Wolf stepped into the wreckage and took hold of her, she tapped him on the chest and invoked her talent. That knocked the wind out of him, in a single powerful gust, leaving him so depleted he had to struggle to gasp. But he managed to get out a few words. "That was mean of you."

"Thank you," Meanie said. "Now get your carcass out of here before I touch you again." It was no bluff, and he reluctantly retreated. What business did girls have with magic talents? They only impeded progress.

But one house remained. Once Wolf had recovered his breath, he approached the third house. It was made of solid impervious brick, so he did not threaten to try to blow it down. This was the occasion for a bit of discretion. "Let me in, trollop," he called politely. "I have big things in mind for you."

Despite Wolf's politeness, there was something about the way he addressed her that Minnie found annoying, so she responded in kind. "By all means, bush-tail," she said as she opened the door and presented her nice bare shoulder. Wolf eagerly put his paw on it, a prelude to much further touching—and froze in place. She stepped back, and he toppled, flaking off chips of ice. Her talent, of course, was the Cold Shoulder.

Then Minnie called in her friends Eenie and Meanie, and the three of them shoved the frozen Wolf into the neighboring sewer and watched him float away. Chances were that he would not be bothering the Three Little Prigs again. Meanwhile, Eenie and Meanie would have to move in with Minnie, at least until their houses were rebuilt. None of them mourned the Wolf. Maybe if he had taken a bath and brushed his teeth it would have been a different story, but they were self-righteously choosy. They knew they could do better elsewhere.

"And that's how it went," Colt concluded. "It seems that Wolf is just not into Prigs, however much he might have desired it."

"Too bad," Goar said. "Still, it pretty much proves the case. I will make notes for my novel. We can choose future prospects more carefully, and get some really interesting stories."

"And maybe mess up some staid Xanth traditions along the way," Colt agreed.

The two exchanged a mental smile. They were in business.

Chapter 2

PRINCESSES

Princess Eve left her seven-year-old son Plato in the competent hands of the governess Zosi Zombie and walked the path from Hades to Xanth. She was going to visit her twin sister Dawn, who had something disturbing on her mind. Eve was really curious what that might be, because Dawn had a virtually perfect life in Xanth, with a great talent, husband, children, and mission in life. It was not like her to be bothered by incidentals. That sort of thing was Eve's province; she was the darker one, in hair and mood. Why just this morning she had suffered a weird dream whose details she had forgotten, but the oddity of it lingered. Something about a Princess and a Frog? No, that wasn't it. Princesses and frogs seldom interacted.

Eve reminisced how they had come to their places in life. They were twin sisters, twenty-six years old, one lovely as the morning, the other lovely as the evening. They were Sorceresses because all the descendants of Great Grandpa Bink had been promised Magician caliber talents by the Demon Xanth. Dawn could tell anything about anything she touched that was alive, while Eve could tell about anything inanimate. In their youth they had been mischievous girls, sometimes naughtily flashing panties to freak out boys, but both had grown up to be more responsible married women. Eve had wooed and won the Dwarf Demon Pluto and become the mistress of his nether realm Hades, colloquially called Hell, ministering to the sorry souls there. Dawn had wooed and won her friend the walking skeleton Picka Bone, and taken residence in the traveling Caprice Castle, collecting and storing surplus puns. Eve had married for status, Dawn for love; Dawn had the better deal.

So why was Dawn disturbed? She had the perfect life. It was a mystery.

Suddenly there was a tavern astride the path ahead. Eve did not remember any such thing along this route; it was the private path the sisters used to visit each other, going to Hell and back, not open for others. Yet here was this establishment, typical of the type that sent many folk to the nether realm. Had she taken a wrong turn while wrapped in her thoughts, and arrived at a bypath?

Eve stooped and touched the surface of the path with one finger. No, it was correct and unchanged. Somehow the tavern had been added to the existing path. How, and maybe more importantly, why? Every citizen of Xanth had a magic talent of some sort, ranging from Magician or Sorceress level down to hardly worth it. Someone must have the talent of instantly building houses, and dropped one here on the path. That man needed a Speaking To—it was surely a man, because women had little truck with such establishments—to be sure he didn't do it again.

Well, maybe she could find out. She walked up to the building and touched the door with her finger. And stood surprised, if not quite amazed. Because the tavern was illusion. That was to say, more apparent than real. She was unable to tell who had made it, because she couldn't actually touch it, just the appearance of it.

Now she was good and curious. Why should anyone plant such a well-developed illusion here on a strictly private path? Illusion was efficient magic, because it required little effort to get an impressive effect, and it could accomplish a lot when it tried. For example, someone might craft the illusion of solid ground that extended over a deep pit, so that anyone who walked innocently along that ground would fall in the pit and possibly get hurt. Nasty men had been known to buy spot illusions for exactly that purpose, to trap pretty girls in locked bedrooms where they had to bargain their way out in a manner they would not ordinarily choose. Men could be such beasts! Not that Eve herself had any such concern; all she had to do was murmur the name of her husband, and the Demon would be there to make very short and quite unkind work of any aspiring lecher.

Eve walked through the insubstantial door and entered the image of the tavern. And felt a change. The building had become real, as she verified with a touch of the wall. Or maybe the door was actually a portal to send a person to the real tavern at another site. At any rate she was now in the main room of it, and her touch had also advised her that she was locked in. An illusion trap indeed!

The room was filled with people and creatures going about their business. Some elves and gnomes were sitting at the bar, glugging from big glass mugs. Some goblins were at the tables, glugging from more ordinary mugs. Some trolls, ogres, and humans were standing around, glugging from yet more mugs. There seemed to be an endless supply of mugs filled with frothy brownish liquid. Yet none of these gluggers seemed to be drunk. Was the drink illusion? Then why should they bother?

Now she realized another thing. All the folk here were male, except for her. If it was a male-only establishment, why had she been admitted? Because the proprietor could readily have enchanted the door to admit only more males.

And there before her was a table with a single huge mug. On the side was printed PRINCESS EVE. She was definitely invited to this party. In fact she had been expected.

One more thing: above the table was a sign floating in the air:

THE PRINCESS AND THE GROG

Curiouser and curiouser. Was that a story title? Then what was the story? And why was it being presented in this manner? There was a certain familiarity about it, and she realized that that was what she had dreamed of. Not a frog, but a grog. So this might be part of a larger story.

Fortunately she did not have to linger perplexed. She could soon unravel the mystery. She extended her finger and touched the mug.

Uh-oh. The mug contained a magical brew that would immediately render the person who drank it quite drunk and incapable of saying no to anything anyone else might suggest. Worse, it would wipe out the memory of whatever happened this day. In fact it was what in Mundania was known as the date-rape drug. The following morning a girl would have only her sore body to hint at what had transpired.

Eve became aware that though the males in the room were theoretically engaged in their own pursuits, all of them were actually watching her. Waiting for her to take up the mug and drink the grog with her name on it. For her to be unable to say no, or to remember next day.

Talk of falling in a pit.

This was certainly deserving of a murmur to Pluto. But she did not like summoning him incidentally. She preferred to handle awkward situations herself. How could she do that?

What about that floating title? That might be the key.

Eve climbed carefully on the table and stood up. Now the title was in reach. She took hold of the first two letters of the last word, GR, and mashed them about to make one new letter: F. Now it said THE PRIN-CESS AND THE FOG.

She knew what that fog would do. She took a deep breath, held it, and jumped down from the table as the liquid in the mug puffed into vapor. In fact it was dense mist. It spread out, surrounding her, as the males converged. She dropped to her hands and knees and scooted along the floor, concealed by the billowing cloud, passing between the legs of an ogre, moving away from the table. Soon she was clear of the fog.

She stood up and looked back. The center of the room was now a mass of vapor shrouded drunk males, none of them able to say no to whatever was happening, and none of whom would remember any of it tomorrow. Which would make explaining it to anyone else difficult.

Princess Eve smiled. It did seem to serve them right.

She walked to the illusion door and stepped through. She found herself back on the path. She made her way around the illusion tavern, not risking its interior again, and resumed her trip along the path. Soon she reached Caprice Castle; the path was spelled to get to it, regardless of where it was at the moment.

She stepped up to the front and knocked on the door. "Aunt Eve!" a child's voice cried. The door slid open to reveal two five-year-old children. One was a cute human girl, the other a cute walking skeleton.

"Hello, children!" Eve said as she gathered them in for a hug.

"Did you bring us anything?" the skeletal boy asked.

"Of course I did, Piton," Eve said. "But you'll have to change form to eat it. It's a cupcake from the pastree I passed along the way." She handed it to him.

Piton shifted to human boy form and took a bite. "Thanks!" he said around a mouthful.

"And one for you too, though you were too polite to ask, Data. A Danish from the same tree."

"Thank you," the girl said, and bit into it.

"Now I'd love to spend the rest of the day with you two, but I really need to talk with your mother."

"I'm here," Dawn said, stepping close so they could hug. The children ran off, still eating their pastree confections.

"What is disturbing you?" Eve asked. "Does it by chance relate to a strange dream or episode?"

"Yes! How did you know?"

"I had one of those myself. In fact, on the way here."

"Tell me all about it."

Eve did. "Someone must have set it up," she concluded. "It could have been significantly worse for me, if I had not been alert and with magic of my own."

"Exactly. Now let me tell you, or rather show you, Princess Rhythm's experience yesterday. She called me on the mirror and relayed the whole thing."

"Princess Rhythm," Eve repeated, surprised.

Dawn smiled. "You do remember the triplets Princesses Melody, Harmony, and Rhythm, the naughty one who got a boyfriend when she was only twelve?"

"And now she is pushing twenty-one," Eve agreed, responding to the teasing. "And about to come out openly with her boyfriend Cyrus Cyborg, now that she is of age to do publicly what they've been doing all along privately. Yes, I may remember her, if I focus hard enough."

"Yesterday Rhythm had an odd dream, if that is what it was. But beware; there are some elements that some viewers might find objectionable."

"I have spent years in hell," Eve said. "I suspect I can handle it."

Dawn gestured to the magic mirror on the wall, and the scene came on.

Princess Rhythm woke and stretched. Today was the day she would visit Cyrus for some close-up one on one. That was not completely surprising, as she did it every day. But soon there would be no further need for secrecy, and their secret love would be no secret any more.

But right now she had an urgent need. She tossed back the cover and flung her pretty legs over the edge of the bed.

And caught herself just in time. She was atop a pile of twenty mattresses that towered so high that it threatened to bang into the ceiling. Despite that, there was an annoying bump, and she knew that there was something below the bottommost mattress that threatened to disrupt her repose. It felt like a hard half pea. She would have to do something about that. Right after she satisfied her pressing urge.

She gazed down from the height and saw a potty sitting on the floor beside the mound of mattresses. That was it! She would just have to scramble down to floor level and—

She paused her thought. There was something wrong with this picture. First, natural functions were seldom if ever mentioned in fantasy narratives, and almost never in connection with girls, and absolutely not with princesses. A true princess had no natural functions as far as fantasy fiction went. Second, she had a competent bathroom in her suite, complete with sanitary facilities. She hadn't used a lowbrow potty in about eighteen years. The moment she turned twenty-one, she would graduate to perpetual pristinity. Third, what was she doing atop twenty mattresses? She had gone to sleep on one. Fourth, she had the feeling that someone or something was watching. An invisible presence, probably male. That compounded the awkwardness.

Rhythm made an effort and held her, um, patience as she pondered. Certainly she was not about to do anything before she came to understand the complications. She looked around from the height of her feathery mountain, and spied what she had overlooked before.

There was a sign hovering in the air, like the title of a story:

THE PRINCESS AND THE PEE

Rhythm stared at the last word, then down at the potty. She suspected that there was a connection. Especially considering her desperate urgency.

Some one or some thing had set this up, and was watching to see how it played out. Smile! You're on Forthright Focus!

Well, she was *not* going to perform for the camera, though she was about to burst.

But what could she do? She was in the scene, and seemed unable to get out of it without following its rules. She could not delay much longer, lest she begin to leak, um, suffer an unprincessly accident.

Then she got an inspiration. That floating sign seemed to define the action. Suppose the definition shifted slightly?

Rhythm scooted across the mattress, causing the tower to wee-waw alarmingly. The sign was just above the end of the mattress. She got cautiously to her feet and reached up to it. Her fingers caught hold of the word PRINCESS but were unable to move it. The title seemed to be fixed.

Ah, but maybe it could be amended. She sat back on the mattress and took hold of the bedspread. She used a sharp fingernail to cut a cloth shape out, then another. Then she stood and used loose threads to tie two new letters to the last word. Now it said:

THE PRINCESS AND THE PEEVE

Lo, her internal urgency was gone, replaced by a new one: she had to go consult with the pet peeve, the most obnoxious bird in Xanth. She understood the peeve had spent time in hell itself, and been ousted when its fowl beak wore out its welcome there. No one knew what kind of bird it was, except that it was a parody. For that matter no one knew its gender either. It typically perched on a person's shoulder and used that person's voice to insult all comers, stirring up trouble. But she had always liked it, to its evident frustration.

Rhythm clambered down the side of the mattresses to reach the floor. She ran past the now pointless potty, not even pausing to change out of her nightie. She had to get to the peeve.

Ordinarily a girl alone in a nightie would not fare well in the dragon-infested jungle of Xanth. But Rhythm was a Sorceress, and the dragons had come to understand that these ladies were not for burning. Now none tried to interfere with her.

In due course, approximately, because it wasn't exactly a course and nothing was due, Rhythm arrived at the peeve's perch.

The nondescript little green bird eyed her disapprovingly. "Only an idiot or a disreputable urchin would go walking alone outside in her nightie," it remarked.

Rhythm produced her little drum, which was always magically within her reach. She bonged on it with one stick so that its magic manifested as a warning ripple. "Only a bird brain would remark on the obvious." Then she stepped close and kissed it on the beak.

"I wouldn't take that from anyone less naughty than you."

"I know. I'm the naughtiest."

The parody sighed. "What brings you here, Princess Naughty?"

"I think I need your help, peeve."

This set the bird back a bit. The peeve had very few friends, and no one ever wanted its presence for long, let alone its help. It fought visibly against the flattery, without perfect success. "What's up, Princess?"

"Do you want the whole story, or a summary?"

"The whole story, of course, tart."

"Right: the summary. This morning someone tried to make me act out the story of the Princess and the Pee."

The peeve laughed so hard it fell off its perch. It scrambled back, still amused. "Oh, I'd have liked to see that."

"Forget it. I'm not *that* naughty."

"Too bad. So how can I help you?"

The parody had a dirty mind. What else was new? "You already have. I changed Pee to Peeve and came to see you. I figure that means you need to be involved."

The peeve considered. "It could be interesting. Especially if they try again to make you do it."

"I have the feeling someone is watching, even now. I want to know who and why."

"I can tell you Why: there's nothing like seeing a naughty pretty girl perform. As to Who—it could be any male in Xanth."

"No. Remember, I'm a Sorceress. I'm proof against ninety-nine and forty-four hundredths of a percent of males. This has to be something else."

"Something beyond Magician caliber magic. That does limit it. So we'd better get help."

"Help? I don't want the whole of Xanth knowing about this nuisance."

"The other Princesses. So as to have all five."

"Oh." That appealed. Rhythm was a Sorceress. When she got together with one of her triplet sisters, their combined magic squared the power.

When all three of them got together, their power was cubed. The two older princesses, their cousins Dawn and Eve, had invaluable knowledge magic. The five of them together could surely crack this mystery.

"And that's the story," Dawn said as the mirror faded out. "They'll be arriving soon."

"Perhaps that is just as well," Eve agreed. "But what about this invisible observer? Is he watching us now? How can we plan anything effective, if the mischief maker knows even as we plan it?"

"You forget, this is Caprice Castle. It is proof against hostile spying. Rhythm and the peeve know that; that's why they didn't mention it. We have the privacy we need."

"That's right; I forgot. It will be good to see the three twerps again."

"Twerps?" the three princesses chorused, appearing in the doorway. Melody was in a green dress, with greenish hair and blue eyes; Harmony was brown throughout in dress, hair and eyes; Rhythm wore a red dress with red hair and green eyes. It was their standard Trio outfit, as though they were three peas in a pod, though they had become quite different young women. "You know-it-alls call us twerps?"

"And hello peeve," Dawn said, laughing. Because the bird was perched on Rhythm's shoulder, and imitating the voices of the princesses, as was its wont.

The twins appeared, both in human guise for the moment. "What a stench," Piton said, wrinkling his little nose. "Did a zombie crow fly in here and poop?"

"No, it's worse," Data said, matching the wrinkle. "It's the peeve."

"Hello, bratwurst," the peeve said in its own voice. "Or do I mean worst brats?"

Then all three laughed. It was obvious that they understood each other.

"The grownups are heading into a big dull discussion," Piton said.

"So let's us three go and get into some mischief while they're busy," Data said.

"That works for me," the peeve agreed. It flew across to perch on Piton's shoulder. "What you have in mind, bonehead?"

"Mom has a pot of Eye Scream ready to serve the guests," Piton said.

"And what about you, meathead?"

"Let's go have a snowball fight with it," Data said.

"I get the chocolate eyes," the peeve said. "You can have the screams."

The three left the room.

Eve looked at Dawn. "You didn't really leave it unguarded, sweet sister dear?"

"Of course not, sinister sister dear. Picka is watching it."

"But he'll turn fleshly and join their mischief," Eve protested.

"And none of them will bother us while we work out our plans," Dawn said.

The three shared most of a glance. Dawn did have a fair notion what she was doing. It would be easier to work effectively when not distracted by man, bird, or children, all creatures who tended to demand more attention than was convenient.

"Shouldn't we notify King Aunt Ivy?" Eve asked.

"I don't think so," Dawn said. "Not until we know who is watching, and why. It's better to keep our plans secret, which we can do only here."

"Also, King Ivy is distracted with the looming Dragon/Human war," Harmony said. "She's searching for a way to head it off, but it's complicated. We surely need to leave her to it."

"Meanwhile I did some spot research with Goggle," Rhythm said. "There have been incidents."

"So?" Eve asked.

"There's a report of a story that didn't play out well, 'Goldilocks and the Three Beers.' Apparently the storyteller didn't have all the elements in place. Then there was 'The Three Little Prigs,' where the Big Bad Wolf went after three village girls. They used their talent to foil him, and he wound up frozen stiff and dumped in the sewer. Next day I was targeted as 'The Princess and the Pee,' and today Eve was caught in 'The Princes and the Grog.' We both managed to avoid the worst, but the incidents are disturbing. Who is behind this, and what does he want? Surely not just peeks at disheveled girls."

"And how does he set up the stories?" Eve asked. "That requires considerable magic."

"Do you think a Demon is involved?" Harmony asked. She was the most sensible of the trio, and destined to become King of Xanth in due course, so naturally was concerned.

"No," Melody said. "I did spot research with Binge, though it made me a bit tipsy, and learned that the dream realm is involved, in a manner."

"The dream realm," Harmony said. "That does make sense. These were like waking dreams, not exactly night or day dreams. But that puts them outside the realm of the night mares or the day mares."

"Yes," Melody said. "They occur only in the morning, the dreams being planted in twilight between night and day. That confirms that the regular dream carriers aren't involved."

"So then who's doing it?" Harmony asked.

"A rogue night colt."

"A colt! But the Night Stallion doesn't tolerate any other male dream horses. They get banished or killed."

"I said a rogue," Melody said. "It seems that somehow he escaped the notice of the Stallion, and is operating in the twilight zone."

"But male horses can't carry dreams," Eve said. "They're drones; they can observe, but not act, in that respect."

"Some drones can act," Dawn said.

"Those ones are promptly banished to drear Mundania," Eve said. "Or to Hades; I see a number there."

"The colt isn't a drone," Melody said. "But you're right. He can't carry dreams. He's in league with a Mundane writer. The man isn't much good at his craft, but he can carry dreams, or in this case, stories. He adapts them from Mundane fairy tales, such as 'The Three Little Pigs,' only with a word changed."

"'The Three Little Prigs'!" Rhythm exclaimed. "That's where he got it, shoring up his weak imagination."

"Then letting the title play out as it would," Harmony said. "He must have done the same with Goldilocks and the Three Beers."

"The Three Bears," Melody agreed.

"But if he's Mundane, how does he get those hackneyed notions to Xanth?" Eve asked. "Because I can tell you, 'The Princess and the Grog' definitely reached me. I don't care what it was adapted from, I could have been in real trouble if I'd drunk that grog. My Sorceressly powers could have become useless if I didn't remember I had them, or that I could summon my husband."

"Who would have been most annoyed if all those lawless males had deluged you with ellipses," Rhythm said. An ellipsis consisted of three significant dots and was essential to stork summoning. It was considered a rather private matter.

"That's where the night colt comes in," Melody said. "It seems the two made a deal, and the colt carries the writer into Xanth, where he can deliver his pesky notions."

"But a night colt couldn't carry a Mundane physically," Eve protested. "He's a dream horse."

"The Mundane is dreaming at the time. The colt carries not the dream, but the dreamer, who is like a ghost. He gallops through the sky while the writer sows his mischief."

"The ghost writer in the sky?"

"That's it," Melody agreed.

"There's something familiar about that," Harmony said.

"You're thinking of the Mundane song 'Ghost Riders in the Sky,'" Rhythm said. "It's about horsemen who ride among the burning clouds, because they lived bad lives."

"Oh, a pun," Harmony said, frowning.

"And a ghost writer is one who writes a book for another person, anonymously," Eve said. "We have those in Hades too."

"Well, it has to be stopped, punny or not," Rhythm said. "This princess is not going to pee for any Mundane hack."

"That it seems is our challenge," Harmony said. "We need to find a way to stop this wicked collaboration between the rogue dream horse and the bad writer."

"Before someone gets hurt," Eve agreed.

"But we can't touch a ghost, literally," Eve said. "And we can't go into Mundania, even if we wanted to."

"A ghost," Harmony said thoughtfully. "Could a ghost stop a ghost?"

"It might," Eve said. "We have ghosts in Hades, too. But they can't be trusted, and motivating one to do anything useful is next to impossible."

"Or Mundania," Harmony said. "Could we prevail on a live Mundane to deal with the ghost writer, such as by taking away his book of fairy tales?"

"So we need a ghost in Xanth, or a live person in Mundania," Dawn said.

"Could a person be both?" Eve asked.

"How?"

"The same way as the writer. Dreaming."

"But we don't have a dream horse to carry such a dreamer into Xanth," Rhythm said. "There's already too much trouble of that kind."

"But if there were another way?"

"What other way?"

"Maybe a magic mirror," Eve said.

"Magic doesn't work very well in Mundania," Rhythm snapped.

"Suppose we crafted a picture?" Dawn asked. "Actually a portal. In Mundania it would be just a picture of Xanth, but if the right person attuned to it, he might step into it and be in Xanth, albeit in a ghostlike state."

"Now that's a notion," Eve said. "But how do we find such a person?"

"Maybe you could pose in dishabille just inside the picture, as if heading for an ellipsis," Dawn suggested with a trace of a fragment of a bit of a smile, "That would bring any Mundane lad leaping into the picture."

"Or you could turn skeleton and do the same with your nice bones," Eve snapped back.

"Girls, girls," Harmony said, though they were five years older than the triplets. However, Harmony's future as King of Xanth lent her a certain occasional gravitas.

"Aww," Rhythm said. "They were just trying to get a little naughty." She of course was the authority on naughtiness.

"Or you could do the Princess and the Pee skit for them," Melody said.

Rhythm opened her mouth for an angry retort, but was overtaken by a passing giggle. That incident had indeed demonstrated the limits of her naughtiness.

"The picture/portal may be a good idea," Harmony said seriously. "We could select a scene that looks downright mundane, only with little details that suggest it is not so. Only an observant person would catch it, and that would be the one we want."

"Let's do it," Dawn said. "The three of you can cube your magic to craft a portal that would translate a person between the two realms, while Eve and I set about making a path that will lead any dream ghost to Caprice Castle, where I can acquaint him with the situation and enlist his aid."

"But would he cooperate?" Harmony asked. "Mundanes can be remarkably obstinate."

"You should know," Rhythm said. "How many years have you been courting that Mundane man and being balked? Have you even gotten him into bed yet?"

"Five years. No. But Bryce is weakening."

"You do know you could marry any man you chose, without even having to flash your panties? You're smart and pretty and the future King of Xanth, for pity's sake. The man's a fool."

"No more a fool than the cyborg who took up with a twelve-year-old girl."

"I used an aging spell and hauled him into a love spring. He couldn't help it."

"Well, I didn't stoop to any such tactics, sister dear."

"Which is why you can't nail him, sister dear."

"Girls, girls," Eve said, imitating Harmony's voice perfectly when she had said it. This time they all laughed. They loved teasing each other about their naughtinesses.

"Let's face it," Melody said. "Cooperation won't be a problem. When Dawn turns on the charm, that mundane man will do whatever she asks."

The others nodded soberly. Dawn, with her talent of knowing everything about any person she touched, could be angelically persuasive.

"But whom do we choose, and how?" Dawn asked.

"That's easy," Melody said. "Make the portal appealing to any young, unattached, suitably impulsive, and not too smart Mundane who passes by."

"Appealing?" Eve asked. "In what way?"

"A smidge of mind reading will do. Just enough to pick up a lurking desire. Then that image can appear on the screen."

"But Mundane men are interested in only one thing," Eve protested.

"Just like Xanth men," Dawn agreed. "So it can show a pretty girl, beckoning."

"We need more discrimination than that," Harmony said. "Better to block that out and tune in to someone who likes nature."

"That should do it," Rhythm agreed.

A glance circulated and came to rest in the center. They had reached their decision.

Just in time. There was a commotion in the hall as man, bird, and children brought their eye scream ball fight to the princesses' chamber. It was about to get messy. But fun.

Chapter 3

PORTAL

The gallery was having a sale of surplus paintings. Tartan had little interest in art, but was curious, so went to look at the offerings. Sure enough, they were dull, boring, and tedious, not his type of thing at all. Not that he could afford art anyway; this was mere window shopping.

Then he passed a painting titled "Mystery," and backtracked to look at it again. It was simply a jungle scene, a path leading back through the trees toward some hidden goal. Completely ordinary. But it held him. Where did that path go? He wanted to know.

There was a bench opposite the painting. Tartan sat down on it and gazed into the scene. Now he noticed that there were words along the base. Well, letters, anyway. BNX MJQB TH AOEUI. What did they mean? The more he tried to focus on them, the more obscure they became.

"May I join you?"

Tartan looked up. There was a young woman in a white blouse and tan skirt, not pretty, not plain, just anonymously ordinary. Much like himself in his white T-shirt and khaki trousers. She even had brown hair and brown eyes, as he did, except that her hair was longer and her eyes more delicate. "Sure. It's a public bench."

She sat down beside him. "I see you are looking at the Mystery painting."

"Yes. I'm no judge of art. There's just something about the jungle scene that interests me. And the nonsensical lettering below it."

"Jungle scene? Surely you mean the flower garden."

Tartan was surprised. "Are we looking at the same painting?"

"I think so. The one immediately before us."

"Mine is a jungle."

"Mine is not. This is curious."

He glanced at her. "You're not joshing me?"

"Not," she agreed. "I am Tara. My name means tower. It's a misnomer; there's nothing towering about me, in any respect."

"I am Tartan. It means commander in chief. That's another misnomer; I've never had any authority of any kind, and wouldn't know what to do with it if by some mischance I had it. In fact as a child I got teased about supposedly wearing a skirt. You know, a kilt, with a tartan, though I never wore one."

"So we are two completely ordinary people. Hello." She extended her hand.

Surprised, he took it, and they shook hands. Small as the gesture was, it moved him. He found himself liking her. He knew this was nonsensical, as she would soon be moving on and he would never see her again. That had always been the way with him and women.

"And I'll bet we have nothing in common," he said. "Except—"

"Except for our eyes and hair, and the fact that we're both attracted to this painting," she said.

He laughed. "And we can't even agree on what it is."

"So let's settle this. That blue rose looks so close and real it's almost as if I could pick it." She reached toward the painting.

"Are we allowed to touch it? Don't want to leave a fingerprint."

"I'll be careful." Her extended finger touched the painting. "Oh!"

"What, prick yourself on a thorn?"

"It's not there!" she exclaimed, drawing her hand quickly back.

"Of course it's there. It's a painting."

"Then what's this?" She held up her hand. It was empty.

"What's what?"

She looked at her hand. "I thought I picked a petal." She brought her fingers to her nose. "In fact I smell it. Here, see what you think." She held her hand out to him.

Tartan sniffed her delicate fingers. There was a definite odor of rose. "Your perfume?"

"I don't use perfume. That's the rose I touched."

Tartan considered. Had she really brushed a blue rose? So he reached to the painting himself.

His finger found no resistance. Instead his hand passed through the surface and went to the path. He picked up a fallen yellow leaf.

"From the path," he said, showing it to her.

"But your hand is empty."

He looked. So it was. "I guess it felt more real than it was."

Now it was her turn to consider. "I think this is more complicated than we realized."

"Maybe we should alert the proprietors."

"Let's explore a bit more first. This is really odd."

"They might think we're tetched," he agreed. "Not only do we see two different pictures, we can touch them, in a manner."

"Do you believe in the supernatural?"

"No, really. There must be some rational explanation."

"That's the way I see it," she said. "But now we've discovered two things about this painting that are really hard to explain in any rational sense."

"Could it be a—a portal of some kind? A window to another place?"

"Why would such a thing be in a gallery, let alone for sale cheap?"

"Why, indeed!" he said. "How about this: someone made an experimental device that connects two places. He didn't want anyone to steal it, so he framed it as a painting and put a nonsensical title on it. Then he died in a traffic accident, and his inheritors, having no idea of its nature, put it up for sale as they liquidated the estate. So it wound up in the gallery, and folk who look at it see just ordinary scenes. Until we picked up on something else, just enough to make us wonder."

She nodded. "So should we tell the proprietor?"

"I don't think so. He'll either figure we're crazy, or worse, steal the portal for himself. It must be extremely valuable."

"It had to have come here because they bought it cheap. We need to buy it."

"Yes!" he agreed. "At least we appreciate it for what it is, even if we have no idea what it is."

"But can we afford it? I have only thirteen dollars with me."

"And I have twelve, and change."

"Maybe they'll accept a bid."

"Let's try."

They got up and went to the office window. "We'd like to buy one of your paintings," he said. "But we don't have much money."

"Which one?" the bored clerk asked.

"It's titled 'Mystery.'"

"Oh, that one. It's nothing. Make an offer."

"Twenty-five dollars," Tara said.

"Sold."

Amazed, they pooled their cash and handed it over. The clerk wrote out a receipt, and they went to take the painting. Soon he was carrying the large padded package.

"Um, there are details we didn't think of, in our rush to get the painting," Tartan said. "Such as where to take it. I live across town. I took a bus to get here."

"I have a third-hand car, but didn't need it for this. My apartment's down the street, in walking distance. We can take it there."

"You don't mind my, um, visiting?"

Tara turned her face to him. "This is bigger than both of us."

That seemed to suffice. They walked to her small efficiency apartment, which was nondescript, what she could afford.

"What now?" he asked as he set down the package.

"I'm so excited about this portal, I just want to learn more about it."

"Me too."

They propped it up against the wall opposite her bed, where there was space for it. It was about a yard high and almost as wide. Tara reached in and failed to pluck a blue rose from her garden, and Tartan failed to scoop up a handful of dry leaves from his jungle path.

"I wonder," she said.

"Are you thinking what I'm thinking?"

"I think I am. That maybe we could enter that realm, whatever it is, and then we'd be able touch it more substantially."

"Yes. Maybe it just doesn't let its things be passed through to our realm."

"I want to step into that garden. But I'm scared."

"Exactly. Let me test it first. If I disappear and am never seen again, the painting is yours to keep."

"That's gallant of you. But I'm nervous that that might actually happen. I don't think you should risk it."

"Someone has to risk it."

"I suppose so. Still—"

"Tara, I'm ready to take the risk. It isn't as if I have a great job or prospects anyway."

"What is your job?"

"I work in a warehouse. I use a small electric forklift to move crates around. It's dull, and the pay's not much, but it's what I could get."

"I keep accounts for a small manufacturer of novelty scarves. I'd gladly give it up, if I had any alternative."

"We're like two mice in the rat race. So let me take a chance, here."

Tara nodded. "Then maybe, maybe—"

"Maybe what?"

"This." She stepped close and kissed him on the cheek. "Godspeed."

Tartan liked that amazingly well, but kept his reaction in check, careful not to take her gesture as more than it was: encouragement. "Thank you."

Tara sat on the bed, gazing at the portal.

He ducked down and put his left foot through the frame. It landed on the jungle path. He shifted his balance and came up inside the jungle scene.

It had worked! He was definitely in it. The air was warm and sweet, with the trace of a breeze. The path led ahead, somewhere.

He turned to look back, half afraid that there would be nothing but more path behind him, so that he was caught in the new scene. But the framed portal was there, showing Tara sitting expectantly on the bed. Good enough.

"Haloo!" he called, but there was no reaction. She couldn't hear him. Could she see him? He lifted his hand in a wave. Tara waved back.

Good enough. He stooped to pick up a dry leaf. But his hand passed through it without more than the suggestion of contact.

Startled, he walked to the nearest tree trunk and patted the bark. But his fingers went through it. The tree was a ghost!

No, *he* was the ghost. That was why he had been unable to take the leaf out, before. However solid he was in the real world, he was only an apparition here.

It was time to get out of here. If he could. He stooped and put a foot through the frame of the portal, then eased himself out. He was back in the real world.

Tara hugged him. "Oh, Tartan, I was afraid you were in trouble!"

"I'm solid," he said, half in wonder.

She laughed as she let him go. "That's my impression."

"But in there I was a ghost. I couldn't really touch anything."

"So I gathered. I worried that you'd died and become a spirit."

"At least you saw me, there in the jungle."

"I saw you there in the garden."

That brought him up short. "Maybe you should try it now."

"Yes. Watch."

He sat on the bed while she hiked up her skirt and put one leg through the portal, then the other. She had nice legs.

Then, in the jungle, she faced him and waved. He waved back. They were in contact, at least to that extent.

She went to pick a leaf off a low branch. Her hand passed through it. She nodded. Then she stepped back through the frame.

He stood to meet her, uncertain whether to hug her, though he wanted to. She solved that dilemma by hugging him again. "You're right! I was a ghost. I couldn't pick that rose."

"You were in your rose garden?"

"Of course I was. Didn't you see?"

"I saw you in the jungle."

She paused. "My better judgment tells me we should back off now. This is downright spooky, apart from the portal aspect."

"So does mine."

"Let's cross together."

"Right," he agreed, laughing. He could no more leave this mystery alone than she could. "But maybe only briefly, then take time to consider."

"I'll fix you a sandwich, when."

"Thank you."

They held hands and stood before the picture. And paused, jointly surprised.

"Did you see that?" she asked.

"The letters under it changed. Now I can read them. They say THE LAND OF XANTH."

"That's what I see too," Tara said. "When we look at it while touching, the letters align."

"But where is this land 'Xanth'? I never heard of it."

"It must be what is in the picture."

"It must be," he agreed. "On with it, then."

They put their feet through the frame. They jostled together awkwardly, which he didn't mind at all, before straightening up inside.

"Oh, my," Tara breathed.

Because now they stood in both scenes. The jungle glade had become a rose garden without eliminating its trees.

Then Tartan realized something else. "I heard you."

"And I hear you. Now that we're both on the same side of the portal."

"And we're solid," he added, squeezing her hand.

"Are we?" She reached for a rose. Her hand passed through it.

He reached for a leaf, with no better result. "We're still ghosts."

"This makes me nervous."

"Let's get out of here."

They exited the picture and were back in Tara's apartment. "I'll fix those sandwiches," she said, letting go of his hand. "The bathroom's that way."

"Thanks." Because his innards had indeed become a bit unsettled. It didn't help that now that he was no longer touching Tara, the letters under the picture had become nonsensical again.

In due course they put a cover over the portal and settled down to eat the sandwiches and sort things out. "So there is another realm on the other side," Tara said. "This 'Land of Xanth.' But only as we see it."

"And we are ghosts there," Tartan said. "We can see, hear, and touch each other, but nothing else. Except the ground, so we don't fall through."

"It's as if only our spirits cross."

"Yes. But in that case, what happens to our real bodies? Where are they?"

She nodded. "I think we need to experiment one more time today."

They experimented. First he went through and looked back. This time he saw his own body sitting beside Tara. He pointed to it, and she looked, surprised.

"I never realized that you were still there," she said. "Until you pointed."

Then she went through, and they verified that she was actually still sitting beside him. It was as if their bodies were invisible until noticed.

Indeed, only their spirits were passing through the portal. Their bodies were alive but without awareness.

They also discovered that they could see, hear, and feel each other in the portal realm only when their two physical bodies were quite close, preferably touching. "Maybe it's like telepathy," Tartan said. "When our bodies are in contact, then our minds can read each other. Since our spirits are in touch with our bodies, that means our spirits can relate to each other too."

"I think that makes sense," she agreed.

"This also means that if one of us wants to seriously explore that realm, the other had better make sure the physical body left behind is safe," Tartan said.

"But I don't want to explore it alone, even if I know my body is safe."

"Neither do I. So what do we do?"

"We go together. We lie down side by side on the bed and sleep, in effect."

"But we can't do that indefinitely. Our bodies have to be aroused every so often to—for—"

"Natural functions," she agreed.

"But suppose we get caught in the other realm and can't return promptly?" Because they both knew they were going to explore.

"I think we need to try one more experiment," she said. "To see if we can rouse our bodies without actually leaving the other realm. Because if we can, then we can explore to our hearts' content, only pausing to tune out there and tune in on our bodies for necessary functions."

"You realize this entails considerable trust?"

"And lying on the bed unconscious holding hands doesn't?"

He laughed. "Got me there. But I was thinking that one person roused while the other sleeps, well . . ." He shrugged.

"And we hardly know each other. So we should give it time, preferably months, to build up that knowledge and trust."

"The same kind a married couple develops."

She looked sharply at him. "This is of course vastly premature, but yes, like marriage. Time is essential. It would be foolhardy to rush."

"Shall we start the exploration tomorrow?" he asked.

"Of course."

He laughed again. "I think we're going to get along. We're compatible."

"We'd better be."

They entered the picture again, one at a time, and verified that by a significant effort of will they really could rouse their bodies, their ghosts becoming senseless at the time. "But it does seem better to do it in turns," Tartan said. "So that one ghost can keep an eye on the other, just in case."

"Yes. But it will entail our losing partial contact, because our bodies will separate when using the bathroom."

"We'll keep it brief."

"I guess it's time for you to go home. Unless you prefer to stay here overnight."

Tartan considered the implications, either way. "I think I'd better go home. It could be a long day tomorrow."

"Fortunately tomorrow is Sunday. Whatever we have to do needs to be finished then, because we have jobs on Monday."

"We do," he agreed.

"Will you trust me with the portal?"

"Oh, yes."

"Then I will trust you. Kiss me."

He hesitated. "Some candor here. I haven't had any regular girlfriend; I'm just too ordinary. I could get to like you a lot, in a hurry, because you seem to be very much my type. So maybe it's better not to encourage that."

"Ditto here. Encouragement at this stage would be foolish."

So they came together and kissed, chastely. It was nevertheless a phenomenal turn-on for him. She was a real live girl!

Tartan walked out to the nearest bus stop. He had a lot to think about, and not just the portal. He hoped Tara was reacting similarly.

By morning he was sure he wanted to pursue the portal as far as was feasible, if not farther. He wanted to know all about this mysterious Land of Xanth. He was also a little bit in love with Tara. But he remained cautious, knowing that there were battalions of things that could go wrong with either association.

Tara welcomed him at the door. "Oh, Tartan, I was afraid you wouldn't come."

"But we agreed I would."

"I know we did. But the events of yesterday were a little overwhelming, and that could have scared you off."

"That portal does make me nervous," he agreed. "But you're the one I want to tackle it with."

"We should reconsider carefully before we get serious about that. It could be dangerous."

"Yes. Baby steps are best."

"Definitely."

They lay side by side on the bed, took hands, and plunged into the portal.

There were the blue roses, and the path through the jungle. "I wonder," Tartan said, looking around. "Could the portal be designed to appeal to us?"

"But we see different things."

"Exactly. I've always been intrigued by paths in forests. I want to know where they go. Whereas you like exotic gardens."

Tara nodded. "Actually I like forest paths too."

"And I like blue roses."

"But they don't really exist."

"As of my acquaintance with you."

"Which seems to be no problem," she said, evincing a faint blush. It seemed that she felt the increasing impact of their association, as he did. "Because when we're here together, we both see both settings."

"Let's follow the path. Maybe there are candy stripe roses."

She squeezed his hand. "Oh, I just thought: probably we don't have to hold hands here, because we're already doing it in real life."

"We are," he agreed.

Cautiously, they released their hands. Both of them remained tangible.

"That's a relief," she said. "Not that it's bad holding hands with you, but I wouldn't want you to disappear if I let go."

"Yes. I wonder, if we twitched, out there, and our hands separated, would we become invisible to each other, or worse?"

"It didn't happen when we tried rousing our bodies separately," she said. "We just sort of went inert, here. But maybe it would be safest to hold hands here when we do take turns out there, just to be sure."

"Yes. And if one of us seems to fade when we're both here, the other should grab a hand. That might reestablish the connection."

They walked along the path through the jungle. They rounded a bend, came to a glade, and stopped, chagrined.

"Do you see what I see?" Tara asked.

"I see a—a dragon."

"A huge sleeping serpent-like creature with wisps of smoke rising from its nostrils?"

"And iridescent scales," he said. "And maybe two hundred glossy teeth."

"Let's get out of here before it wakes."

They hastily backed off. "That was close," he said. "We could have stumbled right into it."

"Or could we? If we're effective ghosts?"

"I forgot about that. Still—"

"The sensible thing to do is get on out of here," she said.

"Let sleeping dragons lie," he agreed.

So they held hands tightly and marched back toward the dragon.

The monster stirred.

They froze in momentary alarm. But it seemed it was only a sleeping twitch, a shifting of position, and the dragon continued its slumber.

"You know, if we're really ghosts, it can't see or hear us anyway," Tara said.

"So if we shouted at it, it would make no difference."

"But we shouldn't gamble on that."

"We shouldn't."

"On three," Tara said.

"Hey, dragon!" they shouted together.

The dragon did not react.

They walked up to it and kicked at its tail. Their feet passed though the tail without contact. They were definitely ghosts.

They pushed on through the dragon's massive tail. There was slight resistance, as if they were walking through thick fog, before they emerged on the other side.

"Oh, look," Tara said. "A sign."

Sure enough, a little sign said DRAGON.

"Now they tell us," Tartan muttered.

"That's curious. Why have a sign?"

"I sure don't know. I wouldn't think the dragon would stay here long anyway."

"Unless it's for us."

"Like a guided tour? I guess it's possible."

"I'm thinking it is."

"I believe we have confirmed two things," Tartan said. "One, that Xanth is a fantasy land, because dragons don't exist in real life. Two—"

"That we really are effective ghosts, here," Tara said.

"I've never been much of a fantasy or ghost story reader."

"Neither have I."

He sighed. "Sometimes I fear that we are too similar."

She laughed. "I can stand it for a while if you can."

They walked on. Soon the path led them to a huge bare mound. "That's the biggest, ugliest ant hill I ever saw," Tartan said.

Then several things erupted from holes in the mound. "Those aren't ants!" Tara exclaimed.

"They're grotesque little men, with big heads and big feet."

"Not men. Goblins, I think."

He paused. "Well, this is a fantasy land. It can have goblins if it wants to."

"Do you think they're friendly?"

"Goblins? I doubt it. But they shouldn't know we're here."

"Oh, that's right. I forgot we're ghosts. Let's look more closely."

They walked right up to the mound, invisible to the denizens. The goblins were about half human height, but looked twice as mean.

Then a goblin woman came out, with her child. She was exquisite, as pretty a person as Tartan could ever remember seeing, and the child was cute. "Wow."

"She's too small for you," Tara said, amused. "And already married, I think."

"I am merely amazed by the contrast. Their women are as lovely as their men are ugly."

"And there's the sign."

He looked. Sure enough, it said GOBLIN MOUND.

They walked on, and soon came to a pit that threatened the path without quite damaging it. Tara peered down into it. "Oh!"

Tartan looked. The pit was swarming with giant centipedes that bore huge claws. A pinch from one of those would be extremely painful. Now they found the sign: NICKELPEDE CREVICE.

"Nickelpedes?" he asked blankly.

"Oh, I think I get it. It's a pun on centipedes. These look about five times their size."

What a groaner. "Let's move on."

They did. "I'm nervous about bugs, and those are the worst I've seen," Tara said.

"Maybe their females are lovely."

She swatted his hand. "You're vulgar. I mean that in the nicest way."

"Thank you," he said, smiling.

They came to a small tree that made them both halt in place. It looked ordinary, with bark and leaves, except that instead of fruit it had assorted shoes. "A shoe tree," Tara said.

"Another pun," Tartan said. "But maybe a useful one, if you're shopping for shoes."

The next thing they came to was signed OGRE'S DEN. As they passed, a figure like a giant gorilla emerged. It pulled up a sapling and twisted it into a knot before throwing it away.

"Ogres make me nervous too," Tara said.

They hurried on. "I wonder," Tartan said. "That ogre didn't see us, yet he seemed to be showing off for us. Does that make sense?"

"No. But hardly anything seems to make sense here."

"I am wondering whether this path is really a guided tour, showing us what this world of Xanth has to offer."

"Or trying to scare us away from it."

"Either way, why bother? Why set up a portal if you don't want folks to use it?"

"A guided tour," she repeated thoughtfully. "Maybe that makes some sense after all. We're supposed to look, and either be scared away, or decide to stay. As if somebody wants us for something."

"I am getting mighty curious. We're two quite ordinary people, nothing special about us. Why would anyone or anything be interested in us?"

"That is the question," she agreed.

There was another glade ahead, with a small hill. And on the hill—

"Oh, my!" Tartan said. "That's the most beautiful creature I ever saw."

"I agree, though maybe for different reasons."

"That, I believe, is a centaur. With splendid—wings. And that's not all."

"Female," she agreed. "Bare throughout."

The centaur filly leaped forward, spread her wings, and launched into the air. In a moment she was gone into the sky.

"And there's the sign," he said. "WINGED CENTAUR."

"I'm impressed."

"I'm mightily intrigued, and not just by her, um—"

"No human woman has a bosom like that."

"This path must be leading us somewhere. I want to find out where."

"Let's go," she agreed.

They walked on at a faster pace. Soon there was an unusual tree, with green tentacles instead of leaves. The sign said TANGLE TREE.

"It doesn't look tangled to me," Tartan said.

Then a deer-like creature bounded by. It brushed the tree.

Suddenly the tentacles came alive. They whipped around the deer. It was hauled into the interior of the foliage. There was a loud crunching sound.

"Now we know," Tara said, shuddering. "Don't get tangled in it."

Tartan was halfway sickened. "Let's move on."

A small dark cloud appeared in the path ahead of them. "There's something interesting here," it said.

They stopped. "A talking cloud?" Tartan asked.

"I heard that," the cloud said. It changed shape, becoming a pretty dark haired woman in a scant halter and skirt. "Whose conversation?"

"Who's what?"

"Dialog, emoting, expressing, pontificating, lecturing—"

"Talking?"

"Whatever," the woman agreed, crossly. "Who are you?"

"I'm Tartan. Who are you?"

"And I'm Demoness Metria." The woman's hair lengthened, her figure became more alluring, and her costume shrank. "Are you alone?"

"Uh, hello," Tara said. "There are two of us."

The woman seemed to look right through her. "Where are you?"

"Right here," Tara said. "Can't you see me?"

"I hear you but I don't see you. What are you, ghosts?"

"Uh, yes, in a manner. We are Tartan and Tara, from the real world."

"You mean Mundania?"

"We are pretty mundane," Tartan agreed wryly.

"And pretty dull, by the sound of you. I like interesting things."

"Sorry about that," Tara said, amused.

"So I'll be on my way." The demoness faded out.

"Well, at least she could hear us," Tartan said. "And it seems that we have met one more example of the things of this realm."

"I suppose, being a sort of a spirit, the way she pops in and out and changes forms, she could relate partially to ghosts," Tara said thoughtfully.

"And the way she couldn't get the right word—does she have a speech impediment?"

"A what?"

"Obscurity, obstruction, confusion, incapacity, inadequacy—"

"Block?"

"Whatever," he agreed as crossly as he could manage.

They both laughed, and moved on.

Ahead, the forest opened out to a large field. There was an elegant castle, complete with turrets and a moat. The sign said CAPRICE CASTLE.

"I think we're expected," Tara said nervously.

"We must be," Tartan agreed grimly.

They walked on toward the castle. The drawbridge was down, so they crossed over the moat and went to the main door. "Here goes nothing, since we're ghosts," Tartan said, and knocked.

To their surprise, his knuckle rapped against the wood, not phasing through it.

The door opened immediately. There stood a phenomenally lovely young woman in a gown as bright as the morning, with a small crown on her golden hair. "Ah, you have arrived! I am Princess Dawn. I'll be your host, this hour."

"You—you see and hear us," Tara said faintly.

"Oh, yes. My friends and I crafted the spell of the portal and path to lead you here. Though I must say I'm surprised to see two of you. We were expecting only one."

"Sorry about that," Tartan said. "I'm, uh, Tartan, and this is Tara. We were both intrigued by the portal, so we came together."

"Do come in. We have much to discuss."

"Uh, thanks, Princess," Tara said uncertainly.

They entered the castle, and were soon in a pleasant day room.

"I would offer you refreshments," Princess Dawn said. "But in your ghostly form you are unable to eat anything solid."

"About that," Tartan said. "How is it that we are in this form, here in this magic land, yet you can see and hear us?"

Dawn smiled winningly. "First I must bore you with some necessary background."

"Nothing about this situation bores us," Tara said. "Our real lives are dull, while this magic Land of Xanth is fantastic. We actually saw a dragon!"

"And a winged centaur filly," Tartan said. "She was a sight to behold."

"Almost too much of a good thing," Tara murmured.

Dawn smiled tolerantly. "Yes, we tried to give you a preview of what to expect here, including some puns. Here at Caprice Castle we collect and store puns, as they are vital to Xanth's existence. If that turns you off—"

Tartan exchanged a look with Tara. "We're neutral about puns. If they are part of the package, okay. It's not as if we have to eat them."

"Don't eat them!" Dawn said. "They are notorious for giving folk pun-digestion so they emit more puns, and repel anyone within range. But we do have to live with them. Recently we suffered a pun virus that was wiping them out and making Xanth desolate, almost as bad as Mundania." She paused. "No offense intended."

Both Tartan and Tara smiled. "Mundania is dull, as the lady said," Tara agreed.

"As who said?"

"There was a—she called herself a demoness—along the way," Tara said. "She could hear us but not see us. She had a—a problem getting the right word."

"Oh, Metria. She's notorious. She's always in search of something interesting. It's best simply to ignore her."

"That's the one," Tartan agreed.

"Here is the background," Dawn said, returning to business. "The folk of Xanth live fairly ordinary lives, mostly, well, dull, except that every person has a magic talent. Talents seldom repeat, with some notable exceptions, and they range from what we call spot on the wall to Magician caliber, such as being able to change instantly to some other form like a dragon or elf. My magic is of the latter class; I can immediately know all about any living thing I touch." She smiled, and the room seemed to brighten. "I can't do that with you, because you are ghostlike in this situation. Seeing and hearing you is the limit of my ability with you. You, being Mundanes, have no magic talents; that is your curse. However, if you came to Xanth physically and lived here for a while, you would gradually develop magic."

"Being a ghost feels like magic," Tartan said.

"Yes. But it is magic three of my cousins crafted, rather than your own." Dawn took a breath. "There is another Mundane who has become a nuisance. He is in league with a night colt who carries him through the morning sky so he can spread mischievous stories that Xanth natives are obliged to animate. We don't like that."

"You become actors in little plays?" Tara asked. "I should think that would be fun, if they don't last long."

"Titles like 'The Princess and the Pee.'" She pronounced the last word so that they could hear the spelling.

Tartan laughed, but Tara was repelled. "I wouldn't want to act that out in public."

"Neither did my cousin Princess Rhythm. Nor did my sister, Princess Eve, when she was threatened with 'The Princess and the Grog.' It was a dangerous drink."

"I can imagine," Tartan said.

"We fear these stories will only get worse," Dawn said. "So we want to stop the Ghost Writer. But we can't touch a ghost, literally. So we need to recruit a ghost for that. Hence the portal."

"But what could we do?" Tara asked. "We can't even touch each other, unless we're touching in Mundania."

"Two things. You might spy on the Ghost Writer by flying into the sky where he is. That may enable you to trace him back to his point of origin."

"In Mundania," Tartan agreed. "But what then?"

"You, being Mundanes, would be able to approach him physically, there, and encourage him to stop his story raids."

"Wouldn't work," Tartan said. "A man intent on making princesses pee in public or drink knockout grog isn't going to listen to reason."

"So we fear," Dawn agreed. "So you will need competent advice. That brings us to the more complicated aspect."

"Which is?" Tara asked, intensely intrigued.

"You will need to adopt Xanth hosts, so you can go about physically in our land, while retaining your ghostly ability to spy."

"And?" Tartan asked, equally intrigued.

"And go to visit the Good Magician, who will have the answer you need."

"I think we need to think about this," Tara said.

"Of course. You should go home and consider it carefully. You can leave your ghostly presences here to mark your places, and return to them tomorrow if you decide to. If you elect not to participate, they will dissipate in a day and the portal will close. Then we will search for another candidate, elsewhere in Mundania."

There was more dialog, but that was the essence. Soon they vacated their ghostly forms and roused themselves in Tara's apartment.

"This requires weeks or months of serious thought," Tartan said.

"And all we have is a day to decide. It would be crazy to plunge in tomorrow morning."

"Absolutely mad," he agreed. "We have no idea what we're getting into."

She kissed him. "I'm glad we agree."

"We'll have to get unpaid leaves from our jobs, because we don't know how long it will be."

"And stock up on supplies, so we can take proper care of our bodies here."

They had of course decided.

Chapter 4

HOSTS

"I'm so glad to see you back," Princess Dawn said brightly. "Now let me introduce you to your hosts, the half demons Ted and Monica. They can see and hear you because of a spot spell. That won't be the case elsewhere."

A young man and a young woman appeared, literally; they had not been in the room until that moment. "Hi," the man said. He was handsome and well constructed with curly brown hair. "I'm Demon Ted. Demented, get it? My mother is the mischievous Demoness Metria. We'll surely be seeing her along the way."

"Metria!" Tartan said. "We met her. You're really her son? She looked, well, teenage."

"Demons look any age they want," Ted said. "Mom likes to look sexy. But she can be a pain in the posterior, if I do say it myself."

"And her trouble with words—is there a reason?"

"Sure. She got stepped on by a sphinx, long ago, and it fragmented her into three aspects. Metria is the mischievous one with a vocabulary problem. Mentia is slightly crazy, though she often makes more sense than mom. And Woe Betide is a perpetual child of five or so. You can't use bleeps in her presence, because of the Adult Conspiracy."

"The what and the what?"

"Bleeps are bad words that children shouldn't hear, so they get bleeped out," he explained. "And The Adult Conspiracy to Keep Interesting Things from Children. Like bad words or how to summon the stork. We swore never to join it when we grew up, but somehow we did, as all children do when they mature. It's a nuisance."

"And I am DeMonica," the woman said. She was a dusky beauty with curves where it counted. "As in Demon and Monica, jammed together until they merged, as my parents were when they sent for me. My mother is Nada Naga, original girlfriend of Prince Dolph, Dawn's mother. He's still got a bit of a thing for her."

"He does," Dawn agreed evenly. "She liked him but never loved him, and was glad when he married my mother Electra." She smiled fleetingly. "Monica's a bit of a tease. They both are. They've been up to mischief all their lives. Which is why I thought they could help handle the Ghost Writer; they'll understand his nature."

"Sure do," Ted agreed. "Princess and the Pee. That's rich."

"Oh?" Monica asked. "How would you like Prince and the Poop?"

"You pee on me, I'll poop on you," Ted said before Dawn's look silenced him.

Tartan found all this confusing. He grabbed on to what seemed to count. "You're to be my host, Demon Ted, and you're half demon?"

"Two for two," Ted agreed.

"And you're to be my host, DeMonica?" Tara asked.

"You're smart," Monica said. "You nailed it on the first try."

Dawn lifted one eyebrow partway, signaling potential annoyance.

"Uh, just how does this work?" Tartan asked.

"Just walk into me and take over. Like riding a horse."

"I never rode a horse."

"A camel, then. No? A yak? An elephant? A caterpillar?"

"How about a car?" Tartan asked.

"We don't have them in Xanth."

"Just walk into him," Dawn said, not quite showing the verge of exasperation. "No parallels necessary."

Tartan wasn't easy with this, but tried it. He walked into Ted.

And found himself to be physical, with a complete solid body. "You got it," Ted said in his ear.

"I got it," Tartan agreed, half in wonder.

"Yes you do," Dawn said, kissing him on the cheek. The touch made his whole head seem to float. He was physical, all right, and she was some woman.

"She never kisses *me*," Ted complained in his mind.

"That's because you've got delusions of importance, crazy T," Dawn said.

"You didn't speak aloud," Tartan said. "How did she hear you?"

"She was still touching us," Ted explained. "So she knew what we were saying. Ignore her and she'll go away."

Meanwhile Tara had walked into Monica. "Well now," she said, inhaling. "This is a better body than my own."

She was correct, but Tartan knew better than to say so. "I hope I'll learn to recognize you in that form."

"Monica says that's no problem. This body can slowly change."

As he looked, the sexy woman shifted by stages into the shape of the original Tara. Unfortunately that made her clothing hang somewhat awkwardly.

"Maybe just the face and hair would suffice," Tartan suggested. "So that no clothing change is necessary."

"That's one way of putting it," Tara said, not entirely pleased. And in two and a half moments—moments seemed to be measurable, here in Xanth—the clothing filled out again, while the head was that of Tara. "Or would you prefer no clothing at all?"

There was a definite edge. "You're fine any way you want," Tartan said quickly. "Maybe we should move on to the mission." Though the idea of seeing her nude in this host was exciting.

"Curious," Ted said in his ear. "I grew up with Monica, and never thought she was sexy. But now through your eyes, I can see that she definitely is."

"Your hosts know the route," Dawn said. "You can get to know each other better as you travel."

"We'll try to," Tara agreed. "Thank you, Princess Dawn."

"Welcome, Tara. We will surely be seeing each other again, in due course." Then she held up her hand in a pause. "Oh, I may have forgotten to mention this, Ted and Monica: your demonly abilities will be diminished while you serve as hosts. No popping off to other locations, no turning into smoky clouds; you'll have to walk and be solid. You'll be essentially human."

"Oh bleep!" Ted swore.

"Sorry about that," Tartan told him, though actually he was relieved. He had no idea how he would handle popping from one place to another, let alone becoming a cloud of smoke.

They walked on out of the castle. Tartan was surprised to find a completely different landscape outside. The castle had been in a glade yesterday; now it was on a mountain slope. He could see that Tara was similarly startled.

"Caprice Castle travels capriciously," Ted explained. "It is now in a new location."

"Foundations and all?"

"It doesn't need them. It stabilizes itself."

"Monica says we need to get to an enchanted path," Tara said.

"Those are safe from dangers," Ted explained. "Actually we half demons aren't threatened by much we can't handle, but yes, an enchanted path is best."

"Okay," Tartan said aloud.

"This way," Tara or maybe Monica said, heading out. Monica, most likely, because of the way her hips flirted. She had very nice legs.

Tara glanced back. "Monica says you're looking."

"Uh, yes," Tartan said, out of sorts.

"Good. She says."

"Yes, it's easier to let us do the routine stuff, like walking," Ted said. "So you can focus on the mission."

"As if we have any idea what we're doing in that respect."

"Go for one thing at a time. Right now, that's safely reaching the Good Magician's castle."

"Here it is," Tara called. Indeed, there was a nice path with slightly glowing edges. They got on it and walked more readily.

"Princess Dawn said we should get to know each other while we travel," Tartan said internally. "Is there something I should know about you?"

"Nothing important."

Tartan wasn't satisfied with this. "Why did you volunteer for this dull duty?"

"That's cutting to the chase. Several reasons. One is that Dawn asked us, and I've always had a minor crush on Dawn and her sister Eve, and of course she knows it. Another is that you are evidently to be a main character for this narrative, and we've always been incidental characters, so this enables me to seem more important for a while. A third is, well, why did *you* volunteer?"

"Because Xanth is an exciting magic world to me, and I want a pretext to get to know it better. I'd also like to have some real adventure in my life, and maybe some romance. The usual. Also, I'd like to do my bit of good, somewhere, somehow, and this seems to be my chance."

"That's it," Ted agreed. "I knew you could formulate it better than I could. Adventure, romance, and doing good. I've never been much for any of those, and this is my chance, maybe."

"You don't have anything going with Monica?"

Ted laughed. "Her? I told you, we grew up together. She's like a sister to me, though she's not related. We're both half demon, but while I'm the product of two garden variety folk, she's the daughter of a prince of demons and a naga princess. Out of my class. She's a great companion, because she's my age and understands demonly ways, but there'll never be any romance there."

"What is a naga?"

"A cross between human and serpent. They live mostly underground and fight the goblins. They can assume either form, but their natural form is that of a serpent with a human head."

"So Monica is only a quarter human?"

"That's right. But since both naga and demons can assume human form, that's what she normally wears, and of course she makes it look good."

"She certainly does!"

"All shape changers look good in their human forms. It facilitates getting along with humans."

"And her motives for this mission are similar to yours?"

"I'm pretty sure they are. She's even hotter for romance than I am. Girls are. But here in Xanth, well, we're crossbreeds. Folk treat us politely, but there's a prejudice. So we have to do more to get noticed."

That did seem to make sense.

"Oh, there's a shoe tree," Tara said. "With some really nice shoes."

"Aren't the ones Monica has on good enough?" Tartan asked.

She smiled. "You don't understand women. I'm consulting with Monica right now." She marched up to the tree and inspected the offerings.

"For what it's worth, I don't understand either," Ted said. "Women go all mushy about shoes, regardless whether they need them." They sat down on the path and waited.

"These should do nicely," Tara said, plucking a pair. She went to a convenient rock, sat down, and lifted one foot, then the other, so she could change shoes. In the process she showed some very nice thigh. "What do you think, Tartan?"

"They're magnificent!"

Ted laughed. "You're not even talking about the shoes!"

"Don't tell."

"I'm so glad you approve," Tara said. She stood and walked in a small circle, testing the shoes. "Yes, they're fine."

"They certainly are," Tartan agreed.

They walked on. "Monica knows, of course," Ted said. "But she's a decent sort, so she didn't blab to Tara."

"Or maybe she just likes showing off."

"That too. Your eyes were bugging. She enjoys doing that to passing males. But she made sure not to show too much; that would have given it away."

"Too much?"

"We'll get to that in due course."

Tara looked into the sky. "What a pretty cloud!"

"Oh for bleep's sake," Ted muttered. "Rhapsodizing over a cloud?"

"Girls are like that," Tartan said internally, appreciating his turn to be instructive. Then, aloud: "Sure is."

Tara smiled. "In fact Xanth is a pretty place. I like it here." Then, after a pause: "Oh!"

"What?" Tartan asked, perplexed.

"Monica just told me. That's not just any cloud. That's Fracto."

"Fracto?"

"The king of clouds. Monica says that he has a bad reputation in some quarters, you know, raining on parades, but I still think he's a fine figure."

"Monica put her up to that," Ted said. "Fracto doesn't like us much, because we've played tricks on him, but maybe you and Tara can get along with him better."

Indeed, the cloud was puffing up splendidly. Now the points of a vapor crown showed on top.

"The cloud can hear us?" Tartan asked, surprised.

"Everything can hear you, when you speak aloud. Most things don't care, but some do. Never insult a volcano."

"A volcano?"

"When someone insulted Mount Pinatuba, he went ooom-pa! and blew out so much ash that it cooled all Xanth by one degree. Others can bury you in hot lava. Things have feelings; you don't want to get on the wrong side of them."

"You're right," Tartan said aloud. "That's one impressive cloud."

"Haa!" It was a screech from another section of the sky. It came from a gross ugly bird flying toward them.

"Oh, bleep," Ted swore. "That's a harpy. They're dirty birds with fowl mouths."

"I gather the enchanted path doesn't protect us from bad language."

"Or from dropped bombs. Better take cover."

But the harpy was already flying overhead. "What do we have here?" she screeched. "Trash folk from Mundania?"

The cloud gave a warning rumble.

"Oh, blow away, foggy bottom," the harpy screeched at Fracto. "This is not your business."

"We're not looking for any trouble," Tara called.

"Well tough eggs, poop-face!" the harpy screeched. "Trouble's looking for *you*."

"I see what you mean," Tartan said. "But if she can't actually attack us on the path, words will never hurt us."

"Oh, do you ever need to learn," Ted said. "Words *can* hurt you. Especially magic ones. But probably she'll egg us."

"Egg us?"

"Their eggs are explosive. Run!"

Tartan and Tara started running along the path, but the harpy followed them. "Bombs away!" she screeched. "One, two, thr—"

At that point there was a flash of lightning. It struck the harpy on the tail, vaporizing several feathers, and knocked the dirty bird out of the sky.

Ted laughed. "I did mention getting along with clouds?"

"You did," Tartan agreed, amazed.

"Thank you, King Fracto," Tara called. "That was so sweet of you." She blew the cloud a kiss. It sailed up to the vapory edge and struck with a splat that left an imprint of a pair of lips. The cloud actually blushed and floated away.

"Point made," Tartan said. "Things have feelings."

They walked on without further adventure. Around noon they came to a rest stop where there were pie plants, milk weeds, and a lone beer-barrel tree. Tartan and Tara might have been baffled by the punnish offerings, but their hosts guided them without mishap.

At one end there was a long low table shaped like a garden tool where several black birds perched, dipping their beaks in mugs of liquid. "Crow bar," Ted explained.

Tartan didn't even groan.

Refreshed, they moved on. The path wound through forest and field, around hills, and across streams. "Oh, this is so adorable," Tara said, gazing across a quiet pond. "This is such a *nice* land."

"Monica will set her straight," Ted said.

Sure enough, Tara paused. "Tar, let's step off the enchanted path for a moment."

Tartan didn't argue. He was curious too.

They stepped off. Tartan felt something at his feet. The grass was curling around his shoes. "Better move on before it starts to feed," Ted warned. Tartan hastily stepped away from the grass. So did Tara, similarly warned.

There was a sound to the side. A contraption formed of shining saw blades was coming toward them. It did not look friendly

"Sawhorse," Ted said. "Stay clear of it if you don't want to be sawed."

They got out of the creature's way. In the process, Tartan stepped in the edge of the pond. "Hey, watch where you're treading!" an angry voice cried.

Startled, he looked—and saw a lady's wet head lifting out of the pool. "Sorry. I didn't know you were swimming here."

"What kind of a girl do you think I am?" she demanded.

"I—I didn't see you. I'm, uh, sure you're a nice girl."

"No I'm not."

He was confused. "Not?"

"You don't know a mermaid when you see one?"

"Mermaid?" he asked blankly.

She lifted more of herself out of the water. She was splendidly nude to the waist. "Well?"

"Uh, no. You look just like a—a lovely woman."

"And what do you think this is?" she demanded, leaning back and lifting her flukes.

"Uh—"

"You're looking for a piece of tail?"

"No! I mean I, I just never saw a—a mermaid before."

"So now you know I'm not that kind of girl."

"Not that kind," he agreed numbly. How had he gotten into this?

"But I could become that kind." Her flukes quivered and separated, and her tail became a shapely set of legs.

"Wow." That was the extent of his ability to talk at the moment.

"Then again, you look to be a fair hunk of a man. Come in and show me what you're made of." Her legs flexed suggestively, their juncture just under the surface of the water. "Have a nice ellipsis with me, handsome."

"Ellipsis?"

She eyed him obliquely. "You've never had an ellipsis?"

"What is she talking about?" Tartan asked Ted.

"In Mundania you call it sex. We're not that crude in Xanth."

"Oh, you mean when they blank it out, but you know it's happening?"

"Exactly."

"I gather from your reaction that you haven't," the mermaid said. She inhaled. "Then let me be your first."

"Don't do it," Ted warned. "She'll give you a hot time, all right. Then she'll drown you and eat you. She's a predator. That's how they catch their prey."

"Uh, thank you," Tartan said. "But I fear you're more woman than I can handle." He backed off.

"Oh no you don't!" The mermaid flexed and leaped forward, tackling him around the waist. Tartan fell backwards into the brush, but she was tugging him back toward the pond.

"What do I do now?" he asked Ted. He was concerned but not frightened, because he knew his host would not let his body be eaten. The mermaid's grip was like steel; she was stronger than she looked. In a moment she might take the first bite of him, and her face was alarmingly close to his midriff. "I—despite everything, I don't want to hurt her. She's too pretty to hurt."

Ted mentally rolled his eyes. But he did answer. "Tickle her."

Oho! Tartan reached down with his hands, stroking her bare back. When he reached her curvy bottom he curled his fingers and delicately tickled it.

The mermaid shrieked. "Eeeee! Nooooo!" she cried, putting five E's and five O's into it. Here in Xanth such things were quantifiable.

This was almost fun. "Sit up and I'll tickle your front too," he said wickedly.

She lifted her front defiantly. "You wouldn't dare, you—EEEEEE!!"

"Good one!" Tara said from the side, applauding. "Capital E's."

"You utter brute!" the mermaid cried, heaving her body away and back into the pond with a splash. "You don't fight fair."

"I'm mundane," Tartan said. "We don't know any better."

"Disgusting! My poor innocent flesh being mauled by an ignorant barbarian." The mermaid flipped over and dived below the surface, providing him one last provocative flash of her legs as she disappeared.

"Let's go back to the path," Tartan said. His feelings were badly mixed.

"But don't you want to wrestle with the nice mermaid anymore?" Tara asked, a smirk hovering suggestively close to her face.

"Not at the moment."

They returned to the path. The hosts had made their point: Xanth was not nearly as safe or friendly as it looked. Mischief could come in a pretty package.

In due course they came to an evening campsite. "We'll stay here the night," Ted said. "You two can go home, and rejoin us in the morning. You must have things to discuss with each other, privately."

"Yes," Tartan agreed. "You've been more than kind, putting up with us duffers for the day."

Tara paused, then approached Tartan. Something was odd about her, in an attractive way. "I am Monica," she said. "Tara gave me leave. I know you think you have been a burden, but that's not the case. You have given us an interesting day, and there surely will be more coming. We volunteered for this mission in the hope that we would find the experience worthwhile, and you are not disappointing us." Then she kissed him.

"Uh—" Tartan said, at a loss for words at the moment. Her kiss had impact.

"Exactly," she said. "Carry on." She stepped away, and he could tell by her change in expression that Tara was back in charge.

"Then we'll see you both tomorrow," Tara said, and took Tartan's hand.

It was that easy. Tartan and Tara focused on their bodies back in Mundania, and in one to one and a half moments were there, lying on the bed, still holding hands.

He realized that the natural functions he had exercised in Xanth were those of his host's body. His own body here felt about to burst, because they had not thought to take a break during the day.

"Oh, my!" Tara said. She rolled off the bed and ran to the bathroom, opening her clothing as she went.

He would have to wait a little longer.

Soon she was back, not bothering to put her skirt back on. "Your turn."

"Thanks!" He lunged for the bathroom and did his business.

"We'll have to eat, and all," Tara said. "But first I have to say I'm sorry I teased you about wrestling with the mermaid. That wasn't nice of me."

"No it wasn't," he agreed, standing by the bed. "But thanks for the apology."

"And I put Monica up to kissing you."

He was astonished. "You did? Why?"

She ignored the question. "Suppose I make it up to you? Tickle me."

"I'm tempted to." Then he realized that she was naked on the bed, having completed her dishabille while he was in the bathroom. "But—"

"Tickle me bare. It's only fair."

Ordinarily he wouldn't have done it, but it had been quite a day and his feelings were unsettled. "Okay."

"Only I get to tickle you back. You have to be bare too."

"Tara—"

"Come on, be a sport."

So he stripped, but was hesitant to join her on the bed. He really wasn't sure of her intentions, and didn't want to go wrong.

She reached out and grabbed him about the waist, much as the mermaid had, pulling him onto the bed with her. She really did want to do it! He tickled her ribs. "Eeeeee!" she screamed, imitating the mermaid as she thrashed about.

She tickled his bottom. "Oooooo!" he groaned, laughing.

Then they were wrestling. Their faces came together, and they kissed each other savagely. What were they heading for?

"Tara," he gasped. "Are you sure?"

"Not at all. I'm severely conflicted. Time for the ellipsis." Evidently Monica had explained about that to her, as Ted had to Tartan.

"Then maybe we should wait, at least until we're in our right minds."

She kissed him again, and this time there was no mistaking her passion. It swept everything else away.

. . .

It was some ellipsis.

They found themselves holding hands again on the bed, as the ellipsis faded. "Tara, this—what were you thinking of?"

"Tartan, I must confess it. When you came up against that mermaid, and she showed you her—her wares, and then you were wrestling with her—I was, I was *jealous*. There, I've said it."

"Tara, you had no need to be. It isn't as if we have any commitment to each other, beyond exploring this magic land of Xanth. We weren't even in our own bodies. And of course she was a vicious predator."

"I know. Don't I know! But there it was. She had a bosom to die for, and when she made legs and flashed you with her whatever, all I could think of was that I could never do anything like that. Or if I did, you'd just laugh, because I don't have anything close to the equipment she does. Or that DeMonica has. So I just needed to prove that, well, if I caught you off guard, maybe—"

"Oh, Tara! You didn't need to trick me. I already liked you. If I'd been sure you felt the same—"

"Maybe not. Monica picked up on my thoughts, of course. She's more experienced than I am, in this venue. She told me that I should go ahead and declare myself, and she would help pave the way by warming you up. So she kissed you."

"That warmed me up," he agreed. "She's one provocative package, when she wants to be."

"Yes. She said none of that would matter if I got you alone and made my play."

"It didn't," he agreed.

"So I provoked a tickling contest, and I apologize for taking it further than maybe you wanted."

"Oh, Tara," he repeated. "I found you attractive all along. I wanted to—to do it with you. I just didn't want to presume, or take advantage. Or make you mad at me, maybe."

"Now he tells me," she said, laughing.

He kissed her. She kissed him back eagerly.

"Whatever it is," he said. "It will do."

"It will do," she agreed.

Then they set about supper and the evening. By mutual agreement they slept on the bed that night, and embraced.

"I guess we're committed now," Tartan said. "Tara, I can't honestly say this soon that I love you, for certain; it's too new and confusing. But I certainly like being with you, and in time—"

She put her finger on his lips. "It will do," she repeated.

Duly prepared in the morning, they took hands again and focused on their hosts in Xanth.

Tartan found himself looking at Demon Ted from outside. There was something weird about his body. Where was he?

"Well now," DeMonica said with an internal smile. "Hello Tartan! You decided to be female today?"

He was in her body! "Oops, no!" He sailed out of her.

There was Tara, looking like herself, emerging from Ted. "We got mixed up," she said, blushing.

"I guess we weren't perfectly tracked." He passed her and entered Ted's body, while she entered Monica's.

"That was odd," Ted said. "I never felt a woman before—I mean, from the inside."

"Neither have I," Tartan said. "I think Monica was amused."

"It occurs to me that there could be an occasion where a woman's perspective would be useful in a man's body," Ted said. "Or vice versa. We should keep it in mind."

"I suppose so. It might stop a predatory mermaid."

"About that: they aren't all that way. Most mermaids are nice. So are most merwomen."

"Merwomen?"

"The seagoing species. They are better endowed, because the sea can be rougher and colder. But they may be less conversant with landly ways."

"Your background thought suggests there's a story there."

"There is. Mela Merwoman lost her merman husband and set out to find another. There were no good prospects locally, so she made legs and walked on land. Since land girls normally are clothed, she went to a pantree and selected suitable panties, and wore them. But she reckoned without panty magic."

"Panty magic?"

"Any male who sees a girl's occupied panties freaks out. Mela was a robustly well-formed creature, and she freaked out legions of males without realizing. Wish I'd been there, but that wasn't feasible."

"Why not?"

"I had not yet been delivered by the stork."

"The stork?"

"I guess you do it differently in Mundania. Here in Xanth the storks receive the three dots of the ellipsis, which carry a lot of information, and take their time to develop a suitable baby, which they then deliver to the mother."

Tartan was amazed, as seemed to happen often in Xanth. "You mean there's no pregnancy?"

"Pregnancy?"

"I guess not," Tartan said.

"You boys must be having quite a dialog," Tara said. "How long do you plan to stand there with your eyes unfocused?"

"A girl's panties freak out Xanth males," Tartan said. "And there's no pregnancy. The stork delivers babies."

"You're joking!" Then her expression changed as she heard from Monica. "Not," she added weakly.

"I'm not saying I believe it."

Tara turned away from him and lifted her skirt.

Fingers snapped by his ear. "Snap out of it," Tara said behind him.

"What—what happened?"

"On Monica's advice I flashed you with her panties. You freaked out. So that much is true, and she assures me the rest is too. Xanth is truly a different realm."

"I freaked out?"

"You were standing there frozen, your eyeballs locked."

"That's hard to believe."

"Slow motion." She faced away again and lifted the hem of her skirt very slowly. Tartan admired her legs, then her thighs, then as the panty line appeared—

She dropped the skirt. "See? You're dizzy."

"I'm dizzy," he agreed. He hadn't actually glimpsed her panties, merely the very edge. That was enough to satisfy him that there was definitely magic.

"A girl can stop a man in mid charge by flashing him," Ted explained. "It's a weapon they have."

"That must be why all the women I've seen here wear dresses with skirts," Tartan said. "No jeans or trousers."

"Of course. Why would a girl deprive herself of her most potent weapon?"

"But I didn't freak out when that mermaid flashed me."

"She wasn't wearing panties."

"You mean a girl's bare bottom doesn't—?"

"Not the way panties do."

"I continue to be amazed. Does Monica freak you out?"

"No. First, because I've known her from childhood. Second, because she prefers to play fair. She's odd that way."

"But if there were a real threat—?"

"She'd use 'em."

"Now I better appreciate why Tara and I might want to exchange hosts at some point. If we had to get past a flashing female, you could do it if Tara were in charge."

"So I could," Ted agreed thoughtfully. "If we saw it coming."

"And that's what you meant, back at the shoe tree, about showing too much. I would have freaked out, and Tara would have caught on."

"Exactly."

They walked on along the enchanted path. Ahead they saw a person sitting on a rock beside the path. As they got closer, it was apparent that it was a lovely young woman, with pure silver hair, and she was weeping.

"Oh, my," Tartan said aloud. "I can't stand to see a woman cry."

"We'll have to try to comfort her," Tara said.

"Yes," he said, gratified by her support. She had said she was jealous about the mermaid, but it seemed that was a special case. The mermaid had been trying to seduce him, or worse. She was not jealous of all other women. "Let's check with our hosts."

"This is not something we know anything about," Ted said. "She's not from these parts."

Tartan glanced at Tara. "Not local," she said. "But she couldn't be on the enchanted path if she were any threat to us."

So Monica's information was similar to Ted's. They approached the weeping girl. "Uh, miss—" Tartan said.

The woman jumped. "Oh! I didn't hear you come." Her face was as lovely as her body, though tear stained.

"We don't know you," Tara said. "We're on our way to the Good Magician's Castle, and saw you here. Is there anything we might do to help you?"

"I just came from there," the girl wailed. "It's awful!"

"He didn't answer your question?" Tartan asked.

"He answered it," she said, and went into another siege of grief.

Tartan and Tara exchanged a look, and it was clear that both their hosts were baffled too. "Let's start at the beginning," Tartan said. "I am Tartan from Mundania, and my companion is Tara, also from Mundania. We are just visiting, using native hosts, trying to perform a mission."

"I'm Emerald," the girl said. "You can see my nails." She held up her hands. Her fingernails were solid emerald green. "I'm a dragon."

"A what?" Tara asked, startled.

"A dragon. I'm in human form at the moment. I could show you, but I'd have to go off the enchanted path to have room. It's a long story."

"This sounds true," Ted said. "She does have a dragon odor."

"Maybe we should hear your story," Tartan said. "If you care to tell it."

Emerald considered. "I suppose I could tell you. It isn't as if we'll ever see each other again."

"Tell us," Tara said encouragingly.

"Thirteen years ago the Land of Xanth was running short of dragons," Emerald said. "Clio, the Muse of History, made a journey out beyond Ptero to Dragon World and made a deal with the dragons to import a number to Xanth, to replace the shortage. Thus came all manner of dragons: Fire, Smoke, Steam, Suction, Tongue."

"Tongue?" Tartan asked.

"Prehensile. They can wrap their tongues around anything and draw it in to eat. Anyway, the dragons resettled Xanth, and all was well for a while. Some dragons were able transform to human shape, being smart enough to associate with humans on an equal basis." She paused half a moment. "I am of that line."

"We gathered that," Tara said.

"But most dragons regard the human form as demeaning, so do not exercise this ability. So a relative few of us practice it." She smiled briefly. "I learned humility early. Anyway, given this rich new territory, the dragons multiplied, and soon there were too many for the land to properly support. They realized that strong leadership was needed. Therefore they conducted elections, without the knowledge of the humans, who might not have understood. They decided on a king, and I am his daughter."

"You're a princess!" Tartan said.

"Yes, unfortunately. A dragon princess. I was well trained in dragonly ways and am excellent at fighting, but still looked down on because I did not mind appearing human, and I can fight also in this form. But I am also empathic, a trait not highly regarded among dragons, as it interferes with hunting and feeding."

"Do you mean *emphatic*?" Tara asked.

"No, that means forceful. *Empathy* means identifying with the feelings of others."

"Such as potential prey," Tartan said. "I can see how that would make killing and eating it awkward."

"Exactly. I have been trained to kill, and I *can* kill, but I don't much like it. I would rather discuss things with humans than eat them. That makes me something of a pariah among my kind."

"We sympathize," Tara said, with three quarters of a smile.

"Not that dragons were preying on humans or other humanoids like elves, gnomes, and goblins," Emerald said. "Part of the deal had been for the two species to be at peace. But some humans were hunting dragons, though they weren't supposed to, and that annoyed many of us. Some humans were getting killed, and they thought it was by dragons, because there were more dragons than ever. Tensions increased between the two species. The notion of war developed, with neither species really opposed to it; each would be glad to be rid of the other. However, my father and I knew that such a war would lead to needless casualties on both sides. So my father sent me to visit the Good Magician and ask for a way to avert the impending war. That is what I did."

"But you said he gave you an answer," Tartan said. "So why were you weeping?"

"That relates to the rest of the story. You see, he told me that the most expedient way to ensure peace was for me to marry a human prince."

"That might do it," Tara said.

"Yes it might," Emerald agreed. "And I think my father had something of the sort in mind when he sent me. But it's no good."

"Why not?" Tartan asked. "You look delightfully human, and crossbreeds happen in Xanth. Our hosts are crossbreeds. I'm sure any prince would be glad to have you, if you promised not to bite him."

"I'm sure he would. But I can't do it."

"But why not?" Tara asked.

"Because what my father doesn't know is that I'm a lesbian. The idea of marrying a man, even a noble prince, horrifies me. It's not the species that is the problem, it's the gender. I just can't do it."

"Oh, my," Tartan said. "Now we appreciate your problem."

"We certainly do," Tara agreed. "But we're just visitors. Maybe our hosts have thoughts."

They turned the bodies over to the hosts. "Hello. I am Demon Ted, a demon/human crossbreed. I don't have any problem with your dragon nature, and I'd be interested in you myself, because you're beautiful, except that I'm not royal and I'm male."

"I am DeMonica, a demon/naga crossbreed. I am of royal lineage. I don't have any problem with your dragon nature either, but my romantic interest is in men."

"And there it is," Emerald said. "My romantic orientation is what dooms my mission. I don't dare return to my father with my mission unfulfilled, yet it is not in me to marry a prince. Oh, woe is me!" She relapsed into tears.

"What Service did the Good Magician require of you for his useless Answer?" Ted asked.

"None. He said my mission was worthy, but he couldn't help me at this time, so there was no charge. He told me to go on my way."

"That was halfway nice of him," Monica said. "Which is about as far as he goes. What will you do now?"

Emerald considered. "I guess I'll go find a nice private spot and end myself, since I have no viable alternatives in life."

Both Ted and Monica winced.

"Look, Emerald," Ted said after the winces dissipated, leaving small smudges in the air. "We just hate to see a pretty creature like you go that way. Why don't you wait here, and once we're done with the Good Magician, we'll come back this way and you can join our Quest."

"Quest?"

"We're helping Tartan and Tara save Xanth from a fate worse than oblivion: torment by the Ghost Writer," Monica said. "Maybe you can help us, in your dragon form, by flying up and intercepting the Night Colt and chomping him. Meanwhile we'll look out for some way to help you in return. Maybe there's something none of us are thinking of yet, but will in time."

"I suppose," Emerald said uncertainly. "At least I could look for a suitable spot to end myself."

"That too," Ted agreed, almost generating another wince. "Now we'll return to being hosts."

Tartan and Tara came to the fore. "We agree with them," Tartan said. "In a magic land like Xanth, there must be a way to ease your burden."

"There has to be," Tara agreed.

"Thank you," Emerald said. "My hope is faint, but that's more than I had before. Just the sympathy of the four of you helps a bit."

They walked on, leaving Emerald there, no longer tearful. "We have to help her," Tartan said.

"We will, somehow," Tara agreed.

Chapter 5

PRINCE DOLIN

"Thar she blows!" Tartan exclaimed as the castle turrets came into sight. There had been no doubt about finding the Good Magician's Castle, because Ted and Monica were familiar with the route, and the path led right there.

"It's beautiful," Tara said.

"Careful, girl. Last time you said that, you wound up kissing a cloud."

"It was worth it."

"Remember," Ted said. "You can't just walk in. There'll be three Challenges to navigate. Monica and I won't be able to help you there; you'll be on your own. That's the Good Magician's rule."

"We'll handle it," Tara said, evidently responding to a similar message from Monica. "But considering that we're on a mission to help Xanth, and the Magician must know that, why should he obstruct our way?"

"He doesn't like to be bothered by folk who aren't serious," Ted said. "So he discourages them."

"Emerald must have gotten through," Tara said. "She was plenty serious. Yet he didn't help her."

"The Good Magician is known for several things," Ted said. "His grumpiness, his obscurity, and his way of always being right in the end. He must have had reason to turn her down."

"I'm not sure I much like him," Tara said. Then: "What?!" The two punctuation marks were clear, not seeming to like being jammed together.

"Monica's telling her what else the Magician is known for," Ted said. "He has five and a half wives."

"Five and a half wives!" Tartan exclaimed. "I thought Xanth was monogamous."

"It is. It's a long story."

"Condense it."

"Humfrey—that's his name—went to Hell in a hand basket and was given back all his former wives for the prior century or so. They had faded out naturally, in time, and been stored there. So suddenly he had them all back: Dara Demoness, the Maiden Taiwan, Rose of Roogna, Sofia Mundane, the Gorgon, and last and least, MareAnn, who is good with horses. She's the half, though she was his first love."

"That's quite a roster," Tartan said.

"I could tell you more. Each has a book-length story."

"I'll pass, for now. So how do all those wives get along together?"

"Just fine. They all have a common trial: Humfrey himself. They take turns, one month apiece. It's like a relay race. So we'll encounter this month's Designated Wife, whoever she is. That's how they bypass the monogamy issue."

"But first we have to navigate three Challenges," Tara said aloud. "On our own."

"Let's do it."

They walked toward the castle, which was set in a pretty moat, with ornamental trees surrounding it. There was no sign of danger. The path led right to the drawbridge, which was conveniently down; they would not have to swim.

A huge head lifted out of the water, perched on a massive serpentine neck. "A moat monster!" Tara exclaimed as the monster eyed them and licked its lips.

"Let's not swim."

"Not," she agreed with a shudder. "That thing isn't even trying to tempt us with a sexy body. It's just hungry."

They rounded a tree and came across several equines sitting up like dogs and using their front hooves to hold little sandwiches. This was odd but not threatening. But as they approached, for the path went right through the group of animals, somehow the scene shifted so that the creatures were blocking the way with their massive bodies.

"Maybe we can go around," Tartan said.

They walked to the side, but that too turned out to be blocked. They tried the other side, only to find yet more bodies. "There appears to be no way through," Tara said.

"This must be a Challenge. We have to find a way to get safely past it."

"Maybe we can climb over them," she said hesitantly.

They tried, but the bodies turned out to be taller than they looked, forming an effective wall. "I don't think we can do it, physically," Tartan said, frustrated.

"We can do it as ghosts," Tara said. "We can part with the host bodies here and go on by ourselves."

"Good idea. Last one out is a rusty pot."

They paused, not emerging. "I can't get out," Tara said.

"Neither can I. We're locked in. So it seems we *have* to do it physically."

"Somehow," she agreed.

"I just thought of something. Xanth is a land of puns. Maybe there's a pun."

"A pun about horses eating appetizers?" Then she groaned.

"What?"

"The pun. I just got it. A sight pun. Horse d'oeuvres."

Now Tartan groaned. But she was right, because the horses faded away, leaving the path clear. They had handled the first Challenge, almost by accident.

But in barely three moments there was another barrier. Floating spheres with little arms and legs hovered across the path, jostling together.

"Why do I suspect that we won't be able to pass by them?" Tartan asked rhetorically.

They tried, and the spheres blocked them off high, low, and to the sides. No passage.

"Another pun?" Tara asked.

"I can't think what."

"They have letters printed on them. Maybe they have names."

Tartan looked. AAA, BBB, CCC and so on. "Designations, at least," he agreed. "Maybe if we get to ZZZ we'll be able to get around the end."

But there turned out to be no end. Instead the orbs started having different combinations, like ABC, ACD, or ADE. That didn't help.

Then he saw one that said ABS. And a light bulb actually flashed over his head.

"I saw that," Tara said. "You got a bright idea!"

"I did. It's crazy, but—"

"This is a crazy place. Out with it."

"Well, if you put the full name to ABS, you get ABS ORB. Absorb. Maybe—"

"That just might be," she agreed.

Tartan went up to the sphere, which was like a beach ball, and spoke to it directly. "Abs Orb, do your thing."

The sphere floated up to the one beside it. There was no sound, but the other sphere disappeared into the first one. Then it floated to the next, and took it in also. It was absorbing them.

Soon the path was clear. They hurried along.

"ABS must be getting pretty full," Tara said.

Tartan glanced back. "Okay, ABS, you can belch now."

And suddenly the sky was filled with sailing spheres as Abs let go.

They had to laugh, but it was relief as much as humor. Another pun solved, another Challenge navigated.

They resumed their walk along the path. And came to an old-fashioned train station. "My grandfather used to speak of these," Tara said. "He said trains were once the main mode of travel, both far and near. They were powered by big hot steam engines that drew anywhere up to a hundred railroad cars behind them. It sounded so romantic."

"My grandparents too," he agreed. "Almost made me long for the old days."

"What, before television?"

"Well, maybe not *that* old," he said wryly. "I understand they still have scenic tourist train tours through the mountains. I always thought if I ever got married, we'd honeymoon there. Nothing to do but see the sights, outside and in."

"Outside and in?"

"Well, I love mountain scenery, but I also love looking at—I mean, we'd be newly married." Had he gone wrong, speaking too candidly?

"It's a date."

Had she just proposed to him, indirectly? He was at a loss for words.

Then she laughed. "I'm teasing you, Tartan."

Oh. He didn't know whether to be relieved or disappointed. Marriage was way beyond his present horizon, yet it had considerable appeal. They had known each other so briefly, yet already experienced so much together.

"I shouldn't have. I apologize."

"No, no, I just—it's a new horizon, is all." He was being clumsy.

If she was disappointed, she handled it gracefully. "I understand. Let's tackle the Challenge."

They entered the station. But Tartan remained in a turmoil of emotions. There was so much more here than just a magic land.

There was a train track, and on it stood a train. There were several cars, with an engine at the front. A real old-fashioned locomotive, with jets of steam puffing from near the wheels. It was impressive.

"The track leads on right across the drawbridge," Tara said. "Obviously we must ride this train."

They approached the nearest car. Its steps were invitingly down. They mounted them and entered the car. It was long, clean, and nice, with plush seats. They sat beside each other in the middle of the carriage, Tara taking the window seat.

Nothing happened.

"Oh, I just remembered," Tara said. "You have to have a ticket!"

"That's right. We need to buy tickets for our destination."

She laughed. "Which would be the Good Magician's Castle."

"Close enough."

They left the car and walked to the station ticket office. But it was empty.

"I guess we can't buy tickets," Tara said. "If we even had Xanth money for them."

"But there must be a way."

They stood on the platform and looked around. "What's on those trees?" Tara asked.

He looked. "Square leaves?"

They checked more closely. "Tickets!" she said. "They're even printed GM CASTLE."

"Just pull off two, and ride the train," he agreed. "In Xanth you don't buy so much as harvest, like with the shoe trees."

But the ticket leaves refused to be picked. They clung tight to their branches.

"We're still missing something," Tara said.

"The pun," he agreed.

They walked around the front of the train. There on the engine was a plaque with the word SELF. "That's its name?" Tara asked.

"Odd," Tartan agreed. "I could see a locomotive called CHARGER or INVINCIBLE. But SELF doesn't make sense."

"A steam engine named SELF. Not like a streetcar named Desire."

Something hovered near Tartan's head, just out of sight. "Incipient pun . . ." he said.

"I see a vague bulb forming. You're getting an idea."

Then the bulb flashed brightly. "A Self steam locomotive. Self esteem engine."

"Self—steam—engine. Oh, that's almost enough to make me retch," Tara said. "I can't even groan fully."

"Let's find out." He walked to the ticket tree and picked two tickets without difficulty.

"Oh, I could kiss you!"

"Not if you're retching!" he said with mock alarm.

She kissed him anyway, with a laughing groan.

They boarded the train again, flashing their tickets. There was a double beep of acceptance. They sat on the seat and gazed out the window. The train started to move.

"We're on our train ride," Tara said. "Too bad there are no mountains."

Something overflowed. "Oh, Tara!"

Then they were kissing, as the train chugged slowly across the moat. If it wasn't love, it was a fellow traveler.

The train slowed and stopped. They stepped down off it.

There before them was a woman. "Hello, Tartan and Tara. I am Wira, the Good Magician's daughter in law. Welcome to the Castle."

"She's legitimate," Ted said. It seemed he could speak, now that the Challenges had been navigated.

"Thank you," Tara said a bit faintly. She was evidently being similarly reassured by her host.

"This way. Dara is eager to meet you."

"Dara?" Tartan asked blankly. "We came to see the Good Magician."

Wira smiled. "Your hosts will clarify that."

They did. "Designated Wife," Ted said. "Wife of the Month. She'll send you to meet the Magician, in due course. She's a dusky beauty."

Soon they were ushered into a comfortable living room. An elegantly robed woman greeted them as Wira faded into the background. "We're so glad to have you here," Dara said. "The Ghost Writer has to be stopped, and you're the ones to do it." She glanced at Tara, smiling. "We almost match, my dear: Dara and Tara, though I may be a few hundred years older than you."

"She is," Ted said. "Demons are pretty much immortal. She's unusual in that she has a soul, so she treats people fairly. That's more than my mother does."

"But you know, we can't serve a year," Tara said. "We're Mundanes, here only by proxy."

"That won't be a problem, dear. Your Service will be to take Prince Dolin on the Quest with you. In fact, he will be able to help you."

"Prince Dolin?" Tartan asked. Ted was drawing a similar blank, and a glance at Tara indicated that Monica had no information either.

"He is necessarily anonymous at present," Dara said. "His aunt brought him here in the form of a ring. The ring contains his soul. If the ring should get lost, the Prince will be lost. We have provided him with a host, who has donned the ring. So Prince Dolin is in effect the same as you: a ghostly visitor animating a local man."

"We understand how that works," Tara said. "But what's in it for the man?"

"Prince Dolin has about a month left to find a local princess or the equivalent to marry," Dara said. "If he succeeds, he will remain in Xanth, an honored prince with some extremely apt connections. In that case, his host, who has only garden variety weed prospects on his own, will become his permanent body, and be effectively a prince. He likes that prospect."

"He would," Ted said. "Taking a princess to bed."

"Naturally you see only the sexy side of it, Ted," Dara said.

"Oh, bleep!" Ted said. "She heard me. I forgot this is the Good Magician's Castle."

Dara smiled with a fair modicum of smugness. "While Monica appreciates the romantic side. I appreciate both, and they are certainly integral. So help Dolin in what ways you can, and he will help you, and with luck all of you will benefit. As well as Xanth, when the Ghost Writer is dealt with. Now here he is." She lifted her voice half a modicum. "Prince."

A handsome young man appeared, well constructed and muscular, wearing a small crown and of course a ring. His flowing yellow hair trailed behind his head. "I am here, Demoness." His voice was low and vibrant.

Tartan could tell by Tara's expression that both she and Monica were highly impressed. If Tara had been jealous of the mermaid's physical appeal, now it was Tartan's turn. The man practically oozed masculine appeal.

"Dolin, these are Tartan and Tara, Mundanes who are hosted by local residents much the same way you are. They understand your position, and you will join their Quest."

"That is good to know," Dolin said. "Thank you, Tartan and Tara, for having me along. I know it is an imposition."

"Not at all, Prince," Tara breathed.

"We also have with us Prince Dolin's aunt, Princess Merari, or Mera for short." She raised her voice another quarter modicum. "Princess."

A young woman appeared, surely no older than eighteen. She was beautiful, with soft brown hair, brown eyes, and a small crown. There was another round of introductions.

"But—" Tara said.

Merari smiled. "I am Dolin's aunt, but complications of spaced delivery make me eighteen, while he is twenty-five. It happens on occasion."

"Oh, of course," Tara agreed somewhat lamely.

"That is only the beginning of the complications," Dara said. "These folk are from an alternate reality that is accessible via Ptero, the moon that circles Princess Idea's head and contains all possible characters. Your hosts will verify this. I will pause three moments while your hosts verify this." She paused three moments.

"It's true," Ted said. "Ptero looks like a tiny moon, but it's a complete world in itself, far more populous than Xanth."

The moments expired, and Dara resumed. "Because there are so many residents on Ptero and its associated moons, all of whom would like to come settle Xanth, there are severe immigration restrictions. Folk can normally visit Xanth only briefly, and via spirit, taking hosts the way the two of you have. Dolin is with a local host, as I explained, and will be able to remain here only if he marries a local princess or the equivalent. But that is not the end of it. He is indubitably a prince, but is under the standard geis."

"Standard what?" Tartan asked. "Geese?"

"Geis," she said, pronouncing it geesh or gesh. "It is a magical obligation that a person can't avoid. In this case, not only is Dolin required to marry a princess if he is to remain in Xanth proper, he is not permitted to be told his own background. He has no knowledge of his past, and will not know it until he figures it out for himself. That means that some local princess may have to love and marry him blind, as it were."

"But what princess would do that?" Tara asked. "He's handsome, but he could have serious hidden faults." She might have been thinking of the pretty but deadly mermaid who had accosted Tartan. Indeed, appearance was not to be trusted.

"Exactly," Dara said. "It is his host who is handsome; we know nothing about Dolin himself. It is a similar case with Princess Mera, except that she does know her situation, but can't tell it. That is why I am doing the talking. Very few folk manage to immigrate from or via Ptero, because of the geis."

"I can see why," Tartan said. "The restrictions seem unnecessarily severe, just as they are in Mundania."

"Um, Prince Dolin," Tara said. "What does your host think of all this?"

The man's expression changed, becoming distinctly less princely and more ordinary. "I'd rather be anonymous," he said in a lowbrow tone. "I'm just an ignorant country boy on my own, not smart or skilled, and my magic talent is just one thing: to know when to keep my mouth shut. I came here to ask how I might better myself, and this is how: being the Prince's host. So leave me out of it." He shut his mouth firmly.

"And what's your talent, Prince?" Tara asked.

"I don't know," Dolin said, surprised.

"It is to do the right thing," Mera said. "Whatever it may be. That much I am permitted to tell."

"Mera brought Dolin here, and will remain long enough to learn his outcome," Dara said. "Then she expects to return to her reality and report to his mother, Princess Taplin."

"So she's joining our party too?" Tara asked.

"No," Mera said. "I will track you from here via a magic mirror. It will be silent, but I will know from the pictures when Dolin finds a wife."

"You'd be welcome to come too," Tara said.

Mera shook her head. "I do not wish to further complicate your mission. The Good Magician has been kind enough to lend me a host and allow me to stay here for the occasion, and that suffices." She smiled a bit sadly. "I would indeed like to explore Xanth more personally, and possibly remain here, but the geis makes that unlikely."

"A lovely princess like you could surely attract a prince," Tartan said. "If you got out in the field, as it were."

"Thank you, no. It is my host you see here, who is lovely. It is Dolin I must secure. His need is greater than mine."

"You know more about him than he does," Tara said shrewdly.

"Yes. But I can't tell. Not until the time comes when he no longer needs my input. He must make it on his own."

"I have no idea how," Dolin said. "But I find I do have a feel for the right thing, and that is to travel with the two of you and do whatever I can for you."

"We'll surely find something," Tara said.

"What foolishness," Ted said. "Just because he's handsome, they're all goggle-eyed."

"Not that you men are ever that way in the presence of an attractive female," Dara said, as her robe turned translucent, showing her remarkable outline complete with dusky panties.

Wira reappeared, snapping them out of their freak. "The Good Magician will see you now, Tartan and Tara."

"Thanks," Tartan said. The two of them got up and followed her out of the room.

"Why do I suspect this is more complicated than we yet know?" Tara whispered to Tartan.

"Because it is," Wira answered.

That shut them both up.

They went up a narrow winding stone staircase and came to a room filled with books. In the center an old gnome pored over a huge open volume. "Good Magician," Wira said. "The querents are here."

"What did she call us?" Tartan asked Ted.

"A querent is a person with a question," Ted replied. "It's Good Magician speak."

The gnome looked up. "Yes it is, Ted, thank you."

"You're welcome, GM," Ted said silently, laughing.

"You have his attention," Wira murmured. "Ask."

"Uh, Good Magician," Tartan said. "How can we solve the problem of the Ghost Writer in the Sky?"

"Go to the Goddess Isis. Only she can resolve it in a suitable manner."

"Oh-oh. That's mischief," Ted said. "And not just because she's the Goddess of Sex."

"But will she help?" Tara asked, evidently prompted by Monica.

"No," the Good Magician said. "You will have to persuade her. That will be more difficult than finding her."

"And how do we find her?" Tartan asked.

"Ask the maid Amara. Only she can locate the Goddess."

"And will she do that?" Tara asked.

"Perhaps."

"And how do we find Amara?" Tartan asked.

"You won't. She will find you, if she wishes. Simply make yourselves available."

Tartan exchanged a look with Tara. Neither of them was quite satisfied.

The old eyes returned to the tome. They had been dismissed.

Wira ushered them out and down.

Back in the living room they rejoined Prince Dolin. "Are things in order?" he inquired politely.

Tara laughed. "They'll have to do. Let's be on our way."

Mera hugged Dolin in an auntly manner. "Be careful, dear."

"I will, Aunt Mera," Dolin agreed dutifully.

Then they were back on the enchanted path. "Where to?" Tartan asked.

"I have no idea," Tara said.

Tartan got an idea. "Prince Dolin—can your talent guide us?"

"I don't know. I learned of my talent only when Aunt Mera spoke of it."

"Maybe we can give it some practical choices. Such as how to find the maid Amara." He pointed. "This way or that way?"

"This way," Dolin said promptly.

"So be it."

They walked this way, which was back the way they had come. And there was Emerald, watching hopefully for them. "We forgot her!" Tara said. "Had we gone the other way, we would have missed her."

"After we promised to take her along," Tartan agreed, almost chagrined.

"This is a friend?" Dolin asked.

"She's a dragon princess who has to marry a human prince to make peace between humans and dragons," Tara explained. "But she can't, emotionally, because she's a lesbian. She was in tears of frustration when we met her, facing awful alternatives. We don't know how we can help her, but we're bound to try."

"That's too bad. I need a princess to marry, and I'm not sure she has to be human, as long as she looks human."

They came up to Emerald. "Prince Dolin, this is Princess Emerald," Tartan said, formally introducing them to each other. "And we are faced with irony: each of you needs to marry, but it seems you are not for each other."

They shared details, and agreed. The two continued to talk as the group walked the path.

When they came to a fork, Dolin chose the one that bore south. Then one that bore west.

The Prince turned out to be an unassuming, decent chap. Tartan liked him, and knew that Tara liked him better. Even Emerald found him acceptable, maybe because he accepted her as she was and made no moves on her.

A castle came into view. "Oh, my," Tara said. "That's Caprice. In a new location. Not the maid."

"The maid?" Emerald asked.

"We're supposed to get in touch with a maid named Amara, whom we should encounter along the way," Tara said.

"Caprice?" Dolin asked.

"Do what we do," Tartan said. "Consult internally with your host for background information."

Dolin paused. Then his face lighted. "The castle that travels!"

"That's it," Tartan said. "We came from there yesterday, when it was elsewhere. This is either a remarkable coincidence, or your talent wants you to meet Princess Dawn."

"I do not know why. My host tells me she's married, with children."

"She is," Tara said. Then a bulb flash over her head. "Her talent! She knows all about any living thing she touches."

"She might know about me," Dolin said.

"Are you allowed to know about yourself, yet?" Tartan asked.

"I do not know. But I assume that if I learn about myself during our travels, this is acceptable, or my talent would not allow it."

They went to the door and knocked. The door opened. There stood Dawn. "What are you doing here?" she asked. "I thought you were on your mission."

"We are," Tartan said. "Princess Dawn, this is Prince Dolin, and Emerald Dragon. He does not know his personal history, and she can't marry a prince. We thought you might help."

"I'll be glad to," she said. "May I touch you, Princess?"

Emerald put out her hand, and Dawn touched it. "So you see," Emerald said.

"I do indeed. Your mission is vital. I know King Ivy is eager to find an avenue for peace between our species. But this is beyond my expertise. I have no advice to offer you."

If there had been any doubt of her nature, there was none now. Dawn knew.

Then Dawn extended her hand to the prince. He took it.

Dawn looked astonished. Then she stepped into Dolin and hugged him closely. Then she kissed him. "I love you," she said, and fainted.

Fortunately he caught her before she hit the ground, and the four of them steadied her in place. "Should I have paused at a pool to wash myself?" Dolin asked, bewildered.

"You smell great," Tara said. "It must be something she learned about you."

Dawn recovered. "Oh, this is amazing," she said.

"Please, Princess, what is it?" Dolin asked. "I did not mean to offend you."

"Oh, you could never do that, Prince," Dawn said. "I just wasn't prepared."

"So what is it?" Tartan asked.

"I can't tell you."

The three of them stared at her. "You know, but you can't tell?" Tara asked.
"Exactly. There's a geis."

Oh, that again. "So what's next?" Tartan asked.

"I think you should go to Hades."

"I did give offense!" Dolin said ruefully.

Dawn laughed. "Not at all, Prince. Go there to see my sister Eve. She's the mistress of Hades. I know she will want to meet you. I'll mirror her and tell her you're coming. Just follow that path." She indicated a glowing path that Tartan was sure had not been there before.

That quickly they were on their way to Hades. "This may not be completely pleasant," Ted said.

"I could turn dragon if there is danger," Emerald said. "But I prefer not to, because it ruins my clothes unless I take them off first, and I don't like going nude when there are men present. They can get ideas."

"Understandable," Dolin said, and she flashed him a smile.

Tartan noticed that this path was paved. Each tile was printed with the words GOOD INTENTIONS.

Surprisingly quickly they passed a sign saying HADES—TOURISTS UNWELCOME.

"Fortunately we're not exactly tourists," Tara said.

Now the forest gave way to a bleak landscape where obscene shapes danced. Before long the shapes realized that someone was coming in, and formed into two luscious women and two handsome men, each of them beckoning seductively.

"Don't step off the path!" Ted warned.

"But suppose one of them is a princess?" Dolin asked plaintively.

Immediately crowns sprouted on the heads of the females.

"Monica says not to believe anything the spooks say," Tara said. "They just want to get us off the safety path so they can consume us."

"My host says much the same," Dolin said.

"Monica says it's too bad we don't have safety pins," Tara said.

"What are those?" Dolin asked.

"She said they are magic pins you can take with you that will keep you safe as long as you keep them. Even in hell."

Tartan laughed. "I would have guessed another use for them, such as to hold up diapers. But what do I know? I'm hopelessly Mundane."

"Are you sure I shouldn't turn dragon?" Emerald asked.

"Don't," Tartan said, speaking for Ted. "You wouldn't fit on the path, and the spooks would get at you in human or dragon form. That would be hell, literally."

"It would," Emerald agreed.

But the spooks had overheard. Now a handsome woman appeared, beckoning to Emerald, along with a lovely female dragon.

They ignored the spooks, much to the spooks' frustration. The females even yanked up their skirts to flash their panties, but the men kept their gazes strictly on the path. Even so, the peripheral images were like fires.

The path led to a somber castle. As they came to the main door, it opened. There stood a beautiful dark-haired princess. "Tartan. Tara, Prince Dolin, Princess Emerald," Princess Eve said. "Do come in. It's so nice to have human or similar company."

The castle interior was much nicer than the exterior. Soon they met a seven-year-old boy with a modest young woman. "This is my son Plato," Eve said proudly. "And his governess, Zosi Zombie."

"Zombie?" Tartan asked, taken aback. "I must say you don't look dead."

"Not at the moment," Zosi said. "I am alive at present, but my normal state is as a zombie."

"Yeah, she's great," Plato said. "Sometimes we visit the zombies. They're real yucky, with bits of rotten flesh falling off."

"Zosi's perfect for him," Eve said. "If he misbehaves too much, she kisses him. He hates that."

Plato made a face, agreeing.

"I'm a dragon," Emerald said.

Plato eyed her. "You look just like a woman," he said disapprovingly.

Emerald reached toward him with one hand. The hand shifted and became a dragon's claw. "I'm not."

"Wow! Let's go flying!"

"Plato, these folk did not come to play with you," Eve said sternly.

"Come on, Plato," Zosi said. "These folk have private business with your mother."

"I know," the boy retorted. "That's why I'm staying."

Zosi pursed her lips in kiss formation. The boy quickly changed his mind, and they departed. The others managed to avoid smiling, at least while the boy was in sight.

Eve contemplated Dolin seriously. "Dawn wouldn't tell me exactly what she knows, except that I would be interested. But I have my own source of information, as she knows. I know all about any inanimate thing I touch. Do you have any associated object?"

Dolin held out his hand with the ring on one finger. "This is my essence."

"Excellent. Let me touch it."

She touched it. She straightened up. "Oh, my!" Then she stepped into him and hugged him, as her sister had, and kissed him. "I love you!" Fortunately she didn't faint. Quite.

"Please, what is it?" Dolin asked.

"Oh, I can't tell you. There's a geis."

The four shared a subdued groan, along with their hosts.

"I'm sorry," Eve said. "I didn't mean to tease you. I was caught off guard despite Dawn's warning. But it's true I can't tell you. You need to find a princess to marry first, or at least to find out for yourself."

"I am hoping to find one." He paused, considering. "Are there princesses in Hades?"

"A number," Eve agreed. "But they're dead. You need a live one."

"We should be on our way," Tara said.

"Oh, stay the night. It is late, and I'm delighted to have company. You're safe as long as you stay in the castle."

"It's more complicated," Tartan said. "Tara and I have to return to Mundania to, er, recharge. We're just ghosts here."

"Oh, of course. Dawn mentioned that too. But your hosts can stay, and Dolin and Emerald. Oops."

"Oops?" Tara inquired nervously.

"I just remembered we only have two vacant suites. Ted and Monica can share one, of course, but it may be awkward for the prince and princess."

Dolin and Emerald exchanged a cautious glance. "I appreciate the problem," Dolin said.

"We can be friends," Emerald said. "We just don't want to have a romantic relationship or to marry."

"Honesty compels me," Dolin said. "I must say the right thing. Your human form is most attractive. I would have thoughts if I saw more of it than is proper."

She was evidently intrigued. "Even though you know my true nature? That my attraction is to females, not males? That I am not remotely human, apart from my appearance?"

"I understand that you were in tears when the Mundanes met you, because of your bad alternatives. That suggests that you have human feelings."

"That's right," she said, surprised. "The human form must bring human sentiments. They must be necessary, because if I married a human, I would have to play the role to make the marriage work."

"That seems likely," he agreed. "You wish to do the right thing by your partner. That makes you appealing in another way. I do not wish to cause you distress, but thoughts are already threatening to reach me."

"That's sweet. I suppose I could pretend you are female, in the dark."

"Please no. It is better that I not see or feel you in dishabille."

"You really are trying to do the right thing."

"It is my nature."

"Suppose I turn dragon?"

He laughed. "That would do it. Just promise not to consume me."

She smiled. "I promise."

"I will avert my gaze when you strip so as to change without spoiling your clothing. Just let me know when."

"I will," Emerald agreed thoughtfully.

"Then it seems it is settled," Eve said, relieved.

"We will rejoin you here in the morning," Tartan said. "I'm sure you'll find Ted and Monica perfectly compatible."

Tartan and Tara took hands and turned ghost, zipping back to their natural bodies. Again they had to scramble for the bathroom, having forgotten to take a midday break. Then, relieved, they came together and kissed. "Do you still find me interesting," he asked, "after seeing Prince Dolin?"

"As interesting as you still find me, after seeing Monica, Dawn, Dara, Emerald, and Eve."

"Touché!" Then they plunged into another vibrant ellipsis. There was no doubt they found each other interesting.

. . .

"You know, Dolin and Emerald do seem to like each other," Tara said as they ate dinner. "Just not as romantic partners."

"Yes. It's too bad, because they could do each other a lot of good."

"A marriage of convenience. Maybe if they don't find what they want, that would suffice. It would be better than suffering failure and possible extinction."

"If they only see it that way," Tartan said.

"We don't seem to be any closer to accomplishing our own mission."

"Tomorrow is another day."

"You know," she confessed as they turned in together, "I wouldn't much mind if the mission took a long time. Fabulous fantasy days, and nights like this."

"I agree. For the first time my life has meaning. Day and night."

"Day and night," she agreed, and kissed him.

Chapter 6

AMARA

In the morning they prepared themselves and made the change back to their Xanth hosts. Ted and Monica were ready. "Now to rejoin Prince Dolin and Princess Emerald," Tartan said.

They knocked on the door of the adjacent suite. The prince opened it, rubbing his eyes. "I may have overslept," he said apologetically. "There were so many things to learn yesterday, I was more tired than I realized. So was my host."

Behind him was curled a beautiful sleeping dragon, pure silver with emerald green edging on her scales, her wings embracing her body like a cloak. "Emerald must have been tired too," Tara said.

"Yes. We talked last night before she changed. She does not have much experience associating with humans, and it may have been a strain on her. She's a nice person."

"I hope she finds a suitable partner," Tartan said. He was careful not to suggest that Dolin might be such a partner, if it came to the starkest choice. Half a loaf was surely better than none.

Dolin snapped his fingers. "Emerald, it is morning," he said.

The dragon's eyes snapped open. A burp of fire issued from her mouth. Suddenly she was the woman, naked, utterly shapely. Dolin put his arm up to shield his gaze, too late. He was suffering a thought. Not quite a freak. So, for that matter, was Tartan. And Ted. So she was a dragon. Who cared?

"Oh for pity's sake," Tara snapped, and Monica's endorsement was in her tone.

"Oh, I forgot," Emerald said, chastened. "I should have waited for you to close your eyes. Did I freak you out?"

"No," Dolin said through his arm. "Please dress."

Now Tartan turned away as Emerald picked up her panties, knowing those would wipe him out. In barely (as it were) a moment and a half she was done. "I'm decent."

The men were relieved. So, evidently, were Tara and Monica. It seemed the women weren't eager to have the men feast their eyes on either bareness or panties.

"You were never indecent," Dolin said gallantly.

She flashed him an appreciative smile. It was evident that despite their formidable differences, the two were coming to like each other.

Princess Eve appeared. "We have breakfast awaiting you downstairs," she said. "Did you sleep well?"

"Almost too well," Tartan said with a quarter of a smile.

In due course they were on the path out of Hades. "We're lucky," Ted said. "Regular visitors have to be ferried across the River Styx, and sometimes the boatman makes moves on the ladies. But this path bypasses that."

"I wonder how the ferryman would feel about a lady dragon?" Tara mused, and the others smiled.

The demons along the sides tried again to tempt them. Now they even assumed the forms of dragons, changing to luscious bare girls. "Oh cut it out!" Emerald snapped. "You're not lesbians."

The spooks actually seemed taken aback. They didn't know how to handle this. They faded out. The foursome moved on, sharing a smug smile.

They emerged in Xanth proper. "Now where were we going?" Tara asked.

"Eve mentioned Castle Roogna," Dolin said. "It seems there's someone I should meet there."

"Not Amara?" Tartan asked.

"We won't find her, she'll find us," Tara reminded him.

"No, this is one Princess Electra, Dawn and Eve's mother," Dolin said. "The name almost seems familiar."

"She had an interesting history," Ted said.

"Tell us," Tartan said, and turned the mouth over to him.

Ted talked as they walked, guided by Dolin's choices of the right paths. "Electra was an ordinary girl, nigh nine hundred years ago, helping the Sorceress Tapis, who made magic tapestries."

"How long ago?" Emerald asked.

"In historical times," Ted explained. "I said it was interesting."

"There's one of the tapestries hanging in Castle Roogna now," Monica said, also speaking for herself. "It shows whatever is happening in Xanth, past and present. The Sorceress Tapis had a marvelous talent."

"Tapis needed the Heaven Cent," Ted continued. "That's a whole 'nother story. Electra's talent was electricity, so she was there to help Tapis get the Cent charged. At that time a princess, actually Tapis' daughter, came to ask Tapis to make a coverlet for her, so she would not get cold during her long sleep."

"Which is another whole story," Monica said. "She was supposed to sleep a thousand years, then be awoken by a handsome prince who would marry her and they'd live happily ever after."

"Meanwhile the Magician Murphy was skulking around," Ted said. "His talent was to make anything go wrong that could go wrong. Tapis didn't like him. She even sent him a tapestry that opened on Hades. That made him cautious. But his curse affected them, and it was Electra who bit the poisoned apple and fell into the casket, taken by the sleep spell. The poor princess was left out. I understand she was most annoyed."

"I almost think I have heard that story," Dolin said.

"So it was Electra who was kissed awake by young Prince Dolph," Monica said. "Almost eight and a half centuries later."

"Not a thousand years?" Emerald asked.

"She got time off for good behavior."

"While asleep? She must be a really good person!"

"So Electra married Prince Dolph," Ted said. "That's another separate story, because he loved Monica's mother, Nada Naga. But the essence is that if you count from when Electra was first delivered, she's now almost nine hundred years old."

"She doesn't look it," Monica said.

"I'm supposed to meet a nine-hundred-year-old woman?" Dolin asked.

"There must be a reason," Ted said.

"There must be," Dolin agreed. "Because I feel it is the right thing to do."

Ted and Monica retreated, leaving the bodies to Tartan and Tara. "Xanth certainly is full of history," Tartan said.

Emerald laughed. "Most places are. We dragons have our histories too."

They paused at a wayside rest stop, and this time Tartan and Tara had the wit to remember to visit their own bodies. "Much more comfortable," Tara said, back in Mundania after they had handled the necessary details.

"It's getting so I feel more at home with the host in Xanth," Tartan said. "My body here is just a body, not very interesting."

She laughed. "I know the feeling. But maybe we can add some interest." She glanced at the bed. "Shall we?"

He was tempted, but hesitated. "Our hosts would know."

"Oh, they would," she said, coloring slightly.

"I wonder if we could ever get to—to do the ellipsis—in Xanth? That would be interesting."

"Our hosts would certainly know then."

He sighed. "They would. We have no privacy there."

"And not much here, really."

So, vaguely disappointed, they returned to Xanth.

"You should have done it," Ted said, reading his mind. "I would have. Ellipses don't grow on trees, even in Xanth."

Meanwhile Tara blushed scarlet. Monica had evidently teased her about doing it in Xanth.

"I suspect we are missing something," Dolin said to Emerald.

"I may have a notion what," Emerald said. "Dragons do it too."

"No need to share," Tara said quickly.

They walked on, and soon came to the huge Castle Roogna, the center of the Kingdom of Xanth, human division. It was magnificent.

But they didn't get to tour it. A woman came out to meet them before they reached the moat. "You must be the Mundanes," she said. "Eve called me. I'm Electra."

"Confirmed," Ted said.

"We are the visitors," Tartan said. "And this is Princess Emerald, a dragon girl, traveling with us. And this is Prince Dolin. We're not sure exactly why—" He broke off.

Dolin and Electra looked at each other, came together, hugged and kissed. "Oh, my!" Electra said. "No wonder."

"No wonder what?" Tara asked, slightly nettled.

"I can't say. There's a geis. But it's amazing. I'm so glad Eve contacted me. I wouldn't have missed this for the world."

Tartan was getting somewhat tired of the geis, but kept silent.

"You seem to be an interesting fellow," Emerald remarked to Dolin.

"I have no idea how," Dolin said. "I definitely felt something. Princess Electra is very important to me. But I don't know how."

"It is vital that you accomplish your mission, Prince," Electra said. "Then all will be known. I certainly hope you find your princess."

"I hope so too," Dolin agreed weakly.

"I must let you go now," Electra said. "We have visitors attending, and I must return to them. I sneaked out on my daughter's behest." She turned and walked rapidly back to the castle.

"She didn't want us in Castle Roogna," Tara said. "I wish I knew why."

Dolin shook his head. "And as far as I know, I'm not even part of your mission. I'm just along on my own."

"Things can be related," Emerald said. "I'm the real tag-along."

"I wonder," he said. Then he looked back. "I have the feeling Amara is close."

"Good enough," Tartan said. "Maybe we'll finally start solving mysteries faster than we're generating them."

"Wouldn't that be nice," Tara said with feeling.

They walked along the path to a nearby rest stop. Tartan realized that these were always convenient, on the enchanted paths, in contrast to the un-enchanted paths.

There was a young woman. She was reasonably pretty and quite shapely; her panties would certainly put men out for the count. Both Tartan and Dolin looked at her with interest.

"Stop it," the woman snapped. "I do not return your interest."

"But we didn't say anything," Tartan protested.

"You didn't have to. You were thinking of panties."

She had them there. "We are looking for Amara," Tara said.

"I am she. I was expecting you, whoever you are."

They introduced themselves, explaining about the ghosts and hosts. "We are looking for the Goddess Isis," Tara concluded. "We understand you know where she is."

"She's locked in the comic strips," Amara said. "Lotsa luck seeking her there."

"Comic strips?" Tartan asked.

"Bands of egregious puns," Ted said. "Found dividing the sections of the world Ptero. Now some have appeared in Xanth proper."

"We are remembering," Tara said. "But we're not clear how they got to Xanth."

"The Goddess can't leave the comic strips," Amara said. "But she can manipulate them somewhat. So she moves them around to suit her. She can be anywhere in Xanth she wants to be, but always in a strip. She's not pleased."

"So all we need to do is enter a strip and we'll find her?" Tartan said.

"Hardly. You have no experience with strips?"

"None. Well, our hosts do."

"You have some fun coming."

"So will you help us find her?" Tara asked.

"Why should I?"

They gazed at her. "There is perhaps something you want in return?" Emerald asked.

"From you folk? I think not."

Tartan was becoming annoyed. "Don't let her play you," Ted warned. "Let Dolin or Emerald handle it." It was evident that Monica was giving Tara similar advice.

Dolin tried. "As you know, my talent is doing the right thing, even if I lack a clear idea what it is. I feel that the right thing is for you to join our party, and perhaps you will help us when you feel the time is right."

"I am not interested in joining your party."

He smiled winningly at her. That smile could melt ice. "Perhaps there is something we might do for you in exchange."

But the ice didn't melt. "I doubt it."

Dolin looked handsomely regretful. "I fear I do not properly understand. Please, will you clarify? I have not been in Xanth long, and lack sophistication in its ways." Tartan could almost see the radiation of sincerity. How could she not be moved?

Amara sighed. "I'm trying to be polite, but you force me. I am asexual, which means I have no interest in getting into an ellipsis or summoning the stork with anyone. You men have been undressing me in your minds. That makes me uncomfortable."

"But—" Emerald said.

"And you're doing it too," Amara said. "That's not my style either."

"These men have been understanding about my orientation," Emerald said. "They have interest in my body, but they do not press me to give it to them. They would give you similar leeway. For the sake of the relationship."

"Relationship? That's the other thing," Amara said. "I am also aromantic."

"Aromatic?" Dolin asked. "Perfume?"

"No. A-romantic. I am not looking for romance either, with or without ellipses. So you folk have nothing there for me either."

The group shared a glance of frustration.

"Then it seems we must leave you to your own devices," Dolin said with sincere regret. "Perhaps we shall meet again soon."

"I doubt it." Amara walked away.

"That didn't play out well," Tara said.

"I felt that the right thing to do was to let her go at this point," Dolin said.

"After wasting our time with her," Emerald said.

"No, my sense tells me it wasn't wasted, merely a necessary preamble."

"Are you sure your talent is working right?"

He laughed. "No. But it is all I have. More even than my absent memory. I have to trust it."

Emerald eyed him. "I say this in the most perplexed way: you are a mystery."

"To myself especially," he agreed.

"But I like you. I don't understand why."

Tartan sneaked a glance to Tara. There could be a reason.

"And I like you," Dolin said. "Though obviously we have nothing for each other."

"Nothing we care to share," she agreed.

It was time to break this up. "What does your talent indicate is the right thing for us to do now?" Tartan asked.

Dolin considered. "We should follow her."

Tartan shrugged. "It isn't as if we have anything better to do at the moment."

So they walked along the path in the direction Amara had gone.

They came to a fork. "Which way is correct?" Tara asked.

Dolin indicated the right side path.

Farther along there was another split. This time there was a sign on the right side: YOU ARE NOW LEAVING THE ENCHANTED PATH. SAFETY IS NO LONGER GUARANTEED.

"That is the one," Dolin said.

"Why would she take an unsafe path?" Tartan asked.

Emerald sniffed the air. "The odor confirms that she did."

"You retain dragon senses in your human form?" Dolin asked.

"To a degree yes."

"Maybe that's why," Tara said. "That other sign."

The others looked. It said TROLL HOUSE COOKIES.

"I love cookies," Tara said. "Maybe she does too."

"This is not to be trusted," Emerald said. "Trolls are bad news."

"There is something I don't quite understand," Dolin said. "What supports that sign?"

They looked more closely. It turned out that there was no physical sign, merely an outline and the words painted in the air. "This is curious," Emerald said. "I have not seen a sign like this before. Has anyone else?"

The others shook their heads. It was new to all of them.

They followed the new path. "Uh-oh," Emerald said. "I smell troll."

There was a scuffing on the path. That seemed to be where Amara had stopped. And not continued.

"My sense tells me that the right thing to do is follow your judgment," Dolin told Emerald.

"Let me turn dragon and see what I can see. Look if you want to." She started stripping off her clothing.

Dolin and Tartan turned their backs. This was not mere politeness; they knew she was wearing panties.

"Done," Tara said.

They turned back. She was holding Emerald's clothing. Beyond her the dragon was sniffing the ground. Then she spread her wings and launched into the air. She ascended above the trees, circled, and flew away.

"We must assist her," Dolin said.

In three and a half moments the dragon was back. She descended rapidly and skidded as she landed, changing to human as she did. "She's in trouble! A troll got her and is going to cook her."

"In his troll house," Tartan said, shielding his eyes. "Now we know the meaning of that message."

"What can we do?" Dolin asked, not looking at her.

"Follow me." Emerald returned to dragon form and crashed through the brush, clearing a new path for them. When the foliage was too thick, she breathed blasts of fire and burned it out.

They came to a pond. In it was an island, and on the island was a small pavilion: the troll house. Amara was tied in vines, perched on a grill. The troll was gathering kindling and putting it under the grill.

"Amara!" Dolin called. "We'll swim across and save you!"

She saw him. "You can't. The pond is filled with loan sharks, and the troll has dragon's bane to repel the dragon."

They saw that it was true. Colored fins cut the water. The sharks were waiting for them to try to cross.

"Loan sharks will take an arm and a leg if you let them," Ted said.

Ouch! Another pun, but a dangerous one.

Emerald returned to human form. "Distract him," she said urgently. "Dolin, come with me." She returned to dragon again.

Tartan had no idea what Emerald had in mind, but trusted Dolin's judgment in following her directions. "The troll is male. I can think of only one way to distract him."

"Yes," Tara agreed, blushing. "Don't look." She started stripping.

Tartan stepped between her and the pond, facing the island. "Hey, dunderhead!" he called. "Get a load of what you're missing!"

The troll looked, and paused in place. Then he shook himself. "You can't freak me! Too far away."

"Is that so?" Tara called. "How about this?"

The troll paused again, longer. Tartan realized that Monica was helping Tara do a better flash. He wished he could see it himself, but did not dare look. It still was not completely freaking out the troll, but it did have his attention. Meanwhile the dragon was quietly flying across the pond, with a man on her back. It was a heavy load, as she was not a large dragon, and they were perilously close to the water, but they made it and landed on the island.

The troll wrenched his gaze away from Tara. He turned.

There was Dolin, sword drawn. "Hie, varlet!" he cried dramatically, and attacked.

The troll, no coward, snatched up a hefty club. He swung viciously at the man. Tartan was concerned; the prince had no memory; did he have any fighting skill? And where had he gotten that sword? He had not had one hitherto.

Dolin sidestepped the swing, closed in, and speared the troll neatly through the center. "Ouch!" the troll said, irritated. He did not seem to be seriously hurt.

"Let the maiden go, unharmed," Dolin said.

For answer, the troll swung again, the club heading right for the prince's head.

Dolin ducked, stepped inside the swing, and pricked the troll again, this time on a foot. "I know that no single stab will stop a troll," he said. "But each wound counts, and you will gradually lose vitality, until at last you expire. I ask you again to let the maiden go."

The troll's fury doubled. He aimed a series of rapid swings at the prince's body. But the prince avoided them all.

"You are beginning to annoy me," Dolin said, and stabbed the troll through an eye. "Now I ask you a third time to let the maiden go."

"Yeah? Or what?" the troll demanded, lifting his club for a rock-smashing blow.

Dolin sighed. "I see you are not amenable to reason or mercy." Then he ran his sword through the troll's right ear so hard the point came out the left ear.

The troll fell, expiring. It seemed he had finally been tagged in a vital spot.

Then Dolin went to Amara and quickly cut her bonds. She clambered to her feet, chafing her wrists. "That troll!" she exclaimed. "He said he was going rape me and then cook me. I don't know which would have been worse."

"You are safe now," Dolin said. "Now you may ride the dragon back to shore."

"That was amazing! It was as if you were only playing with him."

"I was trying to persuade him to be reasonable. He wouldn't listen."

"Aren't you going to make demands for rescuing me?"

"Of course not. That would not be princely. I was merely doing the right thing."

The dragon approached. Bemused, Amara mounted her back, and flew across to join Tartan and Tara. Then the dragon fetched Dolin across, and changed back to human form while Tara shielded her from the men's direct gazes. Tara herself had dressed while Dolin fought the troll. "That was impressive, Prince," she said. "Where did you get the sword?"

Dolin looked surprised. He no longer had the sword. "All princes have swords. It was simply there when I needed it, so I used it."

Amara looked around. "The group of you mounted a rescue operation. Why?"

Tartan shrugged. "We couldn't let you be molested and eaten by the troll."

"But I was nothing to you. I refused to associate with you and went my way. You had no responsibility for me."

"You are a human being," Tara said. "We had to act."

"How did you even know I was in trouble?"

"We followed you," Emerald said.

"Why?"

"It was the right thing to do," Dolin said. "That is my talent: to do the right thing. We did not mean to interfere with you."

Amara took the four of them in with a gaze of assessment. "I brushed you off, yet you mounted a coordinated mission to rescue me, with two of you distracting the troll while the other two sneaked onto the island so you could dispatch him. Thereby saving me a raping and cooking and consumption and possibly worse. Now you ask nothing in return?"

"That is correct," Dolin said.

"Let him handle it," Ted told Tartan. "He may yet persuade her."

Amara frowned. "Because it is the right thing to do?"

"Yes."

"Nevertheless, it seems I owe you."

"Not at all," Dolin said. "The right thing would not be the right thing were it done for profit. We will leave you, now that you are safe."

"This is persuasion?" Tartan asked Ted.

"Wait and see."

Amara remained unsatisfied. "But you need me to locate the Goddess Isis."

"This is true. But you must help us because you want to, not because you owe us anything."

Amara sighed. "I *don't* want to. But I am constrained."

"How so?"

"Because I am serving as a host, similar to three of you. My ghost is impressed by your demeanor and your action, and will speak with you now."

"You're a host?" Tartan asked. "For whom?"

Amara's aspect shifted. She seemed to become taller, more decisive, almost regal. She also radiated potent sex appeal, something that had been absent before. "For me. I am the Goddess Isis."

"Isis!" Tara exclaimed. "We didn't know!"

The mouth quirked. "So I gather. You did what you did because you believed it was the right thing, seeking no reward. All of you."

"Well, yes," Emerald said. The women were talking because the very presence of the goddess put Tartan and surely Dolin at serious risk of freaking out. "We're sort of an impromptu group, becoming friends, and it seems we have some common values. Such as not letting trolls abuse innocent maidens."

"I have not often encountered that, Dragon Lady. I respect such honor, though recently it cost me supreme power in Xanth. You may have helped Amara out of the goodness of your hearts, without thought of gain, but I do regard it as a debt to be repaid. It would have been quite awkward for me to find another suitable host, and probably worse for Amara. What do you want of me?"

"We—we understand that you are the only one who can stop the Ghost Writer from messing with Xanth," Tara said. "We—we want to ask you to do so."

The Goddess frowned, and the nearby foliage seemed to wilt a bit. She was as potent in her displeasure as in her pleasure. "And of course it was one of the Ghost Writer's naughty little fancies that set Amara up to be cooked by the troll. We are not pleased."

"That floating sign!" Emerald said. "A story title!"

"Exactly. I was absent, as I do not join her continuously, and Amara did not recognize it for what it was. She thought it referred to a confection, a kind of cookie. By the time I took note, it was too late. Then the four of you acted in a manner I could not, as here I am merely a spirit with no physical force. Had the troll been female, I might have entered her and dissuaded her from cooking."

That made Tartan wonder: could he have turned ghost and entered the troll? And turned him away from the cooking, etc.? Had he been a fool?

"The troll would have been an unwilling host," Ted said. "That would have been tricky. You would not have the soul power of the Goddess, who has had centuries to develop her craft."

"So you will help us?" Tara asked.

Isis frowned. "I did not say that. Let me explain: I am physically confined to the infernal comic strip, constantly surrounded by abysmal puns. Only my spirit can range outside the strip, and its power is limited. You surely understand."

"We do," Tara said.

"Were I physically outside the strip, I surely could smite the Ghost Writer, one way or another. But unless he should venture into the strip, I am largely helpless to deal with him. Get me out of the strip, and I will certainly help you."

"How can we do that?" Tara asked.

The Goddess laughed without humor. "If I knew that, I would have escaped long since. Certainly the Xanthly authorities will not allow it; it was they who confined me to the strips. It seems that the powers that be in Xanth prefer that I remain confined. We have to hope that there is some other route."

"Oh, my," Tara said. "We shall have to work on that."

"Do so. Meanwhile Amara will remain in your company, and I will check her every so often. She can also summon me at need. Fare well." The aura of the Goddess faded.

Amara was herself again. "Now you know," she said.

"Now we know," Tartan said, recovering his poise once the overpowering visage of Isis was gone. "It may be just as well that the goddess manifest only intermittently, as we men would not be much use in her presence."

Dolin nodded agreement, then focused on Amara. "I sense that there may be a devious route, and it connects to you. We need to know more about you. What is your talent?"

Amara shrugged. "That won't help. It is knowing where something will be, but not where it is now."

"That is curious. Can you provide us with an example?"

"Certainly. A deer fly will be beside the enchanted path by the time we return to it. I have no idea where the deer is now."

Dolin nodded. "Then let us return to the enchanted path. It is certainly safer than this pond."

They made their way back to the path. As they approached it, no deer fly was evident. But as they stepped onto the path, disappointed, the winged deer flew down from behind a cloud and landed nearby. She glanced at them curiously, then spread her wings again and flew away.

"Point made," Emerald said, smiling. "There seemed to be no way to predict that, short of magic."

"So could you know when a way to free the goddess was about to manifest?" Tartan asked.

Amara was surprised. "I don't know. It's possible, but hardly certain."

"Let's find a rest stop where we can relax," Tara said. "So we can get to know you better, Amara."

"Now I am amenable," Amara agreed.

They found the rest stop, and rested, of course. All of them were tired from their exertions and the tension of the rescue.

"I'm just an ordinary girl," Amara said. "Undistinguished until I reached the age of maturity. Then it became apparent that I had no interest in storks, despite that of the boys. Also no interest in romance. But they kept pressing me despite my negations, so finally I departed my village and wandered on my own. One evening as I relaxed, alone, beside a branch of the comic strip, the Goddess approached me, explaining that she wished to learn more about Xanth but could not visit it physically, being confined as she told you. Would I be willing to act as a sometime host for her spirit? She promised not to embarrass me, but mainly just to watch. And I asked what's in it for me? She replied that she could provide me with virtually irresistible sex appeal. I said no way, I already had more of that than I cared for. Then she said that there were times when such appeal could be useful, such as when I might want a favor from a man. For example, if I were hungry and he had food. I would not have to gratify his burgeoning passion; I could make him give me the food just by hinting that I might later become amenable. Or if there were some ugly chore I had to do, I could get a man to do it for me. Men are highly manageable, she explained; their storkly interest is like the ring in the nose of a bull, and they can be readily led, if a girl is proficient in that venue, as she herself was. I realized that she was right; she could be useful on occasion. So I agreed to be her sometime host, and went about my way, avoiding people. So it has been, until now."

"This is not completely proper," Dolin said. "You should help us only if you wish to, apart from the will of the goddess, and travel with us only if that is your own preference, not hers."

Amara smiled at him. "As you know, I am not interested in passion with you, of whatever kind. But you did save my life, and you seem like a fine man despite your mystery. I believe I would like to be your friend, if that is possible without your thoughts interfering."

"He makes a fair friend," Emerald said. "He honors boundaries despite having thoughts."

Dolin considered. "You are not a princess, Amara, so I have no romantic prospect with you. If you keep your clothing on, my mind will not entertain many thoughts. This works with Emerald, even though she is a princess, and with Tara, who has no more interest in me than you do."

"Speak for yourself," Tara said. "When I look at you, I wish I were a Xanthly princess. I do get thoughts, unmaidenly as it may be to confess it."

"Oh," he said, taken aback.

"Don't be concerned. My main interest is in Tartan; I'm just window shopping. But I have come to understand how the sight of an attractive person can affect the outlook of others."

"Window shopping?"

"It's a Mundane phenomenon. Pretty items are displayed in store windows, and we gaze at them and wish we could have them, though we know better."

"I wish I could have my memory."

Tara smiled. "Not the same. You really do need your memory. Most window shops are frivolous."

"Do you regard yourself as Prince Dolin's friend?" Amara asked her.

"Yes, I believe I do," Tara said. "Though I hardly know him."

"None of us really know him," Emerald said. "He hardly knows himself. But he is a friend."

"On that basis I am satisfied to join your group, apart from what Isis says," Amara said. "And to be a friend to all of you, now that you understand my nature."

"This seems to be the right thing," Dolin said.

"So where do we go from here?" Tartan asked. He was glad that no one had questioned him about thoughts, especially when the Goddess had manifested.

Dolin frowned. "I have a certain ongoing awareness of right and wrong, so that I can remain right. It feels right for us to park here for the night, becoming comfortable in each other's presence. But tomorrow feels like a storm. I fear that there is mischief coming, and there will be no right choice, only wrong ones. This alarms me. I have not before anticipated such a pass."

"You're a prince," Amara said. "Princes tend to have powerful talents. Is yours Magician class?"

"I do not know. Perhaps that, too, is masked from my awareness."

"I ask because Magician-caliber talents are thought to have breadth as well as strength. It may be that not only can you do the right thing, you can guide yourself to it."

He shook his head. "I fear not. I see no path to the right thing tomorrow, only confusion. I am uncomfortable."

"That's the thing," Amara said. "If your talent is strong enough to lead you, the fact that this time it seems to be failing is significant. Something quite ugly may be brewing, that none of us can avoid."

"Maybe it concerns only me," Dolin said. "Maybe if I separate from the rest of you, the mischief will spare you."

"No," Emerald said firmly. "If you face mischief, I mean to be there to help you navigate it."

"I agree," Tara said.

"And I," Tartan said.

"And I," Amara said.

"But why put yourselves in possible danger?" Dolin asked.

"This is the nature of friendship," Emerald said. "You could have avoided danger by declining to tackle the troll."

"But that would not have been the right thing!"

"Exactly," Amara said. "We will face your mischief with you, if it is truly yours and not ours anyway. For friendship."

Dolin looked around, but found only agreement with the others. "I am moved."

"I think it is time for Tara and me to go home," Tartan said. "But rest assured we will return in the morning."

The others waved them farewell.

Back in Mundania, they took their turns with the bathroom, then rejoined on the bed. "You can pretend I'm Amara," Tara said, smiling as she slipped out of her clothing.

"I don't know. Is she animated by the Goddess?"

"Of course. Do you think she would touch you otherwise?"

"And you can pretend I'm Dolin."

"I have a better idea. Let's just be ourselves."

"Only I wish we could be so in Xanth, free of hosts."

"That makes me wonder. Could we do the ellipsis as ghosts in Xanth?"

That seriously intrigued him. "We can see and hear each other as ghosts, as long as we're touching here. Can we also touch each other in that manner?"

"Let's find out!"

"But can we go through the portal and not be in our hosts?"

"Let's find out," she repeated. "We can focus on being just beyond the picture, this time."

So, bare, they held hands and stepped through the portal. They made it, and looked back to see their naked bodies lying on the bed beyond. Their hands remained solid to each other.

They tried to make a hasty bed of ferns, but couldn't touch the foliage. So they lay down on the bare ground, but floated slightly above it. So they simply drew each other together in the air. They clasped and kissed so passionately that cute little hearts floated out. Then came an intense ellipsis.

. . .

Afterward—ellipses tended to be followed by afters—they stepped back through the portal and merged back into their bodies. "We did it!" he said.

"And it was just as good as with our physical bodies."

"So now we know: ghosts can have sex."

"On a mattress of air."

Then they got serious. "What do you think threatens us tomorrow?" he asked.

"I have no idea. But I fear it."

"Yet no way will we skip it."

"And desert our friends? Never."

Tartan realized it was true: their friends were in Xanth. They would be there, no matter what.

Chapter 7

LIZARD OF WAZ

They arrived back in Xanth just after dawn. The others were stirring and eating breakfast. "Any news?" Tartan asked.

"Nothing," Prince Dolin said. "Just foreboding and frustration."

"Did you folk get along okay overnight?" Tara asked.

Emerald laughed. "We did. Your hosts are amusing people, full of Xanthly lore and demon magic, and Amara is great company now that she knows us."

"And we like the hosts," Amara said. "As we like the two of you."

Obviously Amara had integrated with the group.

"But no idea what trouble we face?" Tartan asked. "Or how we can avoid it?"

"None," Dolin said. "That is driving me to distraction. I am the one who has not been good company."

"Me too, actually," Emerald said. "I can turn dragon and protect you from most physical threats, such as trolls or goblins. But we doubt this is exactly physical."

"And do you see anything useful to us in the near future?" Tara asked Amara.

"I do not. Just a sign."

"A sign?"

"Words in the air. I can't quite make it out. It seems like nonsense. But it will be hovering above us."

"Words in the air," Tartan said. "Like Troll House Cookies?"

Amara shuddered. "A Ghost Writer sign! Yes, that's it. But not the same words."

"We're here to stop the Ghost Writer," Tara said thoughtfully. "Could he be aware of us?"

"That seems likely," Tartan said. "Because we messed up his nasty little Cookies story yesterday."

"So maybe he is writing a story for us," Dolin said. "One that we may not much like."

"I think we had better avoid it, if we can," Emerald said.

"Agreed," Amara said. "Let's get out of here."

But the moment they stepped out of the rest area, the sign appeared over their heads.

THE LIZARD OF WAZ

"Oh!" Amara exclaimed. "I am Doorthy from Mundania, an innocent girl, and I have just arrived in a tornado because of a freak accident."

Doorthy?

"And I am the Lizard," Emerald said. "Animated by the Wicked Witch of the Vest, and I am pursuing you with the intention of toasting you. The only way you can save yourself is to flee to the Ruby City, the capital of the Land of Waz, which is at the other end of the Yellow Tricks Road, and beg the Wazard of Whiz to help you."

"The Wazard of Whiz?"

"His favorite expression is 'Whiz on it!' You have a problem with that?"

"Yes I do," Amara said. "It's uncouth."

"He's an uncouth man. That's not the half of it. Just call him the Whiz of Waz. Now shall we get down to business?" She turned dragon and began huffing up a bellyful of fire.

"Oh, I must flee!" Amara said, and ran on ahead.

None of the others moved. Tartan found himself anchored in place, mute, and knew the others were too. This was awful! Their own group was being turned against itself.

Worse, he recognized the title. It was a parody of a popular Mundane fantasy story. Just as the Ghost Writer had written things like the "Princess and the Pee," he had messed with another tale, and it seemed assigned them roles within it. Tartan wasn't sure what his own role would be, but knew he would soon enough find out.

Amara ran out of sight. The Lizard did not pursue closely. It seemed that her job was to herd Doorthy to her destination, rather than actually toast her. But Tartan was not much relieved. This story was unlikely to end well for them.

However, Tartan was able to follow Amara in his ghost form, which was not restricted to his host's body. She ran along the path, which he now saw was formed of yellow tiles. She passed a sign saying YELLOW TRICKS ROAD. Uh-oh.

Sure enough, soon one of her feet, which he saw wore a silver slipper, sank into a squishy tile that was not as solid as it looked. Amara stumbled and almost fell. "Bleep!" she swore, and the nearby brush wilted, not able to tolerate such vile language from an innocent maiden.

Other tiles were firm, and she was able to resume progress, though now she stepped more carefully. But now her slipper had gooey grime sticking to it. She had to pause to remove it and wipe it off on the turf beside the path. In the process she showed a bit more leg than was seemly. Was that part of the script? Did the Ghost Writer want to sneak peeks? Tartan was suspicious.

Amara put her slipper back on and resumed her walk. And suddenly jumped off with an exclamation. The tile had become burning hot. Another trick.

She walked past the hot tile section and got on the path again. Only to hear a loud "Ho-Ho! I see your pretty ankles! And that's not all!"

Amara looked around but saw nothing. "Who are you?"

"I am the tile you are standing on. I see your lovely knees, and that's not all."

She jumped off the path again, clearly not much amused. "You know, with an attitude like that, you're not much use as a path."

"Aww. I'm sorry. I'll behave."

She stepped back on the tile.

"Ho-ho-ho! I see your shapely thighs, and that's not all."

She jumped off again. Obviously these tiles were not to be trusted. Tartan, watching as a ghost, sympathized. No woman would care for this kind of loud crude observation.

The way was rougher now that she could no longer use the path. To avoid nettles, she had to make her way away from the tiles, though she kept them in sight as a guide to the Ruby City.

Worse, a storm was brewing. Things fell from it, not rain, but cats and dogs. In fact it was more like a reign, where canines and felines governed.

Most of them bounded away the moment they struck the ground. A small dogfish landed next to her. Its body looked like a fish made out of metal plates, but it had legs, tail, and head, all metal. The front of the head was a small flat screen, and the teeth below it resembled a computer keyboard.

It spied her and swam close, dog paddling.

Swam? Tartan did a double-take. Well, it was as much fish as dog. So it could swim through air. It was also a he.

"Growf!" he barked horrendously, making Amara jump.

"Oh!" she cried, affrighted for half an instant.

But the dog wagged his tail, seeming friendly as he settled to earth.

"What are you?" she asked. Then she realized: "You're a dogfish!"

More wagging.

"And you're a computer, too."

A smiley face flashed briefly on the screen.

A bulb flashed over her head. "And your bark is worse than your byte!"

The tail wagged so hard it made the whole body bounce.

"Well, it was nice to meet you," she said. "Now ta-ta, doggie. I have a fiery Lizard to flee." She resumed motion.

But the dogfish swam along beside her.

"Look, doggie, I'm not looking for a pet. So just be on your way."

He still didn't go.

Amara sighed. "I guess if I'm Doorthy, you must be her dog. What was his name? Tutu? No, let's make it Tata, since you are free to go any time you want to."

More tail wagging and anther smiley face.

They came to a field. Tata woofed horrendously. There in the center stood a giant black crow dressed in straw, perched on a small tower. She halted before it, surprised, looking up. "Who are you?"

"I am the Carecrow," the creature responded.

"The what? Scarecrow?"

"Carecrow. I care for things that need it."

Amara laughed weakly. "I think I need it."

"Then I care for you. What's your problem, apart from those naughty tiles I heard?"

"I've got a dogfish I didn't seek, name Tata, and I'm being herded by the Lizard."

The crow jumped off the tower and flew down to the ground before her. She was as big as Doorthy, shaped like a human woman, but with feathers, wings, and a beak. "Tata is cute, except for his voice, but you're in trouble, for sure. Do you have any idea how to escape the Lizard?"

"I must flee to the Ruby City and beg the help of the Wazard."

"Oh you poor thing," the Carecrow said. "He makes exorbitant demands for his help."

"It must be better than getting toasted by the Lizard."

"That depends on your perspective. Some women would rather die. I might be one of them."

Amara looked sharply at the crow, whom she now recognized as Tara, in another role in the story. "I'm not interested in lechery."

"But it is rumored that he is."

"Well, too bad for him." She shrugged. "So I guess you can return to your perch, Crow. I'll be moving on."

"Wait!" Tara said. "You still need caring. I don't know how I can help you, but I must try. Do you really think the Wazard can help you?"

"The Lizard said that he was the only person who could."

"The Lizard? The one who wants to toast you?"

"That's the one," she agreed. "Animated by the Wicked Witch of the Vest."

"The Wicked Witch of the Vest! She's the one who cursed me!"

"Cursed you?"

"It's a short nasty story."

"Tell me," Amara pleaded. Tata seemed interested too.

"I was once an ordinary girl, like you," the Crow said sadly. "I traveled with a friend, just seeing the sights in new territory, when a flying monkey landed before us. It transformed into an ugly old witch wearing an even uglier vest. 'Who are you?' the witch demanded. 'What are you doing in my forest?'

"My friend tried to shush me, but I was young and impetuous. 'Who are *you*?' I demanded back. 'No one owns a forest.'

"The witch swelled up like a balloon. 'I am the Wicked Witch of the Vest, and this land is my land. Now get out of here before I throw you out.'

"But I was having none of it. 'I'd like to see you try, you prune-faced idiot. And you look like a clown in that stupid vest.'

"She swelled up even more, somehow. 'This vest gives me the power to transform myself or others, you ignorant girl.'

I laughed in her face. 'So you say. Now fly away, monkeyshines, and stop bothering us. I don't care about you at all.'

"She looked so angry that a small storm cloud formed over her hideous head. 'Well, you look like an ugly bird!' she screeched. 'By the power vested in me, I now transform you into exactly that. See how you like that, birdbrain!' And she touched me with a small bent wand she carried. And poof! I was this crow. 'Now you can care all you want. You are the Carecrow.' And she laughed evilly as she changed back into the winged monkey and flew away.

"And so I was wise too late," the Crow concluded. "My friend was powerless to help me. I flew to this field and perched on this tower, trying to think of what to do to rid myself of this awful enchantment. Now you have come along, and maybe you have a good idea: go see the Wazard. Maybe he can rid me of my nemesis, even if he is an old lecher."

"You are welcome to come with me," Amara agreed. "Though I dread trying to follow that naughty peeking path."

"Oh, I know how to deal with that," the Crow said. "I will show you."

They went to the path. "Well now," the tile exclaimed. "Two females to torment! I'll really have a—ooof!"

Because at that point the Crow stomped hard on it. "One lump or two?" she asked, lifting her foot again.

Tata's woof sounded like laughter.

Evidently the tile decided that one lump was more than enough. It was silent.

They stepped onto the path, and there was nary a word. The tiles had been tamed.

There was a sound behind them. Tata woofed warningly. "Oh, no," Amara said. "The Lizard!"

"Hurry!" the Crow said. "If it catches me, it will burn off my feathers and I won't be able to fly. Maybe we can outrun it."

Amara doubted that, but what else was there to do? So they ran along the path.

There came another sound behind them. It was the Lizard, snorting fire.

"She's on the talking tiles!" the Crow said. "They must be teasing her in Lizard talk!"

Amara choked down a giggle and Tata practically fell over with mirth. What could the tiles be saying to get the Lizard so upset? That they could see under her tail, and that was not all?

Then there was a horrendous blast of fire, and the tiles went silent. They did not like getting burned any more than they liked getting stomped. But in that interval Crow and Amara had lengthened their lead, and now could slow to a comfortable walk.

And there beside the path was an odd shape. It looked like an animated stick figure, formed of wooden head, arms, legs, and a somewhat abbreviated midsection. Tartan was drawn into it, and discovered himself in his role: the wooden man. He was no longer observing as a ghost. He was Tartan, and Demon Ted, and the man made of wood, all in one package.

The three paused. "If we may inquire," Amara said. "We are Doorthy, Tata, and Carecrow." That was to say, the roles animated by Amara and Tara. "What manner of man are you?"

The figure took note of them. "I am the Trim Woodsman," he said. He eyed Amara. "I may have chopped the wood to make the door after which you were named." Which surprised Tartan, though his character said it. So the characters did have elements not contributed by their animators.

"That is impressive," Amara agreed. "But why aren't you chopping wood now?"

"That is a brief but sad story. I was trying to chop enough wood to beat a woodchuck's chucking, and swung too hard, and my solid wood heart flew out and was lost in the brush. I can't find it anywhere. Now I don't have a wooden heart. I am heartbroken. I don't have the heartwood to chop any more." Oh, the puns! Even Tata looked as if a groan was stuck in his circuitry.

"We would help you look," Amara said sympathetically. "But we are being herded by the Lizard, and don't dare dally lest she catch us and torch us."

"The Lizard! She'll burn me up!" Yes indeed, now that he was made of wood.

"Maybe you should come with us to see the Wazard of Whiz," Care-crow suggested. "He might find you new heartwood."

"The Whiz of Waz? You think? That would really help."

There was another bellow from the Lizard, closer. "We'd better get a move on," Amara said nervously. "None of us want to get burned."

They moved on along the tiled path. These were new tiles, and one started to speak, but Amara stomped warningly and stifled it. The noise of the Lizard fell slowly back; it was still herding rather than pursuing.

Which was bothersome in its fashion. "Why is the Lizard herding us in the direction of the Whiz, after telling me that was where I had to go?" Amara asked the others. "Does the Wicked Witch of the Vest have some sort of deal with the Whiz?"

"I have heard it rumored that he likes innocent maidens," Trim said. "But that innocent maidens don't like him. Maybe he wants one to be dependent on him."

"Why?" Amara asked innocently.

Trim exchanged a glance with Carecrow. "I don't know."

"Oh come on!" Amara said. "I need to know what I'm up against."

"I guess you do," the Crow answered after an awkward three quarters of a pause. "It's that they don't stay innocent long."

"What does that mean?"

"There's a quality about innocence that, well, some men get their jollies from despoiling it. So an experienced girl like me is in no danger."

"Danger of what?" Amara demanded.

"I lost my innocence long ago, so it can't be despoiled."

Not that long ago, Tartan thought. Not that their experience in their own host bodies in Mundania counted for this wacky story.

"Exactly what am I innocent about, that he wants to despoil?" This was Doorthy speaking, as Amara did have a notion.

The Crow looked uncomfortable. "What do you know about signaling the stork?"

"I know all about it," Doorthy said. "A man and a woman kiss, and it sends out a signal, and after an inefficient delay, the stork brings her a baby. So it's best not to kiss unless you mean it."

For some reason Carecrow and Trim exchanged another glance. Even Tata fidgeted. Could Xanth really be that ignorant? But Doorthy intercepted their glance with one of her own. "What aren't you telling me?"

"There's a bit more to it than a kiss," Trim said. "There's a secret, um, gesture they make that children aren't supposed to know about, per the Adult Conspiracy to Keep Interesting Things From Children." Oh, so that was it.

"I'm not a child!" She put up her hands to break up the glance the two others were attempting to exchange. "Tell me!"

"Well," Carecrow said reluctantly, "it's—"

At that point there was a roar just ahead. Tata barked warning. They all paused, and Carecrow's statement was hopelessly overridden by silence and lost.

"What is that?" Trim asked nervously.

"I'll go see," the Crow said. She spread her wings and lurched into the air. In a generous moment she was gone.

"Should we hide?" Amara asked.

"I don't think so," Trim said. "I don't have the heart to chop trees anymore, but I could chop a roaring beast, I think." He glanced at Tata. "No offense, dogfish. You're not so much a beast as a person."

Tata put on a smiley face and wagged his tail.

They walked on along the path. In three more moments the Crow returned, fluttering down for a safe landing. "It's a scion," she reported.

"A what?"

"A descendant. Someone who has parents, grandparents, etc."

"That's all of us!"

"In fantasy there can be an implication of nobility."

"He's noble?"

"No."

There was half a pause. Not quite enough to be awkward, but getting there.

"Then what was the roar we heard?" Amara asked.

"That's more complicated. He should tell you himself."

"But is he dangerous?"

"No. That's the problem."

There was three quarters of a pause. Trim broke it up before it could fully form and make mischief. "Let's talk to him, then."

They walked on, and soon came to the Scion. He appeared to be an ordinary man in a lion suit. "These are my friends Doorthy, Trim Woodsman, and Tata," Carecrow said. "Friends, this is the Cowardly Scion."

"Hello," the three said almost together, and Tata woofed.

Amara got to the point. "Why did you roar? It frightened us."

"It did? Thank you."

The pause tried to wedge its way back into the dialogue. "Why thank us?" Amara asked, just in time.

"Because that's what I was trying to do. To frighten folk."

"You don't seem very frightening," Trim said.

"I'm not. But I have to try."

"Why?"

"That's complicated."

"Let's go back to the beginning," Amara said, before pauses and complications could overwhelm them. "How did you get into your present predicament, whatever it is?"

"Once I was a bold scion, the latest in a long line of bolders."

"Don't you mean boulders?" Trim asked.

"No. A boulder is a rock. My ancestors were bold, bolder, and boldest. My branch of the family was bolder. We did bolder things than the bolds did, though not as bold as the boldest did. Then one day as I walked through the forest following a new path—"

"You encountered an ugly old witch in a vest," Carecrow said.

"I did. How did you know?"

"Because that's what I did, and she transformed me into an ugly talking crow. You have my sympathy."

The Scion squinted at her. "Not ugly, really. You have some nice lines under that feather cloak."

"Oh," Carecrow said, the tips of her feathers turning pink. "You're not so bad yourself."

Tartan, observing as the Woodsman, had to remind himself that it was the roles they were animating that were speaking, not the spirits themselves. So it was not really Tara and Prince Dolin exchanging compliments, but Carecrow and Scion. Still, he was moved to put in a word or five. "You do look good, Carecrow."

"Oh," she repeated, evidently struggling to align Tara, DeMonica, and Carecrow. "Thank you."

"And the Wicked Witch of the Vest took away my most cherished quality, my boldness," Scion concluded. "Now I am afraid of everything. So I'm trying to get it back by frightening others, but that's not working very well. Even if they are frightened, I remain frightened too."

"You poor thing," Carecrow said sympathetically. "Maybe you had better come with us to see the Wazard of Whiz, in the faint hope that he will be able to help you."

"I don't know about that," Scion said. "I have heard it said that the whiz of Waz—"

There was a bellow from the Lizard.

"Maybe you're right," Scion said. "Let's go."

They hurried on. But now it was midday and they were hungry, and there were unmentionable calls of nature. They needed to find a rest stop where they could safely take a break.

Tartan got an idea. "Our hosts—if we can step out of character a moment—Amara, can you tell where a safe stop will be, even if you don't know where it is now?"

She looked surprised. "Yes. There'll be one in fifteen minutes, just beyond the next hill and dale."

"Thank you."

They walked on, and sure enough, there was a walled enclosure that looked sturdy enough to withstand flames.

They went up to it and found a solid door. They opened it, and discovered a serene courtyard with several pie trees and a water log. They would not go hungry or thirsty here. They entered and shut and latched the door. They were safe, for a while.

There was a knock on the door. The five, including Tata, exchanged a startled glance. Who could that possibly be?

Then Carecrow flew up to perch on the wall. She looked down outside. "No, you can't come in," she said. "You know that." Then she was silent a generous moment. "Well, I'll ask them."

The Crow flew down inside the yard. "It's the Lizard, only Emerald out of character. She wants to know if we can have a truce for lunch. She really doesn't like having to chase us."

"Why not?" Tartan asked, and Amara nodded agreement. "But I think we can't risk actually joining her. Not as long as this awful parody continues."

"I hate this parody," Amara said fervently. She certainly had reason.

So they harvested several fresh pies and Carecrow tossed them down for the Lizard to eat. After lunch and rest the Lizard retreated, nominally to attend to a private function, and they were able to leave the enclosure without hazard.

They resumed their trek. Before long they spied a deep red glow ahead. It was the light of the fabled Ruby City. The houses were giant faceted rubies, and the streets were gold and silver. It was impressive.

The Yellow Tricks Road led right up to the central palace, where they were met by a humble servant. "The Whiz is expecting you. This way."

They were ushered into a large central chamber like a mundane movie theater, with a large screen in front. On this screen played scenes of water: rushing rivers, waterfalls, fountains, geysers, surging waves, and a looming thunderstorm. Obviously the theme of the Whiz.

The screen showed a quiet, deep pool. "Who are you, and what do you want?" a man's voice inquired.

If they were expected, why the questions? But Tartan answered. "I am Trim Woodsman, and I want a wooden heart, because I lost mine."

"Noted. Next?"

Then Tara: "I am Carecrow, and I want to be released from this enchantment, because in real life I am a woman, not a bird."

And Dolin: "I am the Cowardly Scion, and I want to recover my boldness."

And finally Amara: "I am Doorthy. I want to escape being teased by the Lizard of Waz, who said only you can save me."

Now the pictured pool formed into a face. "I can provide you with a wooden heart, Trim. I can release your enchantment, Carecrow. I can restore your boldness, Scion. And I can save you from the Lizard, Doorthy."

He paused. They waited. Tartan knew they were on the verge of the unkind demand.

"But if you want me to do these things for you, you have to do something for me. What do you offer?"

"I will chop some wood for you," Tartan said.

"I will do some housework for you," Tara said.

"I will fight a monster for you," Dolin said.

"What do you want of me?" Amara asked. This was the critical one, because she was the central figure in this sordid drama, and the prettiest girl.

"Nothing."

"I don't understand."

"What I want is the Goddess Isis with you as her host."

So he knew about that! But how?

"For what?" Amara asked guardedly. As if she didn't know.

"Bring her on. I want to talk to her directly."

Amara changed, shedding the innocent Doorthy role and her natural neutrality. She stood taller, and her sex appeal smote them all, male and female. Amara was a pretty girl, but Isis was a beauty. "What do you want of me?" she asked. The words were the same as the ones Amara had used, but the implication was no longer remotely neutral. There was only one thing any man could want of her, and they all knew it.

"Half an hour of wild passion."

There it was.

"No."

No? How could the Goddess of Sex turn down such an engagement? The picture on the big screen became a storm that blasted rain at them so realistically that Tartan had trouble not flinching.

"Every day."

"Make some other demand," Isis said coldly.

"Why not? This is your nature, isn't it? The ultimate mistress?"

"You misunderstand the term. A mistress is the plaything of a man. I am the mistress of mistresses: the governor of men. I do not seek to govern you, and you certainly shall not govern me. Neither will you govern my host, who has no interest in such passion. Give up this chase."

There was half a pause. "You may not properly appreciate the situation, Goddess." The storm on the screen was still intensifying.

"Acquaint me with it," Isis said icily.

"I am the Ghost Writer. The Night Colt watches constantly, and advises me of your activities. He was watching when you manifested before. You are locked in the dream I have crafted. You can't escape it unless I release you. I will release you and your companions only if you give me what I want. If you do not oblige me, you will remain locked in the parody forever."

"You can't lock me anywhere," Isis said, and now the very air around her was precipitating sleet. "I live in the Comic Strip. I have no physical presence in Xanth proper."

"True. But I can lock your host. You will be unable to leave your Strip even in spirit without returning to my power. If you should give up on her and seek another host, I will craft a dream to trap that new host. One way or another you will come to me. Better to do it now and do your companions some good, rather than leaving them to their fates."

"This whole thing is merely your ridiculous story," the Goddess said. She was now standing in a mound of fallen snow. "It has no reality other than your passing narrative. It will end soon, and your captives will be released."

"Not so. It will end when its narrative is complete, or when I terminate it. Its narrative is far from complete. In fact it can continue for several volumes. Goddess, your friends are mine." There was a third of a pause. "It isn't as if I am demanding anything you can't readily grant. Just half an hour a day. You might even enjoy it."

"I doubt it." The entire room had become a frozen lake. Tartan, Tara, and Dolin were hugging themselves to keep warm.

"Well, you can hold out as long as you choose. You may not suffer, but your friends are freezing." The screen was showing a terrible winter storm. That was surely independent of the frigid region around the Goddess, which was a product of her ire.

While that dialogue occurred, Tata had been sniffing around the room. Now he caught a curtain in his metal teeth and tugged. The sheet pulled loose and dropped, and there was a man working a console.

"Ha!" Isis said.

"Pay no attention to the man behind the curtain," the voice cried. "He has nothing to do with you."

Isis strode to the man, caught him by the back of the collar, and hauled him off his chair. "No? Then what's this?" She jammed her fingers on the console. The winter storm dissolved into chaos. "Let's see what work I can make of you." She turned to face the man on the floor.

"Stop!" the man cried. "I'm not the Whiz or even the Ghost Writer. I'm just a hireling doing his business."

The Goddess reached out to touch him on the top of the head with a finger. "It's true," she said, surprised.

The others plodded through the melting slush to join her. "This is all faked up?" Tartan asked.

"Just a stage set," Tara said.

"But you are still in his power," the man on the floor said. "He can come here physically only in the half hour before dawn or the half hour following sunset. That's why he wants you then. But his stories govern the rest of the day. You can't escape them."

"We shall see about that," Isis said. "Let's get out of here." She faded, leaving Amara. "I agree," Amara said. "I'll be bleeped if I'll let the Ghost Writer touch me, with or without Isis's attendance. I don't want any man, let alone the bleeping Ghost Writer."

"Good girl," Tara said.

But it occurred to Tartan that if one of them got close enough to the Ghost Writer to indulge in mad passion with him, that should also be close enough to nullify him and free Xanth of the bad dreams. Still, the others might not see it that way.

They hurried out of the palace, unopposed. There was Emerald, free of her Lizard form for the moment. Tara gladly hugged her. But the hour was late. What would happen when the Ghost Writer came on the scene personally?

"We have to find a private place and consult," Tartan said.

"Anywhere will do," Tara agreed, catching on.

So they stopped on the street. "Here's the thing," Tartan said. "The Ghost Writer works through proxies most of the day; he can't do it directly. When the script gets messed up, as now, we're free. But soon he'll be here himself and straighten it out." He turned to Amara. "If you got close enough to—"

"Forget it," she snapped.

"Then we'll just have to find a way to escape. How can we do that?"

"I have an idea," Prince Dolin said. "I have no memory of my past, but I suspect it's not from the contemporary scene. If we could go where I came from, we might be beyond the range of the Ghost Writer."

"But if you don't know, you can't tell us where that is," Amara said.

"Maybe I can, indirectly. My Aunt Mera is watching us on the mirror. I think she knows what I do not. Such as where I came from."

"But she can't tell you, until you find a princess to marry," Tara said.

"True. But maybe she could tell *you*."

Tara made a whistling shape with her mouth. "Aunt Mera?" she asked the air. "Can you hear me?"

"She said she could see, not hear," Tartan said.

"Oh, yes, I forgot. I need a paper to write on."

They looked around, but found no paper. "Will a wall do?" Emerald asked. "I passed a good one not far back."

"Let's see it."

The wall turned out to be perfect. They found a stick, dipped it in dirt, and used that to write on the wall in huge letters. MERA. HELP!

"I hope she's watching now," Dolin said nervously. "Dusk is near."

Indeed it was. That meant that the Ghost Writer was on his way.

Then Tara brightened. "She's here! In spirit form." The others saw nothing, but weren't concerned. Tara was a ghost here, though occupying a host body, and she could pick up on another ghost. Then she spoke to Mera. "We need to escape to where you folk came from, beyond the reach of the Ghost Writer. Now. It's important." She was silent a moment. "Oh, my!" Then: "Gather round me; she has a spell to take us there. But it's complicated. There's stuff I can't tell Prince Dolin, so I can't speak it aloud. It's amazing."

They gathered around her. "Everyone must be touching," she said. "It's a time transport spell, a potent one, but there's only the one."

"But Aunt Mera can't do time travel," Dolin protested.

"She made a deal with the Magician of Time," Tara said.

"With who?" Dolin asked. "I know of no such character in this episode."

"You don't know, but I do," Tara said impatiently. "She traded to get a Time Bomb. Now get with it while we still can."

It did seem best to follow her script before the Ghost Writer caught up with them. They linked hands, making a circle of five, with Tata in the center.

"Now," Tara said.

Then things changed.

Chapter 8

SORCERESS TAPIS

They arrived in a pleasant walled garden: Tartan, Tara, Dolin, Emerald, and Amara, together with Tata dogfish. There were assorted pie plants, milkweeds, breadfruit trees, shoe trees, pillow plants, and clothing trees, surrounded by colorful flowers. This was obviously a small personal plantation, the kind that a well-appointed household would have so that far-flung foraging would not be necessary.

Tata woofed.

"He smells something," Amara said. They were no longer in the Land of Waz parody, but the dog continued to stick close to her. Evidently he was an independent creature, just as they were, caught up in the narrative they had escaped. "I can tell."

"Fancy that," Emerald murmured, not in a critical way. The two young women got along well, maybe in part because of their mutual disinterest in romancing any man, and Dolin got along with them both, having satisfied them that he did not have romantic designs on either.

Tata walked along a small path between flowers, sniffing something out.

"I heard something." It was a thirteen-year-old girl. "Oh! A dogfish! And people!"

Amara took charge. "Please excuse us, miss. We seem to have barged into your garden. We apologize."

"Oh, it's not my garden," the girl said. "It's Mera's garden. I merely help out. I came to harvest some fresh pies for dinner, and here you all are."

"Whose garden?" Dolin asked. He seemed taken aback.

Then Tartan caught on. Dolin's aunt was named Mera. The coincidence had evidently set him back.

"Princess Merari," the girl said. "Princess Taplin's younger sister."

Dolin seemed to be taken aback another step. His mother's name was Princess Taplin.

Amara clearly picked up on the coincidence. "Perhaps we should introduce ourselves, before we go on our way and leave you alone. I am Amara, an ordinary young woman. This is Prince Dolin. And Princess Emerald. And Tartan and Tara, from Mundania. And Tata Dogfish."

"Oh, he's so cute," the girl said, reaching down to pet Tata, who clearly liked the attention; his faceplate had a smile and his tail was wagging. "I'm Electra."

Now the others were set back. Electra was the Princesses Dawn and Eve's forty-six-year-old mother. This child had the same name? Coincidence was being stretched to the breaking point.

Amara come to the rescue again. "Please, Electra, can you tell us what year this is?"

"Why 237, of course. How could anyone forget that?"

How indeed. This was it seemed the time that princess Mera came from, and Electra, that Mera's spell had returned them to. Electra was indeed a child. Amara looked questioningly at the others. "What's the right thing to do, Prince?" she asked.

"Tell her when we came from," Dolin said promptly.

"We are from your far future," Amara said carefully. "The year 1117."

Electra tittered. "The future doesn't exist yet!"

She was right, yet also wrong. "Perhaps we should talk to—to Princess Mera," Dolin said diplomatically. His aunt.

"Sure. She's setting the table for dinner. Right this way."

They followed her out of the garden and into a pleasant mansion. Well, it was the abode of a princess; they tended to run to mansions. "Mera!" Electra called. "Visitors!"

"Oh? Who?" a melodious voice called back from another room.

"Amara and Tata and their friends," Electra called back.

Then Mera appeared in the doorway. Tartan had expected her to look exactly like the Mera they had met at the Good Magician's castle, by no coincidence. But this was a different girl, a magnitude prettier. Her hair was golden glory, and her figure flirted with absolute perfection.

"Five!" she said, surprised. "I'll have to reset the table. There are only three places now."

"Please, we did not come to impose on your hospitality," Dolin said. "We merely wish to clarify our situation." He seemed unstunned by her beauty. After half a moment Tartan realized why: he knew her as his aunt. Aunts were not stunning, by definition.

"Two of them are royal," Electra stage whispered to Mera.

"Then we really must fete them according to their stations," Mera said. "I will reset the table." She disappeared.

The others looked at Dolin. He shrugged. "It is right," he murmured.

"But we're hardly in fit condition for a royal meeting," Amara said, glancing down at her mussed dress.

"This way," Electra said, and showed them to a palatial lavatory. "There are several chambers, so you can have privacy. Emerge when you are ready. Meanwhile I'll feed Tata." She departed, and the dogfish happily followed her.

"It seems we're committed," Emerald said. "We probably shouldn't have mentioned royalty."

"My fault," Amara said, flustered. "I guess I wasn't thinking straight."

"No fault," Dolin said. "It was proper."

"I don't want to poop the party," Tara said. "But that is not the girl we met in our time. She is absolutely lovely, but I fear you misremember her."

Dolin smiled. "I assure you, that is my Aunt Mera. I know her well. It is that she is now in her own body."

"Oh, of course," Tara said, embarrassed.

"The original," Tartan said. "She practically shines, even when she's not trying."

"She does," Dolin agreed. "She is prettier than Mother Taplin. Of course she's less than half Mother's age, in the future venue. Mother was surely beautiful in her day. They are only two years apart, here."

"You seem to know a lot, Prince," Amara said. "Has your memory returned?"

"By no means. Only that portion relating to her, and that remains incomplete. My memory returns only when specifically addressed by events or special people."

They completed their toiletries and were ready when Electra and Tata returned. The dogfish greeted Amara like a long-lost friend. Soon they were seated around a table set for eight. "But I shouldn't be here," Electra protested, looking at the eighth plate. "I'm the servant, not a guest."

A regal older woman appeared. "Stay, Electra. I have a premonition that you are important to this dialogue."

"Yes, Sorceress Tapis," Electra said humbly. "At least I'll serve the food."

The Sorceress smiled acquiescence. "Then you will join us." She walked grandly toward her chair at the head of the table.

Dolin hurried around to hold her chair for her. "Why thank you, Prince," she said as she sat. "Where did you learn your manners?"

"From my mother, the Princess Taplin," he said. "She told me it was important for a prince to be mannerly."

The Sorceress gave a visible start. "Please, tell me your identities and situations."

Now Dolin did the honors, as they all sat and Electra busily served pies and milkpods. "We are a party from your far future, here to escape an unfortunate situation. This is Princess Emerald of the dragon realm, a dragon in human form." Emerald nodded. Electra, less sophisticated than the others, looked awed. "The maiden Amara, host to the Goddess Isis." Amara nodded, then manifested briefly as Isis, causing all three of their hosts to stare momentarily before recovering their manners. "The Mundane lady Tara, in a host. The Mundane man Tartan, in human host. They are here on a mission to save Xanth from an embarrassing threat. The dog Tata joined us along the way. And myself, Prince Dolin, son of Princess Taplin, your daughter. I greet you, Grandmother Tapis." Clearly, more memories were returning, now that he was in the presence of his grandmother.

Tapis frowned apologetically. "I find this difficult to believe. You came from the Year 1117?" Evidently Electra had told her.

"We did," Dolin answered.

"By what means?"

"Aunt Mera arranged it."

Mera opened her mouth, but Tapis silenced her with half a glance. "What do you know of Mera?"

Dolin considered briefly. "She joined my mother in the future, helping to take care of me. Her talent is—is to travel between realities."

"Who told you this?"

"She did, in my time. She was instrumental in making me part of this party. I love her."

Mera gazed at him with a tightly controlled glance. This was her own future history he was describing.

Tapis considered a good two thirds of a moment. "You must understand, this is not something we can accept just on your say-so. You could be actors in some remarkable play. Do you have any proof of your futuristic origin?"

Dolin spread his hands. "None, Grandmother."

Tapis focused on his right hand, where he wore the ring. "Tell me about the ring you wear," she said, her voice deceptively calm.

"Gladly, Grandmother. It is your ring, which you gave to your daughter Taplin to secure her during her long Sleep, along with the magic coverlet. That coverlet became my blanket when I was young, and now the ring contains my soul. It is invaluable to me."

"May I touch it?"

"Of course, Grandmother." Dolin held out his hand.

Tapis put a finger to the ring. There was a faint flash. "It is indeed my ring."

"Taplin swore never to part with it!" Mera said indignantly.

Dolin smiled understandingly. "It was Mother's most treasured possession. She loaned it to me for a time to enable me to survive. I remember this as I address it."

"To survive?" Tapis asked sharply.

"I do not remember this portion directly, of course, but Aunt Mera told me, and I know it is true. When I was eight years old I happened to be in the vicinity when the Sea Hag was changing hosts."

"The Sea Hag!" Mera exclaimed. "She's notorious."

"Yes. She is a dreadful creature. It seems she lives eternally by taking new young host bodies when the old ones wear out. When I saw it happen she was wroth and threw me to a monster, who consumed me, and I died. Mother was devastated. But she found a way to save me by catching my soul in this magic ring. There it will remain until I marry a princess in the primary Xanth reality, when I will become real there and live again, as an adult. But only there; I can never return to thank Mother, for in her reality I died as a child. Aunt Mera will bring the empty ring back to her once I am secure, and she will be happy, as she has not been in seventeen years."

"Now I understand," Mera said tearfully. "What an awful history. I see now that I must go to help my sister save you."

"I don't understand," Electra said. "How can marriage in another reality restore your life?"

Dolin spread his hands. "This is not a thing I properly understand. But if it is not true, then I am doomed."

"I understand it," Tapis said. "There are many alternates, most of which are possibilities rather than realities. When an alternate person comes to Xanth proper, he or she can stay there only about a month before fading out. But if that person marries a regular resident, and has a child, that child then anchors that person in Xanth, because a child must have a father and a mother. You, Dolin, being royal, must marry a person of your station."

"Yes, if I can find a suitable princess and persuade her to gamble on me," Dolin agreed.

"That would not be much of a gamble," Tara said. "You're handsome and accomplished and nice."

Dolin laughed. "But it seems there aren't many available princesses. Emerald, here, would have been ideal."

"I'm a dragon," Emerald protested. Tata woofed agreement.

"That matters not," Tapis said. "She is a princess, and grounded in reality. She would do."

"Then why doesn't she?" Electra asked.

Emerald sighed. "That is my tragedy. I must marry a human prince to secure detente between the dragons and the humans, so that there will not be divisive war. That is why my father sent me to the human realm. Prince Dolin certainly qualifies, and I like him personally, but I just can't do it."

"Why not?" Electra asked before Tapis could shush her.

"Because I am a lesbian," Emerald said. "I can't bear to marry any man, prince or no."

Mera looked shocked, but did not speak.

"And I respect that," Dolin said. "I would not care to marry a man either."

The others laughed, and Tata woofed, but there was an undercurrent of awkwardness verging on distress.

Emerald took a breath. "But if you can't find your princess, Dolin, and are faced with oblivion, rather than let that happen I would marry you. I value you too much to allow you to die through any neglect of mine."

"I sincerely appreciate the gesture," Dolin said. "And I know you would make a fine wife, one with a certain fire." He smiled briefly. "But I would never inflict such a sacrifice on you. We are better as friends."

"Yes," Emerald agreed, clearly relieved.

"It seems that there are complications quite apart from your presence here," the Sorceress said. "Well, there may be proof of your origin and nature, Grandson, if you care to demonstrate it."

"How is that, Grandmother?"

"It will hinge on your authenticity as my grandson, because of course you do not exist today. Still there are things you should know. Such as Taplin's talent."

"Why yes, I do know that," Dolin said. "It is sleeping."

"Sleeping?" Tara asked. "Everyone sleeps."

"Ah, but this is different," Dolin said. "The rest of us sleep for only a few hours at a time. Taplin can sleep indefinitely."

"Like for several centuries," Mera said.

"But—" Tara said. "But now I think of it, what about, um, natural functions? Didn't she need to eat? And to eliminate? To exercise? Wouldn't her flesh bruise or rot if she didn't move for hundreds of years?"

"That's it," Dolin said. "She is able to sleep without those impediments. Neither did she ever suffer bad dreams. Neither did she age. She woke the same age as she was when she slept. She is the perfect sleeper. That is her talent, which no one else has. That enabled her to reach the future, marry, and signal for me."

"That is a talent," Tara agreed, impressed.

"It also enables her to pass the time when life becomes uncomfortable," Dolin said. "She will sleep until Princess Mera returns with news of me." He frowned. "And if that news is not good, then she may sleep and never wake again."

Tapis nodded. "You do know about her. That is a positive signal. My daughter Taplin departed on her long Sleep only a year ago, on a journey of what you say will be 880 years total. There are three things that I share with my daughters, and if you also share them, then you are authentic."

"I do not know what these may be," Dolin said. "My memory is imperfect, because of complications of my situation. I recall things only as they relate to me."

"One is an ugly little wart on the left little toe."

Dolin looked surprised. "I am in the host body of another man; this is not my true form. But I have had an itch on that toe, as if something should be there. Now I remember as a child, trying to scrub it off."

The Sorceress nodded. "What is your favorite food?"

"Why, I never thought about it before. But now that I do, it is hayberry longcake. I could eat that until I got sick, and still love it."

Mera's mouth dropped open. "Me too," she said.

"And me," Tapis said. "We shall have it today for dessert, as we always do. But perhaps you could have heard of this."

"I could have guessed," Dolin said. "Now I remember how Mother loves it."

"One other thing," Tapis said. "Do you know my talent?"

"Why yes, now that you ask," Dolin said. "You make marvelous magic tapestries."

"How do I make them?"

"Why of course you weeve them."

Tata tried to suppress a woof of amusement.

"I do what?"

"You weeve them with marvelous dexterity and magic."

There was part of a silence.

"I think you mean weave," Amara said diplomatically.

"Yes, weeve," Dolin agreed.

"Uh-oh," Tartan murmured.

"There is a problem?" Dolin asked.

"The word is weave," Amara said. "Are you unable to say it correctly?"

Dolin considered. "Now I appreciate the distinction, hearing the way you say it. If that is correct, then yes, I am unable to say it your way."

"Oh, my," Mera said.

Dolin spread his hands. "If that disproves my authenticity, then I am sorry. I truly thought I was your grandson, Sorceress, and your nephew, Mera. Certainly I should be able to speak the word correctly. I apologize for being an imposter. It was not my intent."

"No," Mera said. "I, too, pronounce it weeve. So did my sister Taplin."

"And so do I," Tapis said. "I do weeve my tapestries."

"They do," Electra said. "None of them can say weave."

Dolin was confused. "But that means—"

"Welcome to the family, grandson," Tapis said with a smile. "I am glad, for it is apparent that you are a fine young man."

"And that my sister didn't give away her ring for nothing," Mera said.

They had finished the meal. Electra stood. "I'll clear."

"Not yet, dear," Tapis said, and the girl sat back down obediently.

"There is more?" Emerald asked.

"There surely is," Tapis said. "How much do any of you understand about alternate realities?"

"Why, they surely exist," Dolin said. "Because I am from one."

"What is the primary reality?"

"That is the one that these good folk occupy," Dolin said. "The one I seek to join."

"How does it differ from yours?"

"I do not know about other respects," Dolin said carefully. "But in it, Princess Electra is a grandmother, as she is not in mine."

"I'm a what?" Electra asked, astonished.

Dolin smiled. "We met her. She is forty-six years old, the mother of twin girls, now adults." He paused. "She welcomed me like a long lost nephew, and the twin daughters did too, as if I were their brother. I don't understand that."

"Maybe I do," Mera said. "Who is your father?"

"Prince Dolph." Then he looked surprised. "The same man Electra married!"

"So you *are* a nephew," Mera said. "Or more correctly a stepson. And a half brother to the princesses. In another reality."

"It seems I am," Dolin agreed, amazed. "Now I understand why Dawn and Eve greeted me so affectionately. They knew."

"How did Electra get to your time, our future?" Tapis asked.

"I am not sure," Dolin said. "I have very little background history of that reality, or of my own."

"I can answer that," Amara said. "It is a significant part of Xanth's known History. The Evil Magician Murphy put a curse on the household of the Sorceress Tapis, and it caused Electra to accidentally bite the apple and fall into the coffin to sleep for a thousand years."

"Not Taplin?" Mera asked. "Then how can my sister be safely asleep right now, on her way to the future?"

"Because that was the prime reality," Tapis said. "Call it Number One. We are Number Two, where the curse did not strike and my daughter departed as planned."

"We're not real?" Mera asked.

"We are real," Tapis said. "Merely not primary. All realities exist, and we are surely in most, but some are more fundamental than others."

"Wow," Electra said.

"I have a problem," Tara said. "If only Taplin had the power to sleep for centuries without harm, how did Electra do it in the other reality? Why didn't she die of old age in her sleep?"

"Oh, I can answer that," Electra said. "My talent is electricity. It imbues me, and protects me. It would have put me into a sort of stasis so that I had no natural functions or aging until kissed awake."

"Ah," Tara said.

"Who did you say I married, there in the future?"

"You married Prince Dolph," Amara said. "He had been enamored of Princess Nada Naga, but he knew that you—Electra—had to marry him or die, so he married you, and soon came to love you. Your daughters are Dawn and Eve, both highly regarded Sorceresses."

"But I'm not royal!" Electra protested. "I'm just a common servant girl."

"Not any more," Tapis said, smiling. "But if Electra took Taplin's place in the future, in that reality, what happened to Taplin here in the past?"

"I believe she married King Roogna," Amara said. "She fared well enough, considering."

"That's a relief," Tapis said. "I would not want her to marry beneath her station."

"That leaves me," Mera said. "If I am to help my sister and Dolin, how do I get back to the future? There is not another apple for me to bite, and I am not at all certain how well I would survive such a long sleep if I did bite one."

"That is the question," Tapis said. "Obviously you do need to get there, lest we be inflicted with paradox."

"I am perplexed," Dolin said. "It was your spell, Aunt Mera, in the future, that sent us here. Are you not able to make another to take us and yourself back?"

Mera shook her head. "Not my spell. I don't do time travel."

"That's right," Tara said. "You made a deal with the Magician of Time. He wanted to get to another reality where he might have a better situation, and you knew you would need a time spell. So you traded. He gave you a Time Bomb set for this time, and you shifted him to another reality. And here we are."

"It is more devious than that," Mera said. "I evidently shifted us into this second reality so that Taplin could have her Sleep, having lost it to Electra before, and in the future I arranged to send the group of you here. But whenever I exert my talent, things change. I may not affect anything in this reality, but rather shift us into another reality. You won't want another alternate; you need to stay in this one. Is that clear?"

"Not at all, Aunt," Dolin said with a smile. The others were similarly confused, Tata included.

"My daughter is a Sorceress," Tapis said fondly. "Her talent can be frighteningly potent and devious. It is best that she not use it unless there is overriding reason. She used it to enable Taplin to take her scheduled Sleep, then found a Self Storage unit to take herself to the future to join her sister so she could help. The alternates seem to vary in their times-cales, so she might indeed shift you back to your future time, but it would surely be a new reality, quite different from the one you came from."

"That won't do," Mera said. "You would be lost amidst foreign realities."

"I still don't properly understand," Amara said. "But this is making me nervous."

"As are all of us," Tara agreed with a shudder.

"This Self Storage unit," Tartan said. "In Mundania they are used to store things so the house doesn't get overcrowded. I gather it's not quite the same in Xanth."

"It is not," Tapis agreed. "A person sets the unit for a given period, then enters and closes the door. She goes into stasis and is aware of no passage of time. But when she emerges, she is when she chose. It is clear that this worked for Mera."

"Exactly. So can we all use another to return to our own time?"

"No. They are rare, and the one she used was the only one we knew of. It might take a century to search out another, and then it would probably be too small for the group of you."

"Bleep," Tartan swore.

The Sorceress looked at him. He was immediately embarrassed. "I apologize for my language. It's just—"

"Let us ponder overnight," Tapis said. "Perhaps in the morning we will have a clearer view of our alternatives."

They didn't argue. The Sorceress was right: they all needed time to think.

"Meanwhile, why don't we show them the Tapestries," Mera said.

"Oh, they would not be interested in that," Tapis demurred.

"Oh, but we would," Emerald said. "We dragons have heard about your fabulous magic tapestries. Isn't there one in Castle Roogna?"

"I did make one for the new King Roogna," Tapis said. "Are you saying that it survived to your time?"

"Oh, it did," Amara said. "It's a huge animated map of Xanth showing anything the viewer wants to see. It is truly fabulous, as Emerald says."

"And you have others?" Tara asked. "I would certainly like to see them."

So they were treated to an impromptu tour of the tapestries hanging on the mansion walls. One was a still life that showed the mansion itself, from its first construction as a baby hut to its final year as a decrepit haunted house. The history of it played out as they watched, then repeated.

"This is cloth?" Tartan asked, amazed. "It's like a TV set!"

"Like a what?" the Sorceress asked.

He explained what a TV set was. "Now that's true magic," Tapis said, impressed.

Other tapestries showed glades where animals grazed, and the animals moved about from one side to the other, occasionally glancing at the spectators. Or pretty fish in a pond, merrily swimming. Or a growing chestnut tree, producing chests of nuts.

One showed a dragon, who took off and sailed into the sky amidst slowly moving clouds. "Oh, I'm in love!" Emerald said, awed. "What a fabulous scene!"

"Then you must have it, dear."

"Oh, no, I couldn't possibly—"

"Nonsense. I make my tapestries to be seen and enjoyed." Tapis took it down, rolled it, and put it into a tubular sleeve for safe transport. It was surprisingly compact. In fact now it looked hardly larger than a thimble. She gave it to Emerald, who handled it as if it were a precious stone signified by her name, and put it in a pocket. Tartan was amazed yet again by the permutations of magic. He knew that the tapestry would revert to full size when taken out and unrolled.

"Oh, thank you so much," the dragon lady said, tears of gratitude flowing. "I will have my father hang it in the Royal Den for all to admire." Then she sobered. "Once the peace is made between our species." Tartan knew what a complication that was.

"Of course, dear," the Sorceress agreed reassuringly.

Then it was time to retire.

"But there are five of you, and we have only two spare guest suites," Electra said apologetically.

"Dolin and Emerald can share a suite," Amara said. "They're royal and they understand each other. I'll share with Ted and Monica; we also understand each other."

"Who and who?" Electra asked.

"Tara and I will return to Mundania for the night," Tartan explained. "Ted and Monica are our hosts."

"Oh," Electra said, trying to look as if she understood.

Emerald took Dolin's arm. "Is it all right if I don't change, tonight? My dragon form crowds things."

"I will try to suppress my thoughts," Dolin agreed.

"Oh, go ahead and have them, as long as you don't try to act on them."

"A fair compromise," he agreed. They entered their room. They truly did know and trust each other. Tartan realized that they actually enjoyed each other's company, now that the ground rules had been worked out. She might even tease him by stripping and washing while he watched. Maybe they were practicing for the possibility that they would have to marry, for their separate reasons. They both stood to lose too much if they weren't prepared for that difficult pass.

"Thoughts?" Electra asked.

She was thirteen, well below the Conspiracy threshold. "They're like brother and sister, teasing each other," Tara said. "Think of it as like tickling."

"Oh." The girl still seemed uncertain.

"We'll see you in the morning," Tartan said when the three were in their room.

"Don't do anything we wouldn't do," Tara cautioned them. That broke up Amara and the hosts. They all had a fair notion what Tara and Tartan were doing in their off time. Even Tata, staying close to Amara, was amused. He had a surprising comprehension of human activities.

Then they were back home in Mundania. "What a picklement," Tartan said once they had dived for the bathroom. "I hope there's some way out for them, apart from the Ghost Writer mission."

"I'm glad that time travel or alternate realities in Xanth don't affect us here." Tara said. "For once I'm satisfied to have no magic."

"No magic? Your panties affect me regardless. I'm starting to freak out."

"Can't have that," she said, pretending shock. "I'll take them off immediately." She did so.

"That's better." They plunged into a ferocious ellipsis.

. . .

That evening, in mussed pajamas and nightie, they discussed it further. "Apart from the several individual problems," Tara said, "How are we going to get back to present-day Xanth? I can appreciate how we can't use another Self Storage unit, and why Mera shouldn't use her talent again; that could mess things up worse."

"The cure could be worse than the illness," he agreed.

"Another thing: did you see how Mera froze when Emerald confessed that she's a lesbian? Monica pointed that out to me. She must be straight laced."

"She soon recovered her poise. I don't think she'll let prejudice interfere with the welfare of the group. After all, she has to get to the present day too."

"About that," she said. "Monica mentioned something to me in passing that I took little note of at the time, but now I wonder. There's a Timeline the Muse of History uses that records all the events of Xanth, or at least all the ones that count. You know, births and deaths and stuff."

"Deliveries and fade-outs," he agreed. "How does such a document relate?"

"It's magic, as are most things in Xanth. Sometimes significant events are inserted retroactively, when hindsight indicates their importance."

"So?"

"So could maybe a person be inserted in the Timeline, and actually be there?"

"That's crazy!"

"Xanth is crazy. Nonsense often works there."

The idea started to take hold. "You're thinking that our trip back in time appeared in the Timeline, and maybe if we recorded that we returned to the present day, then it would happen?"

"Something like that."

"Assuming the Timeline is a physical entity that we might approach."

"Yes. The Sorceress Tapis might know."

"So we could record 'Prince Dolin's party reappears in the present,' and it would happen."

"Or go to the Timeline, get on it in the past, and walk to the present."

"Let's do it!"

She glanced down at her dishabille. "We just did it. Didn't you see that ellipsis?"

"That, too," he agreed, laughing. "You know, Tara, my life changed when I met you, and not just because of Xanth."

"Mine too."

"When Xanth is over, I don't want us to be over."

"Me neither."

"Do we want another ellipsis?"

"Just hold me and sleep."

"Okay." He did.

In the night she nudged him. "I changed my mind. I want an ellipsis."

"May I sneak in some kissing too?"

She laughed. "Yes, of course."

"Okay."

. . .

In the morning they rejoined their hosts. Tata barked, knowing they were there. "Wow!" Ted said. "Twice in one night!"

"We're in love."

Tara blushed. Monica was teasing her too.

"I don't see what you folk see in it," Amara said. "It's just three stupid dots, after all."

"Ask the Goddess," Tara suggested.

Then Amara blushed. Evidently Isis was giving her a bellyful.

They rejoined Dolin and Emerald. "I wonder if there's a magic pill to change romantic orientation," Dolin mused as Emerald donned her dress.

"If we find one, you can try it first," Emerald said, smiling.

They had a fine breakfast served by Electra, and dog biscuits for Tata. "Tell me about my twin daughters," she begged.

"Dawn can tell anything about any living thing," Tara said.

"Eve can tell anything about any inanimate thing," Tartan said.

"Dawn knew my nature the moment she touched me," Dolin said. "So did Eve when she touched the ring."

They went on to tell whatever else they knew about the twin Sorceresses. Electra was rapt. So, surprisingly, was Emerald. And Tata. "It's too bad that Prince Dolin can't share a household with Dawn and Eve," she said. "They're all so great."

"Well, if I find a princess to marry, then I can share a reality with them," Dolin said. "I'd like that. They are fine girls."

"You know you can if you have to," Emerald said.

He shook his head. "I wish I could help you some other way."

"If it should come to that, for both of us, I am thinking it might not be too bad. If I should have to be with a man, you're the one I would want."

"But I would not want to repel you. If we married, we would be required to summon the stork."

"Perhaps I could shut my eyes, clench my teeth, and hold my breath long enough."

Princess Mera looked as if she wanted to say something, but stifled it.

"Very well," the Sorceress said as they finished the meal. "We all have done a fine job of avoiding the salient question, but now it is time. The five of you need to return to your time, and it seems that Mera needs to go there too, but she hesitates to use her talent for reasons we have clarified. Has anyone come up with an idea, however far out it may seem?"

Tartan looked at Tara. Tapis caught the look. "You have a suggestion, Tara?"

"I—it's crazy, but—is there a Timeline?"

"There is," Tapis said. "Does it relate?"

"Could we maybe step on it and walk back to our future?"

The Sorceress considered. "I never thought of that." She glanced at Mera. "Do you suppose that could work?"

"It might," Mera said. "It would be less risky than using my talent, because we could stay in this reality instead of crossing to a new one."

"That was my thought," Tapis said. "But there is a problem."

"There's always a problem," Mera agreed.

"The Timeline is in a largely inaccessible place, by no coincidence, because the Muse of History does not want anyone stumbling on it by accident and interfering with it. It would be difficult to reach unscathed."

"Dragons?" Dolin asked. "Emerald could help us there." He smiled. "That might be less stressful for her than marrying me."

"He thinks he's joking," Emerald said. But she was smiling. They were teasing each other.

"Perhaps," Tapis said. "I don't know. Just that it is designed to be hard to reach. You may find the route too awkward or hazardous to manage."

"Yet if it represents a feasible solution for us," Dolin said, "then perhaps the effort would be worthwhile."

"Shall we vote?" Amara asked brightly.

"Why not," Dolin said, laughing.

They took a vote, all of them, because any change in realities would affect them all. Even Tata participated, evidently having an interest. It was eight to one, with only Mera voting no.

"Why?" Emerald asked her.

"Oh, I think it's the best course. I *don't* want to use my talent again. But I have a nervous feeling about it, as if there is something we are missing. So it's more a vote of caution rather than negation. I will certainly go along with the majority."

"Your nervousness makes me nervous too," Emerald said. "But I see no better alternative."

"Then it is decided," the Sorceress said briskly. "I regret losing you, Mera, so soon after losing Taplin, but it is clear that you must accompany them back to the future." She glanced at Electra. "What of you, dear? In one future you become a princess, mother of Sorceresses. I doubt you can go there now, however, since you are already there, and in the other future your prince marries Taplin."

"I'll stay here with you, Sorceress," Electra said. "You have been like a mother to me, and I am happy here. You need someone to do the chores."

"And you have been like a daughter to me," Tapis said. "I was hoping you would say that, for I dislike being alone. But with Mera gone, there may be too many chores for you."

"I'll manage," Electra promised bravely.

"I remember how sad you were when Father Merlin left," Mera said.

"He didn't die?" Tara asked.

"No," Tapis said sadly. "He was called to Mundania where they needed him. We were married for twenty years, and three children were delivered, before he received the call eleven years ago. I hated to see him go, but there was a young king Arthur who truly needed his assistance. I understand he is doing well there. They are severely short of magic in Mundania."

"Three children?" Tartan asked. "The Princesses Taplin and Mera we know of, but who is the third?"

"Our first child, Jonathan, was delivered a year before Taplin."

"My big brother," Mera said. "We called him the Zombie Master, because of his talent for animating zombies. He fell in love with a pretty girl, Millie the Maid, and zombied himself when he lost her to an evil transformation. We don't like to speak of that."

"But they survived in our time," Amara said. "She was a lovely ghost for something like eight hundred years, but then was restored, and he recovered and married her. They had a long and happy life at Castle Zombie before they retired."

"I'm exceedingly gratified to learn that," Tapis said. She took a breath. "Now you must prepare for your excursion to the Timeline."

"This seems to be the right thing," Dolin said. "But how do we get there?"

Tata barked, startling them all. His bark was still worse than his byte.

"Tata can find the way," Amara said. "He can sniff out any path."

"That is a talented dog," Emerald said.

"Yes. There's something about him," Amara agreed. "He is more than he appears."

"Then it seems to be decided," Dolin said. "We shall search out this Timeline."

Tartan was almost sorry to depart, because the Sorceress was a good host and a fine person. But of course they could not dwell in the past. They had a mission to accomplish in their own time.

Chapter 9

TIMELINE

They organized as a party of six plus a dogfish and bid regretful farewell to Tapis and Electra. They wore backpacks with supplies for the trip,
packed by Electra. Tartan's pack contained sandwiches, chocolate, and a
folded paddle. What was that for?

"I am only sorry that Electra will not get to be a princess," Mera said as
they followed Tata into the jungle. "She is a very nice girl."

"Maybe there will be something just as nice for her here," Emerald
said. "Being royal is not always a pleasure."

"Yes!" Mera agreed fervently. She seemed to have forgotten her wari-
ness about the dragon princess's orientation. The two were the same age
physically, and both were outstandingly pretty. Tartan was glad to see
them getting along.

Tata paused where the path split into several branches. He sniffed each
one carefully. "If I understand his reaction, and I think I do," Amara said,
"he is finding that all the paths lead to the Timeline, but some are more
challenging than others. He is trying to find the fastest and safest one."

"Your talent relates?" Dolin asked.

"Yes. I know that the Timeline will be at the end of any path we choose
by the time we get there. Tata must have reason for being careful."

The dogfish finally settled on a path and swam forward through the
air. They followed in single file: Amara, Emerald, Mera, Dolin, Tara, and
Tartan.

"Woof!"

They halted in line. "A nest of nickelpedes," Amara announced.

"I packed some repellant," Mera said. She dug out a small bag, opened
it, and blew a whiff of dust into the air.

There was a desperate scrambling as the nickelpedes fled. The powder was effective.

They came to the shore. "I forgot," Ted told Tartan. "The Sorceress Tapis lives on the Isle of View. We have to get to the mainland."

"The Isle of View?" Tartan repeated aloud.

"I love you too," Tara replied. "What brought that on?"

"Not the sentiment," he said "The island."

"The what?" Tara asked. Then: "Oh, Monica just told me. When you pronounce it, it sounds like I Love You."

"It's a very affectionate island," Emerald agreed. "As is the Kiss Mee River farther to the east. We dragons fly over both of them all the time."

There was a small rowboat just big enough for six people and a dog. They got in and sat on the benches. Now Tartan's paddle became functional. Electra had of course known. Dolin had another.

They pushed off into the water. Dolin sat near the front and stroked on the left, while Tartan sat near the back and stroked on the right. The craft moved smartly forward.

For all of ten strokes. Then a big toothy serpentine head rose out of the water before them. "Oops, a sea monster," Amara said.

A big green eye eyed them. Then the jaw gaped and the head moved down toward the boat. The thing was big enough to take up a person in a single bite.

"Did you check your right thing sense, prince?" Tara inquired worriedly.

"Yes. We should be fine."

The monster's eye fixed on Amara as one of the tastier morsels. A huge tongue slurped around the mouth. Then the head advanced.

"Tata, do your thing," Amara murmured.

"GROUFF!" the dogfish barked so fiercely that all of them jumped. His faceplate showed a frowny face.

The sea monster rocked back, amazed. Tata followed, swimming out of the boat up through the air toward the head. "RUFF RUFF RUFF **GROUFF!**"

The monster hastily sank back under the surface. It didn't know that the dog's bark was worse than its byte.

But the commotion had attracted other predators. Two small winged dragons converged on the boat. One puffed fire, the other smoke.

"I don't much care to be either fired or smoked," Tara said.

"My turn," Emerald said. She stood, efficiently peeling off her clothing, revealing her fine body. Tartan looked away, partly to avoid freaking and partly to avoid Tara's glare if he did. She didn't want him embarrassing himself or Emerald. Then the princess leaped and converted to her dragon form, spreading her wings and heaving up into the air.

"I saw your legs!" Dolin called after her. "And that's not all!"

Tata woofed appreciation.

Emerald turned her head to snort a small jet of flame toward Dolin. Had she really been annoyed it could have been a big jet. Then she oriented on the two hovering dragons. There was a brief exchange of growls. After that the two turned about and flew away.

Emerald flew to the far beach, landed, and transformed back to human form. They paddled toward her. There were no further disturbances.

"What forms!" Ted said to Tartan.

"Which form? Human or dragon?"

"Both. She's one luscious human creature I'd gladly embrace if I didn't know she'd turn to the other and toast me."

Tartan had to agree. Both Emerald's forms were superlative. It was a shame she had no interest in appreciative males.

"Oh, stop it," Tara snapped. "All three of you." She knew that Tartan and Ted were comparing notes, and that Dolin had thoughts.

"Can't a girl change without getting ogled?" Amara asked.

"She's beautiful, both forms," Dolin said.

"She is," Mera agreed. Actually Mera herself was just as sightly, but she never showed her body the way Emerald did. She was, after all, somebody's aunt.

They reached the shore. Dolin stepped out and handed Emerald her clothing, which she donned without embarrassment. "I believe I speak for all of us when I say thank you for your display," Dolin said.

"My what?"

"Your display of ferocity that scared away the other dragons," Mera said quickly.

"No ferocity there. I merely addressed them in dragon talk and they agreed to leave you folk alone. It's the Winged Monster Convention, which has existed for millennia: we do not interfere in each other's business."

"They thought we were your captive prey?" Amara asked.

"Why else would any of you be watching me? You're nervous about which one I'll eat first."

Dolin laughed, swept her into his embrace, and kissed her. She did not resist; in fact she kissed him back. They truly got along. It was an interesting friendship.

"How will the boat get back to its harbor on the other side?" Tartan asked.

"Either someone will cross from this side," Mera said. "Or someone will whistle from the other side. Then it will go there on its own. We use it all the time."

Tata sniffed out the proper path, and they forged back into the jungle. "Do you think it's far?" Amara asked. "I wouldn't like to be caught out here at night."

"Woof!" Tata called back.

"Oh, that's a relief." She turned to the others. "Not far at all. Just difficult."

The path petered out, facing them with dense and thorny foliage. "Now what?" Tara asked.

Tata pointed with his nose at the densest patch. "Woof!"

"Oh?" Amara asked, surprised. "Are you sure?"

"Woof!"

"All right." She strode directly into the thorn patch.

And through it, unimpeded. It was illusion!

They followed her through a wicked looking tangle. The path resumed on the other side. But soon it led to a crevasse.

"Uh-oh," Mera said. "This would be an offshoot of the dread—well, I forget what it is, but it's awful."

"The Gap Chasm," Amara said. "The forget spell finally wore off it so we moderns can remember, but it must be fresh here in the past."

They stood and gazed down into the crevice. It was too wide to jump across, and so deep that there was only darkness below.

Tata sniffed along the edge. "Woof!" Then he walked out into the gulf.

The others stared. The dog was suspended in the air just above the pit. He was not in danger, because he could swim through the air, but at the moment he was simply standing.

"Oh, it's an invisible bridge," Mera said. "I forgot about that too."

"It was one potent forget spell," Amara said.

"Is it safe?" Tara asked dubiously.

"Yes and no," Mera said. "It is structurally secure. We can safely cross, physically. If we want to."

"Why wouldn't we want to, if this is the way to where we're going?"

"The ogles."

"Eagles?"

"No, ogles."

"Ogres?"

Mera sighed. "I think I will have to demonstrate." She stepped out onto the invisible bridge.

Nothing happened, for an instant. But by the time it filled out to a full moment, there was a gust of wind that tugged her skirt up, showing her very nice legs. She put her hands down to stop it. So far, so good.

Then a swarm of flying creatures zoomed along within the chasm. They were small, but had huge bulging eyes. "Oh, lookee lookee lookee!" they chortled. "Peek peek peek!"

Mera quickly stepped off the bridge so that there was no longer a view under her skirt. The birds fluttered away, disappointed.

"Ogles," Amara agreed.

"In Mundania there would be no problem," Tartan said. "Most of the girls wear jeans."

"This isn't Mundania," Amara said sharply.

Meanwhile Tata was sniffing a bit back from the crevice. "Woof!"

"Oh, my," Amara said. "That will do it." She walked to the dog, squatted, and scooped up two handfuls of dry dirt. Then she walked back to the bridge, and onto it.

Immediately the ogles swarmed in again. "Peek peek peek!"

Amara let them get close under her. Then she hurled a handful of dirt down into their midst. "Oooo!" they chorused, spinning out of control, blinded.

Amara smiled smugly. She walked on across the gulf. Whenever an ogle came close, she raised her other hand, the one that still held dirt, in a threatening gesture. The ogle retreated.

"Well, now," Tara said. She scooped up her own dirt and went to the bridge. Then Mera, and Emerald. And finally the two men and the dog, needing no dirt. They were across.

"And I thought that throwing dirt was only a political device," Tartan remarked. The Xanthians looked at him blankly.

There was a puddle of water. They took turns washing their hands in it.

Tata took the lead again. He rounded a corner and woofed.

There was a boy of about fourteen. "Hello, dogfish," he said.

The others caught up. "Who are you?" Amara asked.

"I'm Eleph. Who are you?"

"I'm Amara. My talent is knowing where something will be. What's yours?"

"Making pigs fly."

Tartan choked back a laugh.

"That's interesting," Amara said. "Can you demonstrate?"

"No."

"Why not?"

"Because I can't find any more pigs. They avoid me."

"That is a problem," Amara agreed. "Maybe I can help you."

Eleph was interested. "You can?"

"I happen to know that there's a herd of pigs soon to be in the vicinity of the Sorceress Tapis' mansion. If you go there you'll find them. Maybe if you agree to do chores, the Sorceress will let you stay there a while."

"I'll do it!" Eleph said joyfully. He jumped up and ran down the path they had come on.

"What was the point of that?" Mera asked.

"Electra needs help with the chores. He seems like a nice boy. It may be fun for them watching the pigs fly. Maybe there's a future there for them both."

Mera nodded. "Good points. They should get along."

Tartan was impressed. Amara had just used her talent to do Electra some good. The aromantic woman might even have fostered a future romance. Evidently she didn't hate romance, merely did not feel the need of it for herself.

They walked on. Now they came to an ogre's den, and the ogre was outside it, twice the height of a man and broad in proportion, squeezing juice from small stones. There was no way to avoid him. Ogres, Ted informed him, were known to be the strongest and ugliest creatures of Xanth, and they were justifiably proud of their stupidity. There would be no reasoning with this one.

"This may be a job for my other form," Emerald said grimly.

"Beware," Mera said. "One of the ogre's businesses is teaching small dragons the meaning of fear. I understand they are quite good at it."

"I will handle it," Isis said, manifesting. "This is part of my deal with Amara: she provides the host, I provide the social expertise."

"But that's an ogre!" Mera said. "They don't understand social."

"I don't work through understanding," the Goddess said, striding forward.

The ogre looked up as she approached. "Me see gee she," he said, surprised.

"That's a compliment," Mera said, surprised in turn.

"Come down to my level, big boy," Isis said. "So I can whisper in your cauliflower ear."

The ogre didn't try to think about it. They could tell, because his head was not heating and the fleas were not jumping off. He simply sat down on the ground with a thunk that cracked the earth around him. "Me Handee. Who you be?"

"Come off the idiot doggerel, Handee. I am no ordinary dull woman. I am a Goddess. Speak to me in real talk."

"Oh, you know," the ogre said, taken aback. "What can I do for you, Goddess?"

Tartan was amazed, and saw that the others were too. The ogre could talk normally!

"It's what I can do for you," Isis said. "My kiss, should I choose to bestow it, will lock you in bliss for five moments and an instant or two."

"Undoubtedly," Handee agreed. "But at what price?"

"My party needs to pass by you to reach the Timeline."

The ogre squinted at her with something other than stupidity. "What do you know about the Timeline?"

"We need to get to it so we can return to our own time, far away in the future. You are clearly here to guard it from intruders like us."

"No. I will not let you pass. Not even for a kiss."

Now Isis squinted at Handee. "So you want to bargain, male thing? How about two kisses? The second will put you in bliss until day's end."

Handee made a smile that wilted the adjacent foliage. "That's more like it, you fascinating female."

"Brace yourself. Here it comes." The Goddess stepped into the ogre and kissed him firmly on the gaping mouth. Small sparks flew out, as if there were an electrical charge. Handee froze in place, an expression of idiotic bliss on his dull features.

"And the second," Isis said. She kissed him again, more firmly. This time his hair lifted from his head as the current was discharged into the air, and small jags of lightning spiked from his fingers into the ground. His expression was set like solidified magma. Blissful rock.

The Goddess backed off and turned around. "Pass," she said. "He won't bother you." She faded. Amara was back, a pretty girl, but hardly the shadow of the Goddess.

Hesitantly the others edged past the frozen ogre. He never moved. He was indeed locked in bliss.

"She did all that with your body," Tara said to Amara. "With only two kisses."

"My body and her spirit," Amara said. "I could never duplicate it, even if I wanted to. But she's right: it is useful on occasion."

"If she kissed me like that, I'd be locked into love with her," Dolin said, awed.

"She does have some conscience," Amara said. "Also, she doesn't want you. She wants to get rid of the Ghost Writer, and probably needs this party's help to accomplish that, since it is your mission. So she'll leave you alone."

"I am glad to know that."

There was a brief shower, containing just water, no dogs or cats. Then the sun came out again, and there before them was a rainbow, the top band neatly tied in a loop. They were at the near end.

Mera laughed. "It got confused! Rainbows are supposed to be unapproachable, with a treasure at the far end."

"Curious," Dolin agreed. "What's this?"

They looked. Right at the end, where it touched the ground, was a little patch of colorful plants. They did not bear fruits, but fancy glasses of sherbet with colored fruit juices. They looked delicious.

Amara glanced at Tata as he sniffed the glasses. "Safe to drink?"

"Woof."

They served themselves to the refreshment. Tartan's was wonderful, and he could see that the others were too.

"That was excellent," Dolin said.

Emerald laughed. "You should see your tongue! It's rainbow colored."

"So is yours," he replied.

It turned out that all of their tongues now sported rainbow hues. "No wonder it was easy to get," Amara said. "The rainbow was having its little joke on us."

"Call it a new fashion," Mera said, examining her own tongue with a compact mirror she produced from somewhere.

"That wets my appetite," Dolin said.

"Whets, dear," Emerald said. As usual in Xanth, spellings were visible.

"Let's take a lunch break," Mera said. "We don't know how hectic it may get this afternoon."

"We'll rejoin you soon," Tartan said. He took Tara's hand and they jumped home.

"She called him dear!" she said as she scrambled off the bed in chase of a function.

"They're friends."

"I wonder. Can a lesbian fall for a particular man?"

"I wouldn't know. I think they're just teasing the rest of us. Putting on an act."

"Emerald and Mera are becoming friends," she said. "They seem to be finding common interests."

"I hadn't noticed."

"Well, you're an ignorant man."

They quickly snacked, brushed their teeth, and returned to their hosts in Xanth. "What, no storks?" Ted asked.

"Didn't think of it in time."

"And you call yourself a man?"

"An ignorant one," Tartan agreed with a mental smile.

Meanwhile the others had finished their snack. It was time to resume motion. They walked on. They came to a small mountain rising from the jungle as if someone had set it down there. The near base of it was a sheer vertical cliff. Three nude women were braced against the cliff. Their upper portions were unremarkable, but their lower portions were remarkably well formed, and their rear views were surely architectural in their grandeur. What were they doing?

A man stepped out to intercept their party. "May I help you?" he inquired politely. "I'm Patrick Joseph Stapleberg, and this is my assignment."

"We're not sure," Dolin said, forcing his eyes from the statuesque maidens. "I'm Prince Dolin, with several companions. And a dog. We're looking for the Timeline."

"The what?"

"The Timeline of Xanth. It lists all the significant events so that the Muse of History can keep track of things when she writes her histories."

"I'm sorry. I'm from Mundania. That must be a detail I haven't yet picked up on."

"What are you doing here?" Mera asked.

Patrick looked at her, evidently appreciating her loveliness. Tartan realized that it was true what was said about men: they judged a woman by her appearance and not much else. "I am entertaining these three Flying Buttresses while they hold up this wall, so they don't get too bored. Otherwise they will resume their flight in the sky, and the wall will collapse. The Muse of History asked me to see to the support of this section, so I am doing it."

Dolin nodded. "The Muse of History. That means we are in the right place, though I can't say I understand how such shapely girls relate to the Timeline." He glanced around. "What is that?" He indicated a large fruit sitting on a table.

"That's my magic apple," Patrick said. "The Muse gave it to me. In Mundania I was a graphic artist, so she got me the tool to use my talent here." He walked to the big apple and touched it with one finger. A lovely splotch of color appeared. He gestured, and the splotch formed into a still life scene. The three buttresses focused on that, smiling. Buttresses were not known to have much mind, but evidently these ones liked the art.

"I see," Dolin said. "They do like your pictures." He glanced back at the others. "Tata led us here, and this area does feel right, but I think we have not yet found what we seek."

"True," Mera said. "We should not bother these good people further."

Tata made a Bark. "**Grouff**!!"

The sound was so loud that it startled the three sturdy maidens. They leaped from the cliff wall and into the air, sailing up into the sky without wings. They were after all flying buttresses. Tartan got only a flash of their phenomenal bare bottoms as they passed overhead, swimming along using the backstroke, but that was enough to freeze him in place with a freak. He was aware that Dolin was reacting similarly.

Then the wall collapsed with a resounding crash, jolting them out of it. Once the solid butts had stopped supporting it, it had been unable to stand.

"Oh, no!" Patrick cried. "I have failed my mission!"

"Maybe not," Amara said. She of course had not freaked out. "Look what's behind it."

There was a tall metallic column covered in carved words and numbers. An obelisk with four sides. The Timeline!

"This is what we seek," Dolin said, gratified. "Tata knew."

"But it must have been supposed to remain hidden," Patrick said. "That was why the Muse assigned me here."

"She won't object to our brief use of it," Amara said. "Our need is great."

"Still—"

"The Muse surely has other sites to protect," Amara said. Tartan was seeing her from behind, but recognized the persuasive aura of the Goddess briefly manifesting. "Ask her. I believe you can contact her via the magic apple."

Still he hesitated. "I don't know."

The aura intensified. Was Isis going to kiss him?

Then the apple flashed.

"But it seems she does," Patrick agreed, surprised. He went to the apple and looked into it. Then he packed it into a bag, folded up the table, and departed with a friendly wave to the group.

They stood before the obelisk. "Now what?" Tartan asked.

"It seems right that we be here," Dolin said. "But I know not how to use the Timeline."

"None of us do," Tartan said. "I guess we thought that your knowledge of the right thing would cover it."

"It will help," Dolin agreed. "But knowing the right course when there are several to choose from is not the same as working out that course for myself. Someone will have to suggest a course before my talent applies."

Tartan laughed. "How about taking a hammer and smashing the Timeline?"

He was greeted with looks of horror. "That's not funny," Mera said.

The suggestion had not been serious, but Tartan realized that even as a joke it was in very poor taste. "I'm sorry. I wasn't thinking."

"But the answer is no, a thousand times no," Dolin said. "That is not the right thing."

Tartan, embarrassed, tried harder. "What about making a wooden tower of our own, with a platform that we can mount to reach the right elevation? I'm assuming that the top of it is our future time."

"That will do," Dolin agreed.

"But getting there is only part of it," Tara said. "What do we do once we're there?"

"Try to chip our own entry onto it?" Tartan asked.

Dolin shook his head. "Only the Muse of History can make an entry."

"Could you turn dragon and fly up there?" Amara asked Emerald.

"And do what? Blast it with fire? I have no hands in my natural mode."

"Carry one of us there?" Dolin asked. "As you carried me across the lake to reach the troll?"

"Yes and no. When I carried you, I had plenty of room to spread my wings wide. Even so, it was difficult, because you weigh as much as I do in dragon mode, and I barely made it across without crashing. Trying to take you up to the top of the obelisk without veering into it would be a challenge, and I could not hover there. I'd have to have you jump off and cling to it. What would you do then?"

"Make a fool of myself," Dolin said. "That is not the way."

"But there has to *be* a way," Mera said.

"I think we're still a few breaths short of a bonfire," Emerald said. "We need to know what we're going to do before we use up our energies building a tower."

Tata sniffed the base of the Timeline. He woofed. They all looked at him.

"He knows something," Amara said. "But it's too complicated for me to grasp just from woofs. I think he's as smart as we are, but he lacks the human tongue. All he has is a woof or bark. So the problem is how he can tell us what he knows."

"He can tell us if we ask him yes or no," Dolin said. "One bark for yes, two for no. Maybe three for maybe."

"Can you play Twenty Three Questions?" Emerald asked.

"Do you mean Twenty Questions?" Tartan asked.

"Seventeen Questions," Dolin said.

"Eighteen and a half," Mera said, smiling.

Amara laughed. "In contemporary Xanth proper, it's Nineteen Questions, cumulative, whatever it may be in other realities or Mundania. Each has to be phrased for a yes, no, or maybe answer, or for a specific number, like how many people are in this party. If you can't get your answer then, you lose. It's normally a game. But let's see." She looked at the dog. "Can you play it?"

"Woof!"

"Good enough," Emerald said. "That's one question. We had better make the others count."

"We had better," Amara agreed. "Because we're in a different reality now, and it may have a different limit. We don't really know how many questions we can use."

"We'll agree on each question," Emerald said. "Then you can ask it, so that we waste none carelessly."

"That is the right course," Dolin agreed.

"We need a strategy of questioning," Tara said. "Maybe proceed from the general to the specific, cutting the unknown segment in half each time."

"So what's a good general question?" Emerald asked.

"First, make sure we're in the right ballpark," Tartan said.

"What kind of park?" Amara asked.

"I mean, the right general area. We don't want to ask how many stars are in the sky or how many fish in the sea; we want to know how to use the Timeline to accomplish our purpose."

"Ah. Like maybe is there an action we can take with respect to the Timeline to get back to the future?"

"I think that will do," Tartan agreed.

"Keep it simple," Mera said. "Tata clearly understands us, but we need to be efficient."

Amara faced the dog. "Tata, is there anything we can do with the Timeline to return to our own time?"

Tata barked once.

They discussed the next question. In due course Amara asked "Does it involve touching the obelisk?"

The dog hesitated, then gave one bark.

Why the hesitation? "Either we touch it or we don't," Tartan said, perplexed.

They discussed it again. This was tedious, but they wanted to get it exactly right. Then Mera got an idea. "Must we touch it in a particular spot?"

One bark.

Back on track. "The proper date!" Tara exclaimed. "Touch it in the wrong place, we go to the wrong time. That's why Tata hesitated. He didn't want to steer us wrong."

"We have to touch the right time?" Amara formally asked.

One bark.

"And that time is the date we came from, 1117?"

Another hesitation, followed by one bark. Hmm.

They paused to consider. Was there another catch?

"Maybe this," Emerald said. "If one person touches the right time, he or she jumps to the future, leaving the rest behind. But the next person who touches it may not land in quite the same place. So we could get separated, and have real trouble getting back together."

"Woof."

"So we'll all have to touch it together," Tara said.

"That could be difficult," Dolin said. "Climbing the tower may be an individual matter, unless we make a big one. Also, the lettering on the Timeline is small."

"Not to mention going overhead in skirts," Mera said. "Men are as bad as ogles."

The men did not respond, as if the remark was not worthy of refutation. But Tartan knew he would find Mera's skirt from below a tempting sight.

"Maybe we can link hands, with one person touching it," Amara said.

"Woof."

"That seems right," Dolin agreed.

"Are there any other cautions?" Amara asked the dog.

Tata gave two barks.

"Good enough," Tartan said. "Now all we have to do is build the tower. We'll have to scrounge for wood. I don't see any lying around nearby."

"Woof."

"Tata can sniff out a path," Amara said.

They followed the dog along a new path. It was marked by a sign: BEWARE THE BRASS.

"Danger?" Amara asked the dog.

A hesitation, then two barks.

"Not exactly," Amara translated.

"Then we had better risk it," Dolin said. "My sense indicates that the right thing is near, if we can understand it."

They resumed their walk. Soon they came to a triple fork, each way marked by a sign. BRASSICA BRASSERIE BRASSIERE.

"Which one?" Amara asked Tata.

The dog sniffed all three paths, woofing approvingly. It seemed they needed to take them all.

"All?" Mera asked blankly.

"But we shouldn't split up our party," Emerald protested. "Someone could get lost."

"Woof," Tata agreed.

"Let's try the left one first, as a group," Tartan said. "Then the second, and the third."

"Woof."

They followed the first. This led to a vegetable garden where there were assorted cabbages, kale, broccoli, lovely cauli-flowers, turnips turning in place, and jars of mustard. That was all.

"All from the mustard family," Tara said. "As adapted for Xanthly puns."

"Well, we won't have to go hungry," Emerald remarked. "But I confess I prefer pie plants."

Tata barked negation.

"These are not for us to eat," Dolin said. "They are wholesome, but it seems for someone else."

"It must be a private garden," Tartan said. "But who would want to grow turnips or broccoli?"

"When I was a child," Mera said, "I had a spinning toy made from a turnip."

Well, that was one reason.

They walked back to the fork, and took the middle path. This led to a quaint tavern where assorted drinks were on the main counter, available for the taking. They were even labeled: BEER, ALE, PORTER, STOUT, GIN, WINE, WHISKEY, and so on.

"All alcoholic," Emerald noted with a certain faint aversion that Mera's expression echoed.

"Well, now," Tartan said. "I could use a refreshing drink."

"No," Dolin said as Tata barked twice.

"What, poison?" Tartan asked.

Two barks.

"It would be wrong for us to drink them," Dolin said. "They are not harmful in themselves, but we must let them be."

"So why were we led to them?" Tartan demanded. "Is some power teasing us?"

"I do not think so. The right course for us, it seems, is merely to know about them."

So, with more reluctance than they had shown at the vegetable garden, they followed the path back to the fork.

The third one got a good deal more interesting. Mostly bare young women were running around a glade, pausing at a pond to view their own reflections. They were all quite shapely, especially when they posed, as they frequently did.

"What have we here?" Dolin asked, interested.

"Nymphs," Emerald said. "They exist in the present too. We dragons have flown over them many times. They play endlessly with their male companions, the fauns, and constantly celebrate in their fashion."

"How's that?" Tara asked.

"They summon the stork. But it doesn't take. That's how they celebrate. The storks completely ignore them. Next day they have no memory of their past. They live endlessly in their happy present tense."

"What possible business would we have with beautiful near-mindless creatures whose only interest is storks?" Tara asked.

"Well," Tartan began, licking his lips.

"No one asked you!"

Tartan shut up.

"They're all wearing bras," Amara said.

"Well, there's a clothing tree with widely spreading bra-anches," Emerald said. "So they're harvesting the bras and playing with them. It must be a new diversion for them, since they really don't need the support."

"They don't," Dolin agreed.

"Which is why this glade is called brassiere," Amara said. "Fortunately there's no pantree here, so they're not freaking any idiots out with panties. The question is, how does any of this relate to us? This isn't getting our tower constructed."

"We can ask," Tartan said.

"Must we?" Tara asked.

"Woof."

"It seems we must," Emerald said. Then, before Dolin could volunteer, "I'll do it." She stepped forward and approached the nearest nymph. "Hello. I'm Emerald Dragon. Will you talk with me a moment?"

"Hello," the nymph replied. "I'm Olga." Indeed, the name was written on her bra. "You're pretty."

"Thank you. We are looking for planks to build a tower. Do you know where any are?"

"Yes. We each have a plank. It makes for a good constitution."

Emerald made half a pause, evidently digesting the pun. "We would like to borrow several planks. Can we do that?"

"Sure, if you do something for us first."

"Uh-oh," Mera murmured.

Emerald was cautious. "I didn't know that nymphs bargained."

"We found this bra tree," the nymph explained. "Now that we have a bit of clothing, we have a bit of wit."

"What do you want us to do for you?"

"We're hungry and thirsty, but we can't get into the garden or the tavern. Both require clothing, more than just bras. Bring us each a vegetable or drink, and we'll bring our planks."

Emerald glanced back at the others, who nodded. It was doable, and it made sudden sense of their recent discoveries. "Agreed. We'll fetch the things while you fetch your planks."

"Wonderful!" Olga turned her head and called out to the others. "Ambrielle! Lilyette! Vanity! Victoria! Bali! Fetch your planks! We have a deal."

"Oooo!" the other nymphs chorused, and ran fleetly into the forest.

Except for one, who hesitated.

"Yes, you can keep your secret, Victoria," Olga called.

"Oooo!" the nymph exclaimed, and ran after the others.

"Get those vegetables and drinks," Emerald said. "While they remember the deal." She snapped her fingers. "You too, men."

Oh. Dolin and Tartan snapped out of the freak the running nymphs had put them in and got moving.

"They'd be real terrors in panties," Mera said, amused. Tata woofed agreement. Tartan privately noted that the dogfish seemed especially interested in Mera, maybe because she was the newest member of the party. When he wasn't with Amara, he was with Mera. Maybe she liked animals, and he picked up on it.

They hurried to garden and tavern, fetching vegetables and drinks. In three moments they returned to the glade, where the nymphs were arriving with their planks. The vegetables and drinks were handed out, and the nymphs eagerly consumed them. Then they followed the party to the obelisk.

Olga eyed the piled planks. "How are you going to fasten them together to make your tower?"

Oops. "We hadn't thought of that," Emerald said.

"Maybe we can help, if you get us more goodies."

There was a brief discussion. Then the party returned to garden and tavern for more refreshments. When they returned, the nymphs had constructed the tower. It seemed they had more abilities than their reputation suggested.

Tartan blinked. The nymphs were now bare breasted. They had used their bra straps to tie the planks together.

There was another round of feasting and drinking. "It's a (hic!) good thing we built this first," Ambrielle said as she finished her drink. "We wouldn't be able to do it now."

"You did a good job," Emerald assured them all. "Soon we'll be on our way. Then you can have your bras back, and your planks. We sincerely thank you for your effort."

"Thath's all righst," Olga said slurrily. "You're nice fholk. Wissh we could do more for you."

Dolin opened his mouth, but Emerald's glance shut it for him. "We'll mount the tower, and I think disappear. Then it's all yours."

"Oshkay," Bali said.

Amara climbed the tower and set herself next to the Year 2117. That was, as it turned out, only about half way up. There was evidently a lot of future to go after their time. Emerald followed, standing below her and taking hold of her ankle. Then Mera, Tara, Dolin, Tartan, with his hand on Tata's back. The two men at the bottom were exerting maximum willpower not to look up. They were ready.

Amara touched the date.

Things changed.

Chapter 10

PTERO

"Well, now," Tartan said. "There's Caprice Castle waiting for us. That's what I call efficient service."

"I shall be glad to meet my half sister Dawn again," Dolin said. "I like her very well."

"But are we free of the Land of Waz?" Emerald asked. "I don't want to be the vicious Lizard again."

Tara smiled. "Amara, what's your name?"

"Not Doorthy," Amara said.

"Doorthy?" Mera asked.

"We were caught in an idiotic parody crafted by the Ghost Writer," Tara explained. "We all had stupid roles to play. Worse, the Ghost Writer wanted the Goddess to manifest in Amara's host body and cater to his illicit passion. You freed us from that by sending us to the past."

"I am glad I came through," Mera said. "I don't remember, as that was my later self."

Tara paused. "Can you be here, if she's here?"

"Yes. She is of what we call Reality Number Two, visiting Reality Number One, using a local host. The same way you and Tartan are visiting from Mundania. I am now here physically. I could not go physically to Reality Number Two, as I am physically already there. There is no conflict."

"That's good," Tara said, looking as if her understanding was incomplete. "Maybe you can meet your alternate self and compare notes."

"Perhaps," Mera agreed. "It could be quite interesting."

"But why is Caprice Castle here?" Tartan asked. "It must somehow have known we would be here, and come for us."

"Princess Dawn must want to verify that we are safely back," Tara said.

"Wait," Tartan said. "There is room physically for only one particular person at a time? That is, none of us could be in any Reality if we were already there as natives?"

"Yes. Fortunately it's not a problem in Reality Number One, because all of you are native or have native hosts. And you, returning there, are yourselves, with no conflict, unlike my situation in Reality Number Two."

"Okay, no problem," Tartan said, relieved though he was not completely clear on the clarification.

They walked the short distance to the castle main door, and Dolin knocked. After a generous moment it opened. An unfamiliar man stood there.

"We may have a problem," Tara murmured.

"I doubt I know you," the man said to Dolin. "But I think I like you." He glanced beyond to the others. "And I really like the lovely ladies. Do come in."

"We thought to see Princess Dawn here," Dolin said.

"Who?"

"The proprietress of Caprice Castle. Didn't she bring the castle here to intercept us?"

"There is no Princess Dawn here, nor has there ever been, worthy as she may be," the man said. "I am Prince Drew, the proprietor of Caprice Castle."

The group exchanged a furtive look. "We *really* have a problem," Tara said.

"Oh, no," Mera said. "We're in another reality!"

"Please," the man said. "I see there is a confusion of some sort, and it must be that Caprice brought me here to help abate it. Come in and sit down, and there will be refreshments as we get to know each other. Perhaps the problem will turn out to be minor."

Tartan seriously doubted that, but didn't argue. Neither did any of the others. They filed into the castle and settled in its main chamber. Punwheel cookies and boot rear drinks appeared by every place.

"First, the introductions," Dolin said. "I am Prince Dolin, son of Prince Dolph and Princess Taplin. My talent is doing the right thing, and it indicates that we were right to come here to Caprice Castle, though it was not our intent."

"I knew you looked somehow familiar," Drew said. "I am the son of Prince Dolph and Princess Nada Naga. My talent is Sensate Focus. We must be half brothers. Though I admit my father never spoke of having relations with any woman other than my mother."

"Uh-oh," Tara said.

"I don't like the sound of that," Tartan said. "What is it?"

"Monica is gone, or at least threatened. I don't understand how, but there's mischief."

"Your host can't be gone. She's still here."

"In a manner."

"She's Nada Naga's daughter!" Tartan said. "By Demon Prince Vore. Not by Prince Dolph."

"Yes. So now she's a spirit too, like you."

"Yes. She's severely shaken."

"Definitely a new reality," Mera said. "After I tried so hard to avoid any such complication."

"A new reality?" Drew asked.

"I am from a reality where Prince Dolph married the sleeping beauty Taplin," Dolin said. "And the proprietress of this castle, in her reality, is Princess Dawn, daughter of Prince Dolph and the maiden Electra."

"Fascinating. How many realities are there?"

"That's indeterminate," Mera said. "I am Princess Merara, daughter of the Magician Merlin and the Sorceress Tapis. My talent is to shift realities. I presume they already exist, and that I become aware of them when I engage a new one. I now know of three. We were trying to remain in what we call Reality Number One. Apparently I messed up, and we came here."

"This would be a dangerously potent talent," Drew said. "I appreciate your frustration. If it is not unbecomingly personal, may I inquire as to how you think it might have happened?"

"I don't know," Mera said, little coils of frustration hovering near her head. "I tried to be careful."

"Please, I am not blaming you, Princess. I am familiar with the manner the exercise of one's talent can have unanticipated consequences, having run afoul of that myself on occasion. It is in my mind that I may indeed be able to help you, and that is why Caprice Castle brought me here to meet you. Suppose we complete the introductions, and then I will clarify my notion."

Drew certainly came across like a prince. Tartan introduced himself and his origin. Then Tara, Emerald, and Amara.

"Woof!"

"And Tata Dogfish," Amara said with a smile.

Drew looked closely at Tata. "This is a good deal more than a dog," he said.

"More?" Amara asked. "How so?"

"I do not wish to bore you with the detail of my talent, but it is relevant in this instance. Sensate Focus is a talent of observation and projection. I can focus microscopically so as to perceive the finest detail of any object, or telescopically to study the farthest stars. I can detect and follow scents, or become immune to stench. I can hear a pin drop, or withstand deafening noise. I can develop an exquisite sense of balance, or be immune to motion sickness. I can see through the crevices in fabrics to a person's flesh, but also can be immune to freakout by panties or nakedness. I can also project sensuality so that my mere touch on a woman's wrist sends her into a daze. I realize you may find this hard to believe."

"I do find it hard to believe," Mera said. "Touch my wrist."

"As you wish." Drew reached out and touched her wrist.

Mera went into a daze. A faint cloud of vapor surrounded her, making her outlines foggy. A generous moment later it dissipated, and she returned to full focus. "I believe you," she said faintly.

"When I look at Tata, I see not only his flesh, but his aura. He is host to a Sorceress, who has been observing and hearing anything he sees and hears. Similarly the way I see your auras, Tartan and Tara, and your dragon essence, Emerald, and the Goddess you host, Amara. And of course yours, Prince Dolin, centered on that magic ring."

"A Sorceress!" Dolin exclaimed. "We did not know of this."

"Perhaps she will identify herself and explain," Drew said. He got up and fetched a magic mirror, holding it before him so that the others could all see it. "Sorceress, if you care to, you may animate this mirror so that you can show yourself and talk with us directly. We are curious as to your purpose here."

The mirror brightened. An image formed. It was a beautiful woman.

"Princess Eve!" Dolin exclaimed. "My half sister."

"Yes, brother," Eve replied from the mirror. "I am glad that you now understand more of yourself, so that I need no longer keep the secret." She looked around. "I am Princess Eve, twin sister of Princess Dawn, married to the Demon Pluto, and the mistress of the realm of Hades. My talent is to know anything about any inanimate object I touch, just as Dawn's is to know about any living thing she touches. Dawn and I were concerned for Prince Dolin, not wanting to lose him so soon after discovering him. So when I found opportunity I borrowed a spell from a minion of Hades and joined the party, lending my talent to the dogfish when it was helpful to you. That way I knew that the group of you was safe."

"That's why Tata was able to sniff out the correct paths!" Amara said. "And to know things we needed to know."

"That is why," Eve agreed. "But I confess I am as mystified as you why you failed to return to the correct reality. Mera was careful not to use her talent again, so you should not have changed realities."

"That I hope to fathom and explain," Drew said. "I have a certain facility with explanations, once I know the facts. Please, Princess Merara, detail your history with this group."

"Call me Mera, Prince." She seemed to remain a trace dazed by his demonstration of his talent.

"Please, Mera."

"Well, actually I can't speak for my future self, because—" She broke off, a puzzled look crossing her face. "Oh, my!"

"There is a spirit hovering near you," Drew said.

"It is—me," Mera said, surprised. "The original me from the other reality. She was watching the group, but couldn't track it into the past, but now that we're back in the future, I mean the present, she just found me. Oh, this is amazing!"

"Tell us," Emerald said.

"I will—I will let her speak directly. I will be her host."

"Hello Aunt Mera!" Dolin said.

"Hello, nephew. I'm so glad you're well. It was the ring I tracked. Its magic signals your location. Now let me see." She considered a generous moment, then summarized for Drew how Dolin was killed by the Sea Hag and the ring imbued with his young soul.

"The Sea Hag," Drew said. "We know of her. We do not like her."

"No one does," Amara said, grimacing. "For good reason."

"Then when the time seemed propitious," Mera continued, "I took the ring to the Good Magician. He recognized me immediately, though I am not natural to that reality. He agreed that Dolin deserved to live. Of course he required a Service for his assistance, and I agreed to exercise my talent on his behalf at such time as he required it. That performance is on account, as it were. Then he arranged for one of his wives to take the ring and switch places with herself in the adjacent reality, thus transferring the ring to that reality. He also provided a host for my spirit to animate in that reality so that I could visit it without vacating Dolin's reality. I needed to retain my physical presence there so I could later report to my sister Taplin on the success or failure of our mission. If I crossed over physically, I would lose that presence and might not be able to return without complicating the situation. As I was, I could simply revert my spirit to my body when the time came." She paused to look around. "Is this relevant? Am I boring you?"

"You're not boring us," Emerald said. "Your participation is more complicated than we knew."

"I believe it is relevant," Drew said. "Please continue."

"The Good Magician also provided a host for Dolin," Mera continued. "I used it to put on the Ring, animating my nephew, but also followed the group he joined with mirrors and my spirit, as I explained to the rest of you. Meanwhile the Good Magician had another visitor, the Magician of Time. He had not found what he wanted in his own reality, so wished to go to another in the hope of better fortune."

"What was he looking for?" Tara asked.

Mera smiled. "Women. He wanted to find a Sorceress to marry, but the ones in that reality were taken. He was interested in me, but I demurred."

"And you traded your talent for his," Drew said. "He gave you a time bomb in exchange for your putting him into another reality."

Mera looked sharply at him. "How do you know that?"

"Because this is where he came to. He is now a guest in Caprice Castle. He told me all about how he got here."

"Oh, my," Mera said.

"And I think I have the answer," Drew continued. "You said you tried to avoid using your talent, so as not to change realities, but you did use it: to help him change."

"I did," she agreed. "But that was him, not me."

"Your talent affects you too, when you use it. Maybe not always directly. In this case it left you in the same reality, but when the party traveled to the past, via that Time Bomb your talent had traded for, and returned to the present, it came to the reality it had touched before. This one."

"Oh! It must have."

"So Prince Dolin and his party came here," Drew concluded. "And your problem is how to return to the one your party started from."

"That's it," Dolin agreed.

"And that is where I may be able to help. Not directly, but I do have contacts."

"Contacts?"

"Princess Ida. She surely exists in your reality, because I think she exists in every reality."

"She does," Amara said. "But her talent is the idea, not traveling between realities."

"Maybe not directly. But indirectly it may be possible."

"We do not understand," Tartan said.

"The world Ptero revolves around her head," Drew said. "On it or its subsidiary moons exists every person who lives in Xanth, or ever did live, or ever might live. We can go consult with our alternates, in case any of them know the answer."

"Oh, that's right," Mera said. "I used it to go from Reality Number Two to Reality Number One. It can be used as a way station."

Tartan did not want to admit how confusing he found this, so he shut up.

"That just might work," Amara said. "But just as coming here from Ptero can be complicated, so going there may not be easy."

"Visits can be accomplished in spirit," Drew said. "That should be easy for those of you who are already riding hosts in spirit form." He drew a breath. "But first I believe you should meet Bernard."

"Who?" Tara asked.

"The Magician of Time. He should be interested, since he was involved in this complication, however inadvertently." He snapped his fingers. "Caprice, if you would be so kind, please notify Bernard that we have company he may find interesting."

There was a musical note. Then a man appeared. He was nondescript, but Tartan could tell immediately he was a Magician. There was something about him.

"This is Bernard, the Magician of Time," Drew said. "Bernard, you should remember Mera."

The man looked perplexed. "I do not see her here."

The form of Mera in Reality Number One manifested. "Here."

"I do recognize you now," Bernard said, surprised. "But I'm a bit confused. Are you the original, or a duplicate in this reality?"

"Both," she said. "My spirit has joined the host body of my other self, who came physically here. This is her real appearance." Mera reverted to herself, significantly lovelier than the other host. "It seems that when I exchanged favors with you, it affected the group I was trying to help. It's complicated."

"I'm sure. I have to beware of paradox when I practice my art, and I don't always see it coming."

"That's it, inexactly," she agreed.

Other introductions followed, including Tata Dog, but there were no further references to Princess Eve or the Goddess Isis, both of whom preferred to retreat into the background for now. Then Drew said "We shall go to Castle Roogna to see the Princess Ida, and thence to the world of Ptero. Are you interested?"

"Actually I am, because my life partner is surely there." Bernard glanced around. "Unless one of you ladies—"

"No," Tara said quickly. "None of us want to remain here. We want to return to our own reality. Especially my host. Desperately."

"As I do not," Bernard said. "So Ptero it is."

"Also, not all of us are princesses or Sorceresses," Amara said.

"Actually, I am reconsidering that," Bernard said. "I am a Magician; I don't need to have another of that caliber in the family. I would settle for the right girl, regardless of her station."

"Good choice," Emerald said. "Princesses can have other qualities you might not appreciate."

Drew picked up the magic mirror. "Princess Ida," he said.

The glass flickered. Then the face of an older woman appeared. "Yes, Drew."

"We have an unusual situation. I am entertaining visitors from other realities, some of whom wish to return to their own. We feel that contact with some folk on Ptero may be beneficial."

Ida laughed. "Unusual? You severely understate the case, Drew, as usual."

"Guilty," he said, smiling. "May I bring them to you?"

"No."

"No?" he asked, surprised. "Is the occasion inconvenient?"

"Not at all. It's that Hilarion and I are traveling, returning to his kingdom for a while. So we will pause at Caprice, if the castle cares to pick us up."

"Immediately," Drew said.

Ida laughed. "Which is literal, of course. Caprice just appeared before our carriage."

"The door is open. Come in."

"So it is. Thank you."

"Ida married Prince Hilarion in this frame," Drew explained to the others.

"In ours too," Amara said. "I suspect she is in all the realities, and maybe he is also."

"I believe I am," Princess Ida said from the doorway. "Otherwise it would be difficult to relate to the myriad alternatives."

They all jumped to their feet, embarrassed. There stood the princess, with a tiny moon orbiting her head. There was no possible doubt of her identity. "We did not see you coming, Aunt Ida," Dolin said apologetically.

"Nor did you need to, Dolin," she said.

Drew was surprised. "You know him?"

"Of course I know him. He's right next door, in the adjacent reality. You're half brothers. But of course you wouldn't know that, Drew."

"I know it now," Drew said wryly. "But you never mentioned him before."

"Certainly I didn't. The concept of alternate realities just confuses most folk who are limited to one." She turned to her husband, a handsome older prince. "Why don't you go take a nap, dear, while I see to these needful folk? There's no need to bore you."

Hilarion nodded and went to a spare couch. He lay down and was promptly asleep. Evidently he was used to her activities.

"She's also your aunt?" Mera asked Dolin during the pause.

"Oh, yes. She's my father's sister."

"I thought that was King Ivy," Emerald said.

"I am Ivy's twin sister," Ida said. "Dolph is our little brother."

"Oh." Now Emerald was embarrassed. "I'm from the dragon realm, and know only a very general outline of your royal family."

"Nor do you need to, Emerald," she said, smiling.

"You know me?" Emerald asked, surprised.

"Of course I know you, dear. Human/Dragon relations are vital if we are to avert internecine warfare. I wish you every success in your quest."

"And do you know me?" Mera asked.

"Certainly, Mera. You and I will be working closely together in the future. Your talent of changing realities is invaluable when there's a mix-up." Ida glanced around. "As seems to be the case at the moment. There seem to be folk from three realities here."

"We need to return to the reality where the Princesses Dawn and Eve exist," Dolin said. "Without complicating things further. We thought maybe someone on Ptero would be able to help us."

"Certainly. That person would be my alternate self on that world. You will recognize her by the world of Pyramid orbiting her head. She will be able to direct you to the people you need to see."

Mera eyed the ball orbiting Ida's own head. "That's a—a world?"

"Oh, I'm sorry, I forgot you are from the distant past, and are not familiar with more recent discoveries. Let me explain, briefly. Ptero, here, may seem small, but it is actually a full world rendered seemingly tiny by the magic of perspective. You will visit it spiritually, with only your souls going there while your bodies remain as anchors here."

"Ah," Mera said. "The way I left my body in one reality while my spirit visited another, so that I could return when the time came."

"Exactly, dear. Also the way Tartan and Tara leave their hosts in Mundania while their spirits explore Xanth. They are parallel processes. Spiritual travel is much safer than physical travel, especially among realities, because returning is so much easier." Ida looked around. "Suppose we get to it now? It will take about an hour." She held up a hand to forestall any objection. "Time is different on Ptero. You may spend days there, but return here shortly after you departed. Drew has been there before; he will guide you. I will nap with my husband while we wait. Then when you return we will resume our separate journeys, missions accomplished."

A glance circled around. This did seem to be the expedient course.

They settled back in their chairs, and Princess Ida released a waft of some kind of incense. Tartan sniffed it, and felt his soul withdrawing from his host's body. "But I'm coming too," Demon Ted said. "I wouldn't miss this for all the worlds."

Tartan saw that the other members of their party were similarly unconscious, at least physically, while their spirits pulled out and floated above their bodies. Both Amara and Isis emerged, Tara and DeMonica, Dolin and his anonymous host, Tata Dogfish and Princess Eve, Emerald, Drew, and Bernard. A party of approximately thirteen.

Drew, who had prior experience, beckoned the others, and they floated toward him. They linked hands and paws, forming a circle. Then they flew toward Princess Ida's orbiting moon, which grew strangely larger as they approached it. By the time they reached it, it was the size of a planet. Then they drifted down toward its surface. Tartan saw that there were mottled patches separated by thin membranes. To the north the planet was deepening blue, and to the south it was red. The western side was green, and the eastern side was yellow. It did not seem to be rotating, or if it was, they were rotating with it.

They descended to a large field and landed on firm sand. They might be traveling in spirit, but they seemed perfectly solid here. The world of Ptero also seemed to be full planet sized, with the same gravity they were used to.

"Oh, it's good to be real again!" Monica said. "Even if only here on the world of imagination."

Only then did Drew release the hands of those he held. "We are here in the designated landing field for visitors," he said. "Princess Ida's abode is to the north; she is currently in her winter residence. We should soon find her. But there are cautions."

"Cautions?" Tartan asked warily.

"Time is not as it is in Xanth. To the west is the future; to the east is the past. We will age as we go west, and youthen as we go east. It therefore behooves us to remain close to the proper path."

"Wait," Tara said. "How far does this go? I mean if we go west, how old will we get?"

"That is different for every person. We can go no farther than our natural lifespan on Xanth. Beyond that we seem to be at a wall, looking beyond but unable to go there. Similarly, we can go no farther east than our age, first becoming children, then babies. The older ones among us can proceed farther."

"I am eighteen," Mera said. "But I date from almost nine hundred years ago. Which age counts?"

"The older one. That may be useful, should we have to veer east; you could carry the babies."

"What, a dozen babies?"

"Maybe you could use a wagon," Tara said, laughing.

Mera didn't laugh. "Let's stay on the straight and narrow."

They walked north, and the landscape soon started turning bluish and the air cooled noticeably. "We'll need warmer clothing," Drew said. "There are clothes horses in a nearby pasture."

They went to the pasture. The horses wore all manner of clothing. In fact it became apparent that they were entirely made of clothing. "But won't taking their clothing cripple or kill the horses?" Tara asked.

"No," Drew assured them. "They will rapidly grow it back. In fact they like being useful."

So it seemed. The horses crowded to the fence, whinnying eagerly.

"Still, we'll have to trade for what we take," Drew said. "There are sugar maples, canes, and beets out of their range."

They went to the plants and harvested pocketfuls of sugar cubes. The fair trade seemed to be one cube for one item of clothing. In Mundania this would not have been a fair exchange, but Tartan realized that this was not Mundania.

Tartan harvested a warm jacket and boots, and the others got similar clothing. Soon their pockets were empty, but they were well dressed for cold weather. The horses seemed to be well satisfied.

They resumed their trek north. "Uh-oh," Drew said as he peered ahead.

Tartan did not like the sound of that. But looking north, he saw dark turbulence in the sky. It was a storm, and seemed to be shaping rapidly into a bad one. Still, could they duck their heads and plow on through the snow flurries?

Then several sticks flew through the air and struck the ground ahead of them. Tartan went to pick one up. It was a cane.

"Oh, no," Tara groaned. "It's a hurry-cane."

"Puns exist on Ptero too," Drew said. "In fact they are more persistent here than on Xanth. Fortunately they are mostly confined to the comic strips."

"Comic strips?" Isis asked.

Drew looked at her, and took a breath. Tartan knew why: the man was really seeing her in her natural beauty for the first time, no longer masked by her host. Stunning hardly described her. Even fully clothed in winter gear she put men at the verge of freaking out. In fact Dolin's host, now a person in his own right, had already freaked out. "Uh—"

She produced a pair of dark glasses she must have harvested from one of the horses. "Put on these snow glasses so that the brightness doesn't blind you." She set another pair on the face of Dolin's host, and snapped her fingers to bring him out of it.

Drew took the glasses, which surely cut down her image to little more than a dark shadow. "Thank you. I can explain about the comic strips. They—"

"I know about them," Isis said. "In fact I live in them. I can handle them."

"Are you sure? They can rot minds."

"I am sure."

"Very well. The storm to our north must have overlapped a comic strip and ripped out some of the puns. Regardless, there is a good deal of physical force there, and we should not risk it. We must veer to the side to get around it. That means—"

"That they risk becoming either too old or too young to function effectively," Bernard said. "Fortunately that is my domain. I can immunize them from the ravages of time."

"Ah, yes, I forgot about that," Drew said. "That will be very helpful."

"Gather around me, folks," Bernard said. "I will detonate a time stasis bomb that will lock you into your present ages, regardless where we travel."

They gathered around him, except for Isis. "I am four thousand years old," she said. "I am already essentially timeless."

"You impress me, Goddess," Bernard said. "You do indeed seem timeless. I wonder—"

"No. I have other business."

Tartan kept silent. Isis might be timeless, but that was not the quality that impressed men. She was obviously used to their reactions, and not much interested.

They walked to the east, skirting the storm. The land turned yellow, and they could see trees and buildings getting younger, but they were not affected. Soon they came to the border of a comic strip.

"I don't think the storm actually crosses the strip," Drew said. "So if we can get through that, then we can proceed north and in due course return to our original route, north of the storm."

"Now it is my turn," Isis said. "Stay close to me and do what I say, even if at times it seems odd or outright crazy. Remember, most of the puns are sight gags made up of illusion, not actually dangerous in themselves. The danger is in getting lost in them, totally confused, so that you can't find your way out of the comic strip. I do know the way out, and here on Ptero I can use it, as I can't on Xanth proper because this is only my spirit, not my actual body. Trust me."

"We do," Amara said. Then to the others: "I have come to know the Goddess well, as we have been traveling together. She is many things, but she is not a liar. She can and will do what she says."

"I believe it," Drew said. "I have observed her." And his observation was something no other person could match.

Isis stepped across the comic strip border, and the others followed close behind. It was some behind, Tartan noted, even through the heavy winter coat. Then Tara slapped his arm warningly, and he focused on their surroundings. He suspected that Tara wasn't really jealous, but was protecting him from making a fool of himself before the others. But he wasn't quite sure.

"Why hello, visitors," an older woman said, spying them. "Uncle, see who we have here!"

Tartan looked. It wasn't a woman, but a small island. Two islands, with pie plants, lollipops, and tea trees on one, and a beerbarrel tree on the other, catering to female and male tastes. It might be nice to rest on those.

"Forget it," Isis snapped. The islands faded back, their feelings clearly hurt.

"Why did you rebuff them?" Tara asked the Goddess. "They didn't mean any harm."

"Those were Auntigua and Uncletigua," Isis said. "Abysmal puns there to distract us at the outset. Get on one of them, and it might be days before you think to move on."

Oh.

"You reject our offerings?" a librarian demanded. "I'll throw the book at you!" He hurled a hefty book so hard it caught fire.

"Dodge it!" Isis cried.

They managed to avoid the flying tome. It crashed through the foliage beyond them and set it afire. Oh, again.

"That's a representative of the censor ship," Isis explained. "They cruise around and use books as weapons rather than education or entertainment. They prefer to burn them."

"But that doesn't make much sense," Tara protested. "If they don't like books they should just leave them alone, not destroy them."

"This is the comic strip," the Goddess reminded her.

Oh, yet again.

They came to a river that was too broad to jump across and surely not safe to wade through. But there was a ferry boat. "I'll take you," the captain called.

"You will not, Harper," Isis snapped, and the boat and river faded out. "He's not a man," the Goddess explained. "He's a malign fairy."

"Harper's fairy," Tartan said with a groan.

"And that water was filled with aqua tics that would have sucked out your fluids."

"Oh?" Bernard asked. "Then what would that linguis tic I see to the side do?"

"It would suck out your language."

Tartan was concluding that they were lucky to have the Goddess along. Some of these puns were dangerous.

They passed through a section with small men wielding little sticks. "Ignore them," Isis said. "Those are only chap sticks."

"Is there much more of this to endure?" Tara asked.

"Not a lot," Isis said. "Avoid those creatures."

They drew back in time to let two disreputable things converge and collide with each other. They exploded into a sickeningly brown stench.

"Diar and Rhea," Isis said.

"Best avoided," Tartan agreed.

Now a sweet melody sounded. It came from a tiny hovering bird. "But the humming bird is safe," Isis said. "And we are at the far border." Then she paused, looking out. "Bleep."

"Bleep?" Amara asked nervously.

"Now I see that the storm does cross the comic strip. We shall simply have to wait to let it pass."

"In here?" Emerald asked with a quaver.

"I see a comfortable spot." The Goddess forged toward a factory building. "This is a fact-ory. It manufactures satis-faction."

Indeed, the closer they got to it, the more satisfied they were. Now the comic strip did not seem bad at all.

"However, we will not remain here any longer than necessary," Isis said. "Lest we become too satisfied to continue our mission."

"I'm glad we have you as a guide," Tartan said.

"You may appreciate why I want to get out of the comic strip," the Goddess said. "I have learned its nuances, but it can become wearing."

"Why are you confined?" Bernard asked.

"To prevent me from conquering Xanth and becoming its queen."

"Which I suspect King Ivy would not appreciate," Bernard said. "Nor the heir apparent, Princess Harmony."

"This is the nature of royalty. Not everyone who wants to rule can be accommodated."

They waited comfortably. Tartan found it odd seeing Dolin sitting alongside his host, but of course he himself was sitting alongside *his* host, Ted, and the same was true for Tara and Monica.

Isis glanced at the nearby border. "Ah, I believe the storm has retreated somewhat. Now we can skirt it and resume our trek."

"No hurry," Tartan said, and several others agreed.

She sent him a piercing look that made him wince. "You are already succumbing to the satis. Rise and follow me."

Reluctantly they followed her on out of the strip. The moment they cleared it, their satisfaction fell away. "What were we thinking of?" Tara asked rhetorically. "We never wanted to leave."

"Exactly," Drew said. "It is possible to get lost emotionally as well as physically. The Goddess has served us well." He glanced at Isis. "I wonder—"

"No."

He shrugged and walked on. Men, Tartan noted, tended to be slow to get the message when loveliness like that of the Goddess was near.

They could see the turbulent edge of the storm to the west. They stayed clear of it, and in due course rejoined their original path going north. It was increasingly cold and covered with blue snow, but they were dressed for it and glad to be back on track.

"And there at last is Princess Ida's winter abode," Drew said. "We have arrived."

"That's a relief," Tara said. "I hope it's downhill from here."

But Tartan feared it would not be.

Chapter 11

CONCLAVE

Princess Ida was vigorously shoveling blue snow out of her walk. She was thoroughly bundled, but there was no mistaking the moon orbiting her head, Pyramid, four triangular sides, blue red, green, and gray. "Why hello, all," she said, and it was plain that she recognized them all. "I had a feeling I would have company today, and Prince Hilarion isn't much for winter sport, so I was clearing the way."

And since her talent was the idea, and what she believed was true inevitably became true, she did have company. It was also possible that she had personal communication with herself on the ground level and the chain of moon level realities; that would surely help her in maintaining the connections between worlds. "We need to meet with our assorted relatives in other realities," Drew said. "Some of us need to cross realities, without disturbing the general order unduly. And some are looking for suitable life partners, myself included, as you know."

"Then you will want the sauna."

"The sauna, Aunt? We did not come for relaxation."

"I know that, dear. Go there and strip down, and I'll round up the others for you. I'm sure it will all work out." Ida returned to her shoveling.

Tartan knew, again, from what he had been told, that if Ida was sure, it was so. That was after all her magic. He chided himself for not quite fully believing.

Drew led them across the snow to a tiny igloo big enough for about one and a half people. "Follow me," he said, and dived into its small entrance hole.

"But there's no room," Tara protested.

"There is room," Monica assured her, and dived in herself.

Tara shrugged and followed her. Then Tartan did, expecting to encounter a total jam inside. But to his amazement, the interior was just large enough for the four of them. It was also quite warm. Drew had already stripped down to his briefs, and Monica to her bra and panties. Tartan was about to freak out, but then a waft of steam fuzzed her outline just enough in those regions to ease the problem. It was evidently a competent sauna.

Tara shrugged and did the same, as she would have sweltered to distraction otherwise. Steam fuzzed her key details too, without quite managing to obscure the fact that they were less pronounced than Monica's.

So Tartan stripped down too. It seemed that the Adult Conspiracy, or whatever it was, was protecting them from incidental mischief.

The others arrived, one by one, and with each one the sauna expanded just enough. It also showed no sign of melting, despite the heat. So it was magic, made to accommodate whatever number of people was needed. He should have known.

Soon they were all seated around a hot pool that burbled up in the center, enjoying the steam bath. Even the Goddess Isis, who probably could have walked through fire if she wanted to. Steam formed a thick blanket around her, but Tartan found that it still wasn't smart to look too closely, lest he freak anyway.

"The others should be along soon," Drew said. "I must say, you girls look fetching."

"You certainly do," Bernard agreed.

"What you boys need to find are girls who aren't on other business," Amara said. "Who are free to settle down with you in your own reality. You seem to be worthy men. We're just not the ones."

"We are looking," Drew said. "But so far luck has not been with us."

"It was the right thing for you to come here," Dolin said. "Aunt Ida said things would work out."

"So she did," Drew agreed. "But in what sense did she mean it? That you would find your proper reality, or that folk like Bernard and I would find our women?"

"I believe she meant it in all respects," Dolin said.

"That is very positive," Drew said. "But as with the Good Magician's Answers, some interpretation may be required."

Another person entered the igloo. "Princess Dawn!" Tartan exclaimed.

"I am so glad to see you, Dawn," Dolin said. "Now I know our relationship. You are my half sister."

"That's wonderful," Dawn said, stripping as she spoke. "The geis prevented me from telling you, but now that you know it for yourself, I am free to acknowledge it." She went to him and kissed him on the cheek. Then she took her place before the central pool. "Oh, this is delightful, after that snow!" She looked around. "Some of you I know. Some I don't. If you will touch hands with me, I will know."

Drew and Bernard reached across to touch her hand.

"Oh, my," she said. "Another brother, and the Magician of Time. I'm impressed."

Another person arrived. This was Princess Eve. Dawn quickly explained about them to the newcomers, and Eve smiled graciously. She too stripped down and sat before the pool. The steam had to struggle to mask the two of them.

The next person to arrive was D. Metria. "What's scrolling here?" she asked.

"Happening, Mother," Ted said before she could go into her routine. "We're having a conclave, and it seems you're invited."

"Oh, Woe Betide would love this. And Mentia. Do you mind if I—?"

"Go ahead," Tartan said.

She glanced at him. "Do you know me?"

"We met on the path to Caprice Castle," he said. "Tara and I were the ghosts."

"Oh, yes," she agreed. "The dull Mundanes."

"The same," Tara said with a smile.

Metria took a deep breath as her clothing dissipated, almost (but not quite) freaking out all the men except Drew. She burst into a ball of smoke, which then fragmented into two and a half sections, which in turn coalesced into Metria herself, a similar demoness with more oomph, and a child.

"Gee," the child exclaimed. "A pond!" She leaped into it, assuming the form of a cannonball, and splashed hot water over everyone.

"That is Woe Betide," Drew said. "Five years old and technically my aunt."

"She is not," the shapelier demoness said. "She is an aspect of your mother, as am I."

"Yes, Aunt Mentia," Drew agreed with resignation.

Mentia turned to the others. "The distinction between the three of us is that Metria has a vocabulary disability, I am a little crazy, and Woe Betide is a brat."

"I am not!" the child cried from the pool, splashing water in her direction. "You take that back, you freak!"

"Quiet, urchin, or I'll throw an Adult Word at you, you little nuisance."

"You wouldn't dare, you meanie!"

Mentia whispered something into her palm, then threw it at the child. Woe dodged to the side, and the word sailed on into the water, where it sizzled villianously before expiring.

"Missed me!" the child cried. "Nyaa nyaa nyaa!"

"Why don't you go out and play in the snow?" Drew suggested diplomatically to the child. "You can have a snowball fight."

"Say, yeah!" Woe exclaimed happily as she rose from the water. Then she paused in place. "But who can I hit?"

"My children Piton and Data will be out as soon as they get their jackets on," Dawn said. "They're your age, Woe. They'd love a snowball fight."

"And my son Plato," Eve said. "He's only a little older."

"Aww, his snowballs smell of dead things," Woe said.

"His governess Zosi Zombie is along to be sure he behaves," Eve said.

"Great!" Woe said, and zoomed out the doorway.

"As is our nanny Jody," Dawn said. "Her musical talent is great for distracting them when they get grumpy."

Eve glanced at her. "I thought Kelei was your nanny."

"She is, in Xanth proper. But here on Ptero we have access to folk from other realities, and Jody is marvelous as an alternate."

"Is any of this relevant to our conclave?" Drew asked. "I'm sure children and nannies are fine for those who have them, but not all of us do."

"Actually, this discussion is the right thing," Dolin said, surprised. "I am uncertain of its relevance, but the feeling is strong."

"Oh, my," Dawn said. "I just realized how relevant it is. I believe we should go out and watch the children have their fun."

Drew shook his head. "Glad as I am to meet you half sisters, I just can't believe that—"

He was interrupted by the entry of another man. "Father!" Dolin, Drew, Dawn, and Eve said almost together, amazed.

"Prince Dolph," Amara said. "The father of these four siblings, by three different wives, it seems."

"The wives are along," Dolph said. "You have to get out of the sauna. A snowshoe is coming."

Tartan glanced at Tara, confirming that she was as confused as he was. So they both stayed out of it.

"A snowshoe?" Bernard asked.

Now they heard a muffled thud. Something huge had struck the ground nearby.

"It's headed this way," Dolph said urgently. "It could hit the sauna."

There was another thud.

They decided to get out, despite not being dressed for it. They scrambled out of the doorway and stood in the deep blue snow. The children were nearby, four of them. So were Dolph's wives, three older women standing together. Tartan recognized Electra, and presumed the others were the Princess Taplin and Nada Naga. Apparently they got along, here on Ptero.

"Mother!" Dolin exclaimed, going to hug the middle woman.

"I'm so glad to see you making friends, dear," Taplin said.

"Yes, but it's complicated."

There was not time for more, as there was another thud. All gazed at the approaching monster.

Which was an enormous shoe. It seemed to be made of packed blue snow, and was the size of a house. And it was moving, as if on the foot of an invisible giant. But there was only one of it, apparently tromping along by itself. Heading right for the igloo/sauna.

"Our clothing is still in there," Dawn exclaimed. "We have to stop it!"

The men exchanged a glance. They seemed to be less concerned about clothing, though faint traces of steam still fuzzed the ladies' key areas.

"I can send it back in time," Bernard said.

"I could turn dragon and toast it," Emerald said.

"Don't do that," Princess Ida said. "The snowshoe is merely going from A to B." Indeed, now Tartan saw a big letter A near the horizon where the shoe might have started, and the letter B in the other direction where it was going. "We don't want to harm it, merely to divert it."

"Let me try," a young woman said.

"By all means, Jody," Ida said. "Drew, perhaps you can help her."

"Yes, Aunt," Drew said, not seeming to understand her suggestion but willing to go along. He went to join the girl, who saw him and smiled with a sudden flash of prettiness.

The shoe landed one giant step closer to the igloo, actually not far from where the people stood. Jody and Drew went out to intercept it.

"Jody is a distant descendant of Jordan Barbarian and Threnody," Ida explained as the others watched. "Her talent is healing music. That is, it makes people feel so much better they want to dance."

Jody came close to the snowshoe and began to sing. Her song was so cheerful that Tartan felt his feet lifting in the beginning of a dance. He saw Drew, closer to her, dancing more vigorously. And then the shoe danced too. It lifted and set down in the same place, thunderously tapping the ground. Then it jumped to the side and tapped there. It continued, traveling sideways, until it was no longer heading toward the igloo.

Jody stopped singing, allowing all of them to relax. The snowshoe resumed its forward motion, missing the igloo and going on toward the horizon.

"That was beautiful!" Drew said. "You diverted the menace without harming it."

"Thank you," Jody said shyly.

"I don't believe we have met before," Drew said. "Are you here on business?"

"I babysit Princess Dawn's children, here on Ptero."

"Oh, that's right; she mentioned it. Are you from her reality?"

"No." She hesitated. "I'm from yours. But you don't have any children to babysit."

"That's because I don't have a wife. I am here to look for one." Then he did a double take. "And Princess Ida suggested that I meet you. I am impressed by your talent. Are you by any chance—?"

Jody blushed.

"Of course she's available, you ninny," Ida said. "Kiss her and be done with it."

Drew hardly even thought about it. He took Jody into his arms and kissed her. Little hearts flew out.

"I see we're going to have to get a new baby sitter," Dawn said. "She'll be tending to her own children soon enough."

"Congratulations," Bernard said. Then, to Ida: "I don't suppose you lined up one for me too?"

"There was no need," Ida said. "She's been under your nose all along."

"Under my nose?"

"Kelei!" Ida called.

Another pretty young woman appeared. "Yes, Princess Ida?"

"Bernard is about to take notice of you."

"Oh." Kelei blushed furiously.

"She's had a crush on you forever," Dawn said. "But you never noticed. Then you left our reality. That wasn't nice."

"I—"

"Show him your talent, dear," Ida said.

The snowscape ahead of them became a scintillating pattern of light and colors, utterly lovely and compelling.

"She diverts the children," Dawn said. "That's why we like her. It's not a Magician class talent, but there are more things than magic in a good relationship, as you may be coming to understand, Bernard. You were looking for a Sorceress when you should have been looking for a compatible woman."

"I stand corrected," Bernard said, plainly impressed with more than Kelei's magic, spectacular as it was. She was fully clothed for the snow, unlike those who had hastily exited the sauna, but had good foundations to support that clothing.

"Let's get back inside before we freeze," Tartan said, fearing that the blueness of his body was not merely snow. Tara nodded emphatic agreement.

They piled back in, including the three women who had been supervising the children, because now Dolph and two wives were doing that, enjoying their time with their grandchildren and each other, with the demon child Woe Betide, and with Tata Dogfish. They were even getting in on the snowball fight. Ida, her business here finished, returned to her house.

The nannies quickly stripped, in the heat of the sauna, confirming their proportions, had there been any doubt. Now Kelei sat next to Bernard and Jody sat next to Drew. Zosi sat next to Eve. She was different; she did not look like a zombie, and Eve respected her enough to trust her son to her care. She surely had an interesting story.

"Her boyfriend is Mundane," Eve murmured to Tartan. "He visits every so often. That's what keeps her from reverting to full zombie mode. Meanwhile she's perfect for Plato, who has a certain taste for the macabre."

Oh.

"Now let's review our purpose here," Dawn said briskly. "Dolin? There are things some of us know but may not be allowed to say, so it is better if you say them." Which was a nice way of including those who had no idea what was going on.

"I originated in what we are terming Reality Number Two, R#2," Dolin said. "I am the half brother of Prince Drew and the Princesses Dawn and Eve, in R#3 and R#1 respectively. I was killed as a child by the Sea Hag, but my mother, Princess Taplin from the distant past, attempted to save me by giving me the chance to live in another reality, one where I did not live and die." He glanced at Taplin, who nodded. "It seems the vagaries of magic allow such things, albeit with serious restrictions. My Aunt Merara, Mera, carried the ring containing my soul to the Good Magician, who enabled us to transfer our spirits to hosts in R#1. If I am able to find a suitable princess to marry there, I will be able to remain as a living man of my apparent age, with the missing portion of my life filled in. To facilitate my search, the Mundane visitors Tartan and Tara allowed me to join their quest to deal with the so-called Ghost Writer who is obliging Xanth residents to play out dream stories he crafts. We were joined by Emerald, a dragon princess presently in human form, who needs to marry a human prince in order to secure a lasting truce between the human and dragon species."

Dolin paused, smiling. "It would seem that Emerald and I represent the answer to each other's quests, but that is not the case. We are friends, and will marry if we have to, but we prefer to avoid this. Because she has no romantic or storkish interest in men, and I hope to find a princess who can fully enjoy such relations with me. Another member of our party is Amara, who in R#1 is host to the Goddess Isis." He glanced at the two, who nodded. "Amara has no romantic interest in either a man or a woman, and while Isis has considerable interest, this is not her mission at the moment. She has agreed to help deal with the Ghost Writer, but is confined to the comic strip and can't act directly outside it. Her interest is to find a way out of the strip that doesn't annoy the powers that be."

He smiled. "As you can appreciate, our several missions were similarly unlikely to be accomplished. But it got worse. The Ghost Writer caught us in one of his stories, a parody of a Mundane fantasy, and we were unable to escape it. He demanded as the price of release that Amara, hosting Isis, engage him in stork teasing trysts. This is objectionable to both ladies. We escaped it the only way it seemed we could, by using one of Magician Bernard's time bombs to vault back to the time of my Aunt Mera, almost nine hundred years ago. There we met the Sorceress Tapis, she of the phenomenal magic tapestries, my grandmother on my mother's side. She was courteous and generous, and we very much enjoyed her company." He paused as Emerald made an expression.

"The Sorceress gave me a marvelous tapestry," Emerald said, in the pause he had made for her. "See." She brought out the thimble, drew out the tapestry, and unrolled it, holding it up for all to see.

There was a murmur of awe as the dragon took wing and flew among the clouds. Anyone who had not been aware of Tapis' magic certainly appreciated it now.

Emerald rolled up the tapestry and put it away just before the pause ended. She had a nice sense of timing, as princesses often did.

"Thank you, Emerald," Dolin said. Then he resumed his summary before it got lost. "We arranged to return to the present time, adding Aunt Mera to our party, whose talent is to shift realities. However such shifts can have unintended consequences, as we discovered to our dismay when we arrived in a third alternate reality, R#3, where we met Prince Drew and Magician Bernard. There may have been a purpose in this diversion, for it seems it has helped both men find what they were looking for, but for us of the original party it is a problem. We came here for this conclave in the hope that some member of it would have a viable notion how we might safely return to R#1."

"I am not clear on a detail," the Demoness Mentia said. "Maybe it's my craziness interfering with my understanding. Why can't Mera just change you back to your original reality?"

"Your confusion is not crazy," Dolin said. "It is because of those unin-tentional consequences. We do not know what other effects such a change might have. We do not want to get lost in yet another reality."

"Such as my host and friend Monica ceasing to exist," Tara said.

Drew looked at Monica. "I am glad to meet you, half sister. You do favor Mother."

"Thank you," Monica said faintly. She had been a bold girl, but the experience of nonexistence had evidently shaken her.

"There is also the matter of control," Mera said. "I do not know enough about foreign realities to be sure of selecting the right one. It might be a dangerous gamble."

"Point taken," Mentia said. "We demons exist everywhere and nowhere, independent of the realities. But when we breed with humans, those chil-dren are limited to the frame where it happens. Fortunately my worser self Metria did not marry elsewhere, so her son Ted remains."

"Nice to have that reassurance," Ted said wryly.

"Worser self?" Metria demanded. "*You're* the worser self."

"So you like to suppose, halfwit."

"Mom! Aunt! Don't get into a catfight here," Ted said. "It wouldn't be seemly."

"Who cares about seemly?" Metria demanded.

"I do," Mentia said. "But of course I'm crazy."

"You certainly are," Metria agreed. "Nothing about you makes sense."

"Accordingly, I apologize for calling you my worser self. I'm the worser self."

"Thank you." Then Metria did a double take. "But if your apology is nonsense—"

"It certainly is," Mentia said smugly.

"You're both worser selves," Ted said quickly. "And I love both of you, and cute little Woe Betide too, pains in the posterior though you all may be at times."

"Well, that's more like it," Metria said, and Mentia nodded agreement.

"We do need to get back to our original reality," Dolin said. "Or in my case, to my chosen reality. I think we now appreciate why Mera is extremely cautious about exerting her power. Yet it seems we need it if we are to return. Is there any safe way?"

"This may be irrelevant," Bernard said. "I believe it was your favor to me, Mera, putting me into the third reality, that tweaked your own reality with its backwash. Now I want to return to my original one, because Kelei is there. Could that change be undone? Reverting us all to R#1?"

"I'm not sure," Mera said. "It may be like working with reverse wood: you never can be quite sure in what manner it will reverse something, and it's not necessarily consistent."

"Reverse wood?" Tara asked.

"That is a type of wood that reverses whatever it touches," Eve explained. "A reverse wood tree growing in a love spring may convert it to a hate spring."

"Or to a love summer, fall, or winter," Dawn said.

"Or a bed spring or fall," Mentia said. "Crazy, no?"

"Point made, thank you all so much," Mera said grimly. "Also, there are many realities, some very similar to their neighbors, and I still could get the wrong one."

"Maybe what we need is a map," Tara said. "So that we will know exactly where to go, without question."

"A map!" Mera said. "Yes, that is what I need, one that shows all the adjacent realities in detail, so I can orient on precisely the right one. But I'm not sure any such map exists."

"It exists," Metria said. "I learned of it one time when I sneaked into the Good Magician's Castle. I'm insufferably curious."

"You're how curious?" Mera asked.

"Endlessly, eternally, infinitely, immeasurably, insatiably—"

"Stop," Mentia said. "You had it right the first time: insufferably."

Metria sent a dagger-shaped glare at her, but it bounced harmlessly off Mentia's shield-shaped deflector.

"Tell me more about the map," Mera said. "It's important."

"It's actually several pages long," Metria said. "One for each reality. They are all bound into the Book of Lost Answers."

"Is that any relation to the Good Magician's Book of Answers?" Eve asked.

"Yes, in a manner. When he gets confused and loses an Answer, it winds up in Lost Answers, a book that mostly writes itself. So that's where the maps of realities wound up."

"So can I go to the Good Magician for it?"

"No."

"Why not?"

"Because the Book itself is lost."

"Lost?"

"Tell her, you tease," Mentia said.

"Lost answers tend to spoil after a while, and the book makes things near it spoil," Metria said. "The Good Magician's wives couldn't stand to have their food spoil before they used it, so the Book disappeared and hasn't been seen or smelled again in some time."

"One of them hid it?"

The demoness smiled. "I doubt that any of them would admit to doing that."

"But I need that Book!"

"Maybe you could ask them. Lotsa luck."

Mera looked so frustrated that Tartan changed the subject for the moment, so that she could cool off and let the steam dissipate. "Something that confuses me: Drew, you just met Jody. How can you be sure she's right for you, long term?"

"I'm sure," Drew said.

"She may be a really nice girl. But surely it takes time to truly be sure."

"I will answer that," Mentia said. "This is Xanth, where things that are crazy in Mundania, like perfect lasting love at first sight, are valid. We don't have the patience for a long, slow, dull acquaintance and verification that the basics are correct. To us, romance is all hearts and storks."

"But—"

"And it works," she continued inexorably. "Your quaint Mundane custom of divorce does not exist in Xanth. Couples stay together in love and fulfillment until at last they fade out. Marriages of convenience may exist, as was the case with Magician Trent and Sorceress Iris, but they tend to become genuinely loving, as was also the case with them. Only in Mundania does the initial attraction of stork appeal wear off, leaving alienated partners. It never happens in Xanth; couples remain loving as long as they both do live, and often beyond that, as is the case with the wives of Good Magician Humfrey." She smiled briefly. "Awkward as it was for him to have them all returned to him from death, simultaneously. They do still love him, grumpy and opaque as he is, and he loves them. Even Metria, devious as she is, has remained with the man she married, as Ted can tell you. Yes, she flirts with and teases other men, but won't actually deliver; I am the one to do that, as I am not married. So Drew and Jody, having discovered each other with a little help from Princess Ida, knew the moment they kissed and the little hearts flew out that this is their love. Had it not been so, there would have been no hearts. The hearts don't lie. Bernard and Kelei know it too, assuming they can get together in R#1. So yes, they are sure, in a way you poor Mundanes can never be, because you lack the magic."

"But these meetings have been largely chance," Tara said. "Suppose Drew had met some other girl first, like maybe Kelei? Would she have been frozen out, because the hearts were holding out for Jody?"

"No, there are many possibilities for couple formation," Mentia said. "But once a match is made it is like striking a fire: it burns regardless of the fuel and may not be put out. The myriad possibilities condense into one, and that one endures, like your quantum physics."

"I wish it were that way in Mundania," Tara said. "In the macro world as well as the micro realm."

"It does happen there on occasion, as you discovered with Tartan."

"True," Tara agreed thoughtfully.

"This is amazing," Tartan said. "How is it that you, D. Mentia, with a reputation for being a little crazy, are coming across as so completely sane?"

The demoness laughed. "The *situation* is a little crazy, with folk from several realities coming compatibly together in a sauna. When things get normal again, then I'll be the contrast. Then I can return to doing slightly crazy things, like flashing my panties at the pool and curdling the water." She stood, hoisted her skirt, and flashed the pool. The water curdled.

Mera took the floor again. "So we need to find the Book of Lost Answers. Does anyone have any notion of where a wife might have hidden it?"

"That would depend on the reality, I should think," Drew said. "Different realities would bring different forces to bear, causing different decisions."

"Reality Number One," Bernard said. "That is where Kelei lives, and where I want to return."

"Where several of us want to return," Emerald said. "My business is there, certainly."

"The business you don't want to accomplish there," Metria said. "Marrying a prince."

"Oh, I'll accomplish it, somehow. I just wish I could do it happily."

"Could you marry Prince Dolin, and each do your separate things without interference by the other?" Drew asked.

"We may have to. But this would violate the theme of instant true love in Xanth, which Mentia has just so eloquently defined. We are friends, not natural lovers. It would leave both of us frustrated, especially when it comes to the ellipsis and the stork. We have to hope that there is some better alternative before we give up and settle for each other."

"Yet you have kissed."

"We'll kiss again, if you wish. We do like each other, and are marvelously compatible, but you will see no radiating little hearts." Dolin nodded agreement.

Drew shook his head. "I see merely sadness."

"Where is the Book of Lost Answers in Reality Number One?" Mera asked firmly. One might almost suspect that she was growing just a mite or two tired of these diversions from the subject.

"I fear we face an impasse," Bernard said. "We must return to R#1 in order to question the wives, about the location of the Lost Book of Magic, but we must have the Book and Map before we do, lest we find ourselves in the wrong reality regardless."

"I don't much like such impasses," Drew said.

"I have a wild idea," Mentia said. "Why don't we go out and join the children in their snowball fight, without putting on our outdoor clothing?"

Tartan looked at her, his eyes trying to penetrate the strategically clinging wisps of vapor despite knowing better. It was as though the eyes wanted to get freaked out, crazy as that was. "That is utterly crazy. Therefore in this crazy context, it has to make some kind of sense. What is the sense of it?"

"That we will soon be freezing cold and miserable," Mentia said. "If we refuse to quit until someone comes up with a viable answer, that will be a remarkable inducement to find that answer promptly."

A glance circled the pool, then crossed it several times, avoiding the floating curds. Then without speaking, they got up and filed out the doorway.

Outside, the fight was going strong. The two half-skeleton children were in their skeletal forms, making them immune to the cold. Piton and Woe Betide had a small fortress of blue snow and were popping up to hurl snowballs at Plato and Data's fort. The sides seemed to be about even, and neither had a decisive advantage. Tata Dogfish was running back and forth between them, as if carrying messages to the warring parties.

The fight broke up when they saw the new adults. "Come fight with us!" Woe called.

The three adults, Dolph, Electra, and Nada Naga, were standing a bit apart, watching to make sure that no one got hurt. Taplin joined them. They looked across as the others boiled out of the sauna. "Have you worked it out?" Dolph called.

"Not yet, father," Drew called back.

"But we're working on it," Dolin called.

"Put on some clothing!" Electra called. "You'll catch your death of cold!"

"That's the idea, Mother," Dawn called.

"*What* idea? To freeze to death?"

"To encourage us to get the idea we need," Eve called.

Baffled, Electra looked at the other wives, but Nada Naga was similarly perplexed. Then Taplin explained the demoness's rationale, and they nodded.

"New sides," Plato called. "Boys against girls!"

"Yeah!" the girls chorused.

Another look circulated. "Why not?" Eve asked. "The boys are bigger and stronger, but we have more girls."

So it was agreed. The two sides lined up, with Dolin, Drew, Bernard, Tartan, Ted, Plato, Piton, and Tata on one side, Dawn, Eve, Tara, Monica, Emerald, Amara, Isis, Mera, Metria, Mentia, Woe Betide, Jody, Kelei, Zosi, and Data on the other. The elders Dolph, Electra, Nada, and Taplin remained neutral, on the sideline. The adults remained in their sauna outfits, while the children remained bundled against the cold.

"Nobody crosses the line," Dolph called. "Stay on your own sides.

"On your mark," Taplin called.

"Get set," Electra called.

"Go!" Nada called.

With that the men stooped to sweep up snow to make blue snowballs. The women stooped similarly, but the effect was rather different, because that position provided the men glimpses into their lowered bras. Even the wisps of steam could not prevail against that, and the five grown men froze in a freak. The women fetched up their snow, made snowballs, and hurled them at the men, scoring on their heads.

That snapped the men out of it. "Don't look directly at their bodies," Drew advised. "Hold your fire a moment. Then aim just below their heads."

The women bent down again to make new snowballs. "Fire!" Drew cried.

The men threw their snowballs accurately into the exposed bras, catching several of the women.

"Eeeee!!" the women screamed in unison, scrambling to shake the snow out. This put the men back into freak mode. Woe and Data tittered, enjoying both sides of the mischances, and Tata woofed.

"Oh, not again," Plato cried, disgusted. "Snap out of it, men!"

This exhortation succeeded, and the men were able to make more snowballs. But the women were learning. This time they faced away from the men as they bent over to fetch their snow. Again the remaining wisps of vapor tried to mask the display, but again they failed. There were simply too many tight panties to cover. And again the women scored on the men. Even the snow was not enough to abolish such a massive panty freak.

"Wake!" Plato and Piton cried together, snapping them out of it.

The women turned away and bent over again. This time the men scored on their bottoms, and some of the snow got inside. "EEEEE!"

At which point the melee dissolved into shivery laughter. Several couples came together, hugging and kissing, to the children's immense disgust. Tartan was with Tara, finding her kisses just as satisfying here on Ptero as they were in Mundania.

"I may have the answer," Amara said. She of course was not occupied with a man.

All paused in their exertions. "Yes?" Dolin asked, as he was not occupied with a woman.

"Get back in the Sauna and I'll explain."

They were happy to oblige. Soon the entire throng was back in the sauna, elders and children included, happily thawing in the steam.

"What is your answer, Amara?" Mera asked.

"It is deceptively simple, which may be why we couldn't think of it before. We thought we had to go to R#1 to find the Lost Book of Answers, but we need the Book to find R#1 for sure. But this is a false dichotomy."

"False? Where is the falsity?"

"We don't need to go to R#1 first. We can do it from R#3, where we are now. As far as we know, the Good Magician is in all realities, as is Princess Ida. He is surely in #3, along with the wives."

"He is," Drew said.

"So we can return to our bodies in R#3 and go see the Good Magician."

"No," Drew said.

"No?" Amara asked.

"You must go see the wives. They are the ones who know where the Book is hidden. The Good Magician is out of that loop."

Amara nodded. "Oh. Yes, of course. But the point remains: we can locate the Book in R#3. And use it to find our way to R#1. No?" She sent out a circulating glance.

The others nodded as the glance intersected them. She had indeed come up with the answer. "Oh, I could kiss you," Mera said.

"Please don't."

They all laughed.

"Now all we have to do is struggle through the comic strip and maybe the storm to return to our point of departure," Tara said.

"Not at all," Drew said. "This is Ptero. We had to travel to reach Aunt Ida, but now that we're through, we can return to reality from here. Remember, this world seems to be the size of a child's ball, from a reality."

"Oh, I didn't know," Tara said. "That's a relief."

"So let's make our farewells to our charming sisters from R#1, and to Kelei for now," Drew concluded. "With reasonable fortune, you will be rejoining them soon, and Bernard will rejoin his love."

"Yes!" Bernard agreed fervently.

"Um, just how do we do it?" Tara asked. "I mean, returning?"

"Merely let go of your condensation and allow yourself to dissolve back into your spirit. It will find its way back to your host."

They bid their farewells, and let go. They dissolved into vapor and floated up off the surface of Ptero. Soon they were far above the world, and the larger reality came into sight: their giant bodies, sitting motionless in Princess Ida's room.

They oriented on their own bodies and hosts, and recovered consciousness. Tartan was back in Ted's host body, and Ted was there too. They stretched, and saw the others doing the same. They were back.

"Welcome," Princess Ida said. "I trust you accomplished your purpose."

"We did, we think," Tartan said. "Your Ptero self helped. Thank you."

"Then Hilarion and I will be on our way. It has been a pleasure interacting with you, and I wish your mission every success." Ida and Hilarion stood and faced the door.

"Wait," Drew said. "Caprice Castle insists on extending its hospitality, at least for lunch."

"Why, thank you, dear; we can stay that long."

"Ah," Drew said, looking around. "I see Jody joined our group after we departed."

"I did," Jody said. "After Princess Ida notified me by mirror message that I was needed on Ptero." She smiled. "I thought she meant just for babysitting. I confess I was surprised to discover her here at Caprice Castle. I did not mean to intrude."

"Never that," Drew said. "Allow me to give you a tour of the castle, now that you are to stay here."

Jody blushed.

"Then I believe we shall tour Caprice." He looked around. "Unless we can offer the rest of you a lift somewhere while we eat?"

"Do you know where the wives are hiding out?" Tartan asked.

"I regret I do not, and it is not on Caprice's itinerary."

"And you, Bernard?"

"I will stay with this party, in the interest of returning to R#1," the Magician of Time said.

"Then I bid you all temporary farewell," Drew said. He was plainly eager to get alone with Jody, and her continuing blush suggested that she had a similar ambition. He took her arm and they departed.

Meanwhile the castle was evidently organizing for a banquet.

That left a diminished group of seven and a half: Tartan and Tara in their hosts, Dolin, Emerald, Amara, Mera, Bernard, and Tata Dogfish, along with Ida and Hilarion. "What now?" Ida asked.

"We don't wish to impose," Dolin said. "If you prefer to rest while we wait on the castle preparations, we can leave you alone."

"Nonsense dear. I have a general sense of what transpired on Ptero, but you can fill me in on the gossipy specifics."

"There are some, actually," Dolin agreed. "Such as the naughty snowball fight."

"I love naughty details," Ida said.

Tartan caught Tara's eye. "We should take our break now, I think."

And Tara blushed much as Jody had.

Chapter 12

ROSES

Back at her apartment Tara was imperative. She dived for the bathroom. "Hurry!" she said as she emerged in seconds. Tartan hurried, of course.

When he emerged, she was naked on the bed. "Fast and hard!" she said urgently. Naturally he didn't question or argue. It was a phenomenal ellipsis . . . . four dots at least.

"Was it the romances or the naughtiness?" he asked as they finally unwound.

"Both. Romance turns me on. But that blue snow in my bra, and then my panties, in front of all those men—I've never done anything like that before, not even close. Not even in my dreams. It was scary and exhilarating to be so bold and wanton."

"I've never seen you so turned on. I love it. I almost saw little hearts flying out. Remind me to slip an ice cube in your bra some time."

"I'd make you eat it, where it lies, before it melts. And it would melt rapidly from my heat."

"And I wouldn't even hurry," he threatened.

"PS, hearts did fly out. They just were invisible here in dreary Mundania."

"I like your heat. But I like you whatever way you are."

"Thank you."

"Do you think we can manage it the way it is in Xanth? Love and storks until we finally fade out?"

"Oh, I hope so!" She kissed him avidly.

"Will we ever get back to Reality Number one?"

"We have to. We have a mission to accomplish."

They quickly ate lunch, brushed their teeth, made passionate love again without even counting the dots, and returned to Xanth.

"I've got to get a girl of my own," Ted said. "You're having too much fun off-screen. Monica says the same."

"You compare notes in our absence?"

"Of course we do. We're old friends. She says Tara's turn-on is turning her on, only she doesn't have a man to spend it with. She's frustrated. I know how that is."

"As I understand it, you and Monica are not related. You can't consider each other?"

"No more than Dolin and Emerald can, though for a different reason. I told you before: we're like brother and sister."

"You did," Tartan agreed. "Maybe one day when you never expect it you'll bump into a girl and little hearts will fly out."

"Let it be soon!"

The meal had been concluded during their absence, and Ida and Hilarion were gone. "You don't suppose those two older folk wanted to get alone?" Tartan asked Ted.

"Well, those details were pretty saucy. Amara let Isis describe them, and maybe she enhanced them some. It turned me on, and I was there."

Tartan laughed. "The Goddess enhances details just by manifesting."

"She does. She stifled it during the sauna and snowball fight, or we'd all have suffered terminal freaks."

"In your absence, Mundanes, some of us focused on the mission," Mera said, clearly understanding what they had been up to. "We devised a plan to locate the Good Magician's off-duty wives. We're sure they are hidden so they won't be bothered by stray visitors, but Emerald will turn dragon and scout for likely locales. Tata will be with her, and he will land and sniff the prospects. He will know if any path leads to them. Then we'll follow."

"Seems viable to me," Tartan said. "I gather Princess Eve is still tracking him?"

"Yes. It's her talent he uses. He loves it."

Soon they were departing the castle. Drew and Jody hardly noticed, being too wrapped up in each other. Little hearts were snagged in the curtains and accumulating in the corners. Tara caught Tartan's eye and squeezed out a faint blush. They certainly knew how it was.

Tartan turned to look back at the castle, but it was silently gone. It did not fly, it simply faded from one place to another.

"Ready, Tata?" Emerald asked. The dogfish wagged his tail. Emerald handed her clothing to Dolin, then turned dragon, and the dog flew up to land on her back, between the wings. Tata could fly on his own, but he was actually swimming through the air, dog paddling, and it was far too slow for this project.

"She's one lovely creature," Bernard said.

"In which form?" Amara asked tartly. But of course he was right: the dragon princess was resplendent in silver with green-edged scales. So was the human form, with the silver hair and green finger and toe nails.

"I was away," Tara said. "So maybe I missed it. Amara, don't you know where something will be? Like the house where the wives are?"

"I do and I don't," Amara said. "The thing being somewhere must be temporary for my talent to work. The wives' house doesn't move, so if I knew where it would be, I would know where it is now, and that nulls my insight. Ordinary talents have limits like that, not necessarily convenient or sensible."

"I believe I can tell the general direction," Dolin said. "That way feels right."

"That's toward the Good Magician's Castle," Amara said. "Only one of them is there at a time."

"Perhaps they remain close by. That makes sense."

She shrugged. "I suppose it does. We might as well walk that way while we're waiting."

In due course the dragon returned. Tata flew off, and Emerald formed. Dolin returned her clothing to her, and she dressed. Tartan realized that this was part of their friendship: she could trust him with details like her clothing, knowing he would not lose it or gape at her. They truly understood each other.

"We found the trail," Emerald said. "On the third landing at a promising intersection. Tata sniffed it out."

"Where is it?" Dolin asked.

"Beyond the Good Magician's Castle, beside the Kiss Mee River."

"That way," he said, pointing in the direction they had been going.

"Yes."

There was a musical note. Startled, Tartan looked. There was a shoe that must have fallen from a shoe tree, but this was no ordinary footwear. It was made of brass, and instead of laces there were keys, and it opened out into a hole like that of a French Horn. The keys depressing of their own accord, and more notes sounded, forming rude musical sneers. "What's this?" he asked.

Tata sniffed it. "Woof!"

Amara laughed. "I can translate that. That's a brassy shoe horn. They care for nothing and nobody. You certainly wouldn't want to wear it."

"I wouldn't," Tartan agreed, annoyed.

"The wives live in a cottage cheese," Emerald said. "It's not far. We can reach it by tonight."

"Um, is that a pun?" Tara asked.

"Maybe to you. It's a cottage made of cheese. They are surprisingly durable."

They walked on. In Xanth, most destinations were reached by walking, and Tartan was concluding that this was no bad thing. They were on an enchanted path, so there were no deadly threats, just puns.

As evening threatened, they came to a camping area. The main shelter had two compartments. "Men can have one, women the other," Amara said briskly. "We'll take turns washing up in the pond. Anyone who wants to peek may do so provided he never tells. It isn't as if there's much left to hide, after that snowball fight on Ptero."

"I'm the newcomer here," Bernard said. "I have eyes now for only one woman, and she's not here."

"Tara and I will go home for the night, as usual," Tartan said.

Tartan and Tara took hands and willed themselves back to her apartment. "I have the feeling that we are slowly nearing the end of our adventure in Xanth," she said. "Do you think we will lose the portal once we're no longer needed?"

"If we manage to complete our mission, and scotch the Ghost Writer, maybe they'll do us the favor of leaving it open. Regardless, we'll still have each other."

"And that's a lot. But I'd still like to visit Xanth some more."

"Amen."

"I also hope that Prince Dolin finds his princess," she said.

"And Emerald her prince," he agreed. "Only that's not a good answer for her."

"I really don't see a better answer than their being with each other, frustrating as it may be for them. Half a loaf, and all that."

"Meanwhile, we still haven't found a way to stifle the Ghost Writer."

"Or even to get Isis out of the comic strip so she can tackle him."

"It's beginning to feel like an unwinnable game," he said.

"Monica says that when the Good Magician is involved, it always works out in the end, however obscure the route."

"That's comforting to know," he said somewhat sourly.

"Monica's pretty experienced in Xanth. She's probably correct. And—"

"And?"

"She's hiding something from me. That's not like her."

"What sort of thing? Maybe we can figure it out."

"An emotional sort. I think she's getting interested in someone she shouldn't."

"What, someone in our party?"

"Maybe. Or someone we met along the way."

"Like maybe Bernard? Whose interest is in Kelei? She'll need to stifle that."

"Yes," she said thoughtfully. "I'm glad I have no such complication."

"I'm glad too. Are we heading for another ellipsis?"

"If you want. I'm satisfied just to be with you."

"Me too," he agreed.

"Are we getting beyond the point of urgency? That smells like love."

"It does. Should I propose to you?"

"Do you need to?"

He laughed. "You can set the date."

"After we solve the problems in Xanth."

In the morning they returned to the group. "Anything happen in the night?" Tartan asked Ted.

"All was calm. But I'm concerned about Monica. She seems moody. That isn't like her."

"Tara is concerned too. She thinks it's emotional."

"Maybe she'll shake it off soon."

"You folk back?" Emerald called. "Time to be on our way."

They resumed travel. Now Tata led the way, knowing the correct path. They passed the fork that led to the Good Magician's Castle and went on toward the Kiss Mee region.

"Do you know about Kiss Mee?" Amara asked Tara.

"It sounds interesting."

"It's very friendly country. But don't drink from the river, unless you want to go into a kissing frenzy."

Tara laughed. "Thanks for the warning."

Then Tata turned off the enchanted path, taking an ordinary one. They followed.

They came to an explosive set of forks, the path diverging every which way as it made its way through a field of tall corn. But Tata had no trouble sniffing out the correct route. "What is this?" Tartan asked. "It looks like a maze." Then he groaned, getting it. "A corn maize."

They followed the dogfish single file. The path switched back and forth, like the route of a snake, and at one point even made a complete loop.

Tara, just ahead of him, stopped. "How can it do a loop without crossing itself?"

"Maybe it forgot that detail," Amara said from behind him.

This provoked Tartan's curiosity. "Wait a moment; I'll backtrack. Keep letting me know where you are."

"Beep," Tara said. "Beep beep beep." She spaced them out.

Tartan walked back around the loop, listening to the beeps. The way curved forward, around, and back again. Tara's signals continued all the while, but remained just to the side, hidden by the thickly growing corn plants. "Did you move?" he called.

"Not a smidge," she called back.

"But I have retraced the loop, and there's no intersection."

"That's impossible. Wait there; I'll join you."

"I'm waiting," he agreed.

Tartan waited, and in a moment and a half she came around the curve. "Or were you just trying to get me alone for a moment?"

"That, too," he agreed, and kissed her. They were not in their own bodies, but it was just as nice, and little hearts did radiate. Then he raised his voice and called to the others. "Are you still there?"

"Immovable," Amara called back.

Tara shook her head. "Impossible, yet it's happening. It doesn't intersect."

"So it's magic."

They retraced their route and rejoined the others. "Some paths are like that, Emerald said. "I could turn dragon and look from above, but I don't have room here to take off, and it would just be blurry anyway."

"I could have told you," Ted said to Tartan. "But I figured you'd rather find out for yourself. This is Xanth, where paths can be one way with no retreat, rivers can do loops in the air, and rainbows are in the shape of bows."

"Thank you," Tartan said shortly.

They came upon a flustered bee. Tara, ever the gentle one, knelt down beside it. "You poor thing? Are you lost?"

"I recognize it," Amara said. "It's a wanna bee. They always want to be something else. Of course it's lost in this infernal puzzle."

"Fly up and perch on my hair, and I will lead you to an open space where you can find your way," Tara said.

The bee made a grateful buzz and flew up to land on her hair.

"How do I love thee: let me count the ways," Tartan murmured. Some girls were afraid of insects of any kind, and tried to obliterate them.

Ahead, the path debouched into a cleared area still inside the cornfield. Tara's bee buzzed happily up into the air and flew away.

A man was standing there looking frustrated. "Uh, hello," Tartan said. "Can we help you?"

"You wouldn't want to," the man said gruffly. His features were indistinct.

Tara stood beside Tartan. "Why not? We're helpful people."

"Because I am AC, the personification of the Adult Conspiracy, widely despised but obeyed."

"Impossible," Tara said. "That's not a person, it's an idea." Then she paused. "I stand corrected. My host reminds me this is Xanth, where unlikely things can become literal."

"What are you doing here?" Tartan asked, similarly reassured by his host. "Shouldn't you be out tormenting children with your ridiculous strictures?"

"Such as bleeping out forceful words and concepts?" Tara added. "So we can't even say bleep if there's a child in hearing range, or even the remote possibility of a child, so that in that way you extend your power beyond all reason?"

"I should," AC agreed without bridling. "But I took a shortcut through the maize and got lost. I can't find my way out. The infernal paths make loops without crossing. Who knows what mischief children will get into if my restraints are not enforced?"

Isis manifested. "What mischief indeed! Children should be encouraged to learn the facts of life, rather than be constantly teased by their absence. Knowledge is superior to ignorance."

"You are mistaken, Goddess," AC said, evidently recognizing her. "The Conspiracy is essential to the preservation of order."

Tartan found this interesting, and was sure the others did too. They all listened closely, letting Isis carry it. How could systematic ignorance ever be justified?

"I have lived four thousand years or more," Isis said grimly. "I have learned much about the human condition, and am seldom if ever wrong, especially when it comes to forbidden desires. I suggest this deal: if you can provide us with three good reasons to maintain this so-called Adult Conspiracy, we will lead you out of the maze so you can resume your work." She glanced around for confirmation, and the others nodded, satisfied with that deal.

AC did not hesitate. "First, the esthetic: children must be shielded from the seamier sides of life, particularly the language. Otherwise in their ignorance they will parrot things like 'Jam your bleep up your bleeping bleep, bleephead!'"

The corn husks at AC's feet curled and smoked.

"He's got a point," Tara said as her ears blushed. "Foul-mouthed children are a menace. I have heard it said that children should be seen, not obscene." Others nodded.

"We'll give you reason #1," Isis conceded.

"Two: the practical. Children must not prematurely learn the secret of summoning the stork, because then they will irresponsibly start doing it themselves and get babies delivered that they are in no way prepared to care for. It takes about eighteen years—longer for some—to gain the maturity and responsibility necessary to properly care for and raise a child. Sad indeed will be the fate of babies delivered to careless and ignorant children. Even if such babies survive, they will be warped."

Tartan was impressed, and he could see that the others were too. Child abuse was not a pleasant thing to contemplate, and it would be inevitable if children were in charge of children.

"But even if the babies survive, it would be a horror for adults, who would soon enough cease to exist," AC continued inexorably. "The phenomenon has occurred in the animal kingdom. It is called neoteny, wherein the juvenile stages learn to breed on their own, cutting out the adult stage entirely. There would soon enough be nothing but children, the adult stage being discarded as no longer necessary. That is a formula for the destruction of civilization."

"Neoteny," Tartan repeated. "I have heard of it, among primitive species."

"Primitive for a reason," AC agreed. "Any advanced evolution is prevented in favor of the wicked joy of breeding young."

"We'll give you reason #2," Isis said thoughtfully.

"Three: philosophical. The most precious thing a baby brings to this world is innocence. The process of maturing is the slow destruction of that innocence, which once corrupted can never be restored. It behooves all adults to safeguard that innocence as long as is humanly possible. That is what makes humanity human, in contrast to the animals. The Adult Conspiracy, frustrating as it may at times be for children, is the first bulwark against the destruction of that innocence. Children don't understand it *because* they are innocent, but it is protecting them in a way nothing else can. Only as adults can they come to appreciate its benefits, and support it."

Isis looked around, spreading her hands. AC had won the day.

"Follow us," Tartan said. "We're on our way to interview the off-duty wives of the Good Magician. We'll lead you out of the maze." Like bee, like personification: they aimed to help.

Tata resumed his sniffing and led them across the field of stubble to the resumption of the growing corn.

Before long they were out, and so was AC. "Thank you," he said. "Is there any favor I can do you in return?"

"No need," Tartan said. "We made a deal, remember?"

AC nodded. "We did indeed. Perhaps we shall someday meet again." He walked away.

There was a streamlet passing by. "Oh, I'm thirsty," Amara said. She knelt and dipped out a small cup of water, and drank it.

"Oh, we forgot!" Tara said. "We aren't supposed to drink the water here."

"The Kiss Mee River," Amara said, stricken. "This must be a tributary, akin to a dilute love spring." She paused. "But I don't feel like kissing anyone."

"Let me try that," Tartan said. He dipped his finger in the water and put it to his mouth. "Oops!" He enfolded Tara and kissed her five times in half a moment before the effect wore off. "It's Kiss Mee all right."

"Then why didn't I—" Amara broke off. "I must be immune!"

"You must be," Emerald said. "That maybe explains your disinterest in romance."

Amara nodded. "It surely does."

"But isn't that a second talent?"

Amara considered. "Maybe not. It may be inherent to my condition."

"But the rest of us had better not drink the local water," Tartan said. "Not that I mind kissing Tara."

"I didn't have the impression you minded," Tara said, smiling.

Tata sniffed the path, and they followed him to, lo, a big cottage cheese. They were there!

"If these are five secluded ladies," Tara said, "maybe we shouldn't approach them in a gang. They may be shy of strangers. Suppose I go up and inquire first?"

"This course seems right," Dolin agreed.

They hung back and waited while Tara went to the door. A hooded woman answered. They conversed briefly, then Tara turned and waved them in.

"We were expecting you," the hooded woman said. "Come in."

"Expecting us?" Tartan asked, surprised.

"AC stopped by. He said you were good folk. He said you even rescued a lost bee from the maize. He's a good judge of people. So we are welcoming you as visitors. It does get dull on occasion, here."

So AC had done them a favor after all.

Inside the cottage, which did not smell of cheese at all, settled on soft chairs, with tea and biscuits, they got to the introductions. "As you surely know, the Good Magician is allowed to have only one wife at a time," the hooded one said. "So we are on monthly rotation. That's fine; we each have five months on our own between sessions. I am the Gorgon, the fifth wife; I do not show my face because it is lethal." The veil she wore seemed to smile. "We are not much concerned with intruders. Any who come are at risk to become stone ornaments."

Isis manifested. "That seems appropriate."

The Gorgon nodded. "AC mentioned you too, Goddess. I am glad to meet you at last."

"If I may inquire . . . ?"

The veil smiled again. "You may wonder why the Good Magician would ever want to marry a creature like me. He did not fear me; he had magic to blank out my gaze and make it harmless. But marriage is a more serious matter. Never mind that when we met he was between wives and his socks were piling up and threatening to obscure the castle in their stench; the premises badly needed a woman's attention. He was by then too set in his ways to change. So I preempted the matter by formally asking him a Question he was obliged to Answer: would he marry me?"

A smile verging on a chuckle overlapped the group of them, wives and visitors alike.

"He made me do a year's service before he Answered, as was his custom," the Gorgon continued. "That was not as arrogant as it might seem. By the time I put his house in order, not only was I thoroughly conversant with it, but I understood him far better than I had before. I could have given it up as a bad job and departed, as he well knew. But, armed with the knowledge of exactly what the job entailed, I stayed, and became his wife. I remained until he went to Hell and fetched back the other wives."

"But then how can you—" Tara started.

"We all die of natural causes in the course of time," the Gorgon explained. "In Hell the others met each other and concluded that on the whole they preferred being wives to being dead. So when he had dealings there, we all returned, and set up the rotation that now obtains. We are technically on leave from Hell."

"Oh," Tara said faintly. "Thank you."

"I am the Maiden Taiwan, the second wife," a petite woman said. "I am technically 183 years old, going by the calendar rather than years of life. They tell me I do not look it."

"You look about thirty," Tartan said.

"Thank you. We do have access to youth elixir, now, but try to use it sparingly."

A lovely young woman spoke next. "I am Princess Rose of Roogna, Wife number three."

A somewhat homely woman was next. "I am Sofia Mundane. He married me to keep his socks in order. They really needed it."

Then came a cute teenager. "I am MareAnn, with the talent of summoning equines. I am a year older than the Maiden Taiwan, but I prefer to be the age I was when I met and fell in love with Humfrey, the Good Magician. We were fifteen." She smiled. "I am known as the half wife; it was a small ceremony. I loved him first, but married him last, because of complications along the way." She smiled again. "At first I was innocent, as I needed to be to summon unicorns. But Hell is hard on innocence, so after that I was ready to marry him, belatedly."

"Missing is Dara Demoness, his first wife," the Gorgon said. "She happens to be this month's Designated Wife."

"We've met," Tartan said. "In another reality."

"You surely have an interesting background story," the Gorgon said.

"We do." Tartan introduced the members of their party, and explained how they got lost in the wrong reality. "We believe that we need to see a good map of the assorted realities, so that we can pinpoint our own and return to it without further error," he concluded. "We understand that those maps are contained in the Book of Lost Answers, and that one of you may know where that Book is. So we come to you to plead for access to that book, so we can safely go home."

There was two thirds of a silence. "This is awkward," the Gorgon said before the silence could become firmly established. "That Book is dangerous. It is true that it tends to make food spoil in its vicinity, contributing to an unkind odor, but the problem is more than that. There are answers therein that deserve to be lost, because they could seriously disrupt life in Xanth and cause needless suffering. We do not want anyone to know where it is."

"We are not seeking forbidden answers, just the maps," Tartan said. "We will be happy to have a—a supervised visit, so that you can be sure we look at nothing else."

"That is not feasible," the Gorgon said. "The Book itself is lost. We do not have it here. The best we could do would be to tell you where we lost it, so that you might search it out on your own. Thus you would have no supervision."

"We could give you our solemn word to look only at the maps," Tartan said.

"But temptation can be a wicked thing," the Gorgon said. "It is hard to be sure who will succumb to it, and the more people there are, the more likely it becomes that at least one will yield, despite having given his or her word."

A glance verging on desperation circled around their group. "Please, we really need this," Emerald said. "Is there any way we can reassure you?"

"There is one way," the Gorgon said. "But you may not wish to do that."

"What is that?"

"To undergo the Test of the Roses."

"The what?"

"Rose maintains a small garden of rather special roses. Their magic makes them respond to the sentiment of the person who touches one. If that sentiment is true, the person may pluck and keep that rose, or give it to another as a harmless gift. But if the sentiment is false, the thorns of the roses will rend that person's hand." The Gorgon made half a pause. "The thing is, the person who seeks to take a rose may not be aware that his (generic he) sentiment is false. He thus risks suffering a grievous scratch, and humiliation. So the roses can be used to verify an uncertain sentiment, such as friendship or love, or to deny it. That is the Test of the Roses."

"But all we want is to see the maps," Tartan protested. "Friendship and love are different matters."

"True. But there needs to be a certain background integrity and com- mitment in order to be a true friend or true love. A person who can take a rose without injury can be trusted. We will trust any of you who success- fully takes a rose. But it may be risky to make the attempt."

"We're a group," Tartan said. "We're not going to leave any of our mem- bers behind because he or she (no generic he) is not ready to take such a challenge."

"We understand," the Gorgon said. "If you are not sure of all of your members, then it is better not to take that test."

"In which case you won't help us find the Book."

"That is true. We dislike phrasing it so starkly, but we long ago discussed it and came to our joint decision. Since even with our help you may not be able to locate the Book, the test could be wasted anyway. It seems like a bad bargain."

"Let's take a vote," Tara said grimly.

What choice did they have? "I will call the roll," Tartan said. "I think for this we need more than a majority. I think we need all of us, hosts included."

"We do," Tara agreed.

They paused, but no one objected.

"Then as I call your name, repeat it to verify your identity, and say yes to taking a rose, or no. Tartan," Tartan said. "Tartan votes yes. Demon Ted."

"Demon Ted votes yes," his host said aloud.

"Tara."

"Tara votes yes."

"DeMonica."

"DeMonica votes yes," Tara's host said.

"Prince Dolin."

"Dolin votes yes."

"Dolin's host."

"Dolin's anonymous host votes yes."

Tartan hesitated. "Can he be anonymous for this?"

The Gorgon looked at Rose of Roogna, who nodded. "What counts is his sincerity, not his name."

Good enough. "Princess Emerald."

"Emerald votes yes. That includes my dragon aspect."

"Amara."

"Amara votes yes."

"The Goddess Isis."

Isis manifested. "Isis votes yes."

"The Magician Bernard."

"Bernard votes yes."

"Tata Dogfish."

"Woof."

"Um, let's do this: if you vote yes, go to Amara. If you vote no, come to me."

The dog walked to Amara.

"And one more, I think. Princess Eve?"

"Woof."

"If you vote yes, go to Prince Dolin. If no, go to Emerald."

The dog walked to Dolin.

"Then we are united," Tartan concluded, relieved. "We will take the roses."

"This is impressive," the Gorgon said. "Both in the members of your entourage, and their commitment."

"We all want to get safely home," Tartan said. "We may be in doubt about other things, but unified in that."

"About doubt," Mera said hesitantly. "I would like to check in the Book for one other thing."

"What is that?" Tartan asked.

"I prefer not to say, at least at this time. It may come to nothing."

"But if it relates to the Book, it must affect the rose you take."

"Yes."

"Does it in any way concern an affair of the heart?" the Gorgon asked.

"Yes. But it complicates it."

The Gorgon pondered half a moment. "Choose one of us in whom to confide. She will judge your case and keep your secret. Will you compromise to that extent?"

"Yes. I choose MareAnn."

The fifteen-year-old young woman stood. "Come to my stall, please."

The two left together. "I continue to be impressed," the Gorgon said. "And curious as, if you will excuse the expression in this context, hell about her concern."

Emerald laughed. "Aren't we all! But she's a good person, even in her mystery, and a vital member of this party. I'm sure she means no ill." The others agreed.

Mera and MareAnn returned. "It will do," MareAnn said. "Her rose should cover this too. Let her check the Book for this one other thing." Then she hugged Mera. "I hope you get the answer you need, my dear."

"Thank you." Tartan noticed that both women had tears in their eyes.

Rose of Roogna stood. "This way, please."

She led them out behind the cottage. There was a nicely cultivated garden with roses of five colors: red, white, yellow, pink, and black. All of them turned on their stems to orient on the arriving group. It was as if they knew what was going on, perhaps better than the people did.

"These are the relevance of the colors," Rose of Roogna said. "Red is Love. White is Indifference. Yellow is Friendship. Pink is Romance. And Black is Death. Each of you thirteen must speak your piece and take a rose. If any of you are rejected, I will not tell you where I hid the Book. To make this quite clear, I will demonstrate."

They watched, uncertain what she meant to do. "This is eerie," Ted said privately to Tartan.

The woman went to stand before a white rose. "I am indifferent to the fate of these good folk," she said. Then she put her hand to the stem.

The thorn moved so swiftly they hardly saw it. Blood welled from the slash on her hand. Tartan winced, and knew that several others were doing the same.

Rose of Roogna tilted a small vial in her other hand, and a drop fell on the wound. Immediately the skin closed up and the flow of blood ceased. "Fortunately I have some healing elixir handy," she said. That was obviously no coincidence.

She focused again on the rose. "I am indifferent to the fate of the nearby nickelpede pit." She reached out to the stem, this time it broke off in her hand, and she held the white rose, uninjured. "That is my rose for today. I must wait another day to take another, but I trust it makes the point. Are there any questions?"

"Yes," Emerald said. "Why would anyone take a black rose?"

"That would bring immediate, painless death to the one who truly desired it," Rose of Roogna said. "On rare occasion there is that need."

"How could that be?" Tara asked.

"One could be the realization that a person's romantic love is not returned."

"Oh. I wouldn't know about that."

"Or that a close friendship is false?" Emerald asked.

"That, too," Rose of Roogna agreed. "It depends of course on the friendship. Most are only casual, but some are as committed as love itself. The roses know."

There were no more questions.

"Then take your turns," Rose of Roogna said. "Each of you must take a rose."

Tartan stepped forward, and the roses oriented on him. He faced a red one. "I love Tara." He put his hand to the stem. It broke, yielding the lovely flower. He handed it to Tara. "For you, my dear."

"Thank you," she said, plainly touched. She threaded the stem through her hair so that the rose became an ornament. "My turn." She addressed another red rose. "I love Tartan." She plucked the rose and handed it to him.

"Thank you," he said, and tucked the stem into his shirt pocket so that the rose was on his chest.

Ted came to the fore. "I am the host, Demon Ted. I am Tartan's friend." He reached for a yellow rose and plucked it without difficulty. He tucked it into his other shirt pocket.

Monica came to the fore. "I am DeMonica. I love a person I will not name." She plucked a red rose without mischief.

The others looked at her. She was in love? The rose confirmed it. But who?

Dolin approached the roses. "I am Emerald's friend." He took a yellow rose and gave it to her.

Then Emerald the dragon princess did the same, giving Dolin a yellow rose.

"I am Prince Dolin's host. I hope he finds his romance, for I will anonymously share it." He took a pink rose.

"I am Amara. I have no interest in romance." She took another pink rose. Tartan realized that the rose did not require romance itself, merely the truth about it.

"I am the Goddess Isis. I am totally different from my host, but I am her friend." She took a yellow rose.

"I am Bernard, the Magician of Time. I love Kelei." He took a red rose.

Now Mera stepped up. "I love someone who doesn't know it." She took a red rose.

"Mera's in love!" Tartan said to Ted. "She never gave a hint!"

Tata stepped up. "Woof."

"I can translate that," Amara said. "He is professing friendship for me."

The dogfish bit at the stem of a yellow rose, and it came away without injuring him.

"Now it is Princess Eve's turn," Tartan said.

"Woof!"

"That's Princess Eve," Amara said. "Friendship for her brother Dolin."

The dog bit the stem of another yellow rose and fetched it in.

Thirteen roses had been collected without mishap. All of them had demonstrated their sincerity.

"One other minor thing," Rose of Roogna said. "The roses you carry are invisible to all but yourselves and those who most love or value you. So you don't need to be concerned about awkward questions."

"What if we accidentally lose one?" Emerald asked. "I would be chagrined, but such things do happen."

"That won't be a problem. You will always know where your rose is, and will be able to track it and recover it."

"That's a relief," Emerald said.

"However, since some of you have exchanged roses, you need to be aware that it is your own rose you can track. That means you will know where your partner is, too. If your partner prefers privacy, you should exchange back."

A glance tried to get started, but dissipated without circling. No one changed back.

They were ready for the Book of Lost Answers.

But what new mysteries they were encountering! Monica loved someone, and so did Mera, and Mera had a secret answer to look up.

"We've got more on our collective plate than just getting home," Tartan murmured to Tara.

"We do," she agreed.

Chapter 13

BOOK OF LOST MAGIC

"We wanted to be sure the Book of Lost Magic would never be found by incidental mischief makers," Rose of Roogna said. "So one night I sneaked out with it alone, though contact with it soiled my dress, and hid it in the dark recesses of a book cellar. Unfortunately I missed the pun, and I think it drifted into the hands of a book seller. He sold it, and now there's no telling where it is. But with your abilities to track and to sense the right thing to do, you may be able to locate it. If you do, you should bring it back to us, so that we can try again to hide it effectively."

"Show us the book cellar," Tartan said.

"This way." She led them to an outbuilding with a slanting cellar door. They pulled open the panels to reveal wooden steps descending into darkness. "I set the book on the top step, intending to return later with a light so I could see to put it in the deepest cellar, but when I returned it was gone. I'm sure it wasn't taken by an outsider, because I locked the door, and the locking spell was undisturbed. The book seller came from below. There might be another access to the surface, but that seems unlikely because we know of none, and we have lived here for years."

Dolin peered into the cellar. "This is the right way."

Tata came up and sniffed. "Woof!" he said, and scrambled down the steps.

"Wait, Tata!" Amara cried, but as with the person she had parodied, Doorthy of Waz, she was too late.

"We need to follow him," Dolin said.

"Not without light," Amara said. "There could be nickelpedes."

"I can freeze them in time," Bernard said.

"I can help," Emerald said. "With both light and nickelpedes." She turned dragon, long and sinuous, and half walked, half slid into the dark hole. Then she breathed a bit of fire, and it lighted the way. If they encountered nickelpedes, that fire could scorch them.

"On our way," Dolin said, and followed the dragon.

"Thank you for your help," Tartan told Rose of Roogna. "We will try to bring the Book back to you when we find it."

"I know you are sincere," Rose of Roogna said. "I wish you success."

"Close the door after us," Tartan said. "Lock it. But check every so often. We'll knock when we return." *If* they returned; he had his doubts about the success of their mission.

They piled on in, in single file, following the retreating dragon light. Fortunately it reflected some from the walls and ceiling, so that they could see the steps. Rose of Roogna obligingly closed the door panels behind them, sealing them in.

"This is eerie fun," Tara said. "As long as I'm with you, Tartan, and my friends."

The subterranean stairway curved as it wended ever downward, far beyond the level where the cellar should have been. "I think this is an access to something other than a cellar," Tartan said.

"So do I," Dolin said. "But it is right that we pursue this course."

The stairway opened out into a larger chamber. But it was foggy, so that they could not see its extent.

"There's something odd about this," Bernard said. "I don't trust it."

"Odd, but not threatening," Amara said.

"I feel giddy," Tara said. "As if we're sort of turning sideways or upside down, only that's not exactly it."

"I feel much the same," Amara said.

"If you become nauseous," Tartan said, "we can retreat." He was halfway hoping they would, because he was feeling strange himself.

"I prefer to move on," Tara said grimly. "We need that Book."

They moved on, and soon left the cave and were in a renewed tunnel with steps. These finally led to another door. Fortunately it was not locked. They pushed it open, and gazed on a decidedly strange scene.

It appeared to be a decorated dance floor, with a giant punch bowl in the center. Raucously loud music was playing. But it was for the birds: all manner of fowls flocked there, strutting in formations, clucking at each other.

Tata ran quietly through to sniff the punch bowl, unnoticed in the bedlam.

Then they were spied. "Fresh meat!" someone screeched. Immediately several dirty birds flew toward them.

"Oh, no," Mera said. "Harpies."

Indeed they were: crossbreeds between humans and buzzards; they had human heads, arms, and breasts, while their lower sections had the legs and tails of barnyard fowl. They were filthy in body and language.

Emerald, still in dragon form, reared up to shield the party from this threat. She breathed a warning bolt of fire.

"Oh, come off it, dragon lady!" a harpy screeched, hovering in place. "We just want to dance with the men. This is the Fowl Ball, after all."

"There are very few harpy males," Amara said. "About ninety-nine percent of them are female. That puts a premium on any males they catch, human or avian. They want to breed."

"You got that right, doll butt," the harpy screeched. It seemed that screeching was their normal mode of speech. "I am Heebie Jeebie Harpy, dance committee slattern. We need three volunteers to dance. You, you, and you." She indicated Tartan, Dolin, and Bernard. "The rest of you sluts can drink yourselves to oblivion for all we care." She indicated the punch bowl.

"This, oddly, is the right thing," Dolin said, surprised. "We men will rejoin you women on the far side, in due course."

"Woof!"

"But that punch is spiked," Tartan said, understanding the warning. "It will do filthy things to our morals."

"You bet it will, hunk pelvis," the harpy screeched. "One taste of that lust elixir and you'll never get enough of us, though you die trying. I mean that in the most randy way."

That was exactly what Tartan was afraid of. "I, uh, already have a girl-friend."

"Well, now you've got a dozen more! You have a problem with that?"

"Yes. I am true to my original girlfriend."

"We'll soon fix that!" Heebie screeched. "We'll string her up by her bra straps and make her glug a gallon of punch. She'll go hog wild. You won't even recognize her then, let alone want her. Which one of these tarts is she?"

"Me," Amara said before Tartan could protest. "Let me at that punch." She strode across to the huge bowl, picked up a giant mug, dipped it in the brew, and drank. She jumped as if punched—of course that was an effect. A small mushroom-shaped cloud formed over her head.

"But—" Tartan said belatedly.

"It is right," Dolin murmured. "Surprised as I am to sense it."

Then Tartan remembered: Amara was immune to love elixir, surely the major component of the drink. She was interceding to save the men from a fate somewhat more degrading than death. But how could she? She might be proof against its potency, but they weren't.

Yet Dolin seemed unperturbed. Did he have reason? Or was getting blind drunk and servicing a dozen harpies part of what was the right thing to do? Tartan had a problem with that.

Amara returned to them, somewhat wavy on her feet, bearing the refilled mug. "This shtuff is great," she slurred. "I can't wait to get into action." For a moment the Goddess Isis manifested, nodding, making her ooze basic sex appeal. "Try it. You'll like it." She thrust the mug at Dolin.

And Dolin took it and gulped a mouthful. He too jumped as if punched, and the mushroom cloud formed. "Whoo! Try it!" He unsteadily held the mug out to Tartan.

What could he do but trust them? Tartan took the mug and gulped a gulp. The punch rocked him, causing him to slop much of the rest of the drink, and he saw the cloud form. But these were only peripheral effects.

The liquid in the mug was plain dull water.

Amara took the mug from him and gave it to Tara, who was standing transfixed. Tara tried a taste, practically radiating disgust, and looked surprised. She passed the mug on to Bernard.

Then Tartan caught on. Amara wasn't simply immune to lust elixir; her touch had nullified it. They were safe from it as long as the harpies didn't catch on.

"Wow!" Tartan said belatedly. "Let's dance, you seductive creature!" He stepped forward and grabbed hovering Heebie by her well-endowed bare front. Any ordinary girl would have screamed and smacked him.

"That's more like it," she screeched, pleased, flapping her wings to maintain the position. "Hover through the fog and filthy air!"

He put his arms around her upper body and hauled her in close. "Oh how we danced on the night we were wed," he sang loudly off-key, remembering a naughty parody. "If you think we danced you got rocks in your head."

"Lovely!" his partner screeched.

Dolin was dancing similarly with another harpy, even slushily kissing her, putting on a good act. So was Bernard. They all knew what they had to do. Meanwhile the other members of their party had quietly faded out. The three men were the distraction, covering for the escape of the others. They had to make it good.

"Lesht get somewhere halfway private," Tartan said.

"Woof!" Tata was standing by a tunnel leading out of the ballroom.

"Over there," Dolin said.

"Not there," Heebie screeched, alarmed. "That's the kraken pool!"

"Kraken?"

"The huge seaborne weed," she explained. "With tentacles that wrap you so it can feed."

"Good. Then we won't be disturbed there."

She looked at him, impressed. "You really are crazy! I like that in a man."

Tartan just hoped the dogfish knew what he was doing. With the Sorceress Eve along he should. Still, it was worrisome. The kraken did not sound like any creature to fool with.

The three men danced into the cave with their partners, right up to the edge of the pool. Several tentacles snaked out and grabbed them. "Eeee—!" Heebie screeched, just like a normal girl.

Then the kraken went still. So did the three hovering harpies, remaining fixed in midair. "I froze them in time," Bernard said. "Let's get out of here."

"Woof!"

They followed the dogfish along the narrow ledge around the pool. It was in easy reach of the kraken, but the weed was not grabbing at the moment. When they got to the far side of the pool there was a larger tunnel going on.

"Now I'll release them," Bernard said.

"—eeek!" Heebie's scream finished behind them. "The kraken got them!"

That was a natural misunderstanding. One moment the tentacles had been reaching; the next, the men were gone. Into the water for lunch, as far as the harpies could tell. So they were free of the dirty birds without complications.

"I'm glad you're along," Tartan said to Bernard.

"Amara did her part; I did mine," the Magician of Time said modestly.

They caught up to the women further along. They were lighted by the glow of the dragon's fire. Tartan hurried to join Tara. "I'm so glad to be with you again."

"What?" she screeched. "Did your harpy girlfriend dump you?" Then she dissolved into laughter.

"I should grab you by your front," he complained. "See how you screech then."

"You can't."

"Why not?"

"It's not bare."

"You can't bare it?"

"Not here," she said and kissed him. "Not yet."

"I'll wait," he agreed.

"Seriously, we really appreciated how you men distracted the dirty birds so we could escape. We know you didn't like having to touch them."

"Well, Amara did her part too, nullifying that punch. But the harpies did have some interesting portions."

She glared. "Oh?"

"Their wings. The way they hovered."

"Oh. Right."

They went on. Soon the tunnel opened out into a truly huge cavern that extended upward as far as they could see by the flickering dragon light. The ground angled down until it came to a brightly lighted floor. It was rock hard to touch, and there seemed to be a reflection of blue sky and white clouds, though there was nothing but darkness above. Was it glass?

"Woof!"

"What?" Amara asked the dog, amazed.

"Woof."

"Okay, I'll touch you," Amara agreed. "So I can better pick up on what you're trying to tell me." She picked Tata up and held him in her arms. "Oh, my!" she said, astonished.

"What's the problem?" Tartan asked.

"This—this is almost beyond belief. But Princess Eve knows."

"Knows what? That we're deep underground and finding a phantom reflection of the sky?"

"It's not phantom. In fact it's not a reflection."

"Don't tell me it's a huge TV screen," Tartan said.

"It's not. It's—it's less believable."

The others gathered around. "You're not being clear," Tara said.

Amara struggled to phrase it. "It's reality."

"Still not clear," Tara said.

"It's really the sky down there. And rock here. We're—we're inverted."

They looked at her. Emerald shifted back to girl form and Dolin gave her her clothes. "I'm having trouble understanding you. Maybe my dragon form has trouble processing information. What does inverted mean?"

Amara tried once more. "When we passed through that foggy cave and felt funny, that was because we were shifting orientation. On one side stone is stone and air is air, as we are used to. On the other side it's reversed. Stone is like air, and air is like stone. Also, up is like down, and down is like up. We changed from being solid creatures passing through air to gaseous creatures passing through stone. Instead of having the main part of the planet below us, it is the sky below us. We feel the same with respect to each other, but we are now quite different than we were." She took a breath. "That's not the floor. Not glass. It's the open sky. We're like holes opening in the rock, which is porous to us, while the air is solid. Inverted."

"I find this difficult to understand, let alone accept," Emerald said. "Is there any other way to phrase it so that maybe we can better grasp it?"

Isis manifested. "There may be a way. I felt that explanation as my host did, and I can make sense of it, though as yet I withhold my belief. I see one possible way to test it quite directly. If solid bodies are now spacious—that is, composed of space—and the air is now rocky, shouldn't it be reversed for our spirits? So that they become solid? If so all we have to do is emerge, those of us who are residing in hosts. We'll find out soon enough."

"Solid spirits," Tartan said. "That's easy to test."

"Then join me as a ghost."

"Wait!" Tara said. "Tartan and I can see, hear, and feel each other as ghosts only when our host bodies are physically touching. Maybe it works the same way with our present hosts. Let's all touch before we emerge."

"That makes sense," Isis said. "I have been in and out of my host a number of times, but have not seen any other ghosts, and I doubt they saw me."

"We didn't," Tartan said, intrigued. "So we can test that too."

Four of them sat on the floor at the edge of the lighted panel and held hands in a circle.

"Woof!"

"Princess Eve too," Amara said, smiling.

The dogfish settled down on their feet, which extended into the center of the circle, overlapping. Now they were five.

Tartan drew his essence out of his host. He tried to float up, but found himself held down. He had to stand firmly on the ground.

The others appeared, standing similarly, with Princess Eve in the center. "Well, I see you," Isis said. "Do you see me?"

"Can you dull it down a magnitude or two?" Tartan said. "I'm about to freak out, even though you aren't wearing panties."

"Clothing does not adhere well to the spirit form," Isis said. But her phenomenal curves fuzzed out a bit.

"We are all naked, of course," Eve said. She, too, was a menace to male eyes. "Best just to get used to it."

"We will try," Dolin said bravely.

"Yes we will," Tara said firmly. She was not close to being as well endowed as the other women were, but Tartan found her just as interesting for purely personal reasons.

"So now we know that one aspect works," Tartan said. "We can see, hear, and presumably feel each other." He squeezed Tara's hand on one side, and Isis's hand on the other. "But are we really solid, or do we just feel that way to other ghosts?"

They let go hands and walked to the bright floor. Tartan knelt and touched it with one hand. His hand passed through it without resistance. Then he took hold of the thin edge of rock bordering the hole and broke off a piece. "I'm beginning to believe," he said.

The others experimented similarly. They all seemed solid.

"Then what of our hosts?" Dolin asked.

They returned to the five hosts, and discovered something else: three of their group were missing. There was no sign of Emerald, Mera, or Bernard. The ones who weren't hosts to foreign spirits.

Then Mera appeared, as pretty as a statue as in person. "I just had to see what you were up to," she said apologetically. "So I touched the circle of you, and willed my soul aloft."

"It worked," Dolin said. "We are now aware of you."

"And I of you. This is amazing!"

"Check the glass floor," Tara said. "But don't fall in."

Mera went to check it, verifying that it was indeed now a hole through which she could fall if not careful. "So we are inverted."

"We are indeed," Tara agreed.

"What does this mean in terms of the Book?"

That made them pause. "Do objects translate the way people do?" Tartan asked.

"They must," Tara said. "Since our clothes translated. It's in our spirit forms we are naked."

"Then the Book must be here, and we can find it regardless."

"It occurs to me that our ghost forms might be useful in searching out the Book," Isis said. "If local folk can't see us."

"We should keep it in mind," Tartan agreed.

"We should rejoin the others," Tara said.

"We should," Dolin agreed.

"Woof," Eve said, smiling.

They returned to their hosts, who now seemed insubstantial. Each of them stepped carefully into the host and sank down inside. Soon they were back to seemingly normal.

"We have confirmed it," Tartan said. "Our spirits are solid. And that bright floor is a hole in the ground opening to the air and sky."

"I am glad to know it," Bernard said.

"As am I," Emerald said.

"I joined them," Mera said. "It is all true."

"Then let's follow Tata to the Book," Bernard said.

They walked across the sky hole, as it was now quite solid to their feet, and resumed walking on dark ground. Or were they? "What exactly are we walking on? Tara asked. "It can't be rock, because we should fall through it."

They investigated, discovering that it was actually a dark tunnel whose air was what supported them. They were walking on top of it. It was leading upward, or, as they now knew, downward into the depths.

In due course they came to a mountain, only in reverse. It would be a giant pit in the ground. The path wound around it, leading to its summit, on which perched a castle. Only this was no ordinary edifice; its foundation was air, and its walls, floor, and roof were evidently air too, with the interior of each chamber being solid stone.

"Whoever built this knew what he was doing," Bernard remarked. "Somehow crafting planks of air."

"And if anything fell into that pit from the normal realm," Emerald said, "it would crash right into the foundation. That seems chancy."

"Goblins probably did it," Dolin said. "They're excellent subterranean craftsmen."

"And who governs it now?" Tara asked. "Maybe we should pause to investigate before just walking up and saying 'Hi, castle minion. We're here to take back the Book of Lost Answers.'"

They paused. "Maybe we should turn ghosts again and look it over," Tartan said. "Perhaps locate the Book. As ghosts we won't be able to touch it, solid as we may otherwise be, but then we can send in someone inverted to get it."

They pondered and decided on a committee of five ghosts, while the others rested. This time they didn't need Tata Dogfish, because it was Eve who knew about things inanimate, and she would be along.

"However, we need to be sure of the rules of exploration," Dolin said. "As ghosts we found ourselves solid, but we remained oriented as before, and the rock remained pervious. It was not a complete transition to the normal realm."

"Just as ghosts obey the normal rules of gravity and direction," Tartan agreed. "They may float, but have to make an effort to leave the ground, and the ground remains down. They are merely people without much mass."

"Mainly, in the manner of ghosts, we were not apparent to regular folk," Isis said. "That's what counts."

"Being invisible and largely inaudible," Tara agreed. "Apart from that, being ghosts is a disadvantage here. We don't want to fall into that mountain space and be lost."

They walked carefully beside the paved path, because the paving itself was made of air that would have mired them ankle deep. They cautiously ascended the mountain to the castle door. It was closed, but they simply walked through it, because it was not solid to them.

It was actually a small castle, essentially a one-person abode. They discovered a kitchen area with a surprisingly comely troll woman preparing a conventional meal. She took no note of them, of course, as she hummed a private tune. There was a bathroom area, a bedroom area, and a study. In the study sat a troll, the evident proprietor. His name was on a plaque on his desk: CON TROLL—BAD ACTOR.

"Can that be coincidence?" Tartan asked, not concerned that the troll would overhear him. "A bad writer sowing mischief in Xanth proper, a bad actor maybe doing something similar in the nether realm?"

"Each of whom has gained access to forbidden knowledge or ability," Dolin agreed. "Which they may be prone to misuse."

"Let's find that Book," Tara said. "This situation makes me nervous."

They moved through the castle, literally, searching for the Book. And in due course found it in the obvious place: under the troll's bed.

"I think we have what we need," Tartan said. "Let's go back and prepare for the official visit."

"This certainly wasn't as exciting as I feared," Tara said.

"Visits to faraway places are seldom exciting," Isis said. "The novelty wears off swiftly, within centuries, even decades, and they become as dull as the local scene."

Back at the camp they returned to their hosts and reported on what they had found. "So now we can go take the book," Tartan concluded.

"Woof," Tata barked disapprovingly.

"Do you mean steal it?" Emerald asked.

"I mean take it back. It doesn't belong to the troll. Some of us can distract him while another takes the Book from under his bed."

"That still smells like stealing."

Bernard shook his head. "I think there is no need to steal it or to take it by force. He may simply give it to us."

"Woof?"

The others looked at him. "Trolls aren't known for generosity of outlook," Amara said. "They are generally mountain brigands who will eat people if they get the chance."

"Trolls differ, like dragons," Emerald said. "Some are nicer than others."

"Point made," Dolin said. "You're the nicest dragon I know."

"Out of a group of one," she agreed, laughing.

"Seriously, I thought most dragons were vicious predators who would as soon toast you as look at you. But knowing you has entirely changed my outlook. I would not marry you by choice, you know why, but it would be no bad bargain."

"There are dragons who think most human folk are vicious predators who would as soon run a sword through an innocent dragon as look at her," Emerald said. "And that dogs are nasty foot biters." She petted Tata. "I knew better, but my association with the group of you has amply confirmed my tolerance. I never want to lose friends like you, Dolin, and you, Monica, and you, Mera, regardless of the outcome of my mission."

"Woof."

"You too, of course, Tata."

"I feel the same," Monica said. "I—I confess at first I was a bit wary of getting to know a lesbian well, of any species, let alone a dragon, but now I don't care about that at all. You're a great friend."

"I love you both," Mera said simply.

"Those three have become quite close during your absences," Ted told Tartan. "As I have with Dolin. We all truly like each other."

"Why do you think he will give us the Book?" Tartan asked Bernard.

"Because you said it is hidden under his bed. That means he sleeps over it. That means in turn that it spoils his dreams, and probably his food too, if he eats in bed. We have but to tell him that. He'll be a happier troll without it."

A look started circling, but gave it up as a bad job and dissipated, because they agreed too rapidly.

Tartan looked at his watch, which seemed to be working despite their inversion. "It's late. Why don't we break for the night and tackle the troll tomorrow?"

This time the look didn't even get started.

Back in the apartment, Tartan and Tara settled their business and flopped on the bed. "Do you think we're getting near the end?" she asked.

"I don't know. With luck we're close to returning to Xanth Reality Number One. But then we still will have the Ghost Writer to deal with. That could be a long unfunny haul."

"And assuming we find a way to nullify the Ghost Writer, and our mission in Xanth is done, what then?"

"You know, I half wish we could stay in Xanth, or at least have continued access to it. I'm hoping we can make that bargain in return for helping out. As long as we're together."

"I'm curious," she said. "Suppose we could be together, but limited to Mundania with our dreary jobs and all. Or that we could be in Xanth, with all its magic, but not as a couple. Which would you choose?"

"Xanth."

Her face froze.

"Then I'd court you there, and hope to win you back, so we could have both."

Her face thawed. "You saw that coming. You played me."

"What can I say? I love you both."

"It will do," she said, nestling into him. Then: "That's interesting, about how Ted and Monica have become close friends with the other members of the group. But it also makes me more curious than ever: who does Monica love romantically, and what question does Mera want to ask the Book?"

"We can all be friends without knowing," Tartan said. "But I agree. I am curious as hades. I hope we find out before this ends."

"Me too."

Then he stiffened, startled. "It's here!"

"What's here, dear?"

"Your rose. In your hair. As bright as always. In the heat of our, um, discussion, I never noticed."

She put her hand to her hair and found it. "That's your rose, that you gave me. But how can it be here in Mundania?"

Tartan checked his shirt. "Mine's here too. I mean yours, that you gave me."

"Maybe we're just imagining it."

"The way we're imagining the whole magic land of Xanth? All right."

"All right," she agreed. "No one else can see them anyway, so there's no problem."

In the morning they girded themselves and returned to the inversion cavern.

"Woof!" Tata greeted them. He was always the first to recognize them, though there was no physical change in the hosts.

"Anything happen we should know about?" Tartan asked, half hoping that one of their two private questions had been answered.

"We agreed to give the troll a fair hearing," Dolin said. "As Emerald says, dragons and trolls aren't all alike."

They set off for the castle, this time stepping firmly on the air tiles. They reached the front door and knocked.

The fair troll lady opened it. "Oh," she said, exactly like a human girl. "Are you looking for Con Troll?"

"We are," Dolin said. "It's about a book."

"That horrible Book of Lost Answers? I hate it."

"It spoils your food," Mera said wisely.

"And that's not all," the girl agreed. "Con hasn't been the same since he found it. I wish he would get rid of it."

So the troll hadn't stolen the Book. Neither had he bought it from a book seller. He had simply found it, so it was his, by his reckoning. Sitting on the book cellar step as if forgotten or lost.

"Allow us to introduce ourselves," Dolin said as they settled into the guest hall, and called off the names of their party. "That Book was lost by the wives of the Good Magician Humfrey. We hope to return it to them."

"I am Trudy Troll, housekeeper and aspiring actress. I certainly hope you take that Book far away from here."

"We do hope to," Tartan said. "But first we should talk to Con about it."

"I will fetch him."

In a generous two and a half moments the troll joined them. "What's this about the Book?" he demanded truculently, which was the normal mode for trolls.

"That book belongs to the wives of the Good Magician Humfrey," Prince Dolin said. "We have come to take it back."

"It won't do you or them any good," Con said con-trarily.

"How so?"

"It has no index, the answers are not listed alphabetically or numerically, and they change randomly. It will answer only one question a day, and that answer is wrong. The thing is useless."

"What do you ask it?" Dolin asked.

"All I want to know is how to become a good actor, so I can make my fame indulging my passion. Instead I get answers such as how to achieve lasting world peace, how to cure cancer, how to escape the comic strip, how to find the perfect human princess to marry, how a lesbian can make a great deal, and how to nullify ghost writing. None of them relate to me!"

Dolin's jaw fell so far his teeth were in danger of falling out. He was not the only one. Some of those answers were ones they were looking for! Isis wanted to escape the comic strip, Dolin wanted to find the right princess to marry, Emerald wanted to secure peace without having to marry a human prince, and they all wanted to nullify the Ghost Writer. All those answers wasted on the troll.

Worse, they were obliged not to use the Book for any of those questions. They had agreed to seek only the key maps to the alternate realities. Plus whatever question Mera had.

"They mentioned wicked temptation," Tara murmured.

Tartan stepped in. "It seems that the Book has the correct answers, but they are lost within its scattered pages. It may be drawing randomly from the answers to prior questions." He made a quarter pause, realizing that they had not yet had the chance to ask any of their questions, not that they were going to. "Or future questions. Or maybe just wished questions. Your answer may turn up in response to another person's question."

"And who is going to waste a good question on the chance that it might give them my answer instead?" Con demanded con-descendingly. "Then share that answer with me?"

"We might," Tartan said. He looked around. "Do we agree that it would be ethical to ask several questions in an effort to get the answer to the one we want, and the one Con wants? We would stop the moment we get those answers, and not question the book further."

The others considered. "We did make an agreement," Mera said. "And we took the roses." Indeed, they all had their roses, which remained fresh and pretty, though the trolls could not see them.

"I don't know," Con said. "If I keep at it long enough, I'm bound to get my answer eventually."

"But have you considered this," Bernard said. "You sleep near the Book, and it sours your dreams. You have been restless and unsatisfied ever since you got it, no? So it is well worth getting rid of."

"True," Con said, con-vinced. "The moment I get my answer."

"Let's see if we can settle this here and now," Dolin said. "Trudy, why don't you fetch the Book?"

The lady troll departed. In barely three moments she was back with the big tome. True to its nature, it had messed up her hair and turned her complexion greenish, even for a troll. "Here," she said, dropping it on the table with an unpleasant thud.

Tata walked up and sniffed the Book.

Tartan thought of something. "Amara, can you tell when and where our maps will be?"

"Here, at noon," she said.

"Now let's ask questions until three answers come up," Dolin said. "The ones for Con Troll, for Princess Mera, and the key maps of the realities we need. Then we will take the Book back to the wives and be done with it, however much we might long to ask for more. Agreed?"

Con barely pondered. "Agreed." And the others nodded. It was a reasonable ethical compromise. If someone got an answer to which he or she wasn't entitled along the way, that was coincidental.

"You first, of course, Con," Dolin said. "Show us how it's done."

Con put his hand on the Book. "How can I become a good actor?" Then he opened the Book, and they all leaned in to read the revealed text.

LESBIANS CAN MARRY IN XANTH.

"See what I mean?" Con said. "Completely irrelevant."

"True," Dolin agreed. He put his hand on the Book, which had some-how closed of its own accord. "How can I find my princess to marry? She needs to be esthetic and capable of loving me in a heterosexual manner." He glanced at Emerald. "No offense, friend."

"None taken," the dragon princess agreed. "We both know the stakes."

Dolin opened the book.

THE PROBLEM WITH MOST MUNDANE COMPUTERS IS THAT THEY LACK FATHER, SON, AND DAUGHTER BOARDS TO GO WITH THEIR MOTHER BOARDS.

"See?" Con said con-versationally.

"Totally irrelevant," Dolin agreed.

Then Emerald stepped up herself and put her hand on the Book. "How can I secure peace between the dragons and the humans?" She opened it.

TRUDY.

The troll lady jumped. "That's my name!"

"Irrelevant," Emerald said with regret.

"We have the answer," Tara said. "I wonder whether we can find the question to go with it?"

"But I asked no question," Trudy said. "I'm just the servant girl."

"But Con did ask. Let's explore this." Tara looked around. Nobody objected. Tartan was curious where she was going with this. "Trudy, why are you working here?"

"I am an aspiring actress. I thought maybe if I associated with an actor on a daily basis, I would be able to learn the ropes, so to speak. What they don't teach in acting school."

"But I'm a bad actor," Con protested.

"Maybe you simply haven't yet found the right role," Trudy said.

"What kind of roles do you prefer?" Tara asked her.

"Romantic," Trudy said dreamily. "But I would take what offers, for the sake of the art."

"Let's see whether you have what it takes. Kiss Con."

"What?" Con asked, startled.

"Give her a chance," Tara said. "She can't be romantic without a part-ner. Actors need other actors to play their roles, don't they?"

"Uh, yes," he agreed, con-fused.

"I think it's called method acting," Tara said. "Trudy, put real feeling into it. Make us believe you mean it."

Trudy walked up to Con, put her arms around him, and lifted her face to kiss him firmly on the mouth. A little heart flew out.

"You're good," Con said, con-tritely. Then he kissed her back. Half a dozen little hearts, give or take one or two, flew out.

"You're better," Trudy gasped. "That certainly seemed real."

"That *was* real," he said con-tendedly. "You swept me off my feet. Oh Trudy, I think with you I could make it. You *are* the answer to my question. Weird that you were right under my nose and I didn't see it. Until the Book told me."

"And you're the answer to mine," she said.

They kissed again. This time so many hearts flew out that it obscured their heads. They more or less faded out of the picture, transported by their kiss.

"So my question elicited Con's answer," Emerald said. "I am beginning to see how this works."

Mera approached the Book. "How can we deal with the Ghost Writer in the Sky?" she asked, and opened the book.

SUN GLASSES ENABLE A PERSON TO SEE IN THE DARK.

"That was your question that you had to get special permission to ask?" Tartan asked Mera. "Any of us could have asked it."

"Perhaps," Mera agreed. "Your turn."

"My turn," Tartan agreed, though he wasn't quite satisfied with her response. He went to the Book. "How can we get the maps we need to get home?" He opened the book.

NOMAN IS AN ISLAND WHERE ONLY WOMEN LIVE.

He sighed. It was another washout.

Tara took her turn. "What *is* the secret for world peace?"

CEREAL KILLERS GET FAT SOON.

One by one they took their turns, including the hosts, but got no relevant answers.

Tartan looked at his watch. "It's noon. We've all asked, but only the trolls have a good answer."

"I think the answer is here," Amara said. "Locked in the Book. Not much help."

"Woof!" Tata barked.

"That's right," Amara said. "Tata hasn't had his turn."

The dogfish put a paw on the Book. "Woof!" Then he scraped the book open. There was a bright map.

"Eve's with Tata," Tara exclaimed. "When he sniffed the Book he knew all about it. He knew Amara was right: the answer was here. It just needed one more question."

They pored over the tome. There were three pages labeled R#1, R#2, and R#3, with a note saying YOU ARE HERE. YOU SHOULD BE THERE. "We're in R#3," Mera said. "I think all I need to do is touch R#1 as I shift, and we'll be home."

"But first we'll have to return the Book to the wives, here in R#3," Mera said. "We promised."

Tartan thought fast. "Maybe the trolls will be willing to do it."

They oriented on the trolls, who were now mostly buried in a mound of little hearts. "Yes, of course we'll return it," Trudy said. "We don't want to keep it here."

"Thank you," Tartan said, and explained where to put the book, and then to knock on the locked door to alert Rose of Roogna.

"No problem," Trudy said.

Now they were ready. "Touch me," Mera said.

They gathered close around her, including the dogfish, so that everyone was touching. Then Mera put her finger on the map for R#1.

Things changed.

Chapter 14

DREAM REALM

They were standing on the slope of the mountain pit. There was no castle here. It seemed that no one had come to build it. Con and Trudy Troll must have set up shop elsewhere, if they even existed in this reality.

"Let's go home," Tartan said.

They marched single file down the mountain and on to the great crystal pool that was the open sky below (above) the hole in the ground. They could not exit via that, of course, in the reversed state. Then on to the kraken pool.

The kraken was there. Bernard made ready to freeze it in time, but it was not assuming a menacing attitude. In fact it looked rather bedraggled. "What's wrong with it?" Mera asked, solicitous even of such a monster.

"There's something in the water on the other side," Emerald said. "It's all churned up, as if Demoness Mentia freaked it with her panties."

"Except that this is not a happy freak," Tara said.

"Sick water," Tartan said. "I wonder."

"Wonder what?" Dolin asked.

"We're in a different reality, but there should be a copy of the Book of Lost Answers here too. Suppose the harpies had taken it?"

Emerald laughed. "They'd soon be fed up with it and throw it away." Then she almost managed a double take, or at least a one and a half take. "In the kraken's pool!"

"Which well might poison the water around it," Dolin said. "Making the kraken sick."

They skirted the pool and came to the section of bad water. "Let me check," Amara said. "If I'm immune to love springs, maybe I'm also immune to sick water." She doffed her clothing, handed it to Emerald, and jumped into the pool. The kraken stayed well away.

Tartan got down and sat at the edge of the pool, to help her if she needed it.

Amara swam down out of sight. Then she was up again, holding something. "The Book!" she gasped, holding it up.

"Oh, I could kiss you," Demon Ted said, borrowing his mouth for a moment as Tartan extended a hand to help her out of the pool.

"Don't do that, Ted!" Amara said, alarmed. Then they all laughed. It was clear that those two got along somewhat the way Dolin and Emerald did, understanding each other.

Soon the pool was clearing. The kraken came to life, investigating, but it made no threatening gesture. "I think it knows what we have done, and is grateful," Tara said.

Amara dried off and dressed. "But if she were interested, I'd be interested," Ted said to Tartan. "She's a great girl, and not at all bad looking."

"Maybe some of Isis rubs off on her," Tartan said.

They entered the ballroom of the harpies. The dirty birds were there. "Fresh meat!" a harpy screeched. Several of them took wing and converged.

Tartan held up the Book. The harpies shrank from it. "Oh, no!" one screeched. "They got the terrible tome!"

"We're just passing through," Tartan said. "We're returning the Book to its rightful place."

"Just get it the bleep out of here. Then come back and have some punch."

"Maybe another time," Tartan said, smiling internally. Naturally they were not falling for that trick.

They forged on across the hall. The harpies gave them a wide berth.

"There seem to be some advantages to literacy," Dolin remarked. "Even relating to such a nasty Book."

They moved rapidly on to what they now knew of as the translation dome. It was essential that they pass back through that and recover their normal orientation. Again they experienced the oddness, the giddiness, but this time they understood its nature.

Finally they reached the book cellar steps. "You may have to sniff the door and figure out how to open it from inside," Tartan said to Tata.

Then the door was opened from outside. "No need of that," Rose of Roogna said. "Mera told me you were coming. So did Kelei."

"Bernie!" Kelei called from behind her.

Barnard launched out of the cellar and enfolded her. Little hearts radiated so thickly that the two were hidden within the cloud.

"All they're doing is kissing," Tara murmured. "I think."

Then Dolin realized something. "Aunt Mera—"

"It's all right," Mera said. "I have been in contact with my R#2 self. She's visiting R#1 by spirit, in a local host. We are not actually occupying the same reality."

"We are not," the other Mera agreed as the two hugged. They looked similar, but not identical, because only one was in her original host body.

"And you found the Book!" Rose said, taking it. "Not that we want it back."

"You were right," Dolin said. "The Book of Lost Answers is dangerous. Where you hid it before was not secure. You will need to find a better place."

"We will do that," Rose agreed.

"We'll be departing now," Bernard said. "If you can spare us."

"Welcome," Tartan said. "You did your part, freezing time at the critical moment."

Bernard and Kelei departed, trailing little hearts.

"That's sweet," Tara murmured. "I'm going to miss that in Mundania."

"Now all we have to do is tackle the Ghost Writer," Tartan said.

"About that," Rose said. "Something occurred to us after you were gone. You should check with the Night Stallion. Surely he could deal with the Night Colt."

"How do we find him?" Tartan asked, interested.

"You go to the dream realm. We have a patch of gourds you can use."

"Gourds?"

"They are gourds with peepholes," Amara explained. "Once you peek in, you can't break the contact until someone interrupts it for you. That's why you always need a nonparticipating colleague."

"We wives will be happy to provide that service," Rose said. "It's the least we can do to facilitate your mission."

"We'd also better rest," Emerald said. "We have suffered much unusual experience recently, and made a long march back."

"There's another cottage nearby," Rose said. "You are welcome to use that. Then in the morning we'll show you to the gourd patch."

So it was decided. They went to the guest cottage cheese, which turned out to be just large enough to provide for them, as such things tended to be in Xanth. The wives brought them a nice dinner. Then, tired in body and mind, they returned.

"Wow!" Tara said, back in the apartment. "We certainly learned new things in that session."

"We did," he agreed. "But are we really any closer to dealing with the Ghost Writer?"

"There has to be a way to nullify him. Which, according to our information, means getting Isis out of the comic strip. I'm drawing a blank on that."

"Let's have an ellipsis."

"Will that get the answer?"

"I doubt it. I just am desperate to do you again, after seeing those two romances work out."

She laughed. "Yes. I thought you'd never ask."

. . .

"Mera never got her answer," Tartan said, suddenly remembering after the ellipsis faded.

"You were thinking of her while you embraced me?"

"Stop teasing me, or I'll kiss you into oblivion."

"I dare you to try."

He tried, but she remained there. "Anyway, I didn't think of Mera until I got the distraction of you reduced. She lost out."

"I'm not sure of that. I don't think the question she actually asked was her original one. That suggests that she did get her answer, in one of the other ones."

"Cereal killers get fat soon?"

"Maybe not that one. But she didn't seem upset."

"Why doesn't she just come out with what's on her mind?"

"She must have a reason."

"She must have," he agreed.

In the morning they rejoined their hosts in Xanth. But Mera's lost answer still bothered Tartan. Should he ask her about it? Then he saw Tara's warning look, and stifled it. Tara surely knew best, in a situation like this.

"We told the wives all about our adventure in the inverse land," Emerald said brightly. "They were amazed. They had no idea that the cellar steps led to such a phenomenon."

"We suspect they were intrigued by the dancing harpies, too," Amara said. "Maybe they want to fetch some of that punch and use it on the Good Magician."

"Naughty wives," Emerald said with half a titter.

Tartan and Tara shared another private look. The wives were older than they looked; they might also be older than they felt. That punch could certainly enliven their lives.

Rose of Roogna appeared at their door. "Ready for the gourds?" she inquired brightly.

"Um, uncertain," Tartan said. "Tara and I are inexperienced in this regard. Is there a beginners' course?"

She laughed. "It's easy. All you have to do is look in the peephole. We will interrupt your gaze in an hour, at which point you will snap out of it. Then you will decide whether to go back in. But you must all be touching each other, to be sure you arrive or return to the same place, together, just as is the case when you visit Ida's moons. The dream realm is huge; it's as big as imagination, and you don't want to get lost in it."

"We just want to see the Dream Stallion," Tara said. "In case he doesn't know what's going on."

"That's Trojan, the Horse of a Different Color. He surely knows. The question is whether he wants to stop it."

"The Trojan horse? Maybe we can persuade him," Tartan said.

"Perhaps," Rose agreed doubtfully.

Tartan and Tara exchanged a private look. Neither liked the sound of that doubt.

The gourds were in a separate little garden. They looked like squash plants with green gourds on stems, not unusual at all.

"Each of you must take a gourd, lie down comfortably, set it before you, and link hands with the others in your party," Rose said. "Only when all of you are linked should you look in your respective peepholes. We will see that you are not disturbed during your session."

"Thank you, Rose," Dolin said. "We truly appreciate your assistance."

"We do," Emerald said. "We know it can be dangerous to use a gourd without a guardian."

Each person settled comfortably in the gourd patch. Tartan sat down on the spongy ground and lifted a gourd onto his lap, its stem trailing like a power cord. Tara sat next to him on his right side and put another gourd on her lap. Dolin was next to her, and Emerald next to him. Amara was next, then Mera, completing the circle on Tartan's left.

"Woof!"

"Oh, of course, Tata," Amara said. She set the dogfish on her lap beyond the gourd, and brought in a smaller gourd for him.

"Now you may peep," Rose said.

Tartan hesitated, as did Tara. Dolin turned his gourd so that the end opposite the stem came up, and looked into the circular peephole there. He froze in place. Emerald, Mera, and Amara did the same, freezing similarly. So did Tata.

"You must join them," Rose reminded them gently. "Otherwise they will be concerned by your absence from the dream."

"Oh, yes," Tara said, and oriented her gourd and looked. She, too, froze.

"Get on it, slowpoke," Ted said.

Tartan was nervous, but knew he had to follow through. He brought his own gourd's peephole around and looked.

He was standing by the gate to a rundown residence on a rundown lot. The whole scene was spooky but completely realistic. He touched the gate, and it was solid and a bit slimy. He felt solid himself. The others were there too, and the dogfish. It was as if they had all stepped from garden to gate without any transition.

"I have heard of this setting," Amara said. "The gourds provide access primarily to the night dreams, which specialize in horror, in contrast to the day dreams. So naturally it's spooky. That's a haunted house."

"Why not a nice dream?" Dolin asked. "Many folk have pleasant dreams at night."

"There are nice dreams, of course," Amara said. "But it seems that it is the bad dreams that have to be specially crafted, as they are intended to punish bad folk for doing their bad things. I understand that once the bad dreams got nullified, and bad folk ran riot, because they no longer feared punishment at night. It's like the adult conspiracy: many folk don't like it, but it does serve a purpose."

"So we have to endure a stupid haunted house?" Tartan asked, annoyed. "When we came here only to see the Night Stallion?"

"There should be a way to bypass it," Mera said.

"Woof."

"Oh, is that so?" Amara asked the dogfish. "By all means show us."

Tata nudged the gate, which creaked open, and trotted across the unkempt lawn to a large sinister tree. He sniffed the base of the trunk. "Woof."

They followed, coming to stand around the tree. "Are you sure?" Amara asked.

"Woof."

She turned to the others. "He says we should knock on the trunk."

"Why not?" Dolin asked. He stepped up and rapped on the bark with a knuckle.

A door slid open. There was a lighted interior.

"But that's bigger than the tree trunk," Tara said. "I can see that from here."

"We call it Mundanitis," Amara said. "Being constantly surprised by magic, as if you haven't seen it before."

"We haven't," Tartan said, coming to Tara's rescue. "Not in Mundania."

Amara and Tata stepped inside. "This is the bypass," she said. "Come on in."

The others joined her. The chamber was indeed larger inside than outside, and there was room for all of them. "It's like an elevator," Tara said.

"What is that?" Dolin asked, and Emerald, Mera, Amara, and the dogfish looked similarly confused.

"It's a Mundane artifact," Tara explained. "You step inside, the door closes, and it takes you to the floor you want."

"That's magic," Emerald said.

"That's science or technology."

"Surely different names for the same thing," Dolin said diplomatically.

The tree door slid shut. Now Tartan saw the panel of buttons on the wall beside the door. They weren't marked. "Do we have to guess where to go?" he asked.

"So it seems," Tara said. "It isn't as if we have a destination in mind, other than finding the Night Stallion."

"Maybe Tata can sniff him out," Tartan said.

"Not if he doesn't want to be found."

Tartan punched a random button. The door slid open. Was that the door opener so they could exit without going anywhere? No, the scene outside was different.

They stepped out. They were now in a kind of forest amphitheater with wide open sky above.

A winged creature swooped down toward them faster than a bird or a plane. It was a bat. It banked and pulled up just before them, then did a fast loop in the air, like an airplane. Then it folded its wings and plummeted, almost smashing into the ground. It flew straight up like a rocket.

There was a bong. The bat flew to a nearby tree and caught a branch, where it hung upside down.

Another bat took to the air. This one zoomed around in an ascending spiral, then did a triple flip and went into a descending spiral.

There was another bong. The bat went to hang on the tree.

A third bat swooped in. This one hovered for a moment, then took off backwards, amazingly.

"They're showing off," Emerald said. "But why?"

"And why before us?" Mera asked. "We're not really part of this framework."

"Woof."

"That's it," Amara said. "Tata got it. They're Acro-Bats, performing stunning aerial displays before a captive audience."

Tartan and Tara groaned almost together. "So this is not a pun-free zone," he said.

"Of course it isn't," Amara said. "Some of the darkest dreams are pun-fested."

"Nevertheless, they are impressively skilled," Dolin said. "Good job, bats."

The bats made an appreciative chirp.

"Obviously the Night Stallion isn't here," Tara said. "Shall we try another address?"

They returned to the tree, entered its chamber, and touched another random button. This time the door opened on a lot with an odd building. It appeared to be made entirely from clothing.

"That's a nice skirt," Tara said, touching that part of a wall.

Mera touched it too. "I have a notion about fabrics, from Mother Tapis's work. Imitation blue chipmunk fur with a Freudian slip lining."

Tartan realized that he was hearing a loose translation, because Mera dated from before Freud's time, assuming there was any parallel in time frames.

"I love it!" Tara said longingly.

The house collapsed, leaving her holding the skirt.

"Oops, I said something I shouldn't! I didn't mean to ruin it!" she said, appalled.

"Maybe you didn't," Tartan said. "I think that's a Wear-House."

"Oh." She thrust the skirt forward, and the house of clothing reformed around it. "That sort of thing could be useful," she said. "Wear the skirt until you need lodging for the night, and it becomes a house."

"We're finding puns," Amara said. "But we want the Night Stallion."

"I wonder," Tartan said thoughtfully. "Could be he's just playing with us."

"Trojan knows about everything he wants to know in the dream realm," Amara said. "The question is, does he want to know about us?"

"He was difficult in my day too," Mera said. "We stayed clear of the gourds."

"Let's try to get his attention," Tartan said. He looked at the house. "I don't think that's a Wear House. I think it's a Where House."

The house shed its covering of clothing and became more ordinary in appearance. "Now let's get inside," Tartan said, leading the way. "Now, House, I want you to be a Ware House, aware and wary of any threats to us. Such as a pesky Night Stallion who wants to mess us up by playing punnish games with us."

The house hesitated. Tartan wasn't clear how that was evident, but he was sure it was so. "All right, so Trojan is your master, here in the dream realm, and you really can't go against him. But maybe you can take us closer to him. Do it."

The door opened. Outside was a new locale. This seemed to be a jungle with huge footprints on the forest floor. "I don't quite trust this," Tara said.

"Ware House," Tartan said firmly. "You can't betray your equine master. But that doesn't mean you can't be true to your nature in other respects. You have just transported us to a new Where, but I want your assurance that it is also safe for us, Ware. Do I have it?"

The house nodded. That was a kind of little dip. "Good enough," Tartan said. "Thank you, Ware. We'll let you go on about your business now."

They went to the door. There on the doorknob was the blue chipmunk fur dress that Tara had liked. "A parting gift for me?" she said, taking it. "Thank you, Wear House. I will wear it with honor."

When they were outside, Tara quickly removed her existing skirt as the men politely averted their eyes and donned the new one. It looked lovely on her. In fact it was downright sexy.

"That dress gives me naughty ideas," Tartan said.

"It's supposed to, because of the slip."

"What do I do with this one?" He raised the old dress she had thrust into his hand as she changed.

"I'll give it as an exchange." She took it and touched it to the wall of the house, where it immediately merged with the wall.

"Dreams can be fun on occasion," Mera murmured.

Now they oriented on the scene they were in. It shook as something pounded the ground just out of sight.

"Are you sure it is safe?" Emerald asked. "I can turn dragon if need be."

"The Ware House promised," Tartan said.

There was an unearthly scream that made the leaves of the trees wilt and drop. "What's that?" Dolin asked, his sword magically appearing in his hand.

Tata woofed.

"A woman in distress," Amara translated.

"He can tell that by the smell of the scream?" Tartan asked.

"So it seems. We had better investigate."

They walked in the direction of the scream. In three moments, give or take an instant, they discovered a solitary brick tower. There was a figure at a window near its top. "That must be the screamer," Amara said.

They stood at the base of the tower, looking up. The figure looked down at them. She said something, but though her scream had carried across hill and dale, her speaking voice was too faint to be properly heard.

"We can't hear you," Tartan called.

The figure considered. Then she dropped a rope ladder down.

They exchanged three fifths of a glance. "Why not?" Dolin asked. Then he took hold of the rungs and climbed up the ladder.

Why not indeed? Tartan followed him up, and so did the others. This was the dream realm, after all; probably they couldn't be physically hurt by a fall, or by whatever the creature in the tower was.

They reached the high window and entered the chamber atop the tower, one by one. And paused.

The lady in the tower was exaggeratedly shapely, with a figure that the term hourglass would hardly do justice to. Further, what they had taken for a rope ladder was actually her rather long hair, plaited into ladder form. So she was captive, while they weren't.

"I am Prima Donna. Rapunzel is my cousin," she said before they asked. "She got rescued long ago, but I still languish. Sometimes it makes me just want to scream."

"We heard," Mera said.

"Why don't you cut off your hair, tie it to the bed, and climb down it to escape?" Tartan asked.

"Cut off my hair?" Prima asked, horrified. "I could never do that! Everyone in my family has long hair. It's our distinguishing mark."

"So it seems it is up to us to rescue you," Dolin said.

"If you would be so kind."

"Would you by chance happen to be a princess, Prima?"

She laughed. "Me? No way! I'm just a humble commoner girl with delusions of grandeur. All I want is to be rescued and carried off by a strong smart male so I can emote on the stage and we can live happily ever after."

And in Xanth it was possible, even likely, Tartan realized. Here was another aspiring actress. But she wouldn't do for Dolin, who was looking for a princess.

"We'll see what we can do," Amara said. Evidently she had an idea.

"We'll check around," Emerald said.

They climbed back down the hair ladder. "I am thinking this is a set-up," Amara said. "Like a challenge to enter the Good Magician's Castle. There must be a way to rescue her, and if we succeed, the Night Stallion will condescend to see us."

A nod circled the group, and Tata woofed. "Even a tale as stupid as one the Ghost Writer wrote might do," Emerald said.

"So we just need to figure out the key to the challenge, and implement it," Dolin said.

"Yes," Amara said. "There should be a hint nearby." She glanced at Tata. "Can you sniff out a hint?"

"Woof." Then the dogfish set off, following one of the lines of big bare-foot tracks. They followed.

That brought them to the owner of the tracks. He was standing in the ones at the end, not yet ready to move on. He looked somewhat like an ogre, though a bit small, being only ten feet tall and weighing barely a thousand pounds. Just enough to make the imprints in the ground as he walked. That had to have been what they had heard before: his feet clubbing the ground.

"Hello," Tartan called before they got too close.

The creature turned. "Are you addressing me?" he inquired in a surprisingly cultured voice.

"We are curious about your situation," Tartan said. "We're visitors here, so there is much we don't know."

"I am a Goesin," the brute said. "That's a contraction of 'Goes In.' As what goes in to X. We Goesinti calculate primes. We remain nameless until we either discover a new prime, or perform some horrendously heroic deed. Only when we earn our names can we seek romance and settle down to family life."

"A prime number?" Mera asked.

He looked down at her as if considering whether she was a romantic prospect. Males tended to have such thoughts when encountering a princess as lovely as she was. "Of course. A number, x, that can be divided only by itself and one. But all the easy ones have been found, which leaves me in a quandary."

"So you are a strong smart male," Amara said. "In need of a woman."

"Exactly."

"New primes may be hard to find. But suppose you heroically rescued a female prime, whom we shall term Prima?"

"That would be fine," the Goesin agreed.

"Then all you have to do is bash down the tower in the glade, and carry off the maiden therein. Her name is Prima Donna."

"Why not?" The Goesin turned around, and his tracks turned with him. He tramped toward the tower.

"That's one smart woman," Ted said to Tartan as they followed.

The Goesin marched up to the tower. "I have come to rescue you," he announced in a voice loud enough to reach the top. "And make you my prime companion. Are you amenable?"

"Very much so," Prima called. "You have my number."

"Excellent." He drew back a ham-fist and struck the wall of the tower. Several bricks dislodged and fell to the ground. He struck again, and more bricks went. After the third strike, the tower gave up and slowly collapsed into rubble.

Prima stepped out from the rubble. Brick dust and fragments coated her body, but she seemed otherwise fit. "My hero!" She flung her hair in a loop that circled the Goesin's head, hauled down his face, and kissed it. Hearts flew out.

The Goesin glanced at Amara. "What's my name?"

"Gusto Goesin," she said promptly. "Conqueror of the dread tower and rescuer of the prime maiden."

"That works for me," he said. He picked Prima up, she not much loath, and carried her away.

"For someone uninterested in romance," Tara said, "You seem to have quite a touch for it."

"I am interested, merely not for me. It's vicarious."

"I'm glad he found her," Mera said. "I was not entirely easy with the way he looked at me." Which was understandable.

Tartan looked around. "Okay, Night Stallion. Have we passed your little test?"

The air over the rubble shimmered. There stood a horse of indefinable color. "Yes," he said.

"A talking horse," Tara said. "Somehow I expected something more, well, grandiose."

"Mundanes don't rate grandiose," the dark horse said. "Hefty equine is about the limit. State your business."

"We have a problem in Xanth that may impinge on your realm," Tartan said. "A Mundane writer of little talent has been writing naughty little skits like 'The Princess and the Pee,' and requiring the folk of Xanth to act them out. He is in cahoots with a Night Colt, who takes him riding at dawn and dusk so they can spread the stories. Then whoever walks into them is caught until the scene plays out. The dreamlets become plays. Do you know anything of this?"

"Yes."

"When the Ghost Writer became aware of us, he trapped us in a skit," Tartan continued. "It turns out that he wants to make a mistress of Amara, here, who hosts the Goddess Isis. They refuse to oblige him."

"The Goddess Isis? The shrew from Mundania?"

Isis manifested, regally furious. "Yes, me, you motley nag! Who the bleep else would it be?"

"So nice to meet you at last, Goddess of the Ellipsis. Many of my dreamers dream of you."

"Of course they do. Without me, and the passions for which I stand, most dreams would be empty and have little appeal. Few would bother to dream any more, depleting your power. You need me, horse face."

"So I do. I also know that you are one capable of nullifying the Ghost Writer. What do you want of me?"

Isis became canny. "Can you get me out of the comic strip?"

"Only in your dreams, Goddess."

"Then what good are you, horse of a different choler?"

"I can enable you to escape the Ghost Writer's daydreams."

"And what do you want in return?"

"Your participation in occasional passionate dreams as an actress. You could lend them a certain authority they would otherwise lack."

"Show me a sample."

The horse dipped his head and kicked out with a real hoof. A painted partition that Tartan had not known was there was knocked down. Beyond it was another scene. "We are filming a bad dream for a lecher who preys on children," the Stallion said. "But so far we have not been able to muster sufficient conviction. This way." He stepped through the hole.

They followed. It was now apparent that what they had thought was a jungle and glade was just a small setting whose boundaries were realistically painted walls. On the other side of one boundary was a camera crew. There was an open face house with an upstairs bedroom where a little girl was about to go to bed.

Two adults were at the door. "We'll be back in an hour, dear," the mother called. Then she and the father exited and closed the door. They walked out of the scene, leaving the child alone.

Now another man came. "They thought I couldn't get in," he said to the camera. "They don't know I jammed the window." He put his hands on the bottom of the window pane and slid it up. There was a squeak.

"What's that!" the child exclaimed, sitting bolt upright.

"Meow!" the man said.

"Oh, the cat." The child lay back down.

The man climbed carefully through the open window. He tiptoed up the stairs. He reached the bedroom where the child slept. He advanced on the bed. "Haa!" he exclaimed as he grabbed the child. "Got you!"

The child morphed into a snake. The head launched forward to bite the man on the arm. "Ooo!" he cried. "A bleeping naga!"

"Cut!" the director said. The cameras turned off.

"There's the dream," the Stallion said. "What do you think?"

"Amateurish," Isis said. "He'd never fall for that. The child lacks conviction. She radiates no terror. And if he did get fooled, you've got the wrong monster. Everybody knows that naga don't sleep in human beds unless they have special reason. That's suspicious. It would be better with a vampire. They are happy to share a bed with a victim, and will even lull him to sleep. Then when she bites him, he knows that he too will become a vampire, and be far more horrified."

"You could obviously do it better," the Stallion said.

"Obviously," the Goddess agreed.

There was a third of a silence.

"Oh, bleep!" Isis swore. "That's the kind of scene you want me to do."

"In exchange for the spell that will enable you and your friends to escape the Ghost Writer's skits," the horse agreed. "You will direct and/or act in a limited number of dreams. That really won't take very much time or be at all difficult for a Goddess of your talents."

Isis looked at Dolin. "Is it right?"

"It is the right thing," he agreed.

"Bleep," she repeated. It was her way of agreeing.

"This is the spell," the Stallion said. "Merely utter the words 'Dream Skit, Scheme Quit.' Then you will be out of it, mistress of your own destiny."

"Wait," Tartan said. "All you wanted was a deal with Isis? Then why involve the rest of us?"

"The Goddess would not come on her own," Trojan explained. "She came only because her host and friend Amara came, and Amara came because her friend Monica came. Monica is integral to your group, loves one of its members, and will not betray its interests, so I had to deal with all of you."

"You're a devious rascal," Isis said.

"So are you, Goddess. You are using this group to try to escape your confinement in the comic strip, and to get a bit of vengeance for the affront of the Ghost Writer's desire of your passion. We are two of a kind."

"Perhaps we are," Isis agreed. "The dream realm is a kind of escape."

"So is Mundania."

"I am trapped in the ludicrous puns of the one, the crazy dreams of the other, and the dreary dullness of the third. The only way I can achieve even the semblance of an interesting life is by traveling spiritually with a Xanth host. It's maddening."

"Perhaps in the future you will visit my realm by choice. We might have an interesting dialogue."

"We might," Isis agreed. It seemed that even the Night Stallion found the Goddess intriguing, and she picked up on that. "I don't suppose you have a little verbal spell to get me out of the comic strip?"

"That's not my realm."

"But what about the Ghost Writer?" Tartan asked, becoming more than a trace though less than a vestige impatient. "Getting out of his ridiculous dream skits doesn't solve the larger problem he represents to Xanth."

"So it doesn't," Trojan agreed. "So maybe you had better return to the waking realm and do your job."

Tartan opened his mouth to let out a furious response. But Tara put her hand on his arm to stifle it stillborn. "What Tartan means," she said smoothly, "is that the Ghost Writer could not mess up Xanth if it were not for the participation of the Night Colt, and that is your bailiwick."

"So it is."

"So are you just going to let the Colt impinge on your domain?"

"Yes."

Now Tara began to evince a faint trace of annoyance that hovered uncertainly in her vicinity. "Why?"

"Because I am old, and just beginning to possibly think about maybe someday eventually retiring from the burden of governing the dream realm. I can't do that until I have trained in a suitable replacement, one who will not incompetently destroy all that I have built. The Colt is the prospect of the moment. I am letting him get in some practice at the periphery, and I am watching to see whether he has what it takes."

"But all he does is spread the nutty stories of the Ghost Writer!"

"That is more than you might think, mistress of the ellipsis. An idea is just an idea until it gets translated into the animation of a dream. A bad idea, or an imperfect scripting, can lead to problems, as Isis pointed out with respect to the child molester. Above all we require competence. That can take time to develop."

Tara fought off the threatening blush sponsored by the reference to the ellipsis. The Night Stallion clearly knew their secrets. "You're not going to stop the Colt?"

"Correct."

"Yet you gave us the spell to escape his dreamlet skits."

"That will simply add to the challenge. Good practice for him."

"So we can't stop the Ghost Writer by depriving him of his steed."

"Your conjectures are marvelously accurate."

"Thank you." The trace of annoyance filled out into a hint.

"You are welcome. Now I must get on about my business, pleasant as this interlude may be. Lovely dress, Tara." The Night Stallion faded out.

"Maybe I should have let you tell him off," Tara said to Tartan. Her hint had become a pique.

"No, your course was correct," Dolin said. "The Stallion was teasing you. He must like you."

"Or dislike me," she said sourly.

"No, he likes you," Mera said. "Otherwise he would not have remained in several lines of dialog with you."

"Now let's get out of this dream," Emerald said. "Ready? Dream skit, scheme quit."

"But that's not supposed to work in a real dream," Tartan protested. And paused, for she had winked out of the scene.

"So we did get something useful," Amara said. "You're next, Tata. Can you say it?"

"Woof!" The dogfish winked out.

The others followed, until only Tartan and Tara's drifting pique of annoyance were left.

Trojan reappeared. "You can take out the Ghost Writer," he said. "Once you figure out how."

"Thank you," Tartan said in a tone that signaled the opposite. He swooped up the pique and said the words.

He was back in the gourd garden with the others. He glanced at Tara as she woke similarly. "Weren't you wearing a different dress?"

She glanced down, surprised. "This is the fake blue chipmunk dress! But that was only a dream."

Rose of Roogna smiled. "Sometimes dreams became real." She glanced at the others. "Did you get what you went for?"

"Part of it," Tartan said. "But not enough."

"Why don't we take a break before tackling the Ghost Writer?" Tara suggested. "We have to plan our campaign."

"Why not?" Dolin asked, picking up on her mixed feelings. She was evidently both frustrated by Trojan's treatment of them, and appreciative of the lovely dress.

Tartan and Tara focused and arrived back at her apartment. "Oh!" she exclaimed.

Because she still wore the dream dress. Which was of course impossible. But then he remembered the roses. If one could appear, why not the other?

"That Dark Horse is really teasing you," Tartan said. "Dolin and Mera are right: he likes you."

"How could he know about the ellipses?"

"No mystery there. He read your mind, which contains the memories of our activities here."

She nodded. "That must make sense. Maybe the dress is illusion."

"Maybe. But that Freudian slip lining is sexy as hell."

"You just want another ellipsis!"

"I apologize," he said, embarrassed.

"Oh, foo." She grabbed him.

. . .

Then they got around to the reason Tara had wanted the break. "Trojan said that Monica loves one of the members of our group. That's confirmation of the emotion I'm picking up from her. But who? We never figured that out."

"We can narrow it down to three: Dolin, Ted, and me."

"It's not Ted. They've been friends from childhood."

"I agree. But if it's Dolin, why doesn't she just say so? She's the daughter of a prince and a princess, so is a princess in her own right, though she never mentions it. She could marry him and solve his problem. If she wanted to. She has to know that."

"Yet it seems she's willing to let him perish instead, or to marry Emerald as a sort of consolation prize. That's indicative. She's not a mean-spirited person; quite the opposite. That leaves you," Tara said. "That's got me tangled up inside."

"Oh, Tara, it's you I love! Monica's a fine girl, and pretty as a picture, and yes, a princess. But she's not for me. You know that. She's magical and I'm mundane."

"I know that," she agreed. "But does *she* know it? I mean, emotionally? You did kiss her."

"I did not!"

"I mean when you kissed me, in the harpy caves, in Xanth. She received it too. She knew it wasn't for her, but it might have affected her."

Tartan was chagrined. He had never thought of Monica when he kissed Tara in that host. "Oh, Tara, I hope it's not me! There's nothing but mischief there."

"Nothing but mischief," she agreed.

"Can't you find out exactly? We seem to have no good alternatives here, but it might help if we knew for sure whom she loves. Then maybe we'd have half a notion what to do."

"I can try," she agreed. "I do have pretty close access to her body, and thus her mind. But what if it *is* you, as seems likely?"

"And she's not saying, because she knows you're my girlfriend. Everything I've seen of her indicates that she's loyal to her friends."

"Yes. That's part of the hell of it. *She's a nice girl.* And she's my friend. She doesn't deserve the kind of heartache we see coming."

"Find out," he said. "Then do what you have to do."

"I will," she said, deciding. She took a deep breath. "Now let's go face the magic."

"Face the magic," he agreed, appreciating the partial pun.

Chapter 15

LOVE AND MAGIC

"We're back," Tartan announced.

"As if we can't readily see the difference," Amara said. "You had an ellipsis, too."

"Why else would we go home?" Tara asked. Tartan knew she was glad to have her real reason masked. She did not want Monica to suspect what they were after.

"You pay so much attention to such a small thing."

Tara didn't argue. She was for once happy to leave the ellipsis as the background. "Have you worked out our itinerary?"

"We have," Dolin said. "We figure that the Ghost Writer has lost track of us during our sojourn in other realms, so we can go consult with the Good Magician to find a way to nullify him."

This was ridiculous; if the Good Magician was ready to give them such information, he would have done so at the outset. Tartan opened his mouth, but Tara put her hand on his arm warningly. Then he caught on: they must have made their real plans while in the gourd garden, where the Night Colt would have trouble spying on them, as the wives had surely protected it. Now they were implementing them, using a false plan as a cover. They were actually setting it up so the Colt would plant a nasty trap of a dreamlet along the way, to lock them in as he had before.

"That makes sense," Tartan agreed. Then he asked Ted, as he knew Tara was asking Monica: what was the real plan?

"It's a counter trap," Ted explained. "We'll walk blithely into the Ghost Writer's story, and play it out until it brings us to confront him, as before. He'll think Isis will capitulate this time, having failed to get rid of him.

Then we'll step out of our roles. That may shake him up so much he'll quit."

"That seems unlikely."

"Plan B is for Isis to address him directly, possibly fascinating him so that he has to do her will. Then he'll have to follow *our* dreamy skit."

"Isis doesn't even like him. I hope there's a Plan C."

"We're working on it."

Tartan glanced at Tara. She caught his glance and sent it back. She had gotten the same update.

They came to the cornfield with the maize maze. Tata, sniffing out the correct path, led them right through it, including the loop that did not cross itself. "Must be a hidden overpass or underpass," Tartan muttered.

"What is that?" Ted asked.

"Mundane magic borrowing from the third dimension. One road passes over the other without intersecting it."

"Be alert," Amara murmured. "He can't strike on the enchanted path, so it must be on this side path."

"Woof!"

They paused. There was the floating sign. THE PRINCESS AND THE HOG.

"Wait half a moment," Tara said. "Wasn't that the title of the skit that Princess Eve was caught in? Is he using them over?"

"Woof."

"Tata says no," Amara said. "That was 'The Princess and the Grog' which she got out of by changing it to Fog."

And the dog had it from Princess Eve herself, whom he was hosting. So this was a different variant, and probably a different story. The Ghost Writer was not entirely without imagination. Almost, but not quite. They still needed to be rid of him.

"What can we do but move on?" Dolin asked rhetorically.

"And play it out so that we can talk with the Ghost Writer himself," Emerald said.

"Who wants only one thing," Amara said with a frown.

"Maybe we can talk him out of it," Mera said.

They were into their act. Tartan remained uncertain how well this would play out, but he and Tara had to play along.

They walked on under the sign. Amara, the one woman in their group who was not a princess, became one, with a cute little crown and a princessly robe. Tata Dogfish, walking beside her, turned into a bright yellow creature. He rolled up, becoming a gold ball. She picked him up and carried him, as he was no longer as mobile as before.

Tartan remembered the story of the Princess and the Frog. The princess had accidentally rolled her ball into a spring and lost it. A frog had agreed to fetch it out from the depths, provided she let him share her life. Eager to recover her precious ball, she agreed, but then was less eager to honor her part of the deal. But her father the king insisted that she do what she had promised, and the frog shared her room and ate at the table with her. Finally she got so mad that she threw the frog against a wall, whereupon he became a prince who had been enchanted into a frog, and the two rode away in his carriage to live happily ever after. That conclusion had never made sense to Tartan. The princess was a brat, undeserving of any such reward. But since when did fairy tales have to make sense? The question was what was the Ghost Writer going to do with it?

Dolin looked unchanged. He walked beside Emerald, also unchanged. Surely they had roles in the story. What were they? And what about the rest of them?

Well, they would surely find out soon enough.

Princess Amara rolled her gold ball along the path ahead, then skipped along to pick it up. She rolled it again, but this time it veered off the path and dropped into a rabbit hole with a startled woof.

Oh, no! Were they to go through the rabbit hole into Alice's wonderland? Was there no limit to the Ghost Writer's plagiarism?

Amara ran to the hole and put her arm in. "O, woe is me!" she wailed. "I can't reach it. I have lost my most precious possession. The hole is too deep."

Also too small for her to scramble into, fortunately.

There was a stirring in the adjacent bushes. A big pig appeared. No, a hog, per the story title. "What's up?" he snorted.

The Princess burst into tears. "I was playing with my golden ball, my very favoritest thing, and it rolled into a rabbit hole and I can't reach it," she wailed.

"Hmm," the Hog snorted, in a nice trick of pronunciation. "That is a picklement. What would you give me if I dug it out for you?"

"Oh, I would give you anything, anything at all, if you will only rescue my poor gold ball."

"Anything?" the Hog snorted with deep dirty significance. Tartan remembered another kind of naughty comic skit, wherein the dialog was between an innocent girl spoken in high falsetto and a lecherous old man spoken in low resonance. Such as his "The whip, the whip, the whip!" and her "No, no, no!" "The whip, the whip, the whip!" "No, no, anything but the whip!" "Anything?" in a tone fraught with sinister implications. And her response as she caught on: "The whip! The whip! The whip!" Had the Ghost Writer heard that skit? This princess might well be better off with the whip.

"Yes, anything!" she blithely agreed. Which was the problem with true innocence.

"Will you take me into your palace and let me share your royal life?" the Hog asked.

"Yes!"

"Good enough," he snorted. Then he oriented his tusky snout and rooted in the ground, scraping out the dirt. In a period of time between shortly and soon he excavated a deep hole. He found the ball, took it in his mouth, and tossed it up out of the hole to land at the feet of the princess.

"Oh, thank you!" she exclaimed, picking up her ball and hugging the woofing out of it. Then she turned and ran back to the palace, quite forgetting the Hog, as her attention span was quite short.

But the Hog followed, and when she entered the palace, so did he.

Now Emerald animated. "Oh, my dear! What's this!"

The Princess glanced back. "Oh, that's just the nasty old Hog, mother. I told him he could come in."

"In that case, so be it," the Queen said without complete enthusiasm.

Dolin appeared. "What's a pig doing out of the sty?" he demanded.

"That is the Princess's friend," the Queen explained.

"Daughter, explain this," the King said sternly.

"He rescued my gold ball," the Princess said. "I told him he could share my life. But you can kick him out, not that I care."

"If you made that promise, you must honor it," the King said grimly, just as any proper parent would.

So the Hog came to live in the palace with the Princess. When it was time for the noon banquet, he had a place right next to her, and was served a royal repast by the cook, Mera. When it was time for her to be tutored in princessly deportment by the royal tutor Tartan, the Hog learned proper manners too. That helped, because after that he no longer relieved himself on the lovely tiles of the floor. When it was time for her to water the royal flowers, he accompanied her to the garden.

Tartan and Tara took their break, as they needed to attend to their mundane bodies. Their hosts would keep the narrative going.

"So far it is playing out as the Ghost Writer has scripted it," Tartan said. "But what happens when that ends?"

"When the Prince hauls the Princess off to his castle? We may have to end it before then."

"I'm still not clear how this will nullify him. Getting out of a skit is one thing, but getting him to stop all the skits is another."

"Monica says that Isis has something in mind. I think she plans to bewitch him with her sex appeal and make him her willing love slave."

"He should be able to get out of that as readily as we get out of his skit."

"Monica says that when Isis really tries, she can just about ensorcel a troll. I gather she made a demonstration one night when we were away. She holds back mainly because Amara doesn't like it."

"Well, according to the Good Magician, Isis is the one who can do it."

"Yet I share your doubt. Kiss me and make me forget all this."

He kissed her, but she didn't forget. So they returned to Xanth, dispirited.

"You missed a boring excursion," Ted told Tartan. "Those flowers are nowhere near the match of Rose of Roogna's garden."

"The crisis will come at dusk, when the Ghost Writer phases into the scene," Tartan said. "That's what we're waiting for."

Dusk came. It was time for the Princess to retire. Tara the maid brought the basin of warm water for her to wash with, and the Hog got cleaned up too. He was now a fairly handsome swine. Then the maid turned down the silken bed covers—and the Hog climbed into the bed.

The Princess stared. "Now wait a moment or three," she said. "I'm not about to sleep with a big fat ugly stinky Hog in my bed."

He was no longer stinky, but that might be a moot point. "Your father the King said that if you promised, you had to honor it," the maid reminded her. "The Hog is with you throughout."

"Oh phooey on that!" the Princess screamed, outraged. She jumped on the bed and pushed the Hog out so that he fell on the floor with a meaty thunk.

"Ow!" he exclaimed, no longer snorting. Then he stood up. The evil spell on him had been broken by the thud, and he had become a Prince. He had also, Tartan realized, become the Ghost Writer, who had taken his place now that it was dusk. "You deserve to be spanked, you undisciplined girl."

"You wouldn't dare!" the Princess said. "I've never been spanked in my life!"

"There's always a first time." The Prince caught her, threw her across his lap as he sat on the bed, hauled up her nightie, and smartly spanked her bare bottom. It was amazingly comely anatomy, rippling splendidly, and Tartan realized that Isis was enhancing it for the occasion. She was beginning her ensorcelment. He had to shield his eyes before he freaked out, even without seeing panties. Could the Goddess prevail?

"Ow!" the Princess screamed more in indignity than in pain. Then she did a double take. "You smacked my bottom! Only the man I marry can do that."

"Indeed," the Prince agreed. "The nuptials will be next week at my castle. But first we'll celebrate our engagement with a resounding ellipsis." He eyed the enhanced bottom with something more than punishment in mind. Isis was scoring. Then he heaved her onto the bed, bottom up. "I trust your inner spirit will do her part."

And would she? Tartan wondered. Assuming Isis had the power to make him her love slave, would she expend it on this ilk? She had balked before.

At which point Amara said "Dream Skit, Scheme Quit," and exited the scene. The others followed suit, including Tata, causing the scene to dissolve.

"What's this?" the Ghost Writer demanded, startled. His own role as Prince had faded with the demolition of the scene.

"This is the showdown, you ludicrous pervert," Amara said. "You have no power over us. There'll be no ellipsis."

"We'll see about that," he said, taking hold of her.

Isis manifested. "Yes we will." She inhaled as she stared into his eyes.

And suddenly the contest was on. The Ghost Writer wanted to have an ellipsis with the Goddess in human host, while Isis wanted to enslave him emotionally without soiling her host's body with his brutish passion. It was something to watch.

"Take off your clothes," he said.

"Take off yours."

They both did so, matching item for item until both were bare. The body that had been Amara became phenomenally shapely. Her hair coiled down around her shoulders and breasts. Her eyes grew luminous. Her lips parted invitingly.

"Wow," he murmured.

"Kiss me," she breathed.

But he suddenly jerked back. "No. Spread your legs."

"If he kisses her, he's done for," Ted said. "Her kisses are magic. I know; she kissed me once, just to demonstrate. I would have become her love slave if she had let me. But it was just to show me."

"But if she spreads her legs, he'll have her without being enslaved," Tartan said. "That's what he wants. Passion without commitment. But what warned him?"

"I think it's the Night Colt coaching him."

"I'll see." Tartan caught Tara's eye, then pulled out of the host.

Tara did the same. The two of them stood together as ghosts.

And there was the Colt, visible to their ghost forms as he wasn't to their solid forms. Sure enough, he was standing by the bed, murmuring something to the Ghost Writer. The horse's mouth did not move, but it was clear that he was communicating. "Telepathy," Tara said.

Isis leaned forward invitingly. "First the kiss."

The Ghost Writer started to lean toward her, unable to help himself. But the Colt nudged him and he aborted the motion. "No. First the legs."

She lay down on the bed. "Then join me," she said, parting her legs. They were phenomenal; Tartan would have been lost, had he been the target.

The Ghost Writer got down beside her, then quickly rolled over to cover her. But her legs snapped shut as she aimed a kiss at his mouth. He barely turned his face away in time.

"Bleep!" they said almost together. Then they both laughed.

"I dare you to tackle me without the Colt coaching you," she said.

"No way! You've got a four thousand year lead in experience."

"Then come to me in the comic strip. I'll have my own body there. Then I'd be free to spread my legs."

"You'd have panties on, and freak me out, then kiss me when I'm out of it."

"At least you're not stupid," she said with a certain hint of dawning respect. Tartan realized that the Goddess liked a good fight almost more than a conquest.

"Bleep! I wish you'd come to me on my terms. We could have such a time."

"We could," she agreed. She put her hands to either side of his head, holding it in place. He tried to resist, but his will was clearly being sapped. Slowly she brought her face to his. "Hold still. This won't hurt at all."

The Colt lifted a fore-hoof and knocked the Ghost Writer on the head. "Ow!" he exclaimed, turning his face away.

"Bleep! I almost had you there."

"You almost did," he agreed, rubbing his head.

"Block off the Colt," Isis said to Tartan and Tara without looking.

They advanced on the Colt, who eyed them warily. He evidently was not used to being seen by others. They formed a wall of two between him and the couple on the bed. He tried to get around them, but they moved in tandem, maintaining the block. He was ghostly, but so were they; he could not avoid them.

"Hold still," Isis repeated softly to her victim. Her face was almost blindingly beautiful. No living man could resist for long.

He held still. Victory was incipient.

The Colt dived under them and came up under the Ghost Writer. Then he galloped away, carrying the man.

"Bleep," Isis said once more. "Dusk is ending and the Ghost Writer has to get back to Mundania before the deadline. I almost had him."

"You almost did," Tartan agreed.

"We ran out of time. If I had more time . . ." She shrugged and faded.

Amara was left naked on the bed. "Oh! I faded out. Did anything—?"

"Nothing happened, unfortunately," Tara told her.

Then the bed dissolved, along with the room and indeed, the palace. It was all part of the crafted dream, now finished.

They had come so close to capturing the Ghost Writer. But Tartan knew they would not get another chance like that. As Isis had said, the man wasn't stupid.

"We'd better call it a day, and try again tomorrow," Tara said. "With Plan C, if we can work it out."

Dolin nodded. "Tomorrow," he agreed.

Back at the apartment, Tartan and Tara commiserated. "She really would have gotten him, but for the interference of the Colt and the time running out."

"Yes. She was irresistible, like no mortal woman." He caught himself. "That is—"

"I know what you mean. I'm no goddess, and wouldn't care to be one."

"But they'll make sure she never gets another chance," Tartan said, relieved that she wasn't offended.

"We've got to think of something new, that they don't expect."

"Did you learn anything more about Monica's secret love?"

"Almost. It's definitely one of us, but I still can't tell whom. If she gets sufficiently distracted, I may be able to tell."

"Then there's Mera. What does she have on her mind?"

"I wish I knew. Women are too good at keeping secrets."

He laughed. "Weird to hear a woman say it."

"Well, women are more complicated than men. Men want only one thing. Women want many things, in differing degrees."

"Speaking of one thing—"

She kissed him. "I saw you coming. Have an ellipsis."

. . .

Next morning, back in their hosts, they found no real progress. "We don't even know if there'll be dream skits out there," Dolin said. "Now that we've shown him how we can escape them. That puts us on an even basis, but it's not enough."

"He can avoid us and make mischief elsewhere in Xanth," Mera said.

"First thing to do is to check the location of the Night Colt," Tartan said. "Tara and I will go ghost and see if he's here."

"I will join you," Isis said, manifesting. "Link with me."

They linked hands so that the Goddess would be able to interact with them as ghosts. They drew out of their hosts, and the Goddess did join them. Her spirit was as shapely as ever, but this time she had a comprehensive dress that masked it sufficiently so that Tartan had no problem. She could turn it off when she wanted to. They looked around, but there was no sign of the Colt.

"There is something I wanted to consult with you about, privately," Isis said. "I have been considering Monica. She bears the signs of a hopeless love, and is troubled. I do not think it is kind to let her suffer longer."

"She loves a man of our party," Tara said. "But we can't tell who."

"I can. I am experienced in the signs. It is Prince Dolin."

"That's a relief," Tartan said. "We feared it might be me."

"No. You are not her type."

"A smart handsome prince," Tartan said wryly.

"She values you as a friend, but you do not turn her on emotionally. No, it is definitely Dolin. But that confuses me. Why doesn't she say so? They would make a perfect couple."

"That is our concern," Tara said.

"I believe it is time to bring this into the open." Isis said. "That may be painful, but not as painful as watching her become suicidal."

"Suicidal!" Tartan exclaimed.

"She is really hurting. Once this mission is done, she will have no further reason to live, as she sees it. That's why we need to act now, before we part company."

"I will do it," Tara said. "I would rather betray her confidence than see her die."

"It is not much of a betrayal," Isis said.

"I am curious, Goddess," Tartan said. "I had understood that you were pretty much aloof from ordinary human concerns. Now you really seem to care. Is this a change?"

"Yes. My association with Amara has taught me more of human concerns and emotions. Amara feels some of them only slightly, but she is aware of them. I have come to care about her, and by extension to care about others." She paused. "Specifically the other members of this party. I have come to regard you as friends, and I find I value that, and would like to keep you as such after the mission is done. Is this unrealistic?"

"Not at all," Tara said warmly. "It's human. But we may not be able to visit Xanth after this mission. We don't know."

"I could visit you in Mundania. That would be limited to spirit form, unless I occupied your body as I do Amara's."

"You are welcome to do that, when," Tara said. "We have seen how it works with Amara. You let her be herself, except when there is need for you."

"That is good. Now we had better return before the others worry."

They returned to their hosts. "No sign of the Night Colt," Tartan reported. "We looked all around."

"That's good," Dolin said. "We shall search out whatever story skits there are today."

"There is something else," Tara said. "It may not exactly be my business, but I think I have to speak."

"Of course," Dolin said. "We value your input."

"It is this: my host Monica is in love." She paused, and Tartan knew that Monica was silently protesting. "She is not speaking of it, but I will."

"Monica loves?" Emerald asked. "Who?"

"She loves Prince Dolin."

"Me!" Dolin said, surprised.

Tara took a breath. "I don't know why she won't say it herself, so I must speak on her behalf. You may not have considered her, Prince, but she is actually an excellent match for you. She is the daughter of a demon prince and a naga princess, so she is a princess in her own right, two fold. She qualifies. She can secure your place in this reality. She's an excellent person in her own right, and she loves you. I think you should marry her."

"Why yes," Dolin agreed. "I have come to know her too. I have thought of her only as a friend, but I could readily love her. But I think I need to know first why she has chosen not to speak of this. She's a sensible person; she must have excellent reason, and it may be that I should heed that reason."

"I will turn the body over to her," Tara said. "She has to speak for herself now." She did so, becoming a passenger in the body.

Monica burst into tears.

"My dear!" Emerald said, hurrying across to embrace her. "What is it? I'm sure we all support you, and will help you in any way we can. Certainly I speak for myself. You are my closest friend."

Monica only cried harder.

They all grouped around her comfortingly, and slowly she subsided and was able to speak. "It is true: I love Dolin. It came upon me gradually as I got to know him better, but it is complete. I wish I could marry him."

"And you should," Emerald said. "Not only will it complete your love, it will grant him status in this reality. What could possibly prevent that?"

"You," Monica said.

"Me? My dear, I do not oppose it. I think it's wonderful."

"It's that your mission is overwhelmingly important. The humans and the dragons are inevitably trending toward war. That will be horribly destructive. It has to be avoided. Only you can stop it, by marrying Dolin. I know you don't love each other, and are not romantically compatible, but this is more important than love. You understand each other and will get along well enough, and your union will avert the war. I can't let my private happiness interfere with that."

"Oh, my," Dolin said. "I have to agree with you, intellectually."

"Well, I don't!" Emerald flared, a bit of smoke puffing out of her nose. "You can love her, Dolin. I know you can. It can be a wonderful union. I can go find some other prince to marry. If I'm lucky, he will be tolerant and let me have my girlfriends. And the war will still be stopped."

"He would not be as tolerant as I would be," Dolin said. "I know you, Emerald, and respect you, and love you in my fashion. You would be better off with me."

"And what of Monica?" Emerald asked. "You and she are my closest friends. How could I ever deny her love, by taking it myself when I don't have to?"

Tartan stepped in. "Dolin, use your talent. What is the right thing?"

The prince considered, then looked surprised. "It is to marry Monica."

"See?" Emerald said. "I knew that was best."

"How is it best?" Monica asked. "How can hurting my friend ever be right?"

Mera strode forward. "I believe it is my turn. Bear with me while I explain."

The others looked at her. What did she have to do with this?

"Please do, Aunt Mera," Dolin said. "I know that you want nothing but my welfare."

"No. I want two things. Your welfare, and mine. Your welfare is with Monica, who can indeed secure your place here and give you the kind of love you will not find elsewhere. Your marriage to her will complete that aspect of my situation."

"Oh, I wish it could!" Monica breathed.

"Now drop the other shoe," Tartan told Mera. "What of Emerald and the war?"

Mera turned to Emerald. "I love you."

"You what?" Emerald asked, astonished.

"I did not marry in my home time, long ago, because I could not bear the thought of marrying a prince, however worthy he might be."

"But why not?"

"For the same reason you can't. I am a lesbian princess. When I met you, Emerald, I knew I had to pursue you, to find out if happiness was possible. That is why I joined your party, and helped you all I could. My alternate who is here in spirit could have seen you through, Dolin, but only my personal presence could accomplish my own dream. As I came to know you, Emerald, and to love you, I knew that it was possible. Except for two things."

"Two?" Emerald asked faintly.

"First I needed to know whether women could marry in Xanth. The Book of Lost Answers gave me that answer, thanks to some other person's question."

"Lesbians can marry!" Emerald exclaimed. "I remember. It was one of the irrelevant answers."

"So I asked a different question, concealing my interest," Mera said. "That gave me half of what I needed."

"And the other half?"

"That my nephew Dolin be safely settled elsewhere. If he could not find another suitable princess in time—the limit of our visit here was one month—then he would have to marry you, to secure both your needs. I could not take that chance from him, and there was no point in advertising my own orientation as long as my nephew's fate remained in doubt. But now that he has found Monica, whom I know to be worthy, I can focus on my own desire. Emerald, marry me. It will secure the truce even if you don't love me yet."

Emerald stood amazed. "This is so sudden! How can I be sure?"

"How can *I* be sure?" Dolin echoed.

"Of course it's new to you, Dolin and Emerald," Amara said. "All this time you thought you were stuck with each other."

"Not stuck!" the two said almost together. Then they dissolved into relieved laughter.

"I don't know why I never thought of you, Monica," Dolin said. "You were right beside my nose."

"Because it was mostly Tara in her body," Amara said. "And she kept her mouth mostly shut when Tara was away. Because she was trying to protect her friend Emerald."

"And I never thought of you, Mera," Emerald said. "I wish I had."

"Because you did not know her nature," Amara said. "None of us did."

"It was my secret," Mera said. "Until I could be sure of Dolin's placement."

"So there we were," Tartan said. "With our problems ready to be solved within our own group, had we but the wit to realize it."

"So why are we discussing it, and taking no action?" Mera asked.

Amara laughed. "Here are your orders: Dolin, kiss Monica. Mera, kiss Emerald. Then you will know."

"It is the right thing," Dolin agreed. "We must do it, Aunt Mera."

Still they hesitated.

"Now," Amara said sharply. "We need to have this settled. Even the Goddess has been seriously concerned."

Thus pushed, Dolin advanced on Monica, and Mera advanced on Emerald. They kissed their targets simultaneously. Two big hearts flew out, orbited the lovers, and crashed into each other, fracturing into a dozen little hearts. Now there was no doubt.

Then the two couples disengaged. Dolin hugged Emerald. "Thank you for being ready," he said.

Mera hugged Monica. "Thank you for rescuing us."

Then Monica and Emerald hugged, and dissolved into tears. These were not unhappy ones.

Once things settled down, Dolin and Monica were safely holding hands, and so were Mera and Emerald. "There are things about you,

Mera," Emerald said, "that remind me of things I like about Dolin, now that I am free to accept them."

"We are closely related," Mera said.

Then Amara thought of something. "Mera, must you return to Reality Number Two? I don't think Dolin can return there."

"No problem," Mera said. "I am not the Mera who brought Dolin here. I am the one who came physically to R#3, and crossed to R#1 with the rest of you. My self of R#2 is already on her way home with the good news about Dolin. Princess Taplin will be pleased."

"But Mera of R#2 can't marry Emerald. Isn't she heartbroken?"

"No. We have been in touch. She is relieved that Dolin has found his princess, and, well, she—" Mera blushed. "She is still with me, in spirit, visiting. Now that contact has been established, we are able to retain it despite being in different realities. I hope you don't mind, Emerald."

"You mean I'll be making love to two of you?"

"Yes."

"I will love you both. Mera #2 started this whole business. I'll always be grateful to her."

Dolin looked at Monica. "Speaking of spirits: you mean I am kissing Tara?"

"The bleep!" Tartan swore. Tara of course was staying out of it.

They all dissolved into another round of laughter.

"That leaves Ted and Amara," Tartan said.

"I am not interested in a romantic relationship," Amara said. "You know that."

"But we do need you a while longer," Tartan said. "Because we need Isis. The rest of the group may break up, now that the couples have formed, but—"

"Wait," Dolin said. "You helped us. We're not through helping you. We can't break up the group until the Ghost Writer is dispatched." The others nodded.

"And we don't want to break up the circle of friendship we have formed here," Emerald said. "We should finish the mission, then retain the group." There were more nods.

"I assumed you wanted time to yourselves," Tartan said.

"We do," Monica said. "But we can have that in the evenings."

"I would like to have a relationship with Amara," Ted said. "But as she said, she's not interested. I would not want to mess up our friendship."

"Let me see what I can do," Tartan told him. Then, to Amara: "If the group continues beyond the mission, do you prefer to be with it?"

"Actually I do," Amara said. "I like the friendships, and we now have a good deal of adventure in common. And I like being with Isis, different as we are. I know the Goddess wants to be here too, as friends with the rest of you. But—"

"If you had a regular male companion, other men would leave you alone," Tartan said. "Just as others left Dolin and Emerald alone, leaving them free to be a couple if they needed to. That might make it worthwhile."

"But he's a man. Soon he'd want ellipses, and I don't."

"I would," Ted said. "She's a pretty girl. And when Isis kissed me, I really wanted it. I can't deny that."

Tartan thought fast. This was the crux. "What about this, Amara: you keep company without romance, but if he wants more, ask Isis to handle it? She could let you tune out for the occasion, as she did when trying to seduce the Ghost Writer. It wouldn't take long, and the rest of the time you'd have a pleasant friend."

"Wow!" Ted said. "I'd really go for that! No offense to you, Amara, but the Goddess is something else."

"Oh, she wouldn't—" Amara paused herself with a dash. "Correction. She would. Because she likes this group too, and wants to be part of it, and this would facilitate that. What I have little or no interest in, she has total interest."

"So it would be mutual convenience," Tartan said. "Ted would keep other men away from you, and Isis could give him something every so often. She certainly knows how."

"But I have to be realistic. She'll never agree to that," Ted said. "I'm no prince or Magician. I'm just a garden variety, curve-hungry crossbreed jerk."

"Let's ask her," Tartan said. "Goddess—"

Then Isis manifested. She didn't need to overhear their whole dialog to grasp its nature. "Put Ted on," she said.

Tartan turned the body over to the host. "But I don't want to upset Amara," Ted said uncertainly. Even slight romance seemed to be fraught with uncertainties.

"Leave her to me," Isis said. "Come here, Demon Ted." She shot him a tractor beam glance.

He went to her, towed by the beam. She kissed him. Little sparks radiated. His feet floated an inch off the ground. It wasn't love, but it was potent.

Tartan was left to his own thoughts in that timeless interval of the kiss. "Amara," he said silently. He knew she could hear him, because their bodies were in close contact.

"No, I don't want to kiss you either," she answered with a mental smile.

He laughed. "Tell Isis when this breathless moment is done that Tara and I need to talk with her at greater length, privately."

"Go to her in the comic strip."

"No, the Night Colt is watching, and the Ghost Writer would know we were planning something. It should be in Mundania."

"She'll need a host."

"I'll tell Tara."

"Will do. Now get out of here before the endless kiss ends."

Tartan withdrew, his spot mission accomplished. Just in time, for the kiss was indeed coming to a glacial close after cramming centuries into an instant.

"Okay," Ted said breathlessly when the Goddess faded and he landed back on the ground.

"Okay," Amara said.

"Let's take the afternoon off," Dolin said. "And the night. Then tomorrow we'll tackle the Ghost Writer." He clearly wanted time alone with Monica.

"Together," Mera said. She wanted time alone with Emerald.

"As a group," Emerald said. Ditto, with Mera.

"As three couples," Amara said. "Even if one lacks hearts."

"Well, Emerald and I lacked hearts," Dolin said. "But it was good."

"And we saw those sparks," Emerald said. "And you're no dragon."

"Tara says it's time to go home before she wets her panties," Monica said naughtily.

Indeed it was. Three romances within an hour would have Tara climbing the wall. Tartan wanted to be that wall.

Chapter 16

GODDESS

Back at the apartment, they didn't even wait on the bathroom. Tara ripped out of her dress and tackled Tartan. She had wall climbing to do. He was supremely happy to accommodate her.

. . . . .

Afterward, exhausted on the bed, they realized what they had done. "That was a five dot ellipsis," Tara gasped. "I didn't know they existed."

"That must be the first of its kind," Tartan said.

Now she dived for the bathroom. "I doubt I'll want another for a week."

"Me too."

After his turn in the bathroom, they flopped on the bed side by side. "It was weird, becoming a passenger instead of the driver," she said. "But Monica had to have her turn."

"You did right. That saves Dolin from a loveless union."

"And saves Emerald from another. Mera was a surprise, though I guess there were hints along the way that we didn't pick up on."

"We had other things on our minds."

"Yes." Then she was taken by a convoluted pause. "What?"

"Oh, I forgot to tell you. The Goddess Isis is coming so we can talk. I think I have figured out how to nail the Ghost Writer."

Tara's expression shifted. "I am here," Isis said. "What is your concern?"

"I believe you can take out the Ghost Writer here in Mundania," Tartan said. "All you need is a human host who can intercept him on his home turf."

The Goddess was thoughtful. "I could do that. But I'd have to stay with him to be sure he didn't return to mischief in Xanth. That's more than I care to donate to the cause."

"But it could be worth your while regardless," Tartan said.

"How so?"

"Well, for one thing—" He broke off, hesitating to broach his notion.

Meanwhile she was overtaken by a pause for thought, then spoke. "I haven't done it in Mundania for some time. Let me see whether it is physically feasible."

"I'm sure—"

"Give me an hour with this host, and we'll know."

"You mean—?"

"Of course that's what I mean. You have no idea of the rapture I can provoke when I indulge. You have never experienced anything of this magnitude."

"But Tara and I just performed a five dot ellipsis. We're worn out, at least in that respect."

"Precisely. May I, Tara?" There was an unsegmented pause, because this was in Mundania where the magic nuances were largely lost. "Good enough."

She had gotten Tara's permission to use her body for sex? That was crazy. But it seemed that the Goddess had taken it as a challenge. Well, after that effort flopped, they would be able to talk.

Tara's body oriented on him. She was already undressed, because they had been too tired to dress and get on with the afternoon routine. Now she sat up and took a deep breath. It was amazing how sexy that made her, even in his present state.

Then she took hold of him and kissed him. Rockets went off.

That was just the beginning. Tartan found himself on a tour that wound through heaven and hell without yielding any awe to either. He spent one or two eternities in almost painfully passionate bliss, but unlike his prior effort with Tara, this did not fade. The Goddess had spoken of rapture; she had understated the case. He could tell that it was not just him; Tara, too was transfixed by surging waves of delight as if borne on a mighty and endless ocean.

. . . . . .

Finally they washed ashore, in subsiding inspirations of fulfillment, totally spent. And knew that they had just experienced a six dot ellipsis. The Goddess had made her point. Or rather, her extra dot.

"It will do," Isis said. "I do seem to retain some of my proficiency here. Now let's talk business."

When they were able to focus, they did talk. "You are physically confined to the comic strip," Tartan told the Goddess. "We certainly understand why you want to get out. But the powers that be in Xanth are not going to let you out, knowing you will merely seduce your way to the top, then rule as Queen of Xanth with a harem of lucky men. Even if your rule was phenomenally benign, you would remain an outsider with power, and the people would chafe. So it's better to keep well clear of that, and that means no release from the comics."

"I appreciate the infernal logic," Isis said grimly.

"But here's the thing: you can have a lot more freedom than you may appreciate. All you need are suitable hosts, whose pleasures you can share. Don't tell me you didn't enjoy that phenomenal ellipsis you just put us through."

"I loved it. Tara has a nice little body with all manner of innocent aspects. But that's hardly the same as being free to do my will in my own body."

"Maybe we can talk some good virile men into visiting you in the comic strip. I'm sure that once one tries it, he'll be eager to return. But going out with the hosts is no bad thing either. You can tour Xanth with Amara, and tackle Ted any time you want. You can go to the world of Ida, what's its name, Ptero, in your own dream body, where all the men who ever even thought of existing are, and most of them would really like to be with you."

"Most?" she asked dangerously.

Oops. "It's a case of the ninety-five percent and the five percent: the ninety five who really want to be with you, and the five who lie about it because their wives are listening."

"Oh. Of course."

"And the Dream Realm," Tartan continued. "You have a gig there, but that doesn't mean you have to stay on the set all the time. All those men who have been told 'in your dreams' will be eager to play out those dreams with you, if you let them. Even goblins, trolls, and ogres will pant for you; you know that."

"I do," she agreed thoughtfully.

"And Mundania, where you will have to stick with one man, but that may be your most rewarding experience of all."

"One man?" she asked disdainfully. "I am the Goddess of Fertility!"

"Yes. And for thousands of years you haven't had the chance to be fertile. What you most truly miss is being a loyal wife and mother, this time with a man who won't get treacherously killed by a rival for the throne, and with a son who won't grow up to kill you himself. Because both will know that without you they are nothing. You can finally have it all, in your little anonymous corner of drear Mundania, as a perfectly ordinary housewife."

"An ordinary housewife!"

"I learned something about Demon Ted, as I used his body," Tartan continued inexorably. "His father is totally anonymous. His mother is Demoness Metria, who keeps his father in a state of perpetual bliss so he doesn't get into trouble. Meanwhile she gads about getting into all the trouble she wants, searching out mischief. Ted sometimes gets disgusted, but what can he do? She's a full demoness, and they can't be constrained. What she doesn't do, her slightly crazy alternate self Mentia does, and her childish Woe Betide. But she serves as a useful example for you. You can have several lives. In Mundania, the loyal dull housewife and mother. In the comic strip, the royal seductress. In Xanth, the companion and friend to those who know you and like you for what you are, with a regular sometime boyfriend. In Ptero, the wild vamp. In the Dream Realm, the mistress of monsters. These are five venues that you can be in any time, as long as you're careful and remember which host you are in. You're not confined at all, any more than Metria is. You can realize all your ambitions, in your fashion, almost simultaneously."

"Stop, or I'll kiss you."

Tartan opened his mouth. She kissed him. Stunned, he shut up.

"You have made your case," she said. "You have persuaded me. I will take out the Ghost Writer so he won't bother Xanth any more. But to do that I must first locate him. How can we do that?"

"I thought you'd never ask. Tomorrow when he rides the Night Colt out to seed his naughty little dreams, your spirit will quietly follow them. When they return to his home in Mundania, you will note the place. Then we will go there and set things up for you. We were recruited because we can operate in Mundania, and we will."

"But the Night Colt can see my spirit form. He'll know what I'm up to."

"Not if the other members of our group distract him. We need to devise a show that will grab and hold their attention, so they don't even think of you."

The Goddess nodded. "You have thought this out."

Tartan laughed ruefully. "I have tried to. But my plan may be full of holes."

"You have given me something to ponder. I will see you tomorrow." She faded out.

Tara took a huge shuddering breath. "That was something, and I don't mean just the ellipsis. You really came through, Tartan!"

"Xanth has given me you. I have to repay it somehow."

"That's so sweet." She kissed him.

"And I'd rather have your kisses than hers."

"Is that your ninety-five percent statement, or your five percent?"

He laughed. "You know, if I didn't love you already, I'd be getting there, you cute little tease."

"Now about that show we will do tomorrow morning to distract the Ghost Writer and the Night Colt. What do you have in mind?"

"I did say there might be some holes in the plan."

"Like having no idea what to do?"

"Something like that."

"Let's work this out. What would distract a man and a colt?"

"A mass orgy?"

She hit him with a pillow. "Get serious."

"Actually the surest way to get a man's attention is with a pretty girl. We know the Ghost Writer already wants Isis. If she did a provocative dance—"

"Is there any other kind she would do?"

"He'd watch," he concluded

"One tiny little problem: Isis won't be there. The dance is to distract him from seeing her as she spies on him."

"Oops. But maybe Amara can fake it."

"Manifesting as the Goddess, in the absence of the Goddess? That's one tall order."

"Awful tall," he agreed.

"But let's consider. Suppose we use the magic roses?"

Tartan glanced down at his own rose. "Considering that they mostly can't be seen, I'm not sure how."

"Not to show, silly. As a theme. The Ghost Writer may think they're imaginary, but we can craft a dance about taking the roses and being true to them. Amara has Isis's rose. Maybe it will lend her the ability to pretend Isis is with her. She will be, really, in the form of her rose."

"Maybe so," he agreed cautiously.

"And there can be plenty of jumping and whirling."

"That will make it seem that Isis is there?"

"Like this." She got up, donned her clothing, and stood before him. Then she jumped. Her breasts bounced and the hem of her skirt flared upward, showing a flash of her thighs. Then she whirled, and the hem rose up almost to her waist, showing her panties. Here in Mundania that didn't freak him out, but he certainly appreciated the effect.

"I am beginning to get your point," he said. "If Amara does that, emulating Isis, he will notice."

"That was my thought. Now let's work out the whole dance, simple so the others can quickly learn it, and as sexy as we can make it without violating the dread Adult Conspiracy."

"You're a genius!"

"I thought you liked me only for my body."

"That, too," he said, joining her on the dance floor.

"Oops," she said, pausing in place.

"I don't like the sound of that, cute as it is when you say it."

"It's that the Ghost Writer is there in person only from half an hour before dawn and until half an hour after dusk, day excluded. We'll have to get there early."

"Very early," he agreed. "Because we'll need time to prepare before he arrives."

"I'll set the alarm."

Then he thought of one. "When it's time for the Ghost Writer to go home, he won't be able to watch the dance any more. Then he may see Isis."

"Bleep! The dancers can't follow them through the sky."

"But we can, as ghosts."

"And he'll know we're tracking him, and will go anywhere but home."

A bulb flashed. "Maybe not. Suppose we continue the dance, as ghosts? So he keeps watching us, and when he gives us the slip, he won't be watching for Isis."

"Maybe that will do," she agreed. "But there are so many Ifs I'm getting nervous."

"All we can do is our best, and hope."

They worked out the dance, had supper, and turned in early. Then in the darkness of the wee hours they held hands, ready to head back to Xanth. "I hope they're not mad about being woken up early," she said.

"Who knows what state they'll be in, after discovering their love?"

"Oh, my! Monica may be clasping Dolin when I arrive in her body. Maybe we better wait until tomorrow."

"No, Isis will have told them it's today. We'd better gamble."

"I'll be so embarrassed, if—"

They arrived. The six members of the group, and Tata Dogfish, were seated in a circle. "About time you got here," Ted said.

"You—you were expecting us!"

"Sure. Amara said you'd be here now. That's her talent, you know. So we turned in early and got up early."

Isis manifested in Amara. "You have a plan."

"Yes, Tartan said. "You will watch in ghost form while we distract the Ghost Rider and maybe the Night Colt with a dance. Then you will follow him to his lair, and mark its location."

"But once he starts home—"

"Tara and I will continue the dance in the air, so he keeps his eyes on us."

Isis and the others looked doubtful, but didn't protest further. Obviously luck needed to be on their side.

"One more thing," Tartan said. Then he explained about how Amara would have to fake manifesting the Goddess.

"I will try," she agreed gamely. "I'm not interested in romance or ellipses, but this is a kind of acting, and I have been learning from Isis."

Tartan and Tara demonstrated their Dance of the Roses by the light of the moon, holding their roses aloft. They knew that the others, close friends as they were, could see the flowers. "The point is to make it interesting enough so he'll keep watching," Tara said as they danced. "That means short skirts on the women, and lots of twirling." She smiled. "Yes, men, we'll flash panties; be prepared."

The group had associated long enough now so that their panties had become familiar and no longer delivered full freakouts; but they still had impact, so the warning was well advised. If they freaked out the Ghost Writer, so much the better; the Colt would nudge him back awake, and he would keep watching. Especially the women, focusing on Amara.

Tara twirled. Tartan saw Dolin's eyes widen appreciatively. He might have had a good night with Monica, but he still appreciated sexy exposure when it presented itself.

They went through their little routine several times, then turned the bodies over to their hosts. Now Ted danced with Amara, Dolin with Monica, and Mera with Emerald. Both members of the last couple wore skirts, and both were marvelously esthetic girls; their twirling was fully adequate. Tartan, now watching rather than dancing, had to yank his gaze away. They might not be interested in men, but they were certainly attractive *to* men. Tata also danced, Princess Eve manifesting as a ghost.

"They come," Amara said. Either she knew from her talent, or Isis had seen them.

They had their dance perfected. They continued it as the Ghost Writer and Night Colt arrived, pretending to be oblivious to their invisible presence. Actually, knowing they were there helped, and maybe the magic roses helped too, because they almost seemed to be visible.

The three couples whirled and twirled, the four women flashing in unison. Amara was especially provocative; she was acting exactly as if the Goddess were with her. Tartan, who was free to look around beyond the group while Ted did the dancing, saw that the Ghost Writer was indeed fascinated, his gaze glued to Amara. Maybe he was seeing what he hoped to see: the Goddess.

Then Amara flung her yellow rose high, intending to catch it. And the Colt and Ghost Writer zipped in and caught it in the air. He could see the rose! That meant that his interest in the Goddess was genuine.

"Hey!" Amara called. "Come back with my rose!" Actually Isis's rose, given to her by the Goddess. Amara's rose was pink.

But the Ghost Writer and Night Colt galloped away into the sky.

Tartan shot out of his host, and Tara joined him. But they knew that Isis was watching, so instead of openly pursuing the fugitives they continued their dance, floating after the rider and steed. Tartan found Tara especially evocative, because now she was dancing in the air and it was easy to imagine that a person on the ground would get a good look under her skirt. Not that the dancers below were looking.

The Colt paused, and the Writer looked back, seeing them. Tartan struck a dance pose and Tara twirled, her Blue Chipmunk skirt elevating exactly as when physical. She was flashing him with her ghostly panties. The Writer noticed, and licked his lips as he watched, interested without freaking. Maybe panties had to have more substance to have full power.

Then the Colt shook him, reminding him of the time, and they resumed their trip.

Tartan and Tara sailed after them, not pursuing so much as maintaining the distraction so that Isis would not be seen.

The Writer made a flinging motion, as if seeding a field. What was he doing?

"Uh-oh," Tara said. "He's sowing dreamlets."

"But they can't affect us in our spirit forms."

"I am not sure of that."

Ghostly forms appeared in the air. They seemed to be emaciated people, flying without wings. What were they? "They look like ghostly zombies. But zombies don't fly."

Then they saw the fangs. "Oh, bleep!" Tara swore. "Those are vampires!"

"Ghost vampires? I didn't know those existed."

"Maybe they don't. Except in the Ghost Writer's sick imagination. Now they're coming after us."

"Ghost vampires to prey on ghost dancers," he said. "I think we'd better get out of here."

They moved back the way they had come, but the vampires moved faster, cutting them off. They formed a large sphere surrounding the two of them, covering above, below, and all directions. They would have to pass through that bubble to get away.

"What happens to spirits that get eaten by ghosts?" Tara asked nervously.

"I think we don't want to find out. Solid vampires suck the blood of living folk, and then the victims become vampires themselves. We might become ghost vampires. I don't think our bodies would like that much."

"Not much," she agreed nervously. "It might ruin the ellipses. We'd be trying to suck each other's blood instead."

"Ugh!"

"I was trying to joke. I don't think I succeeded."

The vampire sphere constricted. It looked all too tight. This was getting ugly.

"I'll charge them," Tartan said gallantly. "Then you zip through the hole I make in their wall."

"And what happens to you?" she demanded. "I'm not going without you."

"Then I guess we'll just have to try to fight them off."

"They'll be ready for that, and there are a lot more of them."

Tartan was afraid, not for himself, but for her. He didn't want her getting bitten by vampires. "Tara, I want you to know that if this is the end—"

She cut him off with a kiss. "Focus," she said urgently. "There must be a way."

Then he noticed something. A curving twisting band of translucence was snaking through the sphere. It looked like ribbon candy, but was big enough to take in a person. What was it? Another of the Ghost Writer's creations?

Then a bulb flashed. "The comic strip!" he exclaimed. "A strip of it must have torn loose and drifted up here."

"I think I see puns in it," she agreed. "But I'm not sure how that can help us."

"Isis! She's physically confined to the comic strip, but she's able to control it somewhat. She could have sent it to help us!"

"Yes! Dive in!" She did so herself.

Tartan followed. Now they were both inside the flat band, looking out. The vampires crowded close, looking nonplussed or nonminussed. It seemed that they hesitated to enter it themselves. What would unmitigated puns do to ghost vampires? It might be no laughing matter to them.

But they weren't giving up. Soon one of their bolder spooks would screw his courage to the sticking point and dive in, and others would follow. This was only a temporary reprieve.

"But maybe we can fight them off from here," Tartan said. "We can throw puns at them. There should be a plentiful supply."

"Yes!" Tara grabbed a foul smelling flower. "Eau de Cay—zombie perfume." She wound up and hurled it out of the strip. It hit a vampire, not having much choice, as they were thickly clustered.

"Eau!" the vampire wailed, deep in disgust. It dropped out of the formation, struggling to get away from the smell.

"But we're spirits," Tartan protested. "We can't handle physical things."

"We're not," Tara said. "See, the plant is still there. I merely grabbed its spirit essence. That's just as stinky."

Well, now. Tartan looked, and spied a set of knives made of cheese. He picked one up, noting that all he got was its essence: sharp Cheddar. He hurled it out at the vampires. It caught one right in the gut, giving it a bellyful. It was certainly sharp! And cheesy. This vampire, too, dropped out of the sphere.

Then Tara spied something really weird: a small crazy train chugging along on its misshapen tracks. "A Loco Motive!" she exclaimed, delighted. "Help me send it out."

They took hold of the tracks ahead of the train and managed to angle them out of the comic strip. The Loco Motive chugged right through and into the massed vampires, who immediately went crazy. What else could they do? This Loco train would make anyone crazy. That took out half a slew of them in a quarter of a fell swoop.

Tartan found an old rusty skate. He threw it at another vampire, who was outraged. "That was a cheap shot!"

"Well, it's a cheap skate," Tartan said.

Tara found a tangle of cord formed into the shape of a Y. She threw it out, and it tangled a vampire, who then decided to go elsewhere. It was a Y Knot, useful for making folk change their minds.

Tartan found what looked like a nose with little legs. He picked it up and flipped it out. It landed on the face of a vampire and tried to run away with the creature's face. It was a running nose.

The vampires finally had enough. Blood was one thing, but egregious puns were too much to digest. They flew away.

The spirit of Isis appeared. "I can move parts of the comic strip," she explained. "So I extruded a ribbon for you. I see you made good use of it."

"Thank you," Tartan said. "It saved us."

"But if you were doing that," Tara said, "what about tracking the Ghost Writer?"

"Oh, I realized that was no longer necessary."

"But the whole point of the dance was to distract him while you tracked him."

"I realized belatedly that when he took my rose, I would know where he was as long as he kept it. We all know where our roses are."

Tartan and Tara exchanged half a glance. They had not been separated from their roses, so had not experienced the effect. But Rose of Roogna had mentioned it.

"So why did he take it?" Tartan asked.

"Well, he's never had a rose of his own, so he doesn't know about their qualities. I think he took it as a bargaining chip. He thought I'd do anything he wanted, to get it back." She smiled. "Now I will take it back, and he will do anything *I* want."

They flew back to their hosts, who had concluded their dance once the Ghost Writer had departed. They explained the situation.

"So the next stage will be in Mundania," Amara concluded, speaking for Isis. "He will not be bothering Xanth further."

"How can you be sure of that, Goddess?" Dolin asked.

Amara stepped up to him and Isis manifested. She kissed him lightly and turned away.

"You are sure," he agreed, shaken.

"Oh, yes," Ted said, and Tartan agreed. No man escaped captivity by the Goddess when she put her mind to it.

"We will report tomorrow," Tara said. Then she and Tartan returned to their own bodies, and Isis joined Tara in Mundania. Both women used Tara's mouth to speak, and Tartan had no trouble telling them apart.

"That way," Isis said, pointing.

"How far?" Tartan asked.

"A day's walk. I'll have to fly."

"Now wait," Tara said. "You'll need a Mundane host."

"So I will," Isis agreed. "That complicates things."

"We'll go together," Tara said. "And locate a suitable host."

"Maybe easier said than done, on short notice," Tartan said.

"Maybe not," Tara said. "Let me get on the Outernet. Goggle or Binge should help." She went to her computer.

"What manner of thing is this?" Isis asked him with Tara's mouth.

Tartan laughed. "I guess they didn't have computers or the Outernet in your day four thousand years ago. It's a way to tap into a global network. You can find out just about anything, in minutes or seconds."

"I thought magic did not exist in Mundania."

"We call it science."

"Here we are," Tara said. "Runaway eighteen-year-old girl in this neighborhood looking for a place to stay. She says she'll suicide rather than return to her abusive home, and she's not fooling. She doesn't trust the authorities, who have let her down before. She wants to disappear from the records. A pimp is closing in. We'd better intercept her now."

"This is truly magic," Isis said.

They bustled out of the apartment and got into Tara's car. She drove to the address where the girl was going and spotted her walking beside the street. Tara slewed to a stop just in front of her, and got out. "We have a deal for you."

"Who are you?" the girl demanded suspiciously. She was plain and ragged and evidently tired, no beauty at her best, and this was hardly that.

Tara took her hand. Isis crossed over.

"Oh my god!" the girl breathed. Then almost immediately: "I mean Goddess."

"First we'll get you cleaned up and dressed," Tara said. "Meanwhile the Goddess will acquaint you with what we have in mind. You are of course free to say no; this is voluntary."

"She already has," the girl said, amazed. "I believe her. I'll take it!"

"What's your name?"

"Nydia. It means a refuge. That's what I'm seeking."

"By day you will be Nydia, an ordinary housewife. By night you will be Isis, a Goddess."

Nydia opened her mouth, paused, then nodded agreement. Tara took her to the bathroom.

Tartan got on Tara's computer and did a Goggle search on the name Nydia. Soon he confirmed her runaway status, and verified that she would be better off on her own, if she could make it. There was not even an active search for her.

The girls emerged. Nydia was now clean and dressed in one of Tara's outfits. The skirt fit more or less, but the blouse was tight, and surely the bra under it was too small. There wasn't much to be done about it until they could launder the girl's own clothes, or buy new ones.

"Now we need to locate the rose," Tara said.

"I know the direction," Nydia said. "Isis knows."

They got in Tara's car and followed Nydia's directions. In an hour they came to the neighborhood, and then to the house.

"Uh, before we barge in, we need to be sure," Tartan said.

"The rose is there," Nydia said. "That's sure."

"Okay. Now the Ghost Writer may not want to go along at first. Isis can convince him, but Isis won't be with you all the time, just mainly at night. So I think it is better to persuade him intellectually and practically at first, then let Isis close the deal. Okay?"

"Okay," Tara agreed.

"I am largely unfamiliar with contemporary Mundania," Isis said. "I have been in Xanth for some time. So I will trust your judgment in this respect."

"Nydia will know the details of the present scene," Tartan said. "She will be your guide for that, once we forge the deal. I will do the talking, at first."

They got out of the car and approached the house, which was distinctly nondescript. Tartan knocked on the door.

A dull man answered. "Whatever you're selling, I don't want any," he said gruffly.

"Oh, but you do," Tartan said. "We're from Xanth."

The man tried to slam the door shut, but Tartan's foot blocked it open. "We've come for the rose," Tartan said.

"It's wilting."

"That's because it's away from its owner. Let her touch it, and you'll see the difference."

"Yeah? Then you'll go away?"

"Maybe."

The man let them in. There was the Yellow Rose of Friendship in a vase. It was indeed wilting.

Nydia walked over and took it. Immediately it brightened and became vibrant. She put it in her hair.

"But you're not Isis!" the man protested.

"Not yet," Nydia said. "You thought to bargain with it for her favors, but you won't get to touch her until you seal the deal." She was obviously speaking for the Goddess, whose presence animated her rose.

"What deal?"

"We are coming to that," Tartan said. "Let's introduce ourselves, sit down, and discuss terms."

"Terms for what?"

"For your surrender," Tartan snapped. "Now get with the program."

"What—"

Nydia reached out and touched him with one finger. The Goddess, again. He shut up.

They took seats in his sparely furnished living room. "I am Tartan Mundane. My companion is Tara Mundane. The third person is Nydia Mundane. Soon you will marry her, and leave Xanth alone."

"The hell I—" But he heeded Nydia's threatening finger, and cut it off. It was evident that Isis could deliver more than merely joy by her touch.

"Tell us about yourself, in relevant skeletal detail," Tartan said.

The man struggled with himself a moment, then went along with it. "I am Goar. My name means 'fighter.' I am a writer. My Uncle Hoarfrost left me enough money to live on, provided I write something every month. The stipend's not generous, but it suffices. I would like to score big and become famous and all that, but so far all I have managed is to adapt fairy tales and spread them across the fantasy land you call Xanth. It's good practice, and seeing how my little stories play out gives me some inspiration. Fortunately I am not hurting anyone, since nothing there is real. It's all in my dreams. Which is why I know you folk are fakes. So what do you really want?"

Tara was interested. "So when you force people to act out naughty skits like 'The Princess and the Pee' you don't think you're hurting anyone, because they are all creatures of your imagination with no other existence?"

"Right. How can an imaginary princess ever be embarrassed? And how do you know about that?"

"And when you try to coerce a Goddess into making out with you," Nydia said, "it's just your way of making an imaginary creature toe your line?"

"Sure. Might as well have a little fun on the side, no? My imagination gets tricky at times, not doing exactly what I want. It's a problem with creativity. So I follow its rules to make it behave."

"So you wouldn't treat real people that way, even if you had the power to do so?" Tartan asked.

"Of course not. What kind of a jerk do you think I am? No writer actually practices what's in his fiction. Murder Mystery writers don't kill people, Romance writers don't have pretty girls in every port, Western writers don't blast away with six-guns, Erotic writers don't have sex twenty times a day. It's *fiction.*"

Tartan sent out a glance that reflected off Tara and finished with Nydia. This guy was not actually a bad person, merely a misinformed one. "Very well. Goar, you are wasting your talent adapting fairy tales. What you really need to do is to adapt the story of the Goddess of the Ages four thousand years ago to a modern day setting. That would be the romance of the age, making you famous, and demonstrate to the world that you are not a talentless hack." He saw the man wince; that was scoring. "You can put in plenty of accurately detailed sex, which you will write from firsthand experience."

Goar laughed. "If only I could! I haven't had a real woman since I can't remember when, if ever. That's why I have to go to imagination, where they abound. I just saw a dance troupe in Xanth with four spectacular girls flinging out their hair and skirts, any one of which I'd love to have in my bed. But let's face it, that won't happen in the real world."

"We'll get to that," Tartan said evenly. "Once you have written the story of the Goddess and gotten it published, you'll earn a lot of money from royalties and movie tie-ins. You will no longer have to live hand to mouth on a meager stipend. You will be able to buy a mansion and staff it with attractive servants. And if you get tired of writing, you can retire and keep your fame."

Goar licked his lips. "Damn, you spin a nice dream. But that's all it is."

"And finally you will spend your nights with the Goddess, doing your homework, as it were. Each morning you will transcribe the fifty forms of rapture she teaches you to the written page, grist for those who read your fiction for other than literary reasons."

"Yeah, sure," Goar said tiredly.

"And you will have no further interest in imaginary lands like Xanth, so you can leave them alone."

"In your scenario, sure. I was getting tired of Xanth anyway."

"Now we are ready for the deal," Tartan said. "You will marry Nydia and take good care of her. She will keep house for you, do the grocery shopping, and the thousand dull Mundane details you won't have time for because of the urgency of your writing. Everyone will be happy, including the imaginary folk in the imaginary land you will no longer bother with."

Goar eyed Nydia. "So that's it. You want to marry off Plain Jane here. Well, I'm not interested."

"Oops," Tartan said. "Did I leave out a detail? By day she is Nydia, as you see her now. No other man will try to take her from you. But by night she will manifest as the Goddess Isis, the creature any man would die for, but she will be all yours. You merely have to keep your mouth shut about that aspect. No one but you needs to know."

"Listen, I'm not buying that crap. So you might as well get out of here now."

Tartan signaled Nydia. She stood, manifesting as Isis. "Come here, Goar," she murmured huskily.

The man's eyes locked on her. "What the—?"

"You will find it worthwhile to obey me," Isis said as she removed her blouse. Her bra, exposed, seemed about to burst. Then she inhaled. There was the snap of something stretched beyond its limit. She really had to do some clothing shopping soon, to get her own sizes, let alone the Goddess's.

Goar was drawn to her as to a magnet. She put her arms around him and drew him in for a kiss. Tartan could have sworn he saw little hearts fly out and melt like heated wax.

Then the Goddess took him by the hand and led him to the bedroom. All his willpower was gone. The deal was being consummated. He was doomed, and would never regret it. Neither would Nydia, whose new life as housewife and Goddess was now secure.

Tartan and Tara quietly departed so as not to get caught in the ellipsis. They drove back toward her apartment. "Do you really think he'll get famous?" Tara asked.

"He won't care if he doesn't. All he'll care about is Isis. Her will will be his command. For the rest of his life."

"Yes, of course." She changed the subject slightly. "That romance—you know how hot I'm about to be, the moment we get private."

"I love your heat."

"But there's one thing that makes me nervous."

"Oh?"

"The picture. The portal to Xanth. Will it still be open, now that we've accomplished the mission? I love you, but I hope—"

"Me too! We'll soon know. We can delay our ellipsis long enough to find out."

"Thank you."

They reached her apartment and entered. They looked at the portal. It seemed unchanged, but that might be deceptive.

A shape got up and looked out from the portal. "Woof!" it mouthed.

"Tata!" Tara cried gladly. Indeed, it was the dogfish.

Then Amara appeared, summoned by the woof. She looked out and saw them. She smiled and gave them a thumb's up signal. Then Isis manifested, and nodded, before fading.

The two departed, walking along the path away from the portal, having delivered their message. The portal remained open. They could visit Xanth any time, and be with their friends there, and enjoy the magic.

"Now it is time for the ellipsis," Tara said. "At least three dots."

"At least," he agreed as he joined her on the bed.

. . . .

AUTHOR'S NOTE

At this writing, I have no idea what the next Xanth novel, #42, will be. I am eighty and a half years old, and the thought of tackling another 100,000-word novel is increasingly daunting. I won't say that this is the last one, but it is beginning to occur to me that the series won't go on forever. This one was a challenge to write; I knew the beginning and the end early on, but the middle 50,000 words or so were blank. So the title is a pun on the song "Ghost Riders in the Sky," but that alone does not a novel make. I have described elsewhere my system for working out my narrative as I go, using a notes file parallel to my text file, and I really do use it. Time and again, I came up against a blank wall and had to struggle to get over, under, around, or through it. Maybe some day scholars will use those printed out daily notes—they are not kept electronically—to see what is really involved in writing a novel, even one filled with puns and totally unbelievable things. I will say this: It does not simply flow effortlessly from the mind; it is hard fought all the way. There are fans who think that if it is not effortless, it is bad; those fans are wa-a-ay out of touch with fantasy, let alone reality.

This novel has less violence and more romance—and, yes, suggestive ellipses—than usual. Including lesbian romance. That will surely outrage some readers. But if I allowed myself to be totally limited by the objections of isolated perspectives, there would be little of interest left. Xanth is, and always was, an adult series, even if most of its readers are young, and adults do have some concerns beyond just eating and sleeping. For one thing, the goddess Isis, introduced in *Isis Orb*, is an intriguing character I knew I wanted to do more with. She is the goddess of fertility, or more bluntly, sex, so she tended to draw the novel in that direction. Leading characters do, at times, take things into their own hands, regardless of the expectations of the author.

Sometimes, I get hung up not remembering something in a prior novel. If there is any trifling detail wrong, a reader will catch me up on it, so I try my best to get it right. This time it was Prince Dolin: I had a bit of information on him, but not enough. I knew there was more, but I didn't want to have to read through one or two prior novels just to get that. So I appealed in my monthly www.HiPiers.com column, and two readers came through for me. Thomas Pfarrer and Scott M Ryan called out the exact paragraphs, and so I was able to establish what little was known about him. Since he is a main character here, that was vital. Thank you, Thomas and Scott; I don't know what I would have done without you. Which, of course, illustrates another truth: where I get my fantastic ideas. From my readers, as you will see in the credits section.

Indeed, my readers are a vital part of Xanth. Some of them read the Author's Notes before they read the novel. Critics hate the Notes, as do some publishers; in fact, nobody seems to like them except the readers. Maybe that's part of the problem with publishing today: The powers that be seem not to know or care what readers like. Which has slowly herded me into self publishing much of my work. But that has consequences: The great majority of my readers were devotees of the mass-market paperbacks, and those are going. It's a problem of dynamics: They print twice as many as will ever sell and pulp the leftovers. When authors self publish, they can't afford that. Indeed, publishers can't really afford such waste any more; chains and stores are going out of business, leaving ever fewer places to display those cheap editions. What wrought this change? Electronic publishing. The readers are flocking to it. My wife is an example. She was a mass-market paperback reader, reading maybe a book a day, and when she was done with them, she'd donate them to library sales a carload at a time, literally. But it got so she couldn't find what she wanted. There were no bookstores within range, and the displays at department stores and supermarkets consisted of "Top 20" titles whose publishers paid for the shelving. No payola, no display. When you read hundreds of books a year, the top twenty chosen by that system lose their appeal. But when she went online and checked what the big electronic sellers had to offer, she discovered she could get any book she wanted, sometimes in seconds, cheaper than a physical copy. Further, she could have a hundred novels there in that one reader. Now she carries her electronic reader in her purse, so she can read anywhere, anytime, such as when waiting for a late appointment at a doctor's office. She doesn't even have to hold the pages open, and she won't lose her place. So she was a hardcore paperback reader, but getting to choose for herself what she likes, rather than what a paid-for shelf offers, trumps that, and now she's a hardcore electronic reader. I'm sure she's one of millions. And I, as a writer, follow; now I publish electronically first and try to make my books available in hardcover or trade paperback for those who prefer physical copies, as I do. I regret losing my mass-market readers, but I hope that they will convert to electronic editions, where they can get just about anything of mine, anytime, sometimes at a substantial discount.

So what about me, personally? Many of my readers want to know. Well, I have, at this writing, been married fifty-eight and three-quarters years, trying for sixty. I do housework, meals, and beds, as my wife is infirm and can't stand on her feet long. One of my mental vignettes is that a feminist-type woman will approach me and say "You claim to make the beds?" and I'll say "Yes." "Can you fold a fitted sheet?" And I will explode, "No one can fold a fitted sheet!" And she will go away, satisfied. If you don't get it, you're not a woman. Ask a woman. I also accompany my wife to doctor appointments, shopping trips, and so on; I don't like to let her go out alone because I want always to be there to support her in case there is any complication. She has CIDP, or Chronic Inflammatory Demyelinating Polyneuropathy, a condition in which the body's own immune system attacks the myelin, or fatty sheathing around the nerves, in effect short circuiting them so that signals can't get through to the limbs. She was slowly being paralyzed, confined to a wheelchair that she couldn't move herself because her arms were weakened as well as her legs, and seemingly doomed, until we got the diagnosis and treatment. Now she is mobile, but limited, and must have special infusions every five weeks. We don't travel. When an arduous shopping excursion threatens, we take along the wheelchair, and I push her around. I love pushing my wife around. :-) She can walk; this merely extends her range so she doesn't overdo it and get in trouble. I remember someone saying of another wheelchair user, "I saw her get up and walk!!" As if that proves fakery. Get educated, folks, and help with a closing door if you see a wheelchair person approaching it. They are people, too, and doors can be awkward to navigate. She does volunteer one afternoon a week at a nearby shelter for abused women, as that is a seated job, mainly answering the phone. When I get a call asking for her that afternoon, I'm tempted to say, "She's at the abused women's shelter," but I'm not quite sure they would understand. She used to cut my hair, but had to stop when the illness came on her, so I stopped getting it cut—I was not going out to a barber and leaving her home alone—and now I wear my hair in a ponytail. Yes, there are men with ponytails; no need to smirk. Yes, men's hair does not grow as long as women's hair; my daughter's hair reaches down to her knees, while mine is maybe eighteen inches. Ah, well. I rather like it; it waves naturally. I tease my wife that if her hair curled like that, she'd wear hers long, too. Meanwhile, she does what she can, and it really helps. She does the laundry, as pushing buttons on the machines does much of it, and she keeps our accounts, which are beyond me, as they are complicated, even with modern computer programs that supposedly make them easy. We have been together a long time, and we've had our ups and downs, including grief. Our elder daughter, Penny, died of cancer in 2009, but we do have our youngest daughter, Cheryl, and granddaughter, Logan.

Meanwhile, I exercise my mind and body, maintain my college weight, and try to maintain an active lifestyle. A few months ago, I tripped and fell twice on my exercise runs, getting scrapes on elbows and knees, and the second one brought me to the emergency room—my wife took me—because my shoulder was freezing up. They concluded that no bones were broken, though there were possible bone cracks, and that I should recuperate on my own. I did, though it was over a week before I could lie down; I slept sitting up in my easy chair. It was longer before I could resume my arm exercises, but I was able to walk in lieu of my runs, and in two weeks, I was running again. Now I run more carefully, my mantra being not speed so much as not falling. So I'm fairly healthy for my age. With the huge exception of my teeth. I take care of them, as I do of my body, but they go wrong anyway. I lost count after a dozen root canals and myriad gold crowns that still didn't necessarily save the teeth. Now I'm getting implants. I have an imaginary trio of busty young women who go into titillations of mirth at the thought of a man getting implants, just as they do when I use girls' hair clips for my ponytail. These are *tooth* implants, girls; they plant the artificial tooth deep in the bone of the jaw, and once it heals it serves as a tooth that never decays, cracks, pains, or loosens. I now have nine implants and am pondering six more. They're great, except that they require dental surgery and months of healing, and cost, all told, about $5,000 per tooth. Ouch! Putting all that money into my mouth really chews me up. I will be most annoyed if I don't get at least a decade's use from them before I visit the bucket that says KICK ME— though, for some reason, no one wants to.

I am a liberal agnostic politically independent vegetarian, as those who read my HiPiers column know. Some like to claim that vegetarians are unhealthy, but I'm a smart vegetarian, watching what I eat and tak- ing half a slew of supplements. For entertainment, I play the card game FreeCell on my computer, which I think is the best solitaire ever, using the version that has the "solver" that tells me when I go wrong. Even so, some games are a real challenge to get through. I read books, which I review in my column, and watch videos I buy on sale or trade for, and I review them, too. I tackle the daily newspaper chess problems and the Jumble word puzzle. My wife does it, too; sometimes, she gets it while I stall out or I get it while she stalls. Sometimes we collaborate to solve one.

What else is new? My agent is negotiating a deal for a Xanth movie option, which may or may not come to pass. Yes, an option is merely when a company buys the right to make a movie for a given period of time. Most options are never exercised, and even when they are exercised—that is, they decide to do it—the movie doesn't necessarily get made. I have had several options exercised that didn't make movies. So nothing is cer- tain, but there's always the hope that this time it will work out. Why do I bother when there's such a high failure rate? Because the movie outfits come bearing barrels of money, and I'd love to see my characters and sto- ries come to a kind of life on the screen. Wouldn't you?

What else? I was asked recently what heading I would like on my memorial. You know, after the bucket. I don't plan on a physical one; I'll be cremated, and my only legacy will be my books, which I hope will last for all time. But I remembered being asked a similar question over a decade ago, in 2002, for my epitaph for a book titled *Remember Me When*

I'm Gone, edited by Larry King. I don't know whether it was ever published, but I reread my entry, and believe it still fits me:

Piers Anthony, maverick, liberal, agnostic, independent, vegetarian, health nut. No belief in the supernatural, yet made his living from fantasy. Wrote readable books, made readers smile, learn, and think; helped some to learn to read, write, publish, and live. Longed to understand man and the universe and to leave the world marginally better than he found it. Tried to do the decent thing.

Note that I don't claim always to have succeeded in doing the right thing, just that I tried. We are all fallible. I'm still trying.

Now for the credits to readers who contributed ideas to this novel. As a general rule, I try to use ideas by new suggesters before using repeats by those who make multiple suggestions, but there are a number of multiples, and I have puns, talents, and ideas left over. It can be tricky to integrate everything and still have a readable novel. Well, maybe next time.

Headache as a life form—Larry Miller

Camelflage—Tim Brazeau

Demon Sun; Talent of making pigs fly; Father, Son, Daughter
    Boards—Josh Davenport-Herbst

The Genie family—Brian Jones

Skeleton with fat bones—Owen Marrow

Pocket Change; Flee Market—Darrell Jones

Talent of making motions slow or freeze—Naomi Blose

Infant Tile—Kerry Garrigan

Shin Digs—Beth Stephens

Tail Lent—Linnea Solomon

Jelly Beans—Stan Niemann

Zombies live in zombie houses, Sawhorse, Dogfish, Diar and Rhea,
    hummingbird hums tunes, Kelei with the color patterns, shoe
    horn, wanna bee (previously suggested by Tina Kelley in *Isis
    Orb*), Eau de Cay; Cheap skate, running nose—Mary Rashford

Knocking the wind out—Steven Normand

Cold Shoulder, and special credit for the Prince Dolin background—Thomas Pharrer

The Pastree, with cupcakes; Self Esteem Engine—Steve and Thomas Pfarrer

Acro-Bats—Thomas Pfarrer

Crow Bar—A Sellers

Emerald DragonGirl—Carina Terry

Horse d'oeuvres; Y Knot—Misty Zaebst

The Orbs, with Abs Orb—Howard Morris

Safety Pin—Alex and Erica Sellers

Amara, Immunity to love springs—Anne White

Talent of knowing where something will be—Randy Gardner

Deer Fly—Jenn Ramme

Walking skeleton suffering from osteoporosis; Raining Cats and Dogs, Reigning Cats and Dogs, Computer Dog with Bark worse than Byte, love spring, summer, fall, winter; Bed Spring, Fall—Tim Bruening

Self Storage—Douglas Brown

Flying Buttresses employed—Patrick Stapelberg

Patrick Stapelberg—Patricia Birkes-Stapelberg

Rainbow Sherbet—Emma Archambault

Magician of Time—Bernard Maynore

Talent of Sensate Focus; the Goesinti—Andrew Fine

Islands of Auntigua and Uncletigua—Dexter Smith

Harper's Fairy, Aqua tic, linguis tic, chap sticks—David Wells

Fact-ory with Satis-faction—Wiley Kohler

Jody, with talent of healing music—Rhonda Seiter

Hate Spring as a Love Spring with a reverse wood tree; Wear-House, Where House, Ware House—Richard Van Fossan

Book of Lost Answers (first mentioned in *Board Stiff*); cereal killer—Laura Kwon Anderson

Personification of the Adult Conspiracy—John-Michael Warner

Fowl Ball—David Seltzer

Sun Glasses to see in the dark—Zed Dechant

Noman is an island—William Elam

Lesbian Princess—Tiffany Butterfield

Cheese knife—Tim Brazeau
Loco Motive—Donna Niemann

And my credit to my proofreaders, Scott M Ryan and Anne White.

If you enjoyed this novel and want to know more of me, you can check
my website at www.HiPiers.com, where I do a monthly blog-type column
and maintain an ongoing survey of electronic publishers for the benefit of
aspiring writers. I do try to help others, as hinted in my epitaph.

ABOUT THE AUTHOR

Piers Anthony has written dozens of bestselling science fiction and fantasy novels. Perhaps best known for his long-running Magic of Xanth series, many of which are *New York Times* bestsellers, he has also had great success with the Incarnations of Immortality series and the Cluster series, as well as *Bio of a Space Tyrant* and others. Much more information about Piers Anthony can be found at www.HiPiers.com.

TALES FROM
THE LAND OF XANTH

FROM OPEN ROAD MEDIA

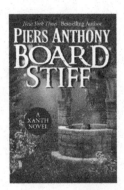

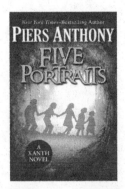

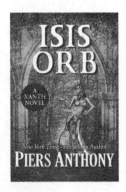

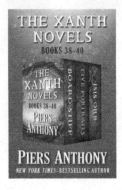

OPEN ROAD

INTEGRATED MEDIA

INTEGRATED MEDIA

Find a full list of our authors and
titles at www.openroadmedia.com

FOLLOW US
@OpenRoadMedia